D0593179

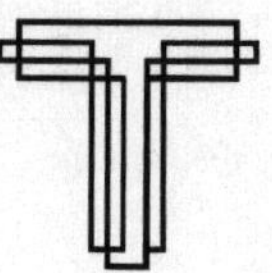

GODS *of* WOOD *and* STONE

A Novel

MARK Di IONNO

TOUCHSTONE

New York London Toronto Sydney New Delhi

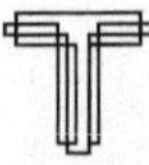

Touchstone
An Imprint of Simon & Schuster, Inc.
1230 Avenue of the Americas
New York, NY 10020

This book is a work of fiction. Any references to historical events, real people, or real places are used fictitiously. Other names, characters, places, and events are products of the author's imagination, and any resemblance to actual events or places or persons, living or dead, is entirely coincidental.

First Touchstone hardcover edition July 2018

TOUCHSTONE and colophon are registered trademarks of Simon & Schuster, Inc.

For information about special discounts for bulk purchases, please contact Simon & Schuster Special Sales at 1-866-506-1949 or business@simonandschuster.com.

The Simon & Schuster Speakers Bureau can bring authors to your live event. For more information or to book an event, contact the Simon & Schuster Speakers Bureau at 1-866-248-3049 or visit our website at www.simonspeakers.com.

Interior design by Kyle Kabel

Manufactured in the United States of America

10 9 8 7 6 5 4 3 2 1

Library of Congress Cataloging-in-Publication Data
Names: Di Ionno, Mark, author.
Title: Gods of wood and stone : a novel / by Mark Di Ionno.
Description: New York : Touchstone, [2018]
Identifiers: LCCN 2017020852 (print) | LCCN 2017024909 (ebook) |
Classification: LCC PS3604.I114 (ebook) | LCC PS3604.I114 G63 2018 (print) |
DDC 813/.6—dc23
LC record available at https://lccn.loc.gov/2017020852

ISBN 978-1-5011-7890-0
ISBN 978-1-5011-7892-4 (ebook)

In loving memory of my brother, A. Paul Di Ionno

Induction Day

Prologue

The guy came unnoticed because all eyes were on Joe Grudeck. But Grudeck saw movement in the far periphery of his catcher's eyes. He knew the geometry of throwing angles and running lines; he knew the large man moving fast against the oblique light of the white tent would get to the stage before anyone could stop him.

The guy was bootlegging something; when he saw it was a sledgehammer and not a gun, he decided to stand his ground. *Joe Grudeck, tough as a lug nut.* That's how a *Globe* writer once described him.

The guy vaulted onstage and went right for Grudeck's bronze plaque. The 12-pound sledge bounced off, leaving a deep dent in the bronzed Red Sox hat on Grudeck's likeness. The second swing came from the heels with the fluid grace of a practiced arc; chin tucked, big shoulders and hips rotating as one, arms extended but tight. The hammerhead hit the bronze Grudeck's throat, shooting off sparks and leaving a jagged fracture down the middle. The plaque fell to the stage in two pieces, and the crash reverberated through the audience, silent in a collective gasp.

This guy was no terrorist, Grudeck thought. No crazy fan. He was dressed oddly, like a mountain man, but he sure knew how to wield that stick. Grudeck didn't waste time thinking who or why, it was go time and the competitive rage that made him a star of several "Basebrawl" DVDs took over. It's why the fans called him *Joe Grrreww*, like a growl. So here we go, he thought, another *SportsCenter* clip.

He shoved the podium over. The sheets of his speech fluttered down. The full water glass bounced on the stage floor, leaving a large puddle. The microphone came down with a feedback shriek. The piercing sound fed Grudeck's blood-rush anger, like flint igniting a grill pent up with propane. *Whoosh!* Grudeck charged and tried to tackle him, but the guy sprawled back and his fists came down on Grudeck's head and neck—*one, two, three, four*—like a sock full of nickels. Grudeck got a buzz in his ears, like the static hum from power lines at night when all else was quiet. *Five, six, seven.* The punches connected like an ax on dead wood and Grudeck's neck felt rubbery. He slid on the wet floor and went to one knee, stuck under the guy's weight, helpless. He took in air deep and got a noseful of the guy's body odor; stale sweat, firewood smoke, and something oily, like gasoline.

Grudeck gasped and coughed, and felt his thighs involuntarily quiver from muscle fatigue. So this is what weak in the knees feels like, he thought. A lifetime of leaving blood and guts on the field and Grudeck never before felt his knees go weak. He wondered if his pants, now sticky with sweat and spilled water, were hanging off his ass. He was afraid of how comical, how stupid, he looked. With his next breath he pulled in the guy's legs and drove up, and they both fell straight back, quaking the stage floor when they fell. Now Grudeck was on top and straddled the guy, set to strike down, but the guy got hold of Grudeck's throat with both hands. Grudeck tried to punch, but couldn't get through the guy's arms. So he, too, went for the throat, and their arms intertwined like cable strands on a suspension bridge. It was then that Grudeck felt the guy's true strength. He pushed Grudeck up with scary, surprising ease. Grudeck dug his fingers into the guy's throat, but the guy only dug deeper. Grudeck fought to breathe and swallow. He felt a stab under his skull and his arms tingled and went weak. But then came more arms, these in blue sleeves, to the rescue. Then came a billy club pressed against the guy's throat, another across his chest. He let go, hands up in surrender. Cops picked up Grudeck and hustled him away; his shaky legs just went for the ride.

There was a woman in white. "You okay, Mr. Grudeck?" He had that tin-can taste of blood in his mouth; he was put in a chair. "Mr. Grudeck?" He felt water running behind his eyes, closed them, then saw the bleeding blue daylight, and opened them quick to make it stop.

Grudeck watched the cops lead the guy out. Young men pushed through women and children and overturned chairs to get closer, throwing balled-up programs and plastic cups at him. The staid induction ceremony was history. The crowd was now part of the evening news. Violent, unexpected news; cell phones recording it from all angles.

Now chairs went airborne. Two cops broke from the phalanx, nightsticks at chest level, but the mob engulfed them. The fans came in tight, fingers like daggers in the guy's face, screaming curses.

Grudeck's mother was led to him. Sal, his agent, on one side, two Hall security guards on the other.

"Are you all right, Joey?" She sounded like she was in a fish tank. "This crazy world . . . I don't understand," she said, taking his face in both hands.

Grudeck looked back at the crowd and saw the bat, a bobbing mast on a roiling sea of chaos. It was his, a genuine Joe Grudeck model, red-wine-stained ash, high in the air. It made Grudeck think of the gleaming silver crucifix he held high, arms above his head, when he was an altar boy at St. Joe's, leading the Mass procession.

His heart banged harder at the thought of his life flashing by. He saw a young first-aid worker step in front of his mother, her white uniform glowing. Angel of Mercy. He saw two girls bathed in dawn light, long-haired angels limping out of his dark Syracuse motel room. Silhouettes in the doorway. One had her panties balled up in her fist, the other trying to snap her jeans, tear-streamed mascara on their faces.

Is that what this is about? Grudeck thought. *After all these years.* His Induction Day, fucked up. His Hall plaque, busted. His speech, never delivered, never recorded for *posterity*, in a puddle of spilled water, ink running. Tear-streamed mascara.

"Mr. Grudeck . . . Mr. Gru . . ." It was the girl in white, voice far away in the upper deck.

He saw his bat, blood-red, waving crazily, now at the head of the procession, and then, like a whip, he saw it come down hard on the big guy's head, the sickening crack of wood on skull. The big guy staggered but stayed on his feet. *Tough as a lug nut*, Grudeck thought. You had to admire the bastard. The big guy twisted away from the blow and looked back at Grudeck. Mutual respect. Blood ran down his face in one jagged stream and dripped off his chin. Again Grudeck flashed to St. Joe's, the painting of Christ bleeding from the crown of thorns, near the entry where he led the boys in from recess, sweaty and laughing, ties and shirttails everywhere.

This was not good. He was drifting away.

"Mr. Gruuu . . ." A translucent green mask on his face, the red stretcher straps tight on his chest, the muted wail of the ambulance siren. He saw the IV bag, and felt the needle go into his arm. Catcher's eyes, still taking it all in, blurred.

The ceiling lights of the ER, the brown face of the doctor. But then the runny, bloody bright blue color of daylight sky came back, and it all got too bright. Everything got whirly, like the lights at Fenway the night he got beaned, only spinning faster.

He was in and out, like airplane sleep, all those road trips. He felt a heavy hand on him, moving a blanket. He heard the bouncing blip of a machine turn to one steady note, the curtain ripped back, hurried feet squeaking on the linoleum floor. He heard the words *swelling* and *cerebral* as his clothes were cut with scissors. He was powerless to object. In and out, paralyzed. So, so tired. He tried to see Stacy's face. *She should have been here*, he thought. Then there were more lights, round like those at the ballpark but right up close, blinding bright, bleaching everything white. Another needle in the arm, everything dissolved. And he was gone.

Winter

Chapter One

Each morning in the black before the Otsego Lake dawn, Horace Mueller took his hands out from under the "Odd Feller" quilt Sally's mother made them as a wedding gift twenty-some years before. The cold air felt like ice on a bruise. Horace was not a religious man, not in the church-kneeling way. But there in the dark he prayed silently to calm the turbulence in his head. "Thank you, God, for letting me wake another day, whether it brings sorrow or joy. And continue to guide me, Lord, to who I am, and what I stand for."

He would lie still and recite those words until he felt a presence; a warm visit in his chest that always made him think of glowing embers of a dying fire suddenly fueled by a gust of fresh air, rekindling. It was God, partnering in his existence, urging him to take on another day.

And then Horace went to work on his hands. He did manual labor, and they hurt, every morning, in some way. Sometimes it was arthritic grating of the knuckles. Sometimes it was nerve numbness burning his palms. Either way, he had to work them back to use. He flexed and extended them, stretching tendons and ligaments, feeling metacarpal bones rise and fall beneath his skin. He bent his fingers back, pulling the skin on callused palms. He cracked each knuckle; the small ones made a snapping sound like twigs underfoot, the fist knuckles made a deeper crack, like bat on ball.

Then it was time to get up and throw an armful of logs into the woodstove. This was Horace's winter ritual: the dawn warming of his drafty farmhouse, circa 1910. It was a headfirst dive into a frigid lake.

On this morning, after a few minutes of hand yawning, Horace put them back under the blanket. The pattern of muslin patches rose and fell as he moved his hands—an invading army under the cloak of darkness—until they found their target: the bunched-up hem of Sally's nightshirt gathered just below her behind. He went under it, then approached the waistband of her flannel pajama bottoms, deftly as he could. He knew his touch was rough; cracked calluses irritated her skin, soft as when they met at Cornell. Horace tried to file them down with an emery board, but it only scuffed the hardened skin, creating little needles that scratched Sally like cat claws. He tried to soften his hands with Sally's moisturizing cream, but it only left his skin plump and vulnerable to the next day's labor; a failed marriage of a woman's lotion and a workingman's hands.

Horace pressed into her, sliding the nightshirt up over the guitar curve of her hip, trying to draw her warmth. He listened as the frigid lake winds leaked through the weathered clapboard siding; the kind of dry cold that sucked moisture out of wood, making the coals in the wood-burning stove burn hotter and faster. He had to get up and get the fire going. But first . . . He arched his back like a waking lion, pushing himself into the humid crevice of Sally's underside. Sally stirred, and backed into Horace with a slight twitch, the faint promise of intimacy. Somewhere, somewhere in her sleep, she remembers, Horace thought. He cupped her butt and pushed forward, leading with his erection, which parted her thighs and ran the full width of her flesh. He reached around her and grabbed the head, and nestled it against the silky fabric of her panties.

Back in college, Horace's favorite time was the heavy-lidded mornings, when Sally woke him with a tug, or her lips. She would fall into him, with that skinny little body. Thin, but strong, the kind of woman that never falls out of shape. Horace would sink into her tenderness. Once there, he tried to lessen his weight. He held himself off Sally the best he could, staying up on his elbows. She would rise up to him, and accept him into her body.

After he became the blacksmith, things changed. He tried to keep his rough fingers off her skin, caressing her head and hair, using just his mouth on her breasts, shoulders, neck, face, and ears, unaware his beard irritated her. Sometimes weeks went by. After Michael was born weeks became months, months became half years. Colicky as a baby, and needing Mommy's middle-of-the-night comfort as a toddler, Michael was between them so much Horace nicknamed him "the human chastity belt." He was almost five when she finally removed him from their bed. But then Sally was afraid their noises, heard through the thin walls of the farmhouse, would wake him. She had a harder and harder time relaxing, and Horace had a harder and harder time convincing her it was all right. And now that she was working out four times a week at a fitness club, well, it reminded Horace of the old saying about boxers who stale by fight time. "They left it in the gym."

So now, on this cold January morning, Horace moved into her . . . if only to prove he was ready.

"Don't, Horace," she said when his prodding woke her. "It's too early. And cold. I'm always cold. Did you stoke the fire yet?"

"Going now."

"I wish to God we'd put more real heat in this house. It gets colder every year."

"I wish to God you'd let me warm you up," Horace wanted to say, but instead squeezed himself out from underneath the covers to not let more cold air in. On quickly went the flannel shirt, long johns, and Wigwams he kept piled on the frayed rush twine chair next to the bed. He tiptoed down the hall barely wide enough to contain his shoulders. The wide-plank floors cried under his weight. He reloaded the stove from the small indoor stack, the wood bone dry, warm and ready to burn, and then went out the back door, to get more from the porch cord. The outside air was nature's cold shower; it shrank his nuts and killed his erection. It was no use to him, anyway. The hard, splintery edges of the split logs dug into his skin and brought new pain to his hands. Just once, he wished his son, now fourteen, would get his lazy ass out of bed and do this. The kid had no problem getting up for early practices in whatever sports season it was. But chores? Or old-fashioned work? Forget it.

Horace stoked the fire, and it spat a few embers onto the floor, which Horace snuffed with his feet. He shut the furnace door and stood, warming his hands, admiring his piece of cast-iron Americana. He found it a couple of summers ago, at an estate sale in a Cooperstown Victorian that was being converted to a B&B. It was rusting away in the garage, junked long ago when oil heat was put in. Horace saw it as a restoration project for Michael and himself. They'd move it home, strip off rust, sand metal back to silver bone, then black-coat it back to good use. But it was baseball season then, and Michael was too busy practicing or playing. After school. Weekends. Always.

So Horace did it alone, like most things these days. He pivoted it from the garage, moving leg by leg, then tilted it into the back of his old Ford Escort wagon. The 489 pounds of cast iron pancaked the car's rear suspension, which creaked and cursed all the way home. It was backbreaking, for car and man. The whole time he was busting his nuts, he cursed Sally for not making Michael help. Mikey had a Legion Ball practice, then Babe Ruth practice. God forbid he miss.

"What's more important? Helping his father on the rare day he really needs it, or going to yet another of a million sports practices," Horace argued.

"What's more important to him, is the question," Sally said. "Not what's more important to you."

That was always the question, and the answer enforced by Sally bitterly defined Horace's fatherhood.

Horace stood in the dark, the room lit only by fire glow peeking through the furnace grates. He warmed and flexed his blacksmith's hands, the palm lines indelibly darkened with the dirty gray stains of bituminous coal. Coal shoveled into the hearth, ash shoveled out, just part of a strongman's work; wielding hammers and pressing bellows and stacking pig iron. His was a lost, ancient craft, with roots older than written history and tools invented in the smoky dawn of civilization. He was an authentic blacksmith, and had the aches to prove it. But he was also an actor, "a living historian" as they said down at the Farmers' Museum in Cooperstown, and an educator. The smithy was first stop on the re-created-village tour. Sparks flew and hammers rang as Horace forged a new horseshoe for groups of scouts, senior citizens, or kids on class trips and delivered this soliloquy.

The blacksmith is a living reminder of a day when strength and function were inseparable; whenever and wherever God's great beasts were domesticated to do heavy work, the blacksmith was the man who kept them pulling, and in the process, forged himself into a beast of a man.

From the discovery of flint and coke and iron, the blacksmith was the strongman who understood earth's metals and minerals, who carried the world forward on his broad shoulders. He was the first to understand the abundance of these God-given gifts in the earth, the first metallurgist, the first maker of weapons, the father of heavy industry, the grandfather of all technology. From the horseshoe to the iron-banded wagon wheel, it was the blacksmith who helped push mankind's transportation forward. From the ancient Hittite blacksmiths came Damascus steel, and the 'smith became the swordsmith and, then, the gunsmith. The blacksmith is ancient, but he endured, because he is the epitome of self-reliance. And here, at the Farmers' Museum, you will see the self-reliant family farm, the self-reliant rural village, the self-reliant America, the one of work and prayer. One that should not be forgotten.

He delivered this with theatrical enthusiasm, reveling in his role of eccentric throwback. He was the star of the village. Anyone could dress up and play chicken farmer, milkmaid, or preacher, or run the apothecary or general store, but Horace put on a show. He made flames leap, like magic, from lumps of black coal, then played in that fire with gloved or bare hands. Horace, the giant, the circus strongman, clanged his heavy tools off red-hot metal with delight. With his dark hair long, his face perpetually tanned and leathered by the constant heat of the forge, Horace saw himself as a mythic figure, the revered subject of Longfellow's ode, an American working strongman like Paul Bunyan or John Henry. He was hardened from the years of wielding heavy tools. At forty-five, with shoulders broad, chest and abdomen firm, arms and legs thick and sculpted, he had never felt physically stronger. *The smith, a mighty man is he.* He could snap a quarter-inch strand of pig iron over his knee, walk a 500-pound anvil across his shop floor, and work an easy eight hours chopping wood or banging out steel. He moved the Glenwood by himself and had to replace two porch stairs at home that splintered under the weight of him and stove. And yet all that muscle could not beat back the encroaching despair that his family, his country, and all the things he wanted to think true were slipping away. So he prayed for purpose, and fought the good fight.

Horace Mueller's hands weren't always black. He had a double master's in history and rural sociology from the ag school at Cornell, but the degree certificates were merely paper extensions of what he learned at home. His grandfather was the last of the New York State hops farmers, and his father tried running an Empire apple orchard, but eventually went to work in tool-and-die for a Syracuse company that made intricate locking mechanisms for bank safes. Competition from Asia drove the company to the brink, saved only by defense contracts. But hatch molds for Navy ships did not require the art of tool-and-die, and Horace's father was let go, into early retirement. Now here was Horace, the next chapter in a family narrative of changing American economy: rural to industrial to information, though Horace was proud he delivered his the old-fashioned way, not through the Internet. Face to face. *Americans should know where they came from*, he sang out to visitors over the ringing echo of hammers. *And know how to grow their own food and make their own goods. Self-sufficiency is a lost art, but you never know when we'll have to go back*, he said with wry humor. *Not with these days of killer storms and tidal floods, and a financial industry that could come crashing down at any moment, like some hollowed-out, termite-infested oak. Cash could dry up. Food distribution could come to a halt. Then what?*

NOW HORACE LET THE HEAT from the stove all but scorch his hands and melt the stiffness. This was the most peaceful moment of his day, and his own excuse for not making Michael get up. Alone, with the glow, in a silent room still dark but now warm. He pulled up a chair and sat, his feet stretched toward the stove, and closed his eyes. This was the life he wanted: simple, with quiet time to pause and reflect. Contemplate. Dream. Be in touch with his spirit, not run from it. He took a few deep breaths, letting his chest expand with air touched by a hint of smoke.

The abrupt sound of the TV from Michael's bedroom killed it. All the years Sally muzzled their sex and now he was over there, TV cranked loud enough to drown out a Roman orgy. It was the morning all-sports highlight show, high-pitched, high-drama, high-volume.

Horace walked away from the fire and down the cold bare floor to Michael's room.

"Michael, hey," he said, knocking gently on the door.

"Michael, hey, Mikey," he said louder a few seconds later. "Mikey, lower that thing."

"COME IN," Michael yelled.

In one step through the doorjamb, he entered the world he'd wanted to escape.

The covers were up to Michael's chin. Only the arm holding the remote was exposed, aimed at his entertainment center with the high-def, flat-screen TV and DVD player, his laptop, and a tangle of phone chargers and iPod earplugs, or whatever they call them. There was the Xbox and Wii, and the gadgets and guns to play them. All of which necessitated a 220-volt line being wired into the house to replace the 110, a few years back. Horace protested the excess, from an intellectual and environmental standpoint, but Sally gave Michael his way. And here, Horace saw, in his own family, the latest chapter of economy: diversion. Disconnection from self and earth through the chronic, electronic connection to entertainment and sports, sometimes disguised as "communication." On Michael's walls were posters of his favorite athletes, captured in some moment of glory. Modern pagan gods, Horace always thought, as he looked around the room.

Michael's shelves held more trophies than books, by far. Every season, every sport, memorialized in stick-on wood veneer, faux marble, and gold-plated-plastic baseball, football, and basketball players. Michael was a good player, and some larger trophies were for more than run-of-the-mill participation. He made all-star teams and travel teams and went to off-season camps. Horace wanted nothing to do with it; it was Sally's thing. When Horace questioned the expense, Sally said they could afford it, but he knew a sucker's game when he saw it. All these private coaches and clinics were a new industry, a modern twist on the old baby-model scams inflicted on the parents of the Baby Boom. Now, instead of dangling Gerber commercials, they dangled college scholarships for sports. And parents paid for the long shot, because everybody thinks their kid is something special.

"Dad, what up?" Michael said, not taking his eyes off the TV.

"Could you turn it down? Your mom is still sleeping."

Michael lowered the TV.

"Want to get up and help me bring in some wood?"

"Nah . . ."

"It's good exercise . . . it'll put some meat on them bones," Horace said, hating his own placating tone, and meek attempt at humor.

"Nah, Dad . . . that's okay."

"C'mon. Help out your old man." Horace reached down and shook his covered toe.

"Dad, no. It's too f'en cold."

Horace let it drop. He stood for a few seconds, frozen by colliding emotions, watching Michael watch the TV. Part of Horace boiled up to want to force the issue. But part of him was deflated. He wanted a boy who wanted to help—to *be* with—his dad. Michael was no longer that boy.

"So how's school going?" Horace finally just asked.

"You know, all right," Michael said.

"What are they teaching you these days?" Horace said.

"You know, the usual," Michael said.

On the TV, in dated blurry color, was a baseball player, clearly from the early 1990s with his longish hair and tight polyester uniform. He was trotting down the first-base line pumping his fist in the air, as his teammates ran out of the dugout, jumping up and down like little boys.

The announcer was all but hyperventilating, . . . *and who can forget this HISTORIC shot . . . tenth inning . . . Game Six, World Series. Joe Grewww jacks one. GET OUT OF TOWN! Red Sox Nation goes WILD . . . Joe Grewww directing "Bedlam in Beantown" with the fist pump . . . an IMMORTAL moment . . . Of course, the Sox lost the Series, but what the hey, Joe Grudeck's going into the Shrine . . .*

Historic shot, immortal moment. A home run in a baseball game, for Christ sakes, and they're making it sound like the Surrender at Appomattox, Horace thought. The hyperbole in this day and age was getting increasingly meaningless. The Shrine . . . a baseball museum. He was about to say so, when Michael disarmed him.

"Hey, Dad, you remember that guy, Joe Grudeck?"

"Yeah, a little," Horace said, suddenly thankful his son had initiated any conversation at all. "I was never big into sports, but I remember him a little. I guess he's an old-timer now. Like me."

Chapter Two

February in Jersey was dismal, year in, year out. Back when he was playing, Grudeck never bitched about pitchers and catchers reporting by the fifteenth, two weeks before everybody else. He couldn't wait to trade the dull gray of Jersey for the calypso colors of Florida. Now that he was retired, he didn't go until the last week of March. They called him "hitting instructor," but he knew the truth. He was a glad-hander. Just like here, at the club.

On these heavy, damp winter mornings, Grudeck woke in more pain than usual. It woke him, circulating in his body like renegade cancer cells. But not silent. Screaming. Waking each day for Grudeck was like coming out of surgery. One minute, you were deeply and comfortably unconscious, helped there by a four-dose of Advil. The next, your nerve endings were on fire. When Grudeck came to, he felt every piece of worn tendon and torn cartilage, all the places where joints now scraped bone-on-bone, hinges weakened by years of overuse. Rotator cuff in his throwing shoulder, shot. Elbow bumped out like Popeye's. Ball joints of hips worn down like struts on a junker. He slowly flexed his stiff hands, trying to bring blood back. He looked at his left hand, his glove hand, the humped back where the metacarpal bones had snapped and sown themselves back together around a couple of surgical pins. His right hand wasn't as ugly, but looked curved even when relaxed, rounded from all those years of gripping baseballs. A hot tingle burned his palms during sleep. Carpal tunnel, they told him. A practice golf swing or drying off with a towel or reaching for a coffee cup could rip a shot of paralysis through his arm, or a buzz of pain muted only by the pins and needles of dulled nerves. His hips, especially the left, his catching side, seized up when he sat too long, ached when he stood too long. Same with each knee. Humidity, or the tail end of eighteen holes, made him limp a little. The Red Sox orthopedist told him he was looking at double replacement somewhere down the line.

"Hips or knees?" Grudeck asked.

The doc laughed. "Both."

And that was before Grudeck retired.

"Don't wait too long past sixty, if you make it that far," the doc said. Now he was forty-six. Sixty was coming.

But his hands, he had to live with. No robot parts for them. They were battered after thirty-some years behind the plate, from Little League to the Bigs. Thirty-some years, hundreds of thousands of pitches hammering his left palm, hundreds of foul tips hitting his unprotected throwing hand. Want to know pain? Split a fingertip.

All that punishment, and Joe Grudeck kept coming.

That's why Boston fans loved him, *all*-time.

First was Ted Williams, then Yaz. But lumped in the next pack, with Foxx and Doerr and Pesky, was Grudeck.

They serenaded him each time he stepped to the plate or threw out a runner or made a tag at home. *Joe GRRR-eww, Joe GRRR-eww*, the "grrr" sounding like a growl because of his pit-bull tenacity.

They loved him for that toughness. They loved him for being white. They loved him for the extra-inning walk-off homer that gave them life in the only World Series he played in. He was just a kid then, a boy hero.

Mostly, they loved him because he stayed. A Red Sock till he tipped his cap good-bye. He was a Jersey boy, and moved back to Jersey when he was done, but Boston still called him its own.

Now he was up for the Hall. First time on the ballot. He knew he deserved it. The fans, and most sportswriters, were for him, because he was a throwback, old Joe Grrreww. Not only in the way he played, but because he never ran off with a big-market owner throwing big bucks at him. Sal called him "the last of the Mohicans," whatever that meant. Other big stars sold themselves, three, four, five times to the highest bidder, but Grudeck stayed. To the end. Just like Williams, Yaz, and the rest, Joe Grrreww was old-school. Last of the company men.

But you get old quickly when you play a young man's game. He held on longer than most, especially for a catcher. Still, he was only forty-one, an age when most men hit their best years, when Grudeck knew he was done. Yesterday's news, except for today. The Hall vote.

Five years since he retired. It went by slowly, slower than all the years he was playing. Five years, waiting for this day. The last big go 'round for Joe Grrreww. His hands hurt more than regularly. What were they trying to tell him? In, or out?

Grudeck ran the numbers through his head: 2,796 hits; 301 home runs; 1,924 RBIs; .289 career batting average.

That was the bottom line. The numbers. Unless you got caught cheating, and Grudeck only used stuff that was legal at the time.

Grudeck was a shoo-in. Wasn't he? The only bad thing was long in his past. Buried by time. Things were different then. The girls were probably ashamed, thought nobody would believe them. Small-town, International League groupies, Grudeck figured. Probably did every guy on the Syracuse Chiefs. But then, they didn't act that way. A little timid. Delicate, too. Either way, the cops never came that morning in Syracuse, or ever, even when his name got big. Joe Lucky.

He looked at the clock . . . 9:00 a.m. Still too early to know.

He was alone with his thoughts, on the edge of his own bed, an arm's length away from a sleeping woman. Janine? Janie? No, Joanie. Joanie MacIntosh. The Cadillac guy's wife. Ex-wife. Soon-to-be ex-wife. Whatever.

He had to get rid of her. When the Hall news came—one way or the other—he wanted to take it alone. He slowly opened and closed his hands, feeling all the moving parts: joints and knuckles resisting, tendons pulling, veins flattening out. He closed his eyes and listened to his hands creak. Like someone walking down wooden steps to a basement. He rolled toward Joanie and shook her, his left hand feeling like a meat hook on her smooth, naked shoulder. The bed smelled like sex and perfume. He was still musky down there, but dead.

"Joanie . . . Joanie, baby, you got to go."

TED WILLIAMS. For some reason, his hand pain always made Grudeck think of Ted Williams. Those were the days, Grudeck always thought. No lockouts, no agent negotiations, no "baseball is a business" talk, even though it was. No constant *SportsCenter* analysis. No national media types in the locker room, watching like vultures, twisting words. Just a handful of friendly newspaper guys. No fans up your ass every minute. Grudeck knew guys from Williams's day had off-season jobs and lived in regular middle-class neighborhoods. He remembered his dad taking him past Phil Rizzuto's house over in Hillside, the town next to Union. Nice place, but in a neighborhood. It was Chuck Grudeck's way of saying, "See. It can happen to you, too."

Man, Grudeck wished he'd played in Ted Williams's day.

Baseball then seemed . . . *sunnier.*

Grudeck remembered the last time he saw Ted Williams, wheelchair-bound with slurred speech, but at Fenway for the opener in '97 or '98.

"There he is, Mr. Red Sox," Williams said to Grudeck through a crooked smile. Williams, a legendary prick, had softened over the years. Got sentimental, even.

Grudeck remembered shaking Williams's cold, clawed hand, a hook of wooden flesh. The "Splendid Two by Four," he thought. It reminded him of dead people's hands, wrapped up in the Rosary, laid eternally on their chest. His dad . . . Coach Rillo . . . his grandparents.

Now, on this cold winter morning, in his luxury condo alongside a world-championship golf course, Joe Grudeck looked at his hands as if they weren't really attached to him, and saw mortality coming for him, too. He would go in the Hall, if not this year, then the next, or the next, and then he would be trotted out once a season for old-timers' day, decaying a little more each year, until.

HE LOOKED AT JOANIE. In the morning light, he saw the dark and gray undersides of her blond-streaked hair. The sheets clung from her shoulder to hip line. She wiggled her ass a little in her sleep. Any other time . . . but right now, somebody was counting the baseball writers' votes, and soon it would be over. He had to get her out of there.

Grudeck sidled up to her, under the sheet. "Joanie . . . Joanie, baby . . ."

"Hmmm . . ." She rubbed that ass of hers up against him. Joanie MacIntosh, with the apple-shaped ass, Grudeck thought.

"Joanie . . . C'mon. You got to go."

He shook her shoulder, then ran his hands down the curve of her hip and gave her a light slap on the rear end.

She fell into his lap at the club bar the night before, and after she threw back a few martinis, they drove to his townhouse overlooking the sixth fairway. Grudeck liked them younger, but there was nothing like a recent divorcée spreading her wings. Especially nowadays, when there's Viagra in the medicine cabinet bull pen.

When they got inside, Grudeck peeled Joanie off him long enough to sneak the little blue pills. "I've got to piss," he said.

"Say pee," she said. "*Piss* is such an ugly word."

As he locked the bathroom door behind him, he thought about all the girls who used the same ruse to slip in the diaphragms they hid from their mothers back in the day, or took those morning-after pills now. Mighty Joe Grudeck, hiding like a schoolgirl.

Now here he was in the morning, numb and rubbery down there, while so much of the rest of his body throbbed with daily aches and pains.

She pushed up against him, harder and with more wiggle.

"No, baby. Not now. Another time. You got to go."

But Grudeck knew there would be no other time. This was a one-nighter, like most. A way to kill boredom, to kill the time between last night and this morning. A way to not be alone. Besides, she was a sponsor's wife, and a club member, to boot.

Grudeck met Joanie a handful of times at the club, usually at some pricey charity fund-raiser where Grudeck glad-handed and signed autographs. Grudeck remembered her because she was a nice-looking bottle blonde, health-club maintained. She was the wife of Jimmy MacIntosh, a local Cadillac dealer. She was tall and elegant and Waspish, and clearly married for money. Her husband was the third-generation owner. What do they say? The first generation builds, the second expands, the third fucks it all up. That was Jimmy Mac. Pudgy and short-fingered, with a monkey face like one of those old-time Irish caricatures from the rag sheets. He spent his days playing golf in Jersey and Florida, while managers ran his business into the ground. The chain his dad built retracted to the original dealership his grandfather started. When Grudeck first met Joanie, he remembered thinking this was the kind of woman—the doctor's wife type—that men like Jimmy Mac married to prove they were making it in life.

Grudeck met Jimmy Mac fifteen years earlier, after he invited Grudeck, through Sal, to play a round at Baltusrol one late October.

"There might be a deal," Sal said.

Grudeck agreed only because he would be home anyway, and was new to golf. He'd never played Baltusrol, but knew it was fancy and challenging enough to host the U.S. Open once in a while. Besides, it would help him take his mind off another World Series without him. On the ninth hole, Jimmy Mac made his pitch. Grudeck never forgot the sight. Jimmy Mac was dressed in a shamrock-colored sweater and sun-yellow pants, and swung a one-iron like a friggin' shillelagh, face blazing red, frustrated by Baltusrol's wicked fast greens as much as failing in the global car market.

"The Germans and Japs are kicking my ass. It's like we never won the Big One. When my father built this business, the only *luxury* cars worth a turd in the whole world were *American* cars, except for Rolls and Bentley. Now we're scrambling for market share in our own country. I need to restore American pride. Something's gotta change. I need a little red, white, and blue. That's where you come in."

He made a name-in-lights motion with his hand. "Joe Grudeck, local sports icon, as American as baseball and Cadillac."

Jimmy Mac spelled out the deal. The cash, off the books, and use of a new, fully insured car, for a couple of TV spots and newspaper ads, and a little glad-handing at dealership parties in the off-season. No more than an hour at the Christmas Sales Event and Presidents' Day. Only an hour, Jimmy Mac promised, to meet preferred customers.

"One or the other, each season," Grudeck countered. "And the car is good. I don't endorse anything I don't use."

This was Sal's rule. He always said, "First, you don't want to look like a hypocrite. Second, you don't want to come cheap."

"I wouldn't want it any other way," Jimmy Mac said as he stuck out his fat hand. "Welcome to the MacIntosh family, buddy."

AND NOW HERE HE WAS, fifteen years later, still in the deal, endorsing Jimmy Mac's wife.

"Joanie. Wake up. Time to go."

She turned toward him and started to grab. Grudeck turned and headed to the bathroom. He pissed, took another Viagra, then tugged at himself until the blood flowed. Joe *GRRR-ewww*, he thought. A man like him had appearances to keep up. Men got the bone-crushing handshake, women got this.

In the full-wall mirror under unforgiving halogen vanity lights, Grudeck saw himself. Still big and broad-shouldered, still strong and sinewy in the forearms and calves. But a thickening layer of soft flesh covered his shoulders and arms and thighs. Gravity tugged his chest, and time stole some muscle density in his biceps, quads, and abdomen. His gut was settling, his hips getting wide. Fat fuck, Grudeck said to himself. He grabbed a handful of belly and saw cellulite. All that club food. Time to seriously get back in the gym, maybe go back on andro, to trim up quick.

Grudeck reached for the giant-sized bottle of Advil and threw down three.

Now he stood before Joanie in his full Joe Grudeckness and gently shook her shoulder.

"Baby . . . Joanie, baby . . . you got to go."

Her eyelids opened and closed, and she looked him up and down with a sleepy gin-and-vermouth hangover smile.

"Omigod, look at you. Uummm. Just the way I remember. Were you like that all night?" Her voice was husky and she came up, mouth first.

He backed away.

"Baby, not now, you got to go. You got to go before the neighbors start talking."

"Oh, shit 'em. Let 'em talk. Serves Little Jimmy right."

Grudeck didn't want to hear it: trophy friend of husband becomes revenge fuck for wife. Not that he was a victim. He just didn't want to hear it.

She grabbed at him, open mouth closing in.

"No, no, no, you don't," he said as he caught her head. "Joanie, I got to get going here. Please."

The Hall news was coming in by mid-morning.

He put on a robe and went to the kitchen and pressed the button on the automatic coffeemaker. The thing roared to life and began to steam and spit. Grudeck looked out the window overlooking the fairway on this cold January morning. The course was empty, the trees around it naked and shivering in the wind. God, Jersey was gray in winter. And barren.

Joanie came out dressed and they had coffee.

"Call me," she said over her shoulder as she left.

Grudeck stayed in his kitchen, looking out the window. Maybe he should call Sal? No, Sal was on top of it.

He turned on the TV. Maybe there was news.

On *SportsCenter* they were talking about him, the same over on Fox. *Joe Grudeck, first time on the ballot. Let him in or make him wait? Our baseball analysts decide.*

Analysts. Like baseball needed to be analyzed. Like it was the world financial markets, or action in Congress.

"Anal-ysts. More like asshole-ysts," Grudeck said out loud, pretty proud of himself for thinking it up.

The first guy—a former *Globe* writer who always acted like a friend—said first-year entry was reserved for only the greatest of the greats. Cobb. Ruth. Williams. DiMaggio.

Look, Joe Grudeck is a Hall of Famer, no doubt about it. But a first-timer? No way. That's the tradition. I know Joe Grudeck, I covered him for years, and if there's one thing Joe Grudeck respects, it's tradition.

The second guy—a TV guy Grudeck knew never left the studio—went the other way.

You just said he's a Famer, no doubt, right? So if he deserves it, he deserves it. First year, second year. What is the difference? Why make him wait?

The serious, combative tone embarrassed Grudeck. Terrorists were beheading people, the country was going back to war, the world was fucked up, but here on *SportsCenter*, Grudeck was the *urgent* issue. Grudeck knew what was coming next: the online poll and the tweets, so anonymous assholes could give their worthless opinions on Grudeck's career. *Tweets*. Stupid word.

Grudeck shut it off. The only thing that mattered was the actual vote, and Grudeck would know soon enough. He sat in the quiet, massaging his hands.

Chapter Three

Immortality came at 10:37. So said the digital clock on the convection oven Grudeck had never once used. His cell phone rang.

It was Sal.

"Joey. You're in . . ."

"By how much?"

Joe Competitive, right to the end.

"Almost unanimous, Joey. Eighty-five percent. And wait, it gets better. No one else made it. You're alone. Jenks and Struby just fell short. No veterans, either. The whole party's gonna be for you."

A few seconds passed. Grudeck didn't know what to say. In his head, "I'm in the Hall" was not shouted with dream-come-true disbelief, but said in quiet matter-of-fact reflection. Expected. Anticlimactic. But real. Like death after a long illness.

"You there?" Sal said.

"Yeah. Yeah, I'm here."

More silence.

"Hey, kid, you know how proud your father would be?" Sal finally said. "He would've never dreamed of this . . . I mean, he dreamed, but you surpassed his wildest expectations."

"I know, Sal, thanks."

"Back when you started, he was happy you just got drafted. When he asked if I could look at that first contract, he was hoping you'd earn enough to buy yourself a little house in Union, before you went to work in a real job . . . like high school coach. That's what he was hoping for. When he got sick and came up to my office to fix his will, the last thing he said was, 'Sal, make sure Joey takes care of what he earns, and make sure he takes care of his mother.' Then you became a star, then a bigger star. Now look at you."

"Thanks, Sallie. Thanks. I couldn't have done it without you."

"Ah, bullshit," Sal said. "But, hell, I did my best, for a small-town lawyer."

"You did great by me, Sal, I have no complaints. Look at my life."

GRUDECK LIVED AT FAR HILLS NATIONAL, on a Tom Fazio–designed golf course in a free townhouse, which he got in exchange for a little glad-handing and playing with members once in a while. Sal got him the deal with Dom Iosso, a billionaire developer, who built the course on the former estate of the car designer John DeLorean, "in the rolling hillsides of New Jersey's estate region," the brochures said. "The equestrian country where Jackie Kennedy Onassis, Malcolm Forbes, Doris Duke, Joe Grudeck, and many other 'rich and famous' made their homes."

Joey Grudeck, son of a Polack sheet metal fabricator and his Italian housewife from down in blue-collar Union, was now one of them. Iosso added him to the brochure when their deal was done.

Rich. A millionaire a few times over. His last contract paid him $8 mil a year for three seasons, all deferred because he was still living off deferments from his previous contract, a six-year deal at $9 mil per. In all, his deferments would pay him at least half a mil per year until the day he died.

And famous. A big name, bigger than any of the CEOs or CFOs he met at the club, the kind of guy his father would have hated. But they weren't household names like Jackie O, Forbes, and Duke, who were all dead anyway. These guys weren't *personalities*; they were just finest-school corporate game-winners. Guys who got rewarded by their boards for skimming quality, reducing work force, and outsourcing jobs, until they couldn't cut it anymore and the boards found new blood. Some were retired, golden parachute guys who failed at places like AT&T and Merrill Lynch. But who knew them? Joe Grudeck, everybody knew.

"CALL YOUR MOTHER," Sal said, "before she hears it somewhere else."

"Sal. Do me a favor. Call her for me. Tell her I'll ride down in a little while. I just want to, you know, absorb it, for a little while."

"No, you should do it, Joe. She should hear it from you. I mean, I'll do it if you really want, but . . ."

"Yeah, you're right, Sal. I'll go."

"Okay. What about the media? I'll write a statement, for now, but do you want to do a presser? Your contract with the club says you got to do it there, but screw that. Do it where you want. Commissioner said you could do it on Park Avenue. Whatever you want."

"I'll go into the city. But I should do one here."

"Like, what, three or four? They'll all want it for the five o'clock news."

"Whatever."

"I'll call Dom and let him know we'll set something up at the club for tomorrow. He'll want his face in there."

"Fine. Good idea."

"And you know, your stock just went up. All the deals we have in place, and the merchandising . . ."

"Another time, Sal. Just give me a few minutes now."

Grudeck put the phone down and thought of a schoolboy joke.

What do you do after you climb Mount Everest?

You climb down.

He was going into the Hall of Fame.

Now what?

This wasn't what he'd expected. He'd expected to be thrilled, elated, choking back tears, all that other stuff. Instead, he felt uneasy. Part of it was what happened in Syracuse. His name would be back in the news, the target on his back. Maybe one of them would sell her story. But probably not.

The bigger part was this:

Now what?

The question he feared most.

He saw it coming a few years ago, playing golf and glad-handing for a living; living off his name. So now what? Five years retired, and still no clue. He'd used the Hall vote as yet another excuse not to answer that question, but here it was.

He shut the ringer off on his phone, and just sat there awhile.

Chapter Four

Horace was in Pompey, sixty-eight miles west of Cooperstown, loading the museum's beat Ford Econoline with some dead farmer's junk: a moldy cider press, a dried and torn leather harness, and a plow so rusted the blades were flaking.

This was a growing pain-in-the-ass of his job. Every time some old farmer or farmer's widow died, the children wanted to donate the "antique" tools forgotten on the property. Horace knew the deal; it was a cleanout before barns, sheds, and farmhouses were razed and land sold to developers. And it helped assuage the guilt for selling Pap's land. His old tools were kept for posterity, they reasoned. At least we did that.

Because of cuts in government arts funding, the museum laid off most of the maintenance staff, so while they were home collecting unemployment, reenactors and craftsmen were asked to do the donkey work. They could choose one of their off days—the museum was closed on Mondays and Tuesdays—for straight time, or do it on regular workdays. Horace took the sixth day. First, he needed the money. Second, if he missed a day, they might find a part-time blacksmith to do his job while he was out collecting junk, and might decide a part-timer was all they really needed. Horace resented this, a double-dagger to the spectrum of the middle class. Not only did he have to work a six-day week to make ends meet, but as a historian with a master's degree, he was taking the job of a Cooperstown townie with (maybe) a high school GED.

Not only that, but these trips never yielded artifacts of value. Anything discovered in these barns, the museum already had in triplicate, at least, and the stuff went from one forgotten corner to another—from some decrepit barn to the museum's huge storage sheds in Cooperstown.

When he made this observation, the bosses countered: "We can't purport to keep farm tradition alive, and then tell well-meaning country folk they should haul Grandpap's cider press to the landfill."

So here was Horace, layered up in Carhartt, hauling junk out of a sagging barn more gray than red, where the surface inches of exposed, weathered wood well outnumbered the chips of remaining paint. The farm was vacant, the barn empty. Everything of value had been sold at auction, the animals sent to slaughter. Inside, the smell of matted, unpitched hay and the acrid residual stench of cow manure was ingrained in the rafters and hung in the damp winter air. It stung Horace's nostrils and his eyes watered. He was alone, on 300-some acres, the sole pallbearer for yet another farm funeral, mourning the dying simplicity of his grandfather's time. This one hit home; Pompey was in Onondaga County, where Horace was from. He tripped on a pitchfork covered by a clump of hay, and stumbled enough to flame his temper. "God *damn* it," he said under his breath, even though no one was around to hear him.

HORACE GREW UP IN LAFAYETTE, a town off Interstate 81, just a thirty-minute commute north to Syracuse. It had been one of a dozen farm hamlets off Highway 20's east-west route through New York State's rural midsection, but when the north-south interstate came through, the city spilled out. Factory workers, looking for yards and driveways, wanted cheap housing off I-81, and developers found a new market for old farmland. The town went from burg to 'burb, just like that.

The Muellers lived in a plain split-level on a 75-by-150 lot, surrounded by houses built in the 1950s, with the same property dimensions, and the only evidence of their agricultural ancestry were stories Horace's grandfather told and a backyard hops patch where the old man grew just enough to brew his own beer.

The grandfather, Helmut Mueller, Horace's "Opa," was the last of the German hops growers who worked for the Busch family in Otsego County. His great-great-uncles brought the know-how with them from the Hallertau region of Bavaria in the 1820s, and transplanted their crops to supply America's growing lager industry. Opa grew up in Germany, but came to the United States as a young man at the turn of the century. But in 1909, a "blue mold" wiped out most of the Hallertau variety, by far the most common in New York State. What the blue mold didn't kill, Prohibition finished off. By the time the taps reopened, the hops industry became entrenched out West. New, disease-resistant varieties were blossoming in the Sonoma Valley, and the long California growing season made West Coast hops cheaper for even East Coast brewers. Helmut Mueller was barely out of his thirties when his livelihood became extinct. He moved out of Otsego County and found orchard work in Cortland. After World War II, those jobs, too, began to disappear as mechanized farming and the new Interstate Highway System made it impossible for local growers to compete with conglomerates. Washington State apples came East faster, and were genetically engineered to be warehoused longer.

When Horace was a boy, Opa taught him to build a hops arbor, and how to tie and nurture the plants, and pick the buds. But the old man's enthusiasm for it was a shallow last gasp, and at night, Helmut Mueller would sit on the back deck, looking lost and detached, like a nursing home patient staring out a picture window into a world he no longer recognized. He would sit, still, with his hands folded in his lap, and look down at the fireflies settled in his hops patch. Next to him would be his homemade beer in a tall glass, covered in running sweat beads, as the contents grew warm and undrinkable.

Horace's father, Hans Mueller, who fought against his ancestral homeland in World War II, came home to technical school on the GI bill, then got work as a tool-and-die machinist at the bank-safe plant in Syracuse. The family moved again, this time to LaFayette. When Hans was laid off in the 1980s, he rented a dormant apple orchard from a grower's widow. With old Helmut's help, he tried to return to agriculture. Horace remembered stacking bushels as a young teen, listening to his father and grandfather grunt to each other in German. But the Macoun apples the dead guy had grown were old-fashioned by then, replaced by sweeter and prettier varieties like Jonagold, Jonamac, and Empire, all developed by Cornell's ag school. Hans Mueller gave it ten years, then quit. Early retirement, he called it, and Horace saw the same resignation on his face that he'd seen on his grandfather's. When Opa died, Horace's father inherited that complete look of the lost; the generation between a man and mortality was erased. He measured his life differently; no longer day-to-day, but in sum total. And so Hans Mueller, like Helmut Mueller, left no legacy of land, or handed-down craft: just a house in LaFayette owned by a distant bank, and a tool-and-die skill for which there was no factory home.

TO UNDERSTAND WHAT HAPPENED, and why it happened, Horace chose history. It came to him one day, thirty years before as a teenager, while he sat under a tree overlooking the valley and snuck a few of his father's cigarettes. It was a late-September twilight, and cloud breaks in the western sky looked lit by torches. Sun rays shot heavenward from the ridge lines on the horizon, like spokes of dusty orange and gold. The beauty of it moved Horace, then a high school senior, to never leave. It was a sign from God, a call to vocation. A revelation.

This land is my land. This home is my home.

Horace sat until twilight became night. The infinite blackboard of stars, and blue wisps of cigarette smoke dissipating like a last breath, made him desperate to find something to hold. What did he have? He had history. Family history, right here. He would stay, and dissect the failures of his father and grandfather and find justice for them through the long lens of historic perspective. They were good men, but men in the wrong place and time. He could redeem them through the study of the unkind unraveling of Rural America by Industrial America in the early twentieth century, followed by Industrial America's postwar shuttering by Global Economy America. Horace knew the national story could be told through one family narrative. When it came time for college, he could see his future in his past.

Horace was smart and got accepted into Cornell's Agricultural College, the land-grant, public part of the university. He was a rural sociology major walking in the door, and out. For the next six years, he collected data, studied trends, and explored theories. He became educated and armed to write and teach, with reverential knowledge, about America's lost agrarian past. His master's thesis, called "The Rise and Fall of the Hops Industry, and Its Lasting Economic and Social Impact on New York Farm Regions," was written from a firsthand perspective, seen from the sullen rooms of his father's split-level.

And his talks at the Farmers' Museum were a continuous update on the loss of small-town country life and character.

In the last ten years, forty million acres of farmland was converted to strip malls or housing development. . . . In the 2010 census, less than fifteen percent of Americans worked in agriculture. In 1910, only fifteen percent of Americans worked outside of agriculture. . . . The rural village spawned small businesses, like the blacksmith shop, which embodied the spirit of invention. Thomas Edison, Henry Ford, the Wright Brothers, all started with small shops in small villages that shaped our nation's industry and history. . . . Invention turned into manufacturing and factory towns were born and thrived . . . and, well, you know the rest. Now they're in China.

And now here he was, Cornell-educated, a craft blacksmith, moving junk out of a barn in Pompey, named like the lost city buried under Vesuvius. The farm, to complete the dismal metaphor, was on Cemetery Road, and overlooked an old graveyard where sandstone markers of the settlers were worn beyond reading. The old church next to it had been abandoned for years; now the building held an antiques shop. Horace found a warped scythe with a rusted blade—there must have been a hundred in the "collection." He broke the splintered handle over his knee and threw it down in the hay. He found an old butter churn, the wood rotted and soft, the tin bands brittle and cracked with rust. He figured it dated back to 1910, the same vintage of three on display at the museum and another half dozen in storage. He tossed it into a stall. Fewer things to move. The rakes and pitchforks went into the same pile. He was tired of lugging dead people's junk.

He loaded the Econoline with just enough stuff to prove he was there, and drove out to Route 20 East. The winter winds infiltrated the van's door seams, shaken loose by miles and time. The heat was blasting lukewarm air and the sweat that soaked his long underwear turned chilly on his back and chest. To make matters worse, the clutch was shot, and Horace had to pump it two or three times on every shift, as the choking smell of burning automotive fluid filled the cab as he headed back to Cooperstown.

Cooperstown, Horace liked to say, was the birthplace of American mythology. James Fenimore Cooper started it with Natty Bumppo, the lone wanderer, the great white conqueror, the "rugged individualist going against the grain." The cliché was built on Natty Bumppo's broad shoulders, from *The Deerslayer* to *The Last of the Mohicans*. Every frontier legend—Daniel Boone, Davy Crockett, Wyatt Earp, even the outlaw Jesse James—was a Bumppo knockoff. Hollywood followed with Gary Cooper, John Wayne, Clint Eastwood, one for every generation. But in Cooperstown, baseball overran that history. Even now in the dead of winter, when the lake ice was ten feet thick and snow-covered golf courses looked like a barren Saharan landscape with airborne white particles whipped up by the Otsego Lake winds, baseball was king.

It was on Route 20, some ten miles out of town, that he saw the new "Cool, Cool Cooperstown" billboard, and it spat right at him. Surrounded by winter's gray and bare-limbed trees, the color and summer theme were even more assaultive and ridiculous; like a puked-up splatter of Day-Glo colors on a subdued Hudson School painting.

They were putting up dozens of them, on every road into town, and Horace fantasized about torching them all on some windy night, to make the fiery point that his staid, historic town would never stand for a cartoon spokesman.

But there he was, "Coop," the grinning baseball, with black shades and a hat on sideways, popping out of a sky-blue background.

"Cool, Cool Cooperstown" was printed in brushstrokes of race-car yellow on royal-blue background; NASCAR colors for the camper crowd, Horace thought. Below it, in smaller letters, were the words *Home of Baaaseballl!* That was the signature line, played on the TV and radio versions of the ads; a comic scream by a cartoon character. The image belonged in some Jersey boardwalk town or a Daytona spring break beach strip, not in Horace's old, dignified, steepled Cooperstown.

The old tourism signs cast Cooperstown in a shadowy Victorian streetscape; a line drawing of an Italianate mansion with a mansard roof and widow's walk, fronted by a wrought-iron fence and gate, all illuminated by a gas lamp. "Welcome to Cooperstown, the Village of Museums," it said, in understated, elegant script. Other old signs had a collage of the museums themselves: the Ivy League–like facade of the Baseball Hall of Fame, the neo-Georgian mansion at the Fenimore Art Museum, and the edifice of the massive stone dairy barns of the Farmers' Museum. Back then, those museums counted. Not now. Not in the *Home of Baaaseballl!*

The museums were run by the Clark Foundation, started by the first family of modern Cooperstown. Stephen C. Clark began the Baseball Hall of Fame, and the Farmers' Museum was converted from the estate of Edward Severin Clark. All were first-class operations, but only the Hall of Fame paid its way. School groups made up most of the farm museum traffic, yawning at exhibits on barn building, crop planting, and family life.

Past the barns were a dozen transplanted historic buildings, laid out to be a typical—but compact—New York rural village, circa 1845. It was all there: the church at the center, the general store, an apothecary, a print shop, a schoolhouse, a physician's office, and the blacksmith shop, all painted in conservative shades of the day. Living historians like Horace, dressed in period clothing, worked their shops. Others performed traditional chores in the working farm just beyond the village. Fields were plowed by draft horses and reaped by antique tools. Cows were milked hand to bucket. And the chickens roamed free before bedding down in the henhouse. It was a beautiful place, a valley hamlet with a view of the lake and the mountain beyond, where Horace lived.

Horace, the historian, started in the archive, thinking the foundation's deep pockets all but guaranteed him lifetime work. But the economy tanked, taking foundation money and donations with it, and Horace, now the blacksmith, entered the modern world of the American workingman. Insecure and changing. The guy who played pastor was first to be cut to part-time with no benefits, and the church became a "special event" facility, booked by corporate event planners as a quirky place to hold a meeting. Next to go were the schoolmarm, the doctor, and the apothecarist—actors, like the pastor, with no special craft or skill. They were replaced, if at all, by interns—usually undergrads or even graduate students from SUNY, working on some obscure mid-state thesis.

The message of the new "Cool, Cool Cooperstown" ad campaign was clear. The Village of Museums—educational, cultured, genteel—no longer appealed to families. Sports had taken over, so the town doubled down on baseball. The old signs were left to fade, battered by the Otsego winters, while the Chamber of Commerce plotted a new direction. When the signs were sufficiently wrecked—demolition by neglect, as they say in historic preservation circles—they were torn down and replaced by the screaming Coop cartoon, a twenty-first-century ad campaign for a nineteenth-century village. And on this winter day, the cheesy signs, with their forced sunny merriment, blared against a backdrop of steely skies and cold, snow-drifted fields, where dead hay and cornstalks poked up like some broken promise of summer.

Cool, Cool Cooperstown.

Home of Baaaseballll!

Not home to anything else.

Just baseball. Out on Route 28, just a few minutes outside the village in Milford, a pantheon to kids' baseball called Cooperstown Dream Park was carved into two hundred acres of fertile valley soil. Horace remembered the dairy farm there; maybe there were two. Yes, one had yellow barns, he recalled, and also had a Black Angus herd for meat. But the verdant pastures were turned into twenty-two lighted fields, with manicured infields with red clay base paths and green outfield fences, and snack bars, souvenir shops, a youth baseball Hall of Fame (whatever that was), and bunkhouses for teams that came from all over America. At least ten thousand Little Leaguers swarmed the place, from June till Labor Day, with their parents, coaches, and siblings. The stretch of highway around it became an alley of chain hotels, pizza, and wings and ice cream joints. They took shuttle buses into the village, toured the baseball museum, and, along with all the other baseball tourists, dropped millions into the economy. Cooperstown counted the money, but you couldn't put a price on what was lost, Horace thought. The soul. The culture. The mission. The nuance of art. Americana. America itself. Call it what you want. It was dying. Worse, nobody seemed to care.

Home of Baaaseballll! bugged Horace on two fronts.

First, it was historically inaccurate propaganda aimed at souvenir-buying tourists. Like Yankee hats made in China, the label was ironically counterfeit. This offended Horace as a historian. Baseball, the so-called national pastime, had no singular home. Cooperstown could not lay claim to being the *Home of Baseball* any more than Yankee Stadium, Fenway Park, or any Little League or sandlot field in America could.

And Cooperstown's claim as "birthplace of baseball" was long ago exposed as a fraud. Horace actually enjoyed telling visitors to his shop the truth.

"If you want to see the real home of baseball, go to the intersection of Washington Street and Eleventh Avenue in Hoboken, New Jersey, and look for a marker in the road," Horace would say. He told them that Cooperstown's life as "Home of Baseball" was not only built on a lie, but the Hall of Fame was built on an artifact from that lie: the "Doubleday Ball."

Stephen C. Clark bankrolled the Hall after he bought the "Doubleday Ball." It was a Frankenstein-stitched, misshapen sphere of leather stuffed with wool and cotton yarn, found in an attic down the road in Fly Creek. Somebody hoodwinked old Clark into believing it was used in the historic first game, which, of course, never happened. Its only historical significance, Horace said gleefully, was this: it was the first piece of junk to be sold as "baseball memorabilia" at a price far exceeding its value. This always got a laugh from the silver-hair crowd.

But, like it or not, the hard truth was baseball is what brought people into town. The Hall drew an easy quarter million a year, ten times more than the Farmers' Museum and the Fenimore Art Museum combined. Worse still, most visitors to Farm & Art were only in town to visit the Hall, which generated 85 percent of the hotel and restaurant revenue. "Farm & Art only" visitors were school groups or geezer bus trips (Farm & Art for old farts, as they said in Clark Foundation circles), none of whom stayed overnight or ate in Cooperstown's restaurants.

Each year, the farm and art museum staffs would be gathered to discuss budget initiatives, a foundation euphemism for cuts. The meetings would be conducted by old William F. Strothford, a thin octogenarian who wore bow ties and lavender or blue seersucker in summer with a straw hat.

Just a week before Horace's trip to Pompey, Mr. Strothford came and gathered the farm staff. Horace looked around at his co-workers, dressed, like him, in period garb, like a carnival collection of farmhands and milkmaids. They knew what was coming, and looked down at their weathered, period footwear, as Strothford explained new cuts.

"I know this is a hardship," Mr. Strothford said. "But with some innovative outreach programs and inclusive exhibits, we are confident this museum can find ways to become more relevant . . ."

Horace raised his hand.

"With all due respect, Mr. Strothford, this museum represents how the region thrived and grew into what it is today. Why is that no longer relevant?" Horace said. "We need more from the foundation. Not less. Cutting our budget, cutting our programs, well, it tells people we are *not* relevant. How can we stay relevant, when it seems this whole town, including our own foundation, is hell-bent on making everything but baseball *irrelevant*?"

There was a patter of applause from the farmworkers, started by a new intern, a big-boned girl with a Slavic face in a milkmaid's dress, who smiled and nodded with approval at Horace. *Natalie? No, Natalia. Natalia Pia-something.* She finished her master's course work at Empire State in Rochester and was immersing herself in her thesis, something about rural transition in the Industrial Revolution. Horace had just met her the week before. It was an unremarkable introduction, on the path between the cow barn and smithy, except that he noticed an Eastern European accent. Ukraine or Belarus? Horace forgot. But when he remarked how the foreign-born seemed more interested in their new country's history than regular Americans, she smiled and said, "Yes, Americans seem to take their historic freedoms for granted, but we find it fascinating."

Horace liked that, and now he raised his chin toward her, in appreciation, and she continued smiling.

Ah, the approval of a woman, so hard fought for—in life and at home—now came to him at the least expected time from a girl born behind the old Iron Curtain. Horace thought of the pioneer days when a man alone on one hundred tilled acres of the Great Plains would take out "matrimonial prospect" ads in papers back East, finding an audience among Civil War widows looking to escape the sad loneliness at battle's end. Grief is love that has lost its home, and the women took trains into the remote West to find a new one in the arms of a frontier stranger.

A man, too, needs a place to put himself, and suddenly there was this Natalia, offering an inkling of a romantic prospect out of the blue, and unexpectedly Horace's irritation with Sally's cool distance from him dropped a notch. Just like that, there was the hope of a future warm place. Just like that. His eyes dropped reflexively to the cleavage above the hand-stitched lace border of her milkmaid dress and she caught him. Still, a smile. Horace gave a little apologetic shrug. *You got me.* She didn't seem to mind.

Horace's fantasy was disrupted by Strothford, who raised a hand to put down the mild sedition.

"I admire your passion, Horace, I really do," he said. "But we must face certain realities. The foundation, and the town in general, must put resources into the entity of greatest return, for the greater good of the community. The Hall of Fame is synonymous with Cooperstown. Twenty years ago, the downtown was filled with antiques shops and art galleries. Now more than half the stores in town sell baseball souvenirs. The Hall is what attracts the conventions and the business groups."

That's when John Grundling, the Farmers' Museum director for all of two years now, piled on.

"And also, Horace, let's not forget it was the Clark Foundation that put us here in the first place, and continues to underwrite our very existence."

Grundling had the annoying habit of stating the obvious with authority. Casual Dress Grundling, Horace called him behind his back. He was boyish in the face, still blond, and wore pressed khakis and a cream-and-dark-green Clark Foundation golf shirt. They're everywhere, Horace thought, these fucking guys with corporate logos on their shirts.

"Let's all remember," Grundling added, "we're all on the same team."

Horace muzzled the urge to shoot back, "No, John, we're on the wrong team. The 'team' is up the street in the Hall."

Instead he kept his mouth shut and collared Grundling after the meeting.

"John, you've got to fight for us. We tell the story of America,"

Horace said. "Why are the relics of dead or washed-up ballplayers more relevant than the traditions and crafts that built this country?"

"Follow the money," Grundling said.

"Okay. Then let's latch on."

"How so?"

Grundling's ignorance about the landscape he supposedly managed irritated Horace, but he tried to explain it without a condescending tone.

"You know the 'Sandlot Kid' statue down at Doubleday Field?" Horace said. "Look how he's dressed. Straw hat, overalls, bare feet. He's a farm kid. Maybe we can create an exhibit on baseball's relationship to farm life. Games played in fallow fields. 'He couldn't hit the broad side of a barn.' 'Can of corn.' Beer and baseball! The Busch family hops, grown right here in this valley. And all that Opening Day sportswriter pap of 'spring hope' comes from a farming mind-set. Seeds were sown with optimism, before the droughts, the floods, the bug infestations, the losses."

Grundling surprised him at first—"Not a bad idea. I'll take it up with the board"—then quickly put on his company face: "But we don't want to step on the Hall's toes."

NOW HERE WAS HORACE, double-clutching the Econoline to throw a downshift each time the truck had to climb a hill. The weary engine compression couldn't overcome gravity, and the truck slowed miserably. Horace had to grind it out, and the smell of burned clutch fluid overpowered the usual fumes of the oil-tinged blue exhaust. "Shit truck," Horace said out loud. Bet the Hall guy didn't drive a shit truck.

He thought about his baseball idea. Maybe it was a way to bring Michael closer to him. It was sports, after all. Michael had changed, and it was more than just growing up. It was growing *away.* Cell phone attached to hand, to text friends or play games or get sports news alerts. Alerts, as in urgent. Crazy world, Horace thought, one filled with constant diversion. He wanted to show Michael something authentic.

He wanted to raise a boy who could do more with his hands than push buttons, and understood the holistic value of crafting something, even if you worked in a place of obscurity, like a farm museum smithy. He believed a man's true character was formed in those dark places, alone, not under the bright lights of the playing field.

Maybe Horace would volunteer to do the research, and get Michael interested. Horace could show him the simple church-picnic rural roots of the game, hand-wound, leather-stitched balls, pedal-lathed bats, burlap bags as bases. Maybe it would lead him to see that Horace's village, Horace's work, was important.

On the winding roads into Cooperstown, Horace decided to ask Grundling to give Michael a summer job, mowing fields, painting fences, helping in barns. Horace envisioned Michael pitching hay and throwing bales in the summer sun, tanned and strong, hair matted with sweat but a smile on his face. He saw them sitting together on a crude bench, shaded by the horse barn, devouring sandwiches from brown paper bags and guzzling the iced tea Sally made.

He saw Michael captivated by Horace's passionate and detailed stories of the hops industry nurtured by their German ancestors. Michael would learn their history, their family history. What an exercise in perspective! Perhaps even . . . *relevance!*

After work they could walk across Lake Street to the art museum and rediscover the collections. Horace took Michael there often when he was little to show him the detailed New York farm-town streetscapes of Fritz Vogt, and the dreamy, muted Hudson River landscapes of Thomas Cole. His *Last of the Mohicans* scenes hung there, painted in the months after the publication of Cooper's famous book. He imagined Michael growing ambitious to read Cooper, like generations of farm boys who turned pages by candlelight and dreamed of adventure; boys with imaginations as expansive as the fields and forests around them, where they played Natty Bumppo on his Leatherstocking adventures. Boys who were apprentices in his character: loner, leader, fighter, peacemaker; virtuous or murderous, whichever the situation called for.

Tight-jawed, iron-willed, fearless, and incorruptible, able to adapt to enemy turf and win. Always win.

"Look around you, son," Horace would say. "Cooperstown may not be the birthplace of baseball, but it is the birthplace of something bigger. It is the birthplace of American manhood."

This pleasant daydream brought calm to Horace's soul. He let out a deep breath, expunging the anger "Cool, Cool Cooperstown" brought on.

And just then, the drivetrain dropped out of the Econoline. Horace heard a bang, felt the power go dead in his hands, then a spark-flying scrape of metal against pavement. He pulled off the road and perched it on a drainage ditch, and dented the fender with his foot.

THE FLATBED TOW TRUCK pulled into the gravel horseshoe driveway of the old stables, where Hank Greenwald came out to meet it.

"Dropped the trans," Horace told him. "Thing's useless."

"Thing's old," Hank said with a smirk. "That don't make it useless. Everything's fixable, till it's not."

Hank's father had worked for Ambrose Clark, who built the stables and barns now used for storage and horticulture development. Across the street, where Ambrose's racehorses trained and grazed on a hundred acres, was the new Clark Sports Center with state-of-the-art fitness toys, and the town's baseball diamonds and soccer fields. It was on those fields that the Hall hosted its annual induction ceremony.

Old Hank had worked on the estate since he was just a boy.

"Only place I'd ever been," Hank liked to say. "I'm the last of the Ambrose farmhands."

Hank wore the uniform of the foundation, cream-colored work clothes with forest-green patches and an embroidered *Hank* over the pocket of his work jacket.

"Just call me Mr. Cream Jeans," he liked to say.

Hank waved the tow truck over to the storage stables, opposite the garden greenhouses on the property, and slid the giant bay doors open on their rollers.

"Easy as the day she was made," Hank said.

Yes, the barns were in remarkably good shape for their age, in some ways better than new. Rural decay was like urban decay, thought Horace. A by-product of poverty. When there was money, like in the Clark Foundation, things stayed in shape. People, too. Hank was at least eighty-five, trim, fit, and strong through work, despite smoking a half pack of Pall Malls a day.

Inside he had the wheel of a freight wagon, circa 1880, balanced on a vise, rebanding it with a strip of galvanized steel.

"Old one rusted off," he said. "Ain't authentic but it'll hold better."

The van was dropped, and as they unloaded the junk tools and equipment, Horace told Hank about his plans to work with Michael—and why.

"Everything is changing so fast, Hank, a boy doesn't even have a chance to breathe fresh air anymore, let alone work up a palm full of calluses," said Horace.

"It's a good idea, Horace. A damn good idea," Hank said, taking a smoke out of his jacket pocket. "Reminds me a little of me and my dad. I got all the schooling I needed from my dad and Irish Jimmy Henkins, who knew everything there was to know 'bout thoroughbreds. And when I look around this place, I see all my daddy built and I maintained. Fences. Gates. Ring posts. Even the birdhouses. He put in that flagpole over there, straight as an arrow with nothing but his eye."

Horace looked at the pole, towering over the barn, the American flag straight in the winter breeze, the Clark Foundation colors and logo below it.

"Made every one of them stalls his self," Hank said, gesturing toward the barn. "Wood, iron, and all. Got his initials in some of 'em. He's been gone thirty-some years now, but his work is still standing. A young boy should see his daddy's work."

"That's what I'm thinking," Horace said. "The kid only sees what he wants to see. His games, his gadgets. Sits there with plugs in his ears."

Hank let out a big sigh, then took a long deliberate drag of his cigarette.

"Nah, that's no damn good. You got to be out in the world to see it change," he said, exhaling. "Look over there, at that Sports Center. When most people around here look it at, they see a new building, a big gym, the induction hoopla in summer. When I look over there, I see the whole damn thing, old and new. I see Mr. Ambrose's training track, and Irish Jimmy leaning over the rail with a stopwatch, watching the colored exercise boy work some t-bred into a lather. I see my daddy on a tractor, grading the track, the dust flying up behind him. I see a field of mares and their rickety-legged foals. I see me and my daddy, repairing the split-rail fence some stallion kicked down. That's what I see."

Just then, the sound of hammer strikes echoed across the empty playing fields. Both men looked toward the noise. Over at the Clark Center, two young men were putting in a roadside sign that said:

Baseball Hall of Fame
Induction Day
July 26
Congratulations Joe Grudeck!

Chapter Five

Grudeck was on his way to Union, to tell his mother, thinking about his father. The day Chuck Grudeck lived for, he wasn't here to see. Life cheated some people that way, Grudeck knew. Irony, the driving force of the universe, like his dad said.

He turned Jimmy Mac's new Cadillac CTS onto Route 78, an interstate descent from the wealth-belt hills, where Grudeck now lived, to the industrial basin of blue-collar Jersey, where Grudeck was from.

Grudeck hadn't lived there full-time since he left for rookie camp, a week after his high school graduation, three months after his eighteenth birthday. That was almost thirty years ago, when his dad took three days off from the fabricating plant and drove him down to Winter Haven. With Joey's new steamer trunk and duffel bag in the backseat of the family Malibu, they made Florida in twenty hours, stopping only for gas, food, and the bathroom. Joey slept most of the way, resting up. His father drove in silence, not even AM radio.

"This is your *destiny*," his father said in his ear as they hugged good-bye. "*Your* destiny. You were destined for this, from the time you could walk."

Now, in the fast lane of the interstate, Grudeck thought about how much his dad sacrificed, but also what he gained. Yes, he created Joe Grudeck, but in exchange got to be Joe Grudeck's father. Yes, from the time Joey could walk, Chuck Grudeck put a glove and bat in his hand, or a football or basketball, until Chuck put Joey in wrestling in sixth grade. Basketball was for *moolies* anyway, his father said. When Joey got old enough to join teams, Chuck Grudeck took the night shift at Jenn-Air, where he shaped galvanized casings for heating and cooling vents, so he could coach his son.

"I'm not going to put you in the hands of some jerk," he always said.

Chuck Grudeck was a good coach, simple as that. He put in the time, and drilled his teams on fundamentals. "Play right, play better" was his motto. And they won easily with Joey in the lineup. Still, Grudeck remembered his father being fair. He let other kids pitch and bat cleanup. He made Joey sit out two innings a game, so other parents couldn't piss and moan about their sons' playing time. In football, he put him on the line for the second half.

"Clear a path for so-and-so," his dad would whisper to him on the sidelines. Joey would be lead blocker, knocking down kids the whole way. With Joey blocking, every kid on his team got the thrill of scoring a touchdown, which made Chuck Grudeck a hero with the parents.

He was a hard-ass in only one area: sportsmanship. His boys behaved on the field. No football spikes, end-zone dances, no trash talk or number ones.

"Win the World Series or the Super Bowl, then you can put up number one," Chuck told his players. "Until then, there's always somebody better."

Joe Grudeck held these values as a major leaguer. Play with hustle, not strut. He demanded the same from his teammates.

Like this legendary Joe Grrr-eww story: The Red Sox acquired a young Dominican slugger named Pujo Gutierrez. Grudeck at the time was a ten-year vet, at the very top of his game and team captain. Pujo batted cleanup, just ahead of him in the line-up. One night at Fenway, Pujo hit a long, long home run over the Green Monster, then took a slow, slow trot 'round the bases. Grudeck got drilled in the hip with the next pitch. That's baseball. Grudeck headed to first, stoic but stung. But in the locker room after the game, Grudeck called Gutierrez over to his stall.

"Hey, Pujo, look at this," Grudeck said, and showed him the bruise on his hip. Then, he swung a right hook into Gutierrez's thigh, sending him to the floor with a charley horse.

"Now we're even, motherfucker," Grudeck said. "Think about your teammates next time you're tempted to rub somebody's face in shit."

That was the Chuck Grudeck in Joe.

IT WAS THIRTY-ONE MILES from Grudeck's condo to his boyhood home on Stuyvesant Avenue, mostly on Route 78. He was on the final leg now, where six lanes were blasted through the traprock of the Watchung Mountains, creating half-pipes of brown outcrops. On the ridge, a panoramic view of urban Jersey opened up, from the Manhattan skyline east to the rise of Staten Island south. Life down there was work. Real work. Rail lines. Port cranes. Power plants. Smokestacks. Planes coming and going, like blinking stars. Middle-class 'burbs, with church steeples and water spheres peeking out over treelines. Grudeck first noticed it the night of his father's funeral, when he took off from Newark Airport to rejoin the team. As he rose above the Jerseyscape, he thought of all the people down there like Chuck and Sylvia Grudeck; all the people not like him. He escaped their obscurity. He was the most famous person ever to come out of his town, a "baseball icon," as the sportswriters say. He left, but didn't. He always came back, but wasn't invested. Not in Union, not anywhere.

Grudeck came off the highway and onto Morris Avenue, Union's main street. But the traffic, always the traffic, made him impatient, so he made a couple of turns and ended up on Lehigh Avenue in the industry section where Jenn-Air used to be. Lehigh Avenue was the tax base in the old days—DiGi Automotive Products, Armstrong Binding, Holman Plastics, East Coast Corrugated Boxes, Jenn-Air, and Liberty Dairies, a milk-processing plant. Places his friends' fathers worked. Sponsors of Pop Warner and Little League. Some of those plants were replaced by clean corporate offices. These names—Schering, Comcast,

Bank of America—were part of the new economy: pharmaceuticals, communications, money, run by the kind of guys Grudeck played golf with these days. Jenn-Air, where his father worked forty-five years, and a few others were vacant, with "Available" signs out front, for God knows how long. Lehigh Avenue ended back at Morris, and Grudeck turned toward home, through the downtown.

The Union center was old, built up in the 1920s, and beat up ever since. Some of the old stores, killed by highway big-box stores, now had signs in Español for international phone cards and money orders. But other places, like Lutz Pork Store and Green Pharmacy, were hanging on. His mother was a customer for decades, and some had personalized autographed pictures of Grudeck on their walls. *To the guys at Lutz—makers of world's best Polish sausage, Joey Grudeck.*

He drove past the town hall, a Colonial-style complex with a bronzed eagle in a clock tower. As a kid, the clock always said "you're late" as he ran home for dinner. As he passed it now, he could almost smell the woody air of fall, when dark came too early, or the fresh-dirt scent of spring, when the extended daylight tricked him into thinking he had more time. All those days, and seasons, he ran past that clock, his sneaker treads packed with mud; the days when his body had elastic immortality, no hand pain, no joint inflammation, just the strong, hard rubber muscles of youth.

He drove past Connecticut Farms School, the public grammar school. He remembered thinking it was a dumb name. They weren't in Connecticut and there weren't any farms. But it was the first town name, later changed to Union right after the Civil War. Still, the name "Farmers" was stuck on the high school sports teams. Grudeck hated it. It was a mushy name, implying no strength, speed, or bad intent, no animal prowess or heroic quality. Just a name from a forgotten past.

He passed the old brick church, which dated back to George Washington days. Grudeck knew this only because he got caught vandalizing it. He was just in fifth grade when he became the only kid who could hit a ball out of St. Joe's schoolyard and onto church property. First, it was into the adjacent cemetery. Then the church, on a bounce. It wasn't long until he could reach it on a fly, and then it wasn't long before he broke a tall, arched window.

The minister saw the whole thing: a gaggle of boys pointing toward the church, the biggest boy's long stride and perfect swing, a swing so easy but so muscular, so tuned but so natural, it could only be a gift from God. He saw the launch, and the high, arcing trajectory of the ball. He lost it in the sky, then heard the clatter of broken glass in the sanctuary as the boys jumped on the batter in celebration.

The minister grabbed the ball and went straight to Sister Jacinta, the principal at St. Joe's. The boys were still buzzing when she came at them like a thundercloud, dark gray, angry, and swirling, with her heavy nun's dress trailing in the wind she created. Behind her was the minister, hurrying to keep up, white hair rising like a cumulus cloud over his black church suit. The sister had the baseball in hand, and waved Grudeck over with it.

"Mr. Grudeck . . . you lose something?" she asked.

Grudeck looked at her, mustering all the innocence he could in his face.

"This look familiar?" she asked, holding the ball up to his face.

"Umm . . . I think. That might be the ball I just hit over into the churchyard."

"The church*yard*?"

"Yeah, I mean, yes, Sister. The church over there, 'cross the street."

"I know where the church is. Did you see it land in the church*yard*?"

"No, I was running . . . you're never supposed to watch the ball after you hit it," Grudeck said. Maybe this bit of Little League wisdom would be convincing.

"Well, as a matter of fact, Mr. Grudeck," Sister said, "the ball didn't land in the church*yard*, it broke a church *window*. And Reverend Angus here says it looked to him like you did it on purpose."

Angus. Grudeck heard his buddies stifle giggles as soon as they heard the name, which caused Grudeck to smirk, which caused Sister to say, "Oh, so you think this is funny? I'm not sure your father will think it's funny when he has to pay for the window. And I don't think Reverend Angus here thinks it's funny."

There it was again. More giggles, this time louder. Grudeck bit the inside of his mouth, enough to taste blood. He didn't want to answer, afraid he might bust out.

"So, you *do* think this is funny?" Sister asked, now tossing the ball up and catching it in one hand, over and over, like a cop tapping his nightstick.

"Nosister," Grudeck finally managed.

"And did you do it on purpose?"

"No, Sister, I didn't think I could hit it that far."

"But you *were* aiming for the church?" she asked.

Grudeck was trying to think how to answer that when, after a few long beats of silence, Angus rescued him.

"I think the point here is, you boys should be more careful, lest we grown-ups take you for vandals," he said. "Now, I saw the whole thing, and it looked to me like you boys were delighted the window was broken. So, what I would like is for you boys to come down to the church after school and clean up the mess, and then do some yard work in our cemetery this weekend to earn the money to pay for that window. Maybe along the way, you'll learn something about the history of our church—and our town—so you'll think twice next time."

The boys went after school to sweep up the glass, and on Saturday, with rakes, work gloves, and leaf bags. Angus asked the boys to clean the graveyard of leaves and twigs, dead flowers, and Christmas grave blankets.

"While you're at it, study some of the gravestones. Look at the names and dates. Understand that all these people once walked where you walk today, and that someday, you will seem as lifeless and distant to a future generation as they do to you," Angus said. "What lives on are ideals and traditions and the places we form those things. Like churches. The church is evidence of our existence. It gives us immortality."

Reverend Angus, having made his point, then departed.

"Reverend Anus," Eddie Spallone said. "Reverend Ang-hole."

After a few hours, the minister brought them some lemonade. The boys sat on the grass as he rambled on about the church's history and its patriot pastor, Reverend James Caldwell, whom the British tried to kill during the Revolution. Instead, it was his wife who was gunned down on the steps of the parsonage before they burned the church down.

"Her murder, and the burning of our first church, didn't dissuade the Fighting Parson," Angus said, going into sermon mode. "Instead, with his wife not yet buried, he rallied the Americans at the Battle of Springfield a few days later, and they drove the British out of New Jersey once and for all. He was a true American hero; a leader of mythic proportions in his time, who remains the most famous person ever to come from our town."

Grudeck remembered how bored he was with the whole thing. He just wanted to get the work done and get out of there. He had a Little League double-header that day.

Now Joe Grudeck drove past the triangular park on the south end of town, where there used to be a big "Welcome to Union" sign sponsored by Liberty Dairies. The sign was above a 3-D billboard, a kitschy Jersey landmark with two protruding plastic cow heads coming out of it, even though there were no dairy farms within fifty miles of Union. It advertised Liberty's milk and ice cream products, and was a bulletin board for town news, especially high school sports, spelled out in headline style. Grudeck's father took pictures of some.

COLONIAL CONF. CHAMPS!
Farmers beat Linden, 4–0. J. Grudeck, 2 HR.
STATE CHAMP!
Grudeck repeats hvywgt win.
FARMERS BEAT E-BETH!
Grudeck 3 TD in T-day game.

Later, the Liberty Dairies bosses added another banner below "Welcome to Union." It said, "Home of Red Sox star Joe Grudeck," later amended to "Home of Baseball All-Star Joe Grudeck."

The cow-head sign came down when Liberty Dairies closed in the '90s, replaced in the triangular park with a tasteful and upscale "Welcome to Historic Union" sign, this one with a cannon and a picture of the old church and a Stars and Stripes in the background. It was all very clean and Colonial; no high school results, no mention of Grudeck.

But as Grudeck drove by on this day, he saw a wide plank of wood nailed to the bottom of the sign, with hurried, hand-painted black letters that said, "Home of Joe Grudeck, new Hall of Famer."

He wondered if Reverend Angus was still around. So much for your Reverend Caldwell, Grudeck would tell him. I'm the most famous person who ever came from this town.

THE HOUSE ON STUYVESANT AVENUE was his parents' first, and only. "Stay put and pay down your mortgage," his father always said. "That's how you build security."

Grudeck had no such worries. Or permanence. After rookie camp, he was off to Waterloo, Iowa, to finish the year in A ball. The next summer, he started Double A in Louisville, then Pittsfield, Mass. By the end of the season he was in Pawtucket, with the Triple A Red Sox, in the International League. It was on a bus trip to play Syracuse that Grudeck first visited the Hall of Fame with his team, never dreaming . . .

As a minor leaguer, Grudeck lived in motels, at reduced rates, that had sponsorship deals with his teams. In Louisville, he tried rooming with two teammates but they were slobs, so back he went to the Motel 6. In Pittsfield, he rented a room from an old couple who took in minor leaguers and came to every home game, but their chumminess made Grudeck squirm. He moved to a Budget Inn on Route 7. In Pawtucket, he stayed at the Marriott Residence Inn a few blocks from the ballpark. When he was brought up to Boston in August, he kept the room and drove fifty miles to Fenway. He bounced between clubs the rest of that season and started the next year at Pawtucket, too, but was called to Boston in July for good. He lived in residential hotels, arranged by the team in his first couple of years, then rented an apartment in a Tudor building in Cambridge, not far from Fenway, then moved into a modern condo in Back Bay, and finally, when he was a star, bought a renovated townhouse in Beacon Hill.

Each time he moved, he paid someone else to do it, lock, stock, barrel. Sal arranged the utilities and paid his bills, and hired decorators to make the place nice. Grudeck's only instructions: "Nothing too girly."

Two of the decorators were recent graduates from Boston's School of Interior Design; both beautiful—one compact and dark, the other willowy and blond, with that summers-at-the-Vineyard look. After they set up his house, they put their imprint on his bed, couches, recliners, kitchen counters, bathroom vanity, and wherever else they wrapped themselves around Grudeck. Both swore they never got involved with clients before. The girl who did the townhouse got a little too comfortable. She made suggestions for high-end furnishings she "absolutely loved," knowing there was no limit to Grudeck's budget or boundaries to his absent taste. He said no, suspecting a gold digger. When she asked for a key to Grudeck's place, so she could wait for him on home-game nights, he cut it off right then.

"Why?" she asked through tears.

Grudeck made it quick.

"I don't have to explain myself to you," he said.

Polish cleaning ladies came twice a week to change sheets, do laundry, and wash dishes, even when he was on the road. It was the routine, never interrupted. If he had a girl over, which was often, he left sex-soiled sheets on the bed until the Polish ladies came. If he brought a new girl home before the cleaning ladies came, well, so be it. Grudeck took perverse delight in that. He didn't know why exactly. He'd always heard from married teammates that wives could sniff out other women on them, even after they showered. Not changing the sheets, Grudeck reasoned, was his way of marking his territory. Truth was, he liked living alone back then. He slept with his big body spread out on the bed, without having some girl's head pressing on his shoulder, making his rotator muscles sore, especially his throwing side. He liked not being nudged because he was snoring, and not stifling his curses when charley horses gripped his calves or foot arches in the middle of the night. He liked ripping gas in the morning, spared of female admonishment, as his bowels grumbled from postgame clubhouse buffets of chicken parm, baked ziti, chicken and broccoli stir-fry, and sandwiches.

One of the Polish ladies had an attractive daughter, late twenties. They surprised him once on an off day, while he was still in bed. "Mr. Joe," the mom yelled as she unlocked the front door, as she did most times to no answer. "We clean."

He yelled back "okay" and stayed in bed until the door opened and the girl appeared. She turned flush and tried to exit. "Oh, sorry, Mr. Joe," she said through a thick accent.

"No, sweetheart, it's okay."

She began to dust the room and wiped down the surfaces. The girl, uncomfortable at first, relaxed and smiled over at him several times, first shyly, then with the confidence of a woman in control. She wore snug jeans and a T-shirt and knew Grudeck watched her butt wiggle and breasts shake as she cleaned. He told her she was very pretty, and when she looked over, she saw he was tenting the sheets. Her eyes stayed on it and her eyebrows flashed up with a giggle. Grudeck knew the deal was done. Grudeck reached for his wallet and extracted several hundred-dollar bills.

"Do something nice for me," he said.

She giggled a little more, took the money, held up one finger as if to say "Wait a minute," and left. She returned with the vacuum cleaner, yelled something in Polish to her mother on the first floor, then shut his bedroom door. As she bent to plug it in, Grudeck came up behind her, naked and fully erect, and reached around to undo her pants. She turned the machine on, and it wailed with cover noise, as she squirmed her jeans over her ass and down her thighs. He all but picked her up and knelt her over the bed. She reached back and guided him in. She was dry and it was a little rough, but eventually moistened. His head was spinning with the suddenness, and easiness, of it all, and he lasted only a minute or two before he pulled out and finished by rubbing it between the cheeks of her ass and exploding on her back. He rolled off, she got up, went into his bathroom, and wiped herself clean. He heard the toilet flush and then she was back, pants up, and proceeded to vacuum. He got back under the covers, and when she was done, she wrapped up the cord and said, "Thank you, Mr. Joe," and left.

It was the first time he'd paid for sex. No pressure. No guilt. Just sex. Easy, bodily function sex.

Now, twenty years later, he was still at it. When he moved into the club, he zeroed in on a Hispanic waitress named Darlena. He'd been there only a few weeks and was nervous about looking like a hound among the members. But he didn't want to go home alone every night, either.

Darlena was no kid, maybe mid-thirties, but with smooth mocha skin, a fit body, and a pleasant service smile. She called him Mr. Grudeck, and the times she waited on him, he left a large cash tip, usually two fifties folded and peeking out from a coffee saucer. They made small talk as she looked nervously around the room, but she let out scant details of her life; single mom with two preteens in Catholic school, up from Perth Amboy, worked here and a yacht club on Raritan Bay, ex-husband a deadbeat. "Maybe I can help," he said, and let it hang there. She didn't object that night as he left her a two-hundred-dollar tip.

The next time she was on, Grudeck waited for her in the staff parking lot, standing in the shadows by the kitchen Dumpster. She came out, undoing the fitted black jacket the waitresses had to wear.

She didn't seem surprised to see him when he made himself known or when he said he'd *had a few drinks* and asked *for a ride up the hill* to his condo. As she drove the old Corolla, Grudeck reached for his wallet and pulled out two hundreds.

"You could have called a cab for less," Darlena said.

"I could have walked. I wanted to talk to you about something," Grudeck said, then added, "We're both grown-ups, right?"

She laughed and said, "Uh-oh. I think I know where this is going." But she didn't seem angry, or tell him to go fuck himself.

"Look, I don't want to insult you. You're a hardworking woman, and I'm a guy who's . . . alone. We can have an arrangement. Nothing weird. Just normal."

"Normal prostitution," she said, and now he thought she might be pissed.

"I wouldn't call it that," he said. "I'd call it mutual generosity. Between friends. You do something nice for me, and I'll do something nice for you."

She laughed again. "I tried dancing once, but I've never been a whore."

"Don't say it like that. I don't want you to be a whore," Grudeck said. Joe Bullshit. "It's not like that. I want to help you; I see how hard you work."

"Then what exactly do you want?" she asked.

"Just enough to help me relax," Grudeck said.

"Hand only?"

"Just enough."

It was just that at first, two times a week. They had signals. If Grudeck was alone at the bar at closing time, it meant his door was open. She would let herself in, and flop down on the bed, and wait. Or he would call her cell right before she got off. He was never rough, or forceful, but she moved from hand to everything in a matter of weeks and Grudeck increased the tips. And he was a very good tipper; enough to pay the tuition at Assumption and her rent most months, and eventually buy a used BMW. And she would always leave as stealthily as she came, right after he fell asleep. She would take the hundred-dollar bills he left out and lock the door behind her.

EVERY OFF-SEASON, for his entire career, he returned to the Stuyvesant Avenue house, a modest but solidly built Cape Cod. Early in his career, he'd have Thanksgiving and Christmas at home, and knock around town until spring training. After he discovered golf, he came home for the holidays but took a few weeks here and there in Hilton Head or Palm Beach. He'd return to Union for two weeks before "pitchers and catchers" in February, and when the season opened, he'd unlock the door of his Boston place and find it just the way he'd left it, cleaned twice a week, even during the off-season.

Grudeck drove to his parents' house; it looked the same as long as he could remember. Brick-faced first floor, wood siding up top, painted white.

When he was in high school, his father spent one weekend to frame and Sheetrock the second-floor walk-up attic, converting it into a long bedroom. Grudeck had to pretty much live down the median of the room, where the ceiling peaked. In the low eaves, his father put a desk and bookcases, which mostly held trophies and ghostwritten sports autobiographies for teens. The room now remained much as Joe Grudeck left it before rookie camp, a museum diorama to his youth athletic triumphs. The only significant difference was the bed. His boyhood bed, a sturdy twin, became too small and too unsteady for Major League Joe. In his first full year with Pawtucket, Joe had his mother order a queen-sized mattress set and the deliverymen squeezed it into a corner of the room. He asked her to order a new bed for his parents, too, and they went around and around before she finally relented.

It was a few years later—his first time as an All-Star—he asked them to look for a bigger house up in Summit or Short Hills, the best neighborhoods around, but they refused.

"This is where we live, Joey," his mother said. "Why move? And then drive all the way down here for church? Or to see our friends? It doesn't make any sense."

So he paid to improve the house. He had the electric, plumbing, and heating upgraded throughout, including central air. A few years after that, he sprung to expand the kitchen with all new appliances (including laundry so his mother didn't have to go down the basement stairs), and added a master bath off their bedroom with a Jacuzzi, which they never used.

He offered to have the house sided, but his father liked the look of the wood. So every few years, Joe Grudeck would pay to have it painted, inside and out. Every five years or so, he'd offer to move them, or redo all the fixtures, or buy new appliances, but they always refused.

"Save your money, Joey," his mother said, and Grudeck tried to explain to her just how much $5 million a year was. "Ma, I could buy you ten new houses for that. Let me buy you one, and I'll put the money for the other nine in the bank."

After his dad died, Grudeck offered to move his mother into a luxury condo in downtown Millburn. She said no.

"Your dad is gone. That's enough change for now. I'd rather be alone here, where I'm used to it."

He offered to buy her a dog for companionship.

"Like I need someone else to clean up after now."

He offered to pay for a housekeeper.

"I don't want some stranger cleaning my house."

They went through it all again when he retired and moved to the golf course. He again suggested a dog. She sniffed him out.

"Lookit, I know you're busy, Joey. I don't expect you to come around every day now you're retired. I don't need a dog. Truth is, I have plenty of friends, and plenty to do. *Puhl-lenty.*"

That was true. While Chuck Grudeck never stopped being "Joe Grudeck's father," Sylvia Grudeck had stopped being just "Joe Grudeck's mother" a long time ago. When he left home, she stopped being a spectator in his life and went on with her own. Active, is what they call ladies her age, but that was too passive a word for Sylvia Grudeck. She was busy. She ran the Rosary Society at St. Joe's, and volunteered in the literacy program at the Hannah Caldwell School library. She got involved in the Union Historical Society, even though as "an Italian who married a Polack" she at first thought she'd be out of place among the "blue-haired ladies." But then, Union didn't have many blue-haired ladies.

In all those places, she was known for her contributions and vitality, released from being just "Joe Grudeck's mother."

All those years, Joey's sports kept her from creating the normal rhythms she wanted in her house. Family dinner, Saturday house-cleaning, Sunday church, all came second to Joey's games. Her life was spent on bleachers, in cycles of blending seasons. Football started in summer's last heat and ended in finger-numbing cold. Wrestling filled the daylight hours between bleak mornings and early nightfall, in dimly lit gyms, followed by the dash to freezing cars in dark parking lots. Baseball began with spring's lingering chill and went through to Jersey's oppressively sticky summers. Then football was back. She was the packer; lunch and snacks, water bottles, sweatshirts and gloves, oh, and seat cushions. All those hours on aluminum or wood planks gave her hemorrhoids. She was a spectator, jammed in among many, trying to find the right angle for comfort on unforgiving seats, or sitting in fold-up field chairs that made her hips ache. She used the hours Joey was at school for the lonely work of running her house, and shopped to make wholesome meals. But many times food would go cold on the stove, when Chuck and Joey came in late from practices and admitted they "grabbed something" on the way home. She mopped the day's muddy cleat marks, only to have tomorrow's brought right back in. She washed and dried and folded Joey's uniforms for the next game and the next and the next.

Then the blur of Joey's childhood ended and, just like that, he was gone almost ten months a year. Baseball took him, and kept him on such a tight schedule—all those games, in all those cities, and thank God, she didn't have to sit through them all anymore. Still, she missed him. When he played in New York, he could only join them for a late breakfast in the team hotel, before getting the bus to the ballpark.

Sometimes they went to Boston, but she stopped after Chuck died. But even before that, for ten months a year, for more than twenty years, she saw him only a handful of days for a handful of hours.

And then he would come home, and it was like he'd never left. Sleeping, eating, talking sports with his dad, going to the gym, doing God knows what around town until he left again for his golf vacation, then spring training. He left a boy, and as the cycle of seasons quickened with time, retired a middle-aged man. Sylvia watched in quiet despair. His sports dominated her life as a young mother, and they would leave her life as an older mother unfilled. Yes, she hoped for the usual: that Joey would someday find a girl and settle down into a grown-up life. Yes, she dreamed of Joey living nearby—around the corner, the next town over—with his agreeable wife and three, four adorable kids. Sylvia could babysit after school, and take them to the park, or go shopping with the girls while Chuck threw around the ball with the boys. But now Chuck was gone, and she, well, she kept busy.

Grudeck was a perfect mix of his parents. He got his height and long arms and legs from his father's Polish side, and the breadth of his shoulders, strength of his back, and sturdiness on his feet from his mother's Southern Italian side. He had his mother's prominent "guinea profile" in nose and chin, and her dark hair, still more black than gray. Certainly, his fierceness as a competitor came from his mother, although his easygoing off-field manner was more like his dad.

But Sylvia Grudeck was not an emotional woman. Even as she aged, she was strong and sturdy, easily able to lug bags of kielbasa and other groceries from Lutz's five blocks away and unafraid to tackle heavy yard work or shovel out after a blizzard. Joe always detected a hardness about her, an aloof shell, maybe a trait passed down from the poor, barren-earth farmers who were her ancestors.

Chuck Grudeck had some dark corners, too, well hidden from the "great guy, great coach" face he put on in public. He found no pleasure in his work; eight hours a day, doing the same thing, over and over and over. Nobody better or worse than the next guy. Assembly was assembly; joyless work for an hourly wage. Something you *had* to do, not wanted to do.

He derived all of his life's enjoyment—more than that, all of his *identity*—from the sports heroics of his son.

Chuck Grudeck may have made Joe Grudeck *what* he was, but Joe Grudeck also made Chuck Grudeck *who* he was: Joe Grudeck's father.

In the end, that was all.

In the years before his father died, Grudeck often wondered, *What if I'd sucked? What then? What would have happened to him?*

Joe Grudeck aided his father's escape from an ordinary life by being an extraordinary son. His talent propelled his dad from run-of-the-mill factory worker to star maker, local legend, pillar of the youth-sports community.

But it wasn't enough to fill Chuck Grudeck's loneliness. The rare times Joe Grudeck moved unnoticed through the house, he detected his parents' distance from each other. His father, on his nights off, watched a game . . . any game . . . on TV, until dozing off. His mother, in the kitchen with the daily *Star-Ledger*, read every word, to make the evening disappear. On weekends, as Chuck rushed through the yard work to get Joey to his games, his mother was in the house, dusting and vacuuming with equal haste. Their conversations over dinner centered on Joey's games and matches, or nothing. The rare times Sylvia didn't go, she got the blow-by-blow.

"Tell Ma how you did today, Joey."

"I pinned the kid from Irvington in thirty-six seconds?"

"You shoulda seen it, Syl . . . Joey picks up this big colored kid like he was nothing . . . and bam! Right to his back. Flat. The place exploded."

Each night, a different story, but with the same ending. Wrestling season, Joey won. Football and baseball, Joey's team won because of Joey.

Both years Joe Grudeck won the state wrestling championships, his father sat matside with the coaches, and rushed out to clumsily hoist his son in the air. When Grudeck's teams won their state football titles, his dad charged onto the field with the kids as the seconds ticked off.

It took Joe Grudeck years to understand, but the burden of it all—*What if I'd sucked?*—kept him coming home to Union. His father needed him. He needed him to be Joe Grudeck, so he could be Joe Grudeck's dad. Joe Grudeck had to stay close. To not do so would have made his father a nobody.

When his dad died seven years back, McCracken Funeral Home had a line down the block. It was a miserable night in late July, misty and damp when rain wasn't falling. Grudeck knew he was coming to the end of the line as a player, and his dad getting sick was a double shot of looming mortality. But he never expected him to go that quick. He would have liked to have spent more time . . . but family doesn't come first in the bigs. The team does.

Joe Grudeck flew in from Detroit to stand by his mother. He stood stoic and strong, sweating in his black suit, knee and hip aches dulled by Advil, and accepted condolences from hundreds of people he'd known his whole life. The kids he played with, now grown into paunchy men. Their parents, now gray and stooped. The other men who coached in town, some older than his dad, now unsure in their step. The remaining Jenn-Air workers, down to one shift as the company outsourced work to a sheet-metal factory in Vietnam. For four sessions over two days, Joe shook all the sweaty hands, giving as firm as he got, even as his own hand swelled and stiffened. He took the back slaps and hugs, ignoring the burning sensation in his throwing shoulder. He listened to stories and compliments about his father, with such intent sincerity his face muscles ached. And not for one minute was he ever convinced all those people were there for his dad. They were there for him.

The night after the funeral, Grudeck boarded a plane in Newark and settled into a first-class seat. During the plane's ascent, Grudeck looked out the small window at the expanse of lights below; the lights of his town and the surrounding towns like his, the lights of thousands of homes like his, filled with people like his parents, all shrinking away beneath him, becoming blurred behind wisps of clouds. Or was it the tears gathering in his eyes?

One light—his father's—was extinguished. And then it hit him. Grudeck, too, was marching down his own timeline. He only had a few years left to play, and then he, too, would fade away. He would no longer be a man of the moment, he would be a man of memory. He would be a living relic. Dead as a player. Alive as something else. What would that be?

He pushed his face closer to the plane window, suddenly overwhelmed by these terribly sad facts: all his fame did not buy his father a single extra minute of time, nor would it eternally preserve his father's legacy. It was all coming to an end. His dad was dead and Joey was getting too old to play. Too old. Who would care about Chuck Grudeck anymore, when Joe Grudeck was too old to play? Here, above it all, he saw it so clearly. He leaned into the window well so the overattentive first-class stewardesses could not see his face.

It was the last time he'd cried.

Not when he retired.

Not on Farewell Joe Grudeck Night at Fenway.

Not this morning, when he found out he'd been inducted.

Chapter Six

Grudeck turned in his mother's driveway, got out, and opened the glass storm door with a G design in wrought aluminum. Sylvia Grudeck was in the kitchen, washing her morning coffee-and-toast dishes, when her son filled the doorway.

"Joey! What a surprise," she said as he gave her a quick kiss on the cheek. "Is everything all right?"

How could she not remember this was Hall announcement day? he thought.

"You should have told me you were coming . . . I have a church meeting this morning . . . but let me put some coffee on."

Grudeck let her.

She waited for him to ask, *just once,* if he was interrupting her day, but he didn't. Not today, not ever. She found this grating, and found herself feeling guilty for being irritated as she filled the glass coffee carafe with cold water.

"Ma, I have news."

"Good news, I hope."

"Yep, good news. I got voted in. I'm in."

She forgot today was the day. Completely forgot. She let the carafe rest in the sink and turned to hug him, now more flush with conflicted feelings.

"Oh, my God. Oh, Joey, your father . . . the Hall of Fame? . . . He would have never dreamed. Oh, Joey . . . so proud, he would have been so, so proud." Tears came to her eyes as she held her son.

Here it was, the culmination of Chuck's life and, well, hers, too, but Chuck was gone, and she was not. She searched for the right superlatives.

"This is just wonderful, terrific, Joey. Ever since you were a little boy . . . The Hall of Fame!"

"Yep, me, right there with Ted Williams, Babe Ruth, Joe DiMaggio, all of 'em."

"I don't know what to say. Well, let's see . . ." she stammered, trying to marry his big news to her already planned day, ". . . let's see . . . I have a church meeting at eleven thirty . . . and we're packing lunches for the soup kitchen after . . . and, oh, forget it . . . I can skip it. Oh, my God . . . the Hall of Fame! . . . I can just, let me call Father Ed and tell him I'm not coming!"

"No, Ma, don't do that. I just came to tell you before you heard somewhere else. I got to go see Sal, and then there's a press conference, and, you know . . . Tell ya what. I'll drive you over."

"And then how will I get back?"

There was some snap in her voice. "I mean, I planned to drive myself," she said, righting herself. "Like I always do."

They moved to the Formica-topped kitchen table, a yellow-speckled relic from the 1960s, still sturdy as Gibraltar, and sat in the matching plastic-cushioned chairs. They were silent for almost a minute as Sylvia Grudeck dabbed her eyes.

"Think about how many times we sat here," he said. "The number of meals . . . I've probably eaten a hundred thousand meatballs at this table."

His mother snorted a laugh.

"Yeah, and these old things are coming back in style. Can you believe it?" she said. "I saw them in Huffman Koos last week . . . a set like this was two thousand dollars! I was with Rose Tartaglia and we were laughing! I said, 'I could have a garage sale, sell my old junky set as an *antique* and make a few hundred bucks.' "

Sylvia Grudeck didn't sit long. She jumped up to get the coffee and grabbed a pack of anisette toast from the pantry.

"Let me make you some eggs," she said.

"No, Ma, I've got to go."

The kitchen wall phone rang.

"Let me just see who that is . . ."

"Sure, Ma . . ."

It was her friend Mrs. Erminio, to say Joey was on TV.

"Oh, thanks, Bet . . . Joey's here . . . I will . . . Yes, I will . . ."

"Betty Erminio says congratulations," she said when she hung up. "And you're on the sports station right now. Tony was watching."

They went into the living room, and Grudeck found the remote on the reading table, right where his father always kept it. On *SportsCenter* he saw his young self, a near rookie smiling in the sun, then behind the plate. Then a still shot of his rookie card.

The announcer, a young black hipster, was saying stuff like . . . *Mr. Lunchbucket, yo, now enshrined . . . last of the hard-knuckled catchers, true that . . . Mr. Icon of Beantown . . . gave blood at the office ev-er-y day . . . Mr. Everyday, Joe Grrreww, going in the Shrine.*

He kept the patter up during the highlights, Grudeck throwing out a runner, Grudeck watching his World Series home run, and then the two moments everybody seemed to love the most.

The first, a still photo of him knocking out Willie McCombs, was one for the ages. Like Ali standing over Liston. Namath aiming his finger to God. Larsen jumping into Yogi's arms. Joe Grudeck showing the ball, Willie McCombs starched at his feet.

It happened in his second year, when McCombs was the fastest man in baseball and played with spikes-up aggression. He tried to score from second on a blooper in the gap, and the throw from right field one-hopped to Grudeck, braced at the plate. Grudeck knew what was coming. McCombs's only chance was to broadside this kid catcher with a shoulder to the ribs, knock him on his ass, and get him to drop the ball. But McCombs lowered his shoulder. Grudeck swung a two-handed tag around hard, aiming for McCombs's head. Glove, ball, and fist—the front line of Joe Grudeck's shifting weight—landed square on McCombs's jaw like a perfectly timed backhanded left hook. A one-punch knockout. He was out, all right, out at the plate and out cold. He fell on his back, arms stiff and quivering at his sides. The Fenway crowd, on its feet and screaming already in anticipation of the play, exploded in a guttural, nuclear howl: 37,000-something people expelling all that was in their lungs at once. Grudeck never heard anything like it. The sound reverberated through his head and chest, deep into his brain and lungs. He suddenly felt light-headed and light-footed. A tingle gripped the back of his neck and his sphincter.

This is what *glory* feels like, he thought at that moment, and seeing the picture brought it all back. Every time.

A guy from the Associated Press got the shot. Joe Grudeck, his mouth open and twisted in emotion, holding the ball like a battle trophy over the prone McCombs. The AP moved the picture internationally. The tabloid *Herald* and staid *Globe* both used it big on Page 1, with a rare identical headline: "OUT AT HOME!"

One play, one moment, the first Joe *Grrrewww* legend was made.

The second, a video, was an ugly, nasty spectacle, always shown in Grudeck highlight clips and a greatest hit in "The Best in Basebrawls" video collections.

On the night he choked out a young slugger named Felix Ruiz, Grudeck was in mid-career and the best-hitting catcher in the AL. It was the final game of a weekend trip to Yankee Stadium in late August, with the teams battling for first. The Yanks won the first two, racking up double-digit runs in each game to the delight of their front-running fans. Growing up in Jersey, Grudeck loved the Yankees, but playing there in a Red Sox uniform poisoned his boyhood memories.

Now it was late Sunday afternoon, the sun sinking on another Red Sox season. Grudeck tried to keep his teammates up, constantly chattering. It was humiliating. Joe Cheerleader, forced to resort to high school rah-rah stuff to fire up a team of fucking quitters. The anger began to spew out of his gut, a toxic, molten flow that dried his throat and burned in his ears. In the top of the eighth, a rookie reliever named Gannon—Gannon the Cannon—pitched Ruiz high and tight. Ruiz faced the kid and grabbed his crotch. The fans went wild, especially all the New York Puerto Ricans who came to see Ruiz play. Grudeck became incensed.

"Hey, it's a day game, there's a lot of families here," Grudeck bitched through his mask. "How 'bout some respect?"

"Fa yu, man," Ruiz said, and spat across the plate.

"Fa me?" Grudeck came back, mimicking his accent. "Those are American dollars they're payin' you, Pedro. Try learning English."

Ruiz ignored him and let another stream of tobacco juice go, this time angled more closely toward Grudeck.

"Watch yourself, Pedro," Grudeck said.

Then Grudeck called for another pitch inside. Gannon shook him off. Grudeck called it again.

The kid shook him off again and stepped off the rubber. Grudeck yelled "time" and bounded toward the mound. The kid looked alarmed as Grudeck bore down on him.

"Hit him," he hissed at Gannon. The kid blinked.

"Hit him," Grudeck said again.

"I don't know, Joe . . ."

"I'm not asking. I'm telling you, hit this son of a bitch, right now," Grudeck said. "Right now, you decide if you want respect in this league. If you do, drill this bastard. Right in the hip. Or the back. Hit him in the head, I don't give a fuck. But hit him now. I'll take care of the rest."

The kid did as told. A fastball to the hip. Ruiz jumped back, but not quickly enough. Ruiz dropped his bat and started toward the mound, pounding his chest, cursing in Spanish. He didn't get far. Grudeck threw off his mask and helmet, ditched his glove, and was right on him. He spun him by the shoulder, so they were face to face, and Grudeck heard the howl in his ears. Was it the crowd or the rush of anger disguised as adrenaline?

"Wha . . . wha da fa?" said Ruiz, hands out.

Grudeck shoved him—just hard enough to let Ruiz come back with a straight overhand right. Grudeck stepped inside it and put Ruiz in a neck-twisting headlock, then flung him over his hip to the ground. Grudeck landed with his big lats against Ruiz's chest and felt the guy's ribs collapse. He was hoping a few had broken. He squeezed Ruiz's neck, trying to break that, too. Then he took his top hand and ripped the thick braided gold chain off Ruiz's neck and tried to shove it in his mouth.

"Now what . . . Now what do you have to say, you spic fuck," Grudeck spat down. "Open up. C'mon, big mouth. I'll shove this spic chain down your spic throat."

By now the benches were emptied and Grudeck saw legs multiplying around him and hands pulling his uniform.

Ruiz struggled but Grudeck had him plenty tight with just one arm. With his fist closed around the chain, Grudeck punched Ruiz hard in the face . . . one, two, three times . . . driving his flat nose even flatter into his dumb skull. Then there was a scrum of bodies, a forest of pin-striped and gray legs, arms flailing and grabbing. Joe Grudeck went back to a two-handed headlock and squeezed until . . . he wanted to hear a snap. He wouldn't let go, even as the blood pumped out of Ruiz's split nostrils, even as his mocha skin turned a sick shade of purple. Men pulled at Joe Grudeck's arms, someone punched him in the ear, and someone kneed him in the back, but he wasn't letting go. Joe Grudeck wasn't letting go until . . . he wanted to see Ruiz's head explode like a blood-filled balloon.

"Jesus Christ, Joe, you're killin' him."

All around him, people were trying to pry him off. They dug fingers into his forearms . . . but Grudeck flexed, and tightened his grip. It was then he heard Ruiz whimper and go slightly limp.

"Joe, that's enough, Joe! Joe, the guy's out!"

It was then he looked in Ruiz's sick, broken, swollen face, and whispered, "Fa me? No, fa you. I could kill you if I wanted to, you big spic pussy."

And then he let go.

The boos and curses came down on him as he walked to the dugout, ejected from the game. Stuff was flying. It was Seat Cushion Day and they came down around him like a flock of Frisbees. The crowd sound pounded through his head and heaving chest, and he felt almost as glorious as the day he starched Willie McCombs. He looked over at Ruiz. Still purple. Trainers around him checking his neck. He was sitting on the grass, all shaky like a just-knocked-out fighter. Which is what he was.

Another *Joe Grrewww* moment.

That night in a New York hotel room he flipped channels, catching all the sports news, and saw the highlight over and over. A suspension was coming, but everyone loved a baseball fight, especially a bloody one. Over the next day, the sports talk show hosts rehashed it all, bickering and yelling, attacking each other like Grudeck attacked Ruiz. Some complained there was no room in baseball for brushbacks, others argued pitchers had a "historical right" to move batters from the plate. Some cried that today's hitters were a bunch of posturing babies too soft to take one for the team, others said a pitcher who drilled a batter had to expect to be charged. But there was something everyone agreed on: Joe Grudeck was right to defend his pitcher, Joe Grudeck was a stand-up guy, an old-school player, a throwback to the days when teammates stood up for each other and guys played with heart. Joe Grudeck beating Felix Ruiz's ass . . . now that was baseball.

THE GRUDECK SEGMENT of the broadcast ended and the announcers moved on to other things.

Grudeck clicked it off, sitting in his father's recliner, imitation leather worn soft on the armrests from the oils of Chuck Grudeck's hands.

"Enshrined," his mother said. "They say that like you're some saint. If they only knew?" She gave a little laugh. *Joey, her bad boy.*

If she only knew, Grudeck thought, letting the two girls from Syracuse visit and trouble his mind for a few seconds.

"But I wish you could get them to stop using some of those pictures," she said. "So violent. Can't you get them to stop?"

No, Grudeck said, he couldn't get them to stop.

"That's what they loved about me when I was a player."

It was the Grudeck lore; last of the old school, the last of the Mohicans, like Sal always said. It was why he was revered in Boston, respected everywhere else. He was like a living ghost from a past most fans thought was better, when baseball was in black and white, and great ballplayers like Ted Williams went to war and liked fishing and were regular guys, just like them.

"You always were such a good player, without all that," his mother said, but the past tense of both their sentences hung in the air, forcing a long silence.

"So . . . what are you going to do now?" Sylvia Grudeck finally asked.

"Sal set up a press conference for later and I gotta do some radio and TV . . ."

"No, Joseph, I mean like in the future," she said. "What are you going to do now? Like with the rest of your life?"

Chapter Seven

Sally Mueller stood in her "ratty robe" at the kitchen window, and held a mug of tea up close to her chin. The warm moist steam rose and enveloped her face, giving comfort against the dry cold of the Otsego Lake morning. She covered the mug with her hands, letting the moisture soothe her skin.

In winter—between the cold, the firewood, and the wet laundry—her hands got red and dry and chapped no matter how much lotion she lathered on them. Her hands made her feel she was aging fast. Time was disappearing and she had little to show for it. The word *little* bounced around in her head. She asked for so little. A little house, a little job security for her family, a little happiness. It all seemed so *attainable*, so American middle class. So little to ask for. And somehow, little by little, it slipped away.

She tightened up the robe, a heavy old terry-cloth thing Horace gave her for a birthday a decade or more before. It was maroon then, bright, but had since faded to the color of dried blood. She blew the steam toward the window, hoping the heat would defrost the ice crystals that formed inside. They were beautiful, glassine mosaics of nature's art—when they were outside. When they were inside, they reminded Sally how much she hated this house. As the crystals dripped away, the window cleared. Sally looked around the property: the bare, unpruned tree branches like varicosities against the gray sky; Horace's frozen clothes and yellowed long underwear, hanging like inverted skeletons on the line; the dead stalks and sticks of the garden; Horace's metal sculptures from his early days of blacksmithing littered the side yard and were entangled in overgrown grass, looking like rusted wheelchairs and walkers at some abandoned sanitarium. She looked down the narrow, rutted dirt driveway, always muddy in summer and rock-hard in winter, leading up from Chicken Farm Hill Road, then at the firewood stacked on the sagging side porch. The chimney above it was in need of repointing, the roof shingles around the chimney were thin and cracked, and like the weathered clapboard on the old house, leaked warm air out and let cold air in. Inside, the smell of stale smoke from Horace's woodstove permeated everything. More than once, Michael's friends got accused of sneaking cigarettes after hanging out at the Muellers'.

Sally turned away and did the math in her head. How much to fix? How much more debt?

She opened the kitchen drawer where she hid the bills, the wood-on-wood screech of cabinet resistance echoing her own trepidation to see the numbers in black and white. The stack, kept under three woven placemats and an assortment of ladles and cooking spoons, was thicker than ever. These relentless mailings by creditors must keep the post office in business, she thought. It was time to work, and the first order of organization was to cull the bundle of duplicate warning letters, and burn them in Horace's stove. At least it was good for something. Next were the bills she had to pay: the cancelable services. The ones Horace would notice if plugs were pulled: electric, cable TV—not that he watched, but he would wonder about the silence. Then car insurance. God forbid Horace ever got pulled over in that pile of junk he drove and found the insurance lapsed. Then he would ask questions and more questions in that relentless way of his and Sally would have to admit how broke they were. Beyond broke. Behind in the mortgage, maxed out on credit cards, unqualified for a home equity loan because of bad credit and a worse house. Sally once tried to add a measly $15,000 or

$20,000 to the mortgage, just enough to clean up her credit cards. She forged Horace's signature on all the requisite paperwork, and took an afternoon off to meet the appraiser hired by Bank of America. He pulled in, scanned the outside, and never bothered to knock. Just like that, he was gone. She ran outside to stop him, but was left standing alone in gray dust kicked up by his tires.

She knew what he was thinking.

White trash.

No two words scared her more. But here she was, in her cold kitchen in her ratty robe living below her modest expectations.

LIKE HORACE, SALLY HAD ROOTS in New York State farming. Unlike Horace, it was dead to her. Gone, and best forgotten. She *lived* what Horace often romanticized. She *saw* the body-bending effects of farmwork on her father, whose shoulders sloped more with each passing year, and the hump in her mother's back, and the limps both had by their early sixties, hips fused and knees bowed from carrying sacks of seed and stacking hay bales and milking cows and loading feed and shoveling shit.

Her job was the chickens, and she could still smell the henhouse; the chicken blood and excrement and rotten eggs seeped into soil and soul, and became entrenched in your nostrils and gut. That smell, it stuck like the gluey goat manure in the traction ridges of your boots.

Sally's family had apple and pear orchards in the rural hills of Romulus, high above Cayuga Lake. Her father tried to convince her grandfather in the mid-1970s to give up the barn animals and fruit trees, and follow other growers into the wine business. The state tourism board was trying to make the Finger Lakes Region the Napa Valley of the East, her father said. The future was in grapes.

Her grandfather resisted.

"He wants to be a gentleman farmer, not a working farmer," Grandpap complained.

"The apples from Washington State are prettier, and prettier is what sells," her dad would say. "Wine is the answer, but he's too stubborn to see it and too old to change his ways. That's what's killing us."

Grandpap finally agreed to let her father experiment with grapes on limited acreage. Her father, taking what the land gave him, tried to develop a series of wines that were apple- and pear-based with a hint of grape, rather than the other way around. But the products lacked the refinement of the Cabernet Sauvignons, Rieslings, Pinot Noirs, Chardonnays, and ice wines of the region.

The wine-tasting tourists were much different than the vacationers from the old Cayuga Lake cabin days, those machinists and bus drivers and cops and government employees from Yonkers or Albany or Schenectady or Syracuse, towing aluminum rowboats packed with tied-down plastic coolers and sleeping bags, ready to rough it in some "rustic" lakeside bungalow. The new tourists were Ithaca highbrows and Manhattanites and Park Slopers; the Arts & Leisure crowd. The wineries were another gallery, a place to envelop oneself in a culture foreign enough from white-collar life to count as an experience.

In her awkward teens, Sally saw these people as erudite and sophisticated. These were New Yorkers, and Sally found herself feeling backward, clumsy, and poor in their company as they came to her farm to try, and reject, her father's fruit wines.

Sally worked the tasting room on weekends all through high school, filling plastic goblets like a bartender as the tourists sipped and meandered around, looking at old black-and-white pictures of her family working the orchards or the packhouse. Her favorite was of Grandpap, pipe and straw fedora, with one foot up on the running board of a '51 Ford pickup with "Romulus Orchards" stenciled on the door.

After years of trying, her father never did produce wines good enough for the Finger Lakes Winery Tour. Still, the signs on Routes 96 and 414 directed a sustainable number of seasonal tourists to their farm atop a hill on Marsh Corner Road, which intersected both county highways.

The tasting room was a converted packing shed, Sheetrocked and painted rose. It was not a wine gallery, no glass tables or craft-period furniture. Just Sally, and her counter of plastic glasses, flustered and intimidated by New Yorkers in their weekend Ralph Lauren or downtown black, talking about balance and depth and pigmentation. She blushed as they asked questions she could not answer about process, or how their wines compared in composition, say, to the Johannesburg Rieslings. When she explained the wines were apple- and pear-based, she could hear the subtle derision that blunted their feigned interest.

"Oh, that. You mean like Boone's Farm? The stuff we used to drink in high school?!"

"So, is it something you can drink with . . . ?"

She stumbled through, feeling so . . . *inferior* . . . a word often whispered about her father's concoctions. She knew what they were thinking. Upstate hick. Trailer trash, getting drunk on cheap fruit wine. Okay, so there were two trailers on the property—for seasonal help. But her family lived in a Federalist brick house, sturdy and meticulously kept by her mother. The surrounding farm, too, was always tidy, with no broken machinery left rusting in the fields. The barns and storage sheds were painted apple-red every few years, the fences bright white. Her dad had the long driveway paved once they started selling wines.

But the wines were a failed experiment that left the farm not quite a winery and no longer a full orchard. Through Sally's adolescence and teen years, her father and Grandpap fought over its future, often bitterly. All their hard work yielded only enough to meet loan interest. They had land, and all the money went to sustain it. Her father wanted to sell, but Grandpap refused.

"This was my father's land, goddamnit."

So they stayed until Grandpap died. Her father, ambition soured and in debt, sold the operation to a Wall Street couple who, within five years, developed a Cayuga White that won Gold Medals at the New York Wine and Food Classic four years running and a dry Riesling that won twice.

The farm was sold just as Sally went off to college, on scholarships and loans, and her parents moved to a small apartment on the back-streets of Skaneateles, where they got jobs in little lakeside tourist shops. She never returned home.

All these years later, now sitting at a tin-top table in a drafty farmhouse with cold air whispering in the cracks, the failure of it all resounded in the walls around her. *White trash.* She graduated Cornell, had a good job managing the billing department of a medical group, wore nice clothes, and bought Michael everything every other kid had.

Still, the words haunted her. She'd wanted something better, for herself and Michael, but . . .

She shuffled the bills and said his name out loud. "Horace."

This house, this life. Sally remembered how it all started, more than twenty years ago. Horace was the farm museum archivist then, and they had a nice, affordable apartment on the second floor of one of Cooperstown's massive Stick-style Victorians. Sally loved to come home, to park in the crushed-stone driveway and imagine the dark, imposing house was all hers. She would look up at the eaves and angular turrets, the decorative molding painted a brooding shade of hunter green, over gray shingles. Horace was doing research and writing, in what Sally thought was only a layover job between his master's and PhD, and wherever that would take them. Chapel Hill, Ann Arbor, maybe back to Ithaca. Princeton? She could only dream. Then, one night he told her about a conversation he'd had with the museum's blacksmith. Horace was researching a Conestoga wagon wheel exhibit, so he wanted to ask the blacksmith about wheel bands.

"I walk in and we talk. After a while he says, 'You're a big man, so why don't you do real work?' " Horace told her.

"What a jerk," Sally said.

"No, he was just ball-busting," Horace explained. "So I say, 'I do real work. I analyze life back then and explain why things were done.' "

"And he says, 'Hah! You don't have to be a professor to know that. For survival! That's why it was done. You want to understand *back then*?

Then put your hands into the fire. Leave the study to schoolgirls.' And then he held up his hands. You should have seen them, Sally! They looked like he was wearing thick gloves of skin, layers of healed burns and cuts and cracks and calluses."

Sally remembered the admiration in Horace's voice, and Horace was not one to fawn. The blacksmith was a Hungarian named Melle Kovacs, and Horace began to visit him daily and return home each night with another bit of his story. He was from the Puszta countryside and came from a long line of blacksmiths. But like Horace, he was educated, with a degree from Szent István University in agricultural sciences.

"I learned much theory, but I never forgot the *practice* of making something lasting with my hands . . . this metal thing that would last for the ages, made the same way through the ages," he told Horace. "Let me tell you something, my friend. I tried working in my field, horticulture and plant development. But those were sciences of patience, not energy. The blacksmith practices a craft of *violence*. It appeals to the man deep inside, the fire core. You hammer and forge and you have something to show for your work in the time it takes the metal to cool."

Horace told Sally he was *intrigued*, and when Kovacs offered to teach him the basics, he agreed.

Sally asked why.

"I don't know; to do something different. Plus, the guy's got a point. I'm trying to understand history through study, locked away in a room full of books and articles. Maybe I can understand more by living it."

And just like that, interest quickly turned to obsession. Horace told Sally he spent his life *doing too much thinking and not enough doing. I'm getting soft. I want to live my life as a creator, not some sidelines critic.*

For the rest of that summer, Horace spent his spare time in stealth apprenticeship, watching as the Hungarian wielded the hammers and tongs of the craft with hands impervious to the flying sparks of the fire or the bits of molten metal that assaulted them daily. It was primal man at his best, Horace thought, and the primitive tools spoke to him.

Those tools, in the hands of a strong man, reduced one of nature's hardest elements to exactly what mankind needed: a weapon, a tool, a horseshoe. Horace said when he worked with those tools—when his forearms were engorged with blood and his hair became soaked with cooling sweat and he felt his historian's hands getting hard as blisters turned to calluses—that he realized old Kovacs was right. To understand history, to appreciate when life was hard, you had to live it. Mimic it, at the very least.

"This is a more authentic life," he told Sally.

"To be a reenactor?" Sally wanted to say, but she kept quiet, hoping the phase would pass.

Instead, Horace expanded his relationship with the tools. He learned about the weights and head speeds of hammers, the grip strength in the tongs and cutting force of the chisels. The tools felt like natural extensions of his arms and hands, and there was much to learn; knowledge in its most physical form.

The historical papers now began to feel dead to him, like brittle autumn leaves, he told Sally. Yes, the history of farming in the Leatherstocking Region was a history *close* to him. Yes, it was his grandfather's, and ancestors' before. But not his. This work, this real work, could be his.

Sally saw no future in it, and said so, but Kovacs coaxed Horace along, telling him he was a natural.

"You know, I'm getting ready to retire—my hands can't take it anymore," the old man told Horace. "They're going to need a new blacksmith. Why not you?"

Horace went to the museum director at the time, Dr. Vanderoot, who had grown the place from a ragtag collection of plows and tools to a living historical village. When Horace asked if he could transfer from archives to the smithy, Dr. Vanderoot was all for it.

"Anybody can study history," Dr. Vanderoot applauded, slapping the arms of his captain's desk chair, "but it takes a special man to forge it! A bad pun, yes, but I say, 'Do it!' "

Horace did. He immersed himself in the dirty work, and gave up his intellectual pursuits without once consulting Sally or weighing the impact on her. His transformation into a man she did not marry had begun.

FALL SEMESTER, SOPHOMORE YEAR. Two bright New York State kids admitted into the public side of Cornell, the ag college, and thrown in with the smart (and rich and more sophisticated) kids from Connecticut to California.

She was shy and kind of pretty, right off the farm, nervous as all get-out to be in Ithaca, afraid she might not be up to the challenge of an Ivy education. He was tall and long, dark hair falling over his forehead, with strength of conviction to match the breadth of his shoulders, without shame for his state upbringing.

They shared a few classes, but during a discussion of *Elmer Gantry* in Am Lit 201, it happened. Unintimidated by his fellow students, or Professor What's-his-name, a Columbia-educated New Yorker, he spoke his mind about the mean portrayal of country folk as mush-brained suckers in early-twentieth-century novels. Horace argued that Sinclair Lewis made cartoon characters of rural people in the fictional town of Zenith, and had the novel stereotyped blacks in a similar way, it would have fallen off the academic world's approved list. He then went a step further and surmised that Lewis was a "sellout," who was just giving New York editors what they expected, or worse, wanted.

"He was from Sauk Centre, Minnesota, for God's sake, he should have known better," Horace said.

"That's a fairly grand and preposterous supposition, Mr. Mueller," the professor said.

But Horace dug in. It was his turf. He argued the novel was not a great book, but a predictable "yawn" about morally corrupt, Evangelical preachers preying on country rubes. Once again, religion and country folk were turned into punch lines by "so-called sophisticated people who did not know how to seek divinity within, or from the earth." Horace said that, all manned up, leaning forward on his desk, shoulders squared to their widest, aware of the silent snickers and sideways glances around him.

The professor argued that the portrayal was accurate.

"The proof of stereotyping lies in your certainty that I'm wrong," Horace shot back. "There's the real danger: you believe what you've read in a novel is more valid than what I've lived."

Checkmate, Sally remembered thinking, filled with admiration for Horace's ballsiness, and she felt something stir in her, something innate. Was that when she fell in love with him? Or was it a few days later, when he came up to her after class and simply said, "Walk with me." It was a gentle order, an invitation delivered with confidence, without waver or fear that she would not accept, and that feeling came back. She learned at that moment where the expression "swept off her feet" came from and they walked up to the magnificent gardens of the Cornell Plantations under a brilliant blue autumn sky.

Without a trace of self-consciousness, he guided her by the elbow over the brick pathways. He placed his hand on her shoulder or low on her back to usher her through some narrow walkways ahead of him. He made her giggle at the names as he enunciated them slowly . . . the W. C. Muenscher Poisonous Plants Garden . . . the Muriel B. Mundy Wildflower Garden . . . He joked that "Triphammer"—the name of the footbridge over the falls below Beebe Lake—didn't exactly inspire confidence.

They walked around the lake (she cut her environmental chemistry class), talking easily about everything—the world, their dreams, and how those dreams might fit into the world. As the sun went down, he took off his flannel-lined jean jacket and put it over her shoulders. It was enormous. She felt like a little girl dressing up in her father's coat. It was warm from his body heat, and she felt safe. Safe and warm. From that first day, until he went crazy, that's how Horace always made her feel.

IT WAS ALWAYS COLD IN ITHACA; in her room at Balch Hall, where the environmentally conscious university kept the heat at 65, and later in the apartment they shared on Eddy Street where the radiators would stop clanging in the middle of the night and ice crystals would appear like intricate etchings on the windowpanes each dawn. "Our art collection," Horace would say as he enveloped her in his arms and warm determination to someday make it all right. He was earnest, as they used to say. And together, they were a serious young couple, not given to drunkenness or other campus stupidity. They fell in with kids like them, young people who cared about pollution, American corporate imperialism, corruption of the political process, the falling national intellect led by the news and entertainment industries. Stuff like that. Their friends were kids from all over America, and Sally was exploding with a sense of worldly growth. They were all groping for something to believe in—and something to leave behind—and found one another. They gathered in dorm rooms and later in shabby Ithaca apartments to sip wine and talk passionately about big ideas.

Horace's big idea was to cure "modern alienation" and the nation's "ethical breakdown" by returning to small-town life.

When someone would argue that small-town life was too confining, Horace countered that it was "liberating, in its own rigid way."

"You know what's expected of you and what to abide by," Horace said. "It cuts down on moral confusion; I think positive creativity can spring from that"; and then he ticked off the famous farm-town inventors, writers, and artists, from Thomas Edison to William Faulkner to Jackson Pollock. He even threw in Sinclair Lewis, because it suited his argument.

Sally thought Horace's outlook was noble and sweet, and, of course, naïve, when he spoke of a society going back to American basics: Ten Commandments, Bill of Rights, and common sense.

"Politicians and the controversy whores in the media convinced us we have no common ground," he liked to say. "They exploit our differences, rather than explore our similarities. On every issue, they work the extreme fringes, left and right, giving platforms to special-interest groups. The voice of the great middle is never heard."

When he said these things in front of their friends, Sally saw in Horace a dynamic potential leader, someone with a vision to help make things right, through writing, teaching, or maybe even politics. She saw a man who could make an impact. And she couldn't wait to get him alone underneath the assortment of sleeping bags and cheap comforters they used to keep warm. He wrapped these around her like a queen's robe when she straddled him and found the right place and rhythm; rubbing against his hard belly where it felt best for her and not having his significant length be too intrusive. Horace didn't seem to mind, as she went and went again. "Just ride me, baby," he would whisper, with one giant hand on her ass and the other clasping the quilt at her neck to keep her warm. When her greed and energy expired, she would collapse next to him, and he would get on top of her, bearing all his weight on his knees and elbows. He would blow the perspiration cool on her breasts and lick it off her belly. He went farther down to remoisten her, and sometimes he stayed long enough for her to go again. Or twice. After, she would pull him up and guide him in, with both hands. She loved using both hands, and kept one wrapped around him to keep him from going too deep too fast. Not that she had to worry. Horace understood their size difference. "Am I hurting you? I don't want to hurt you. Did I hurt you?" he would say, always careful, always considerate.

THE ROLE SHE FIRST WANTED in correcting the world was ecological science, but the head-spinning explanations of atmospheres, biospheres, hydrospheres, and lithospheres, and the math- and science-heavy curriculum of chemistry, physics, biology, geology, and hydrology, were too much for her. Environmental science sounded like a noble idea as a freshman, but as a junior, the *-ologies* and *-spheres* were coagulating into one sticky mess in her mind. So she decided to switch to education.

She remembered the day she told him she was going to quit science. Careful, considerate Horace turned on her, with a quick, condescending judgment that shocked her.

"Horace, I feel like gorging out," she said. "It's too much for me. Maybe I'm not smart enough."

"It's not about intelligence, it's about commitment," Horace spat out. "If you're committed enough, you can make it work."

But she couldn't. Not surrounded by people who spoke in a language she couldn't comprehend and who wrote in formula riddles she couldn't decipher. She wasn't smart enough for it to be easy, and (maybe Horace was right) not committed enough to hack through. She quit, and Horace couldn't hide his disappointment.

SALLY PLUGGED IN HER LAPTOP and thought of the incongruity of the scene. The science quitter, now here in her ratty robe, at a tin table in an antiquated kitchen, paying bills online and watching their checking account diminish in real time. It fell in chunks of odd numbers: $86.57 for cable and Internet, $109.19 for car insurance, $120.24 for cell phones, $90.76 for electric . . . $406.76 gone, just like that. Another month of making a partial payment on the mortgage. Another month of minimum credit-card payments that didn't even cover the climbing interest on her maxed-out cards. One step up and two steps back. So expensive, just to live. She hid all this from Horace because she knew what he would say. Unplug. Simplify. Reject the brainwashing of the communications economy. Did Michael really need 24/7 *SportsCenter* updates on his phone? For Christ sakes, Sally! She could hear his voice as if it were in her head.

It started when he became the blacksmith. Next came his desire to "authenticate" their home life. The mansion apartment was too confining.

"We own no land," he said.

He wanted a farm. A few chickens, a vegetable patch. A life of "self-sufficiency," no matter how meager.

"I don't want to grow my own food. Who has time?" Sally said. Then, remembering the sinkfuls of bloody feathers from childhood, added, "Jesus, Horace, if you've ever plucked a chicken, you'd never want to do it again."

Oh, the sick irony when he found this house on Chicken Farm Hill Road just a little more than a mile from downtown, but a world away.

But she followed him here, to the two acres and a house "with potential" hidden off the unpaved part of the road with a winter view of the lake. She hoped his "own two hands" mantra would manifest itself in home-improvement carpentry and other finishing work. Instead she ended up with a yard of rusting sculptures of twisted band iron.

THEY WERE MARRIED IN THE SUMMER after senior year. It was the logical next step. Horace got a teaching assistantship and went for his master's. Sally was thankful she got her teaching certificate and supported them (barely) by teaching third grade at Immaculate Conception in town.

While Horace was buried in his thesis, Sally hid from him that she hated teaching, that the sound of shrill children's voices gave her headaches, and the small-time politics and cattiness of the staff reminded her of high school. She suffered through two years there, and when Horace got his degree and job in the museum archives, she only pretended to apply for teaching jobs. It was the first time she lied to him about anything, and maybe that was the first big step away. She told him jobs in Cooperstown schools were scarce, and she went to work for a dental practice as an office manager. Again, Horace was disappointed, and her arguments that the job paid better than teaching didn't help.

"You have so much to offer, and you're going to shuffle paper."

Horace never said it, but Sally could hear him thinking it: She quit.

Again. But what did Horace expect? Somebody had to pay the bills and provide good insurance. History, and teaching, weren't doing that.

And in bed, she was no longer a queen. He banged away at her sometimes as if he hated her not living up to *his* expectations, and stopped asking if it hurt. She was a married woman now.

In the archives, he was writing papers and researching the exhibits. She thought he would eventually get bored, go for his doctorate, and find a college teaching job, and that would be that. Good, clean, secure work, with tenure and benefits and a pension at the end of the day. She saw herself as a faculty wife, circulating within a university community, enjoying the arts, becoming involved in charities and civic affairs. Sophisticated and cultured, leaving behind the farm girl who feared being called "white trash."

Then Horace became the blacksmith.

All these years later, Sally could never figure out why. Did he have the soul of a great actor, losing himself in character? Or was he just afraid to compete in the modern world? Was he a complicated man trying to find a simpler time, or a simple man beaten down by complicated times?

White trash. She knew in her heart she wasn't. But there were the realities. The drafty house. The woodstove that made her cough like a smoker and made her clothes smell like they were bought at a fire sale. Horace's beat-up Ford Escort, spewing blue exhaust all over town. More than any of that, the look on her face. She saw age and bitterness creeping in, like she'd seen on her mother and other farm women when they hit their mid-forties. Life would not turn out the way they wanted. It would turn out the way they had expected.

She was tired, as her grandfather used to say, of not having two nickels to rub together. It would be nice not to be broke for a change, to have a husband who wanted nice things. All the bickering over money, justifying every little household purchase, wore her down.

"Why would you buy a teapot when you can boil water in a pan?" Horace once asked her when she came home from Walmart with a whistling teakettle, on sale for $3.96.

She was tired of the inconvenience of their lives. Drying clothes on the line, because the amps in the house couldn't support a modern dryer. Not flushing pee in the toilet because Horace didn't want to overtax the septic (and chided Sally about how much toilet paper she used). Getting frozen firewood from the porch to warm the house every winter day when she came home.

She was tired of his wiry beard hair scratching her neck and face. Tired of him climbing on top of her with his crushing weight. Tired of his smell.

About ten years ago he stopped using deodorant or deodorant soap. He instead announced he would wash only with Octagon or Lava, soaps traced back to the nineteenth century. The Octagon was a big, waxy brown bar that came in a paper wrapper. It lathered up yellow and had an oily smell to it. The Lava had granules of pumice that got out the deep coal dirt of Horace's hands, but chewed up his skin and left his fingertips like sandpaper. Sally could find neither at the local grocery store. She had to make a special trip to Tractor Supply. She complained about the inconvenience, and the fact, she tried to say gently, at first, that neither worked well.

"Horace, you stink!" she finally said.

"I work hard in a hot place," he said. "I smell like a man who works hard in a hot place."

"You smell like a man who sleeps under an overpass. Which would be fine if you lived alone, but you live with me. Why can't you use a better soap?"

"These soaps are authentic to my times."

"Your times? You live now. Besides, it's *offensive* to me! Doesn't that count for anything?"

Horace made a better effort to wash up after work, but the stench, though not as biting, still lingered, and only made Sally more tired of Horace.

Tired of the dead weight of the thick legs and hard arms he threw over her at night, which made her own arms and legs go numb. Tired of him wanting her, and tired of not wanting him. Tired of feeling like she wanted to scream.

Mostly, she was tired of Horace's voice and the way he tried to steer Michael. If the kid wanted to watch a game on TV, Horace warned of "joining the American army of fat-assed spectators." When he wanted to play himself, Horace warned of choosing "sports over intellect and meaningful work."

Later, when Michael starred, especially in baseball, Sally argued that he attacked his games with the same passion, the same slightly scary violence, as Horace put into his work.

"Look, Horace, he swings that bat with as much might as you swing an ax."

"Working in the woodpile has purpose," Horace countered. "It's how we heat the house."

Horace worked weekends, but when he came to Michael's weeknight games, he stood off alone, away from the bleachers, his blackened nineteenth-century work clothes matching his dark face.

"You could pretend to be enjoying it," Sally said.

"I don't have to live vicariously through my kid," Horace replied. "I'll leave that to the 'dude' dads."

In his first few years of Little League, Michael couldn't wait to tell Horace how he did on those Saturdays and Sundays. "Dad, I went two for three . . . Dad, I hit a home run . . ." But then he stopped, almost as if sports were a refuge from Horace, not something to share, like most fathers and sons. Horace happily saw it as a pass; relieved to have Michael's implied permission to stop coming. But for Michael, it was only to spare himself from more Horace lectures.

Those never ended. Everything was a "life lesson." Nothing ever just *was.*

Sally remembered when Michael was nine or ten and she gave him a cheap handheld video game for his birthday. He figured it out quickly enough, and loved to play and play. Horace had it all figured out, too.

"Watch him," Horace told her. "Watch how he becomes mesmerized. Look at how he gets conditioned to play until he loses. Sound familiar?"

"What? What are you talking about?" Sally said.

"Gambling! Play until you *lose.* I'll bet you anything casino corporations are behind these games. Bally's started out making pinball machines, did you know that? Same stuff, just shrunk down. Now the government's in on it. Casinos, lottery. The perfect marriage of diversion and statehouse greed."

Sally dared not say it, but she thought a trip to one of the Indian resorts might be fun. Just to do something different. To see the gaudy lights and people. Maybe a show, just for a change. Sally dared not say it, but she thought Horace was turning into a paranoid nut, a crazy conspiracy theorist, headed toward becoming an even crazier survivalist.

MICHAEL, TOO, GOD BLESS HIM, learned to let it roll. He would let his face relax into this impassive mask when Horace started. It was a great weapon, one of stoic control that translated into power. A facial version of the silent treatment. Horace, exasperated, called him "brain-dead" a few times.

But when he played, well, that's when all the anger seemed to come out. When other kids hit, their aluminum bats made a sharp *ping!* When Michael hit, it was a deeper sound, very much like Horace burying the ax head into a piece of seasoned wood. Michael ran hard, slid every chance he could. His throws from the outfield were uncoiled with his whole body, a transfer of his weight that would leave him stumbling forward as the ball sailed as if shot by something mechanical.

She was proud of him, yes, but a little unnerved by the intensity with which he played, and how much he wanted, make that *needed,* to win.

In Legion ball, he broke a boy's leg sliding into second. The boy stayed down, crying in pain, afraid to move. The field was cleared as the ambulance came and carted him off. Sally watched Michael in the dugout during the long delay, spitting sunflower seeds and joking with his teammates. She was embarrassed by how insensitive and unconcerned he acted. Afterward, as they walked through the parking lot with her carrying his bat bag, she asked him if he felt bad. She was a few feet behind her son, now a head taller. He didn't look at her when he said, "Part of the game."

He'd been such a sweet little boy, and she knew he was spoiled. And she knew she'd done it. But she had to overcompensate for Horace. She remembered how that started, too. The exact moment. Michael was in first grade and he was with her in the grocery store. A liquid baby bath soap with a rubber-headed Winnie-the-Pooh caught his eye and he reached for it. His simple infatuation with the toy was touching and it warmed her heart. But the money . . .

"Can I get this?" he asked, innocent and hopeful.

"No, babe, it's the same stuff in this bottle," Sally said, holding up the generic brand, "but this is two dollars cheaper. You think that plastic Winnie-the-Pooh head is worth two dollars?"

Michael put it back.

"You sound like Daddy," he said.

Sally bought it for him.

Those four words—*you sound like Daddy*—slapped her. She didn't want to sound like Daddy. She didn't want to be like Daddy.

SALLY LOOKED AROUND THE KITCHEN. No dishwasher. A two-slice toaster. No microwave. Her teakettle and the pan Horace used to boil water for his coffee. Her feet felt the cold through the worn linoleum floor. These were just the material things. The other things, the respect mostly, the need for a little kindness, maybe some adoration once in a while . . . well, like the old days. Maybe she would find it all on her own, a new adventure, free of Horace beating her down. She was far from spoiled; she resented Horace for making her feel that way. That's how he would spin this. She *quit* on me. She *quit*. On *me*. Twenty years, and she just quit.

She moved through the house, her tea now tepid, the cold from the wood planks now chilling her throughout. She turned on the shower and the mineral-crusted fixtures whined in protest; somewhere behind the Sheetrock, the pipes vibrated. She waited for the water to turn hot, but knew the best she would get was lukewarm. She stood under the water and cried.

When she was done, she stood in front of her mirror, on this bleak March morning in her ratty robe, steadying herself for the daily transformation from mountain hausfrau to service economy professional woman. Her black flare-legged suit and taupe turtleneck were laid out on the bed over her mother's "Odd Feller" quilt, and her modest gold necklace and bracelet were in their place in a baked clay log cabin jewelry box Michael made her in school. Many days, dressing to leave the house, dressing to join the real world, not this life Horace had sentenced them to, made her feel, well, alive. But on days like this, when she felt so tired of everything, she found less joy in it. Spring seemed so far away.

She took off her robe and was naked in the cold room. She looked at herself in the dim mirror over the unrestored antique vanity. Not bad. Good hips and waistline, everything else still north of middle age. She moved in closer to examine herself and saw the timeline in her face. The age wrinkles were coming, the grays were creeping in. Time was moving. And she was stuck, unhappy. She shivered. Nothing was ever going to change—except she would get more lined and more gray and more unhappy—until she changed it.

She looked out the bedroom window at the barren trees on the property. Barren trees, barren woman, she thought. She felt as cold and empty as the yard.

All she wanted—all she ever wanted—was a normal life. Now all she wanted was out. She wanted a divorce, she now knew, but felt strangely detached from the decision, like she was somewhere else, floating. She tried to bring herself to feel something. Something besides tired.

Chapter Eight

After the Hall vote, Sal booked Grudeck everywhere. Two days of press conferences; first at the commissioner's office on Park Avenue, with print reporters at Fenway hooked in, then live studio interviews with all the national morning shows in New York, then up to New England. *SportsCenter*, *SportsCenter Classic*, the Yankee TV network, Madison Square Garden TV, New England sports TV and radio, WFAN and ESPN radio, for call-in shows where hosts and fans ranted about sports, 24/7.

Same stuff, same questions, different day, different host names, in New York, Bristol, and Boston. Same glare, same Grudeck, self-conscious about the makeup some sweet thing just put on his face. Sign a few autographs for cameramen, producers, and tech guys on the way in.

"My kid's a big fan," they would say.

Grudeck bounced from set to set, each time in fresh clown pancake, talking about his career and lunch-pail image.

"Does anybody in America carry lunch pails anymore?" he wanted to ask. My old man did, he wanted to tell them: punched out fabricated metal on a night shift. Lunch-pail kid? No, more like brown bag, peanut butter and jelly, and the park water fountain. He learned sports on town fields, with his friends. Not like today with sports camps, travel teams, private coaching, strength and conditioning warehouses, parochial school recruiting. Kids coming up today were the best athletes their parents' money could buy. He didn't say all that, though. He had an image: Joe Good Guy. In his heart, though, he was Joe Punk Out. Once in a while, he wished he just told the truth.

While Grudeck talked, the TV stations ran the usual clips; Series home run, fight with Ruiz, still photo of McCombs starched at the plate. Same old, same old. Grudeck, gunning someone out. Grudeck, hand over heart, helmet and mask in hand, during the National Anthem. On radio, they talked about those images, those Joe *Grrreww* moments. No one asked the big questions, though.

Is it still fun?

Why did it all change?

No one ever asked, "What do you really think?"

Maybe no one wanted to know.

What did he really think about the media, these guys up your ass every minute of every day, more interested in your life than you yourself?

Or what did he really think about fans, clingers-on desperate to belong to your universe. They buy a ticket, turn on the TV, wear a hat, T-shirt, jacket, and they belong. "Red Sox Nation." Live for the team, die with the team. Scream into cameras in the ballpark or bars. From the players' point of view, it was all kinds of stupid. But it paid their enormous salaries. Suckers born every minute. And that was the players' dirty little secret: fuck the fans. They pay, we play. They watch, we play. And for all that phony emotion, especially the despair and anger, their asses were never on the line. All that hero worship. It's what led those two teenaged girls to his motel room in Syracuse that night. Because he was a ballplayer, just a minor leaguer then, at that.

He came off the field and out the gate of MacArthur Stadium in Syracuse, covered in base-path dust, hair matted with sweat, game jersey stripped off to let his drenched baseball undershirt cool. The night before, Grudeck became only the second player to drive a ball over the 434-foot ballpark's deep center-field fence and he did it twice, so a thicker crowd than usual came out to see the big kid catcher from Pawtucket. He didn't disappoint; in his first at-bat he rocketed one out and the crowd jumped to their feet and stayed there as Grudeck circled the bases.

As he stepped from the brilliant white field lights into the dimmer, fluorescent shadows of the parking lot, a crowd waited for him. He dropped his bag and started to sign autographs. A fire in the Chiefs' old ballpark the season before had left the locker rooms still blackened and without water, so visiting teams had to shower in their motel across the street. His teammates trudged off to their rooms, cleats scraping pavement, leaving Grudeck with a fan gaggle of mostly kids with parents and a few geezers.

"I seen Richie Zisk do it before you, he was the only one," an old-timer told him. "Then I seen you do it three times in two games!"

Grudeck noticed the two girls, at the back of the cluster, making no effort to move forward. The dark-haired girl lit a cigarette and gave the blonde a puff. When she took it back, she blew smoke rings in Grudeck's direction. They stood there, just out of the swath of light until the last fan was gone, and Grudeck moved toward them, into the shadows.

"So, what's going on?" he said.

The dark-haired girl flicked her thumb at her friend and said, "She wanted to get an autograph for her little brother but was too shy to ask."

"You have something to sign?"

"Uh, no . . . my shirt! You could sign my shirt."

"Front or back?" Grudeck asked.

"Have him sign the front, Rache," the dark-haired girl said.

"No, no, no," Grudeck said. "Turn around and I'll sign the back."

The blonde pirouetted and gathered up her hair off her neck and Grudeck took a Sharpie to the material, feeling the point jump over her thin bra straps.

"Okay, then," Grudeck said, and picked up his bag, but lingered enough for the dark-haired girl to ask, "Hey, would you mind buying us some beer? We have money, and a car."

"How old are you?"

"Seventeen," the girls said simultaneously, but Grudeck guessed younger.

Grudeck didn't tell them he was only twenty, just two years removed from high school and not legal age either. The bar next to the motel had served him and other players the night before, so he said, "Okay."

"What are your names?"

"Amanda, and this is Rachel," the dark-haired girl said.

"Tell you what, Amanda and Rachel," Grudeck said. "I'll go to the bar over there, and pick up a couple of sixes and take them back to my room. Meet me there. Room Seventeen, around back."

The blonde, Rachel, gave her friend an I-don't-know look.

"Don't worry. We'll just hang out," Grudeck said.

"Yeah, Rache, we'll just hang out," Amanda agreed.

THEY WERE WAITING IN A CAR parked outside his room. Amanda was in the driver's seat of a beat Datsun, smoking. Grudeck, with three sixes of cold cans in his bag, let them in and went to get ice. When he got back, they were draining their second, sitting at the table by the front window.

"I've got to shower," he said.

"Can we watch?" Amanda said.

"Amanda!" Rachel squealed.

"Kidding!"

After the shower, Grudeck stroked himself to his full length, blood-engorged and thick, not fully hard but showy. He wrapped himself in a towel and stepped back into the room.

"Don't look," he said, but the towel came off before either girl could avert her eyes.

"Whoa!" Amanda said, as Rachel blurted out a laugh.

"I said, 'Don't look' . . ." Grudeck said with fake embarrassment, and reached for a pair of sweat shorts and a clean Pawsox T-shirt. He faced them as he pulled the shorts on.

He sat on the bed, and they made small talk. He was from Jersey. They had just graduated high school. Rachel played field hockey. Amanda sucked at softball. Rachel was headed to SUNY Binghamton. Amanda to county. Yes, he'd been to Syracuse before, a few times. Last season, too. No, he wasn't married.

"Do you smoke weed?" Amanda asked, fiddling in her purse.

"No," Grudeck said. "Bad for the wind. But you go ahead."

He got up and blasted the fan, and opened the bathroom window as the girls passed the joint and got more giggly. In the haze of marijuana smoke and litter of empties, Rachel moved to the bed, stretched out, and fell asleep. Grudeck, Gentlemen Joe, covered her with the flowery blue-and-gold bed cover.

"You're a nice guy," Amanda decided.

"Then do something nice for me," Grudeck said. It was the first of many times he would say it.

"Oh, I don't know . . ." she said, being cute. "We don't want to wake Rachel up."

But when Grudeck stood in front of her and kissed her, she came back at him, pushing as much tongue as she had into his mouth. He pulled away to take himself out of his shorts, and guided her down. She took it without hesitation, unpracticed and sloppy. Grudeck put his hands around her heavily pierced ears, and helped her back and forth. But after a few minutes, he just took over himself and finished.

"I think we should go," she said, as he went to wash up.

"No, just stay. Don't wake her up. Lie down, too. You shouldn't drive like this."

Amanda got into the bed next to Rachel, with Grudeck next to her. She turned away from him, toward her friend, but he pulled her close and felt her relax in his arms. They dozed off that way.

GRUDECK SAW THE LINES OF DAYLIGHT around the room-darkening shades when he woke with a full morning hard-on. The girl in his arms was fully clothed, but he reached around and undid her jeans. She was still passed out, drunk and stoned, and didn't wake until he had eased her pants and underwear down below her hips.

"Hey!" she said. "Wait."

But he put his hand over her mouth and whispered in her ear, "Shh. We don't want to wake . . ."

"Rachel," she reminded him.

She didn't struggle but didn't help, either, as he pulled her pants off. He grabbed her by the hip and flipped her on her back, and looming above her, opened her legs. He looked to her eyes, but they were closed.

"This okay?" he asked but pushed into her before she could answer. He went in hard, and easily gathered her up in one arm. She felt light and lifeless as he pulled her upper body into him while thrusting below. She let out little noises, even as she stiffened in his arms. He grabbed her tighter, saying, "Shhh, baby, shush, babe. It's okay," and suddenly Rachel, startled, faced them.

"Mandy! What are you doing?"

Grudeck stopped. *Now what?*

"It's okay," Amanda said, as she tried to squirm out from under him. Grudeck held tight, and started up again.

"This is what you came for isn't it?" he said to Rachel. *"Isn't it?"*

The harshness in his voice scared her, and all she could manage was to shake her head no. As Rachel tried to get out from under the covers, Grudeck reached out and grabbed the back of her neck with his right hand to keep her there.

"Isn't this what you came for?" he said again. "To have a little fun with a ballplayer? So let's have some fun."

"You're an asshole," Amanda said. "Get off of me."

But Grudeck pulled Rachel's head down, next to Amanda's on the pillow, and with his left arm he hooked both girls by the neck, pressing their faces together. With his right hand, he groped them both, first over their clothes, then underneath.

When he roughly unsnapped and unzipped Rachel's jeans he asked again, "This is what you wanted, right?"

When he was done, Rachel was whimpering, and Amanda said, "It's okay, Rache, we were drunk."

"She's right, Rache," Grudeck said. "It's okay. You were drunk."

He lay on his back and watched them pull themselves together and walk out into the morning light. After they left, he took a hot shower, scrubbing himself with the rough, cheap motel washcloth.

Chapter Nine

"It's good you're doing these talk shows," Sal said as he drove from a midtown parking garage after a segment on *Good Day New York*. "It'll help you with your speech."

The speech. It was never far from Grudeck's mind. It started with a congratulatory call from a guy named Strothford, who described himself as "the old caretaker of Cooperstown" and talked about the Hall and its mission.

"Preserving History, Honoring Excellence, Connecting Generations," Strothford said. "Not only will your plaque be immemorial, but we archive your speech. Perhaps your words will color your life for those to come."

He thought of his mother's question—What are you going to do *now*?

Question, or challenge? Yeah, he could go another thirty, what, forty years being Joe Grudeck, but each passing year, being Joe Grudeck would mean less and less. A fading light of a diminishing star. And then, just like that, he would go black—blink!—then into infinite, eternal nothingness.

He wanted to count for something, but his impact as a player was already gone. The Red Sox won a couple of Series without him, after not winning any with him. His few "hits and games for a catcher" records were in reach for several active guys. So, what was immortal?

What could he do that nobody else had done? He'd have the bronze plaque, like the other 302 guys. But what else?

Maybe the speech. He could tell the truth. Most of it. Something changed him in Syracuse, he knew that now. Made him more . . . detached.

The old guy had said, "Color your life."

What life? Outside baseball, he was a guy wandering sideways, with no real attachments except to his fame. The words *Connecting Generations* ate at him.

For Grudeck, there were no daughters or sons, nieces or nephews, to tell stories of the real Grudeck. Who knew him, anyway? Really *knew* him. Since the phone call from Cooperstown, Grudeck thought about this constantly. His baseball "immortality" told him just how mortal he was. Who would outlive him to tell his stories? Articles, and highlights, and taped interviews didn't explain what Grudeck was *really* like. Or what he believed in. Not like a family would. Connecting generations? Not Grudeck.

But maybe the speech . . .

He brought it up to Sal that day, leaving the studio, as he stretched out in Sal's Buick LeSabre.

"Sallie, I'm thinking . . ."

Sal knew what it meant when Grudeck called him "Sallie," like Chuck Grudeck used to. It meant he needed a friend.

"What?"

"I don't know, the speech. I think I want to make a good speech."

Sal looked at him over his half-glasses.

"What, kid? What's bothering you, kid?" Sal said again, now stuck in traffic on West Sixty-seventh. "It's just a speech. You've done a thousand. You get up there, thank everybody. Say you couldn't have done it without them. Talk about your dad, all your good memories, how blessed you are. Maybe you get a little choked up, and sit down. That's that."

"I don't know, Sallie. I want this one to be different."

Grudeck looked out the window of the Buick, at hundreds of people hurrying down the city street. All the anonymous nobodies. Grudeck was a somebody; he could jump out of the car and be *recognized.*

And yet . . . all those nobodies probably had somebody. Husbands, wives, kids, parents, siblings. Grudeck had his mom, and Sal . . . and fans.

"I don't know, Sal. Lately, I've been thinking," he said, not turning. "You know something? I've never been anybody's best man. I've never been a godfather. Not even a fucking Confirmation sponsor. How's that possible, all the guys I know?"

"What's bothering you, Joe?" Sal said, more serious this time.

He didn't say it out loud, but a sentence formed in his head: *I love nobody and nobody loves me.* Just thinking it embarrassed him. What was he, a fifteen-year-old girl? Chrissakes. But Jesus, he felt lonely, right now, in midtown Manhattan, being driven by a seventy-something-year-old man, Sal, who was his best, maybe only, true friend. Maybe. Grudeck had made him rich. What if he hadn't? What if he'd sucked? Then what?

Sal looked at him with a frown of concern.

"Nothing. I'm all right, Sal," Grudeck said.

"It's just a fucking speech, kid. You've done a million of them."

GRUDECK WAS NO GREAT SPEAKER. He didn't like it; it was just another way for people to get a piece of you.

Early in his big league days he did a bunch of off-season Meet Joe Grudeck dinners for Little Leagues, Babe Ruths, Legion ball, just to add to his income.

"If they pay a grand, give 'em a five-minute speech," Sal used to say. "For two grand, give 'em the same speech twice. Just make sure it's cash, otherwise you have to file a 1099, and the IRS gets a third."

And that's how it was. Grudeck, the guest of honor, hulking out of a business suit and choked by a buttoned collar, would tower over the dais in front of a banquet room at some Moose or Elks lodge, or VFW or Legion Hall in Braintree, Needham, or Walpole or back home in Jersey. He'd sit through iceberg salad and chicken something-or-other, then listen while the Whatever League president gave the audience the usual bullshit: How great it was for a great guy like Joe Grudeck to come speak to a great bunch of kids and their parents. As if Grudeck were there for free. As if there weren't a brown bag of twenties and fifties at the end of the night.

Grudeck would rise to big applause and the guy who introduced him would shake his hand, pull close, and whisper something like "You have no idea how thrilled our kids are!"

This was done so kids and dads alike would think the league president somehow knew Grudeck well enough to invade his space, like they were personal friends.

When the applause died down, Grudeck would start with the same joke, fed to him by Sal.

"Thank you, thank you very much. I guess there aren't many Yankee fans here tonight."

He then launched into the stock speech: play hard, stay in school, be a good sport, stay away from drugs, and if you tried your very, very best it made you a winner, no matter what. Next to each boy was a dad, nodding in agreement, happy to have Joe Grudeck up there reinforcing the same b.s. they gave their sons at home. When he was done, the president would come back up—another handshake and intimate whisper—and tell everybody Grudeck had agreed to hang around for autographs. At a side banquet table Grudeck would sign balls, baseball cards, and event posters, and shake the moist, grubby hands of boys and fathers. The men would always squeeze harder than necessary. Even in those days, Grudeck felt the wear and tear on his hands. He would then go into the bathroom and scrub his hands under hot water to rinse off the germs, get his bag of cash from the club treasurer, and climb into a waiting Town Car, provided by the group, to go home.

Later, when he was making big money, he only did charity work. The Red Sox offered him for the $10,000-a-table fund-raisers for Children's Hospital and the Greater Pilgrim Fund, where the silent-auction tables were filled with Grudeck-autographed bats and balls, signed and framed photos and jerseys. He posed for pictures, scrawled his name on programs. Joe Glad-hand. In the end, there was no brown bag. Just his hand-scrubbing ritual, then home with some wealthy divorcée or old-enough daughter.

Sal, too, asked him to do a few gratis fund-raising events. Sal's wife was Jewish and on the fund-raising board of MetroWest.

"All the Jews in the world who make money, and I marry the one who only knows how to give it away," Sal used to say.

So Grudeck did the circuit: the Maplewood Country Club for Beth Israel Hospital in Newark, Temple B'nai this or that for United Jewish Charities. He knew it was important to Sal. Delivering Joe Grudeck made Sal feel like a big shot, accepted by his wife's crowd. And that crowd—doctors, lawyers, real estate developers, and their thin, ageless blond wives—never seemed to get tired of Grudeck, who always opened with the same line.

"It's a great honor for me to be here, to be among people who consider me the second-greatest catcher ever to come out of Jersey—after Moe Berg!"

No matter how many times he used it, he always got a big laugh. Berg was a legend among this crowd. He was little more than a bit player for the White Sox, Indians, and Red Sox in the '30s, but did spy work during World War II, which made him a Nazi slayer. Hell, he was bigger than Sandy Koufax with old Jews.

Truth was, Grudeck had never even heard of Moe Berg. Sal told him the story and fed him the line. "All the old Yids from Weequahic High say they remember him, but the truth is he played at Barringer with the *paisans.* One of my uncles from down there knew him pretty good."

But all those gigs didn't require a real speech, a keeper. The Hall of Fame induction did.

A FEW DAYS AFTER THE CALL FROM STROTHFORD, Grudeck got a certified letter from the director of the Hall's library, talking about its "vast amount of material."

"Your speech will become a permanent part of our archives, available for future scholars to read and study, for insight into the culture of baseball in your times. Please view your speech as an opportunity to reveal not only your personality but also your thoughts, in your words, on the game we all cherish. While your plaque gives a brief biography and the statistics that made you induction-worthy, your speech can present your human side: the man behind the ballplayer."

The letter was so . . . *somber*, like he had to deliver the Gettysburg Address or something.

Again, the language haunted him. "Your thoughts, in your words" meant words no longer filtered through sportswriters, or twisted by a sports talk host, or edited for television. No misquoting here.

And the "man behind the ballplayer" sounded as if the people at the Hall knew there was a real person lost inside *Joe Grrreww.*

That morning in Syracuse, after the girls staggered out, he got up and looked at himself in the mirror and saw something different. The kid in him was gone. He was twenty, already a sports mercenary, hardened by his small fame. Those girls . . . he took what *he* wanted, what *he* deserved. He was Joe Grudeck. Fuck everybody else. He changed.

Now was his chance to tell the truth—mostly—about how fucked up things were. And maybe figure out how fucked up he got.

"I'M NOT SURE WHAT I WANT TO SAY, SAL," Grudeck said on the drive home from the TV show. "I want it to be right. You know, maybe even important."

"So, say what you feel," Sal said.

"I'm not sure anybody wants to hear that."

"Tell you what. I'll pull some old speeches. Might give you some guidance."

A few days later, Sal dropped off two 11-by-15 envelopes for him at the club, stuffed with induction speeches from the last few years.

"Where'd you get these?" Grudeck asked, as they ate breakfast in the club dining room.

"Online. Jesus, join the century. The Hall has their archives on the Internet."

"For what?"

"For what . . . for when guys like you want to see other guys' speeches. For research. For guys who write books about baseball. For professors who teach courses about baseball."

Grudeck called the busboy over and asked him to get the girl from the club office. When she came to the table, Grudeck asked for a stack of club letterhead and a few pens.

"I have to write a speech," he said.

"Does it have to be on club stationery? It's more expensive than plain paper," she asked.

"Whatever."

When she returned with three legal pads and a fistful of Bics, Grudeck tipped her fifty dollars to bring it all to his condo. Sal went home, and Grudeck played eighteen holes, filling out an arranged foursome with three vice presidents from Lucent Technologies.

After a nap, dinner, and a couple of beers at the club, Grudeck opened the envelopes where the girl had left them. The names, all familiar, spread out before him, two dozen in all. Sal had gone back and got some of the greats. Hard to believe he was going to be one now.

Grudeck began to read, holding papers at almost arm's length until his eyes could focus. For the first time, he realized he might need glasses.

Sal was right. Most of the speeches blurred with sameness. First, like Sal said, everybody thanked everybody, family, coaches, teammates, fans, then talked about playing catch with their dads and their love of the game. Next was how this moment exceeded all their dreams, and about the humility of being surrounded by the all-time greats. One after another, Grudeck thought how hollow it sounded. Humility? All those thanks were sent out to those who supported *him*, who coached *him*, the fans who loved *him*. Every speech. *His* family, *his* teammates, *his* experiences, *his* playing days, *his* highlights, *his* accomplishments. In naming everyone, they spoke only of themselves.

Grudeck saw it clearly now. His life, too, became all about him, the ballplayer. He let it happen. Prisoner in his own castle. Slave to fame. Fuck, he hated himself. But that was the truth. A star first, a person second. Check that: a star first, nothing second. It was that way right from the start, back to his first year in Little League, when he played for Ficchini Stationery.

Mr. Fich came to see his boys play on Opening Day, and Joey hit two home runs and pitched a shutout. Later that day, Joey and his friends were in town, up on Stuyvesant Avenue, and stopped into Ficchini's for some candy and soda. They picked out stuff and pooled their money at the counter. No one ever stole from Isadore Ficchini. Not with those grappling-hook hands and long, sloped shoulders. He looked more like a retired heavyweight than a candy-store owner. Plus, there were those rumors . . . Isadore the Stevedore, they called him. Mr. Fich did some job rigging down in Port Newark.

As Mr. Fich began counting the kids' money, he looked down at Joey Grudeck, still wearing his uniform.

"Hey, you play for me?"

"Yeah."

"You're the kid who hit the home runs today, right?"

"Yeah."

"The pitcher, right?"

"Yeah."

Mr. Fich reached over the counter and slapped his shoulder with a heavy hand.

"Hey! Hey! Attaboy!" He pushed the money away. "Forget it, kid! Treat your friends. It's on me today."

His friends grubbed up some more candy. And from then on, everything changed.

Being with Joey got you free candy and soda. Being with Joey meant you were cool in high school. Being with Joey meant you got the girls that couldn't get Joey. All through school Grudeck couldn't ever remember being alone, except at home. He also couldn't remember a conversation that didn't revolve around him.

Just that day on the golf course with the Lucent guys, same thing. Grudeck hit first and moved on, leaving the three execs to talk about business strategies, corporate lineage, stock prices, and all the other bullshit they came to the club to pretend to escape. But when Grudeck was among them, it was all about him and his moments, or his take on sports these days.

Now, reading the speeches, Grudeck realized he had talked about almost nothing but himself for thirty-five, forty years now, maybe more. Even toward the end with his dad, Grudeck never had a heart-to-heart with him about the illness. Or death. Or life, as each came to know it. The talk was the same as always. Joe's prospects. Joe's games. Joe's stats.

When his dad was first diagnosed, it was kept from his son, because Chuck Grudeck didn't want Joe distracted during the season. As the cancer progressed, in the brushfire way pancreatic does, Grudeck was called home. He hopped back and forth as much as he could, sometimes overnight from Boston, New York, or Baltimore. The last time they spoke, Grudeck had a day off before a three-game series in Detroit.

In what both knew might be their final moment, Chuck Grudeck lay still with a gray ghost of unshaven stubble on his hollow face, his neck and shoulders withered, and pronounced violet surgery tracks on his colorless skin. Through labored, rattling breath, he spoke only of his son's current season, and another pennant race both knew he wouldn't live to see.

It felt like those community service trips Grudeck made to Children's Hospital. After "Hiya, Jimmy, how ya feeling?" it was all about

Grudeck. The season. The team. How great it was he'd come. The kids would perk up and yak, as long as their strength allowed. But the only thing they had in common with Grudeck was Grudeck. He remembered how it made him squirm. A kid was dying, and Grudeck was getting all the attention from the kid's parents, the nurses, the kid himself. Grudeck, a stranger, an image, just a ballplayer. Not someone who loved the kid or even knew the kid, or the extent of his suffering.

The last visit with his father, there was no perk-up. Grudeck sat by his bed and held the hands that had held him as a baby, and taught him how to swing a bat and throw a football. Those hands were skeletal now, the veins hard over raised metacarpals, under papery skin.

"So, you going to Detroit?" his father managed.

"Dad, just rest."

"How'd you do in Cleveland? The regular nurse brings me a *Star-Ledger*, but she's on vacation."

"I did okay. Nothing spectacular. We took two of three. I had a three-run homer in the opener. But look, just be still. Close your eyes. I'm here."

"Okay, but hit a homer for me, will ya, Mr. Grudeck? And I promise I'll get better."

Chuck tried to laugh, but was consumed by a dry coughing fit. His son lifted a cup of water to his lips, and then Chuck Grudeck drifted off, into a peaceful, predeath sleep. Morphine had finally blunted the pain, much like cancer had blunted his life.

Grudeck stayed through the night. His mother relieved him at dawn, so he could catch a flight to Detroit. Chuck Grudeck died at 8:49 that night, in the second inning of an 8:05 start. Grudeck wasn't called until the game was over, as was his father's wish.

GRUDECK KEPT READING, reading long after he got tired, longer still after he got bored. His hips were aflame and he rolled his head on his neck, trying to loosen the tightness. He wanted to come across just one speech, just one, that said something important, or at least *insightful.* Instead, he tumbled into his bed, and fell asleep with the packet on his chest.

In a dream, he was a boy, lost and alone in a museum hall of cathedral proportions and grandeur. Lining the halls were hundreds, maybe thousands of suits of medieval armor. One plaque said, "Richard the Lionhearted, the warrior of the Crusades." Grudeck knew they were empty, but they scared him just the same. He was a lost boy, looking for someone he thought might be trapped inside. He stood on his toes, lifted the faceplate, and peered into the blackness of the hollow suits. "Hello . . . Are you there? . . . Are you in there?" He went from one to another, his fear and panic growing as each suit came up empty. All that gleaming steel, no man inside.

He woke, with sweat pooled at his sternum and his hair damp.

It was after two o'clock when he called Sal.

"Sallie, sorry to bother you."

"Joe, what the hell? Everything all right?"

"It's this speech thing. I want it to be different," Grudeck said.

There was a pause.

"Sal, you there?"

"Yeah, I'm just trying to figure . . . what's bothering you, kid?"

"I don't know, Sal. Everything changed. I changed. It was fun, at first, then it wasn't. It got too, I don't know, big or something. Too important. It's out of whack."

"You complaining? I mean, let's face it, Joe, most people think you're living every man's fantasy."

"They think. They don't know what I've sacrificed." Grudeck hated the sound of it, the second it came out of his mouth. "I mean, there's been trade-offs."

Sal was quiet again.

"So, what's bothering you, kid?"

"I don't know . . . I think I want to say something that puts things in . . . perspective."

"Okay, kid, but remember, perspective depends on who's *perspecting*. I mean, your take on things might not wash with other people."

"But there's things other people don't know."

"So again, I ask, what's bothering you?"

Now it was Grudeck who was silent. He felt so . . . *unfocused*, and finally said so.

"Well, then, that's what you need," Sal said. "Focus. Tell you what. Come down next week, and we'll talk it out. We'll figure it out. I promise. I'll take care of it."

They hung up, and Grudeck wondered how he could once focus hard enough to see the rotation of the red stitches on a 95-m.p.h. fastball, but now couldn't zero in on his own feelings.

Spring

Chapter Ten

After he heard that final museum budgets were approved, Horace went to see Grundling, in blacksmith garb with leather hat in hand, to ask if the summer youth work program had been chopped.

"It wasn't easy, but I was determined to keep it," Grundling said. He leaned forward and picked up the Conestoga covered wagon he kept on his desk. "We need to show these kids what we do. We're a dying breed, Horace. We need to create the next generation of living historians."

Horace resented the "we." Grundling was no living historian. When was the last time he'd busted a blood blister forging a horseshoe, or took a metal flint in the eye? Never. He spent his days head in laptop, playing with Excel in the comfortable director's office, not with tools, not breathing coal smoke eight hours a day. Still, Horace had to kiss his ass.

"Well, John, I'm glad you see it that way, and I wonder if we can get my son started down that path this summer," Horace said.

Grundling leaned back in his chair, still holding the wagon.

"How old, Horace?"

"Fourteen."

"Hmmm . . . fourteen . . . I don't know. The rules say sixteen, Horace."

"The heck with the rules, John," Horace said, not in anger but with a phony co-conspirator's tone. "You know he's one of . . . us. He was chasing around chickens here while still in diapers. I taught him how to work the bellows for me when he was six. This is a kid who knows not to walk behind a horse."

"Seems I haven't seen him here in a while, Horace."

"Well, you know, sports," Horace said. "That's why I thought a job this summer . . ."

"But he's only fourteen, Horace. Isn't there some other way for him to earn money?" Grundling asked.

A buzz, a hum like a tuning fork, dizzied Horace's brain.

"It's not about money, John . . ." he said, but his anger was tumbling and he couldn't finish.

Naturally, Grundling would think it was about money. It was always about money with these spreadsheet guys.

Horace knew that whatever he said next would have to mask his disrespect for Grundling. Horace knew he was a corporate climber out to impress the foundation that he could "do more with less." Flip a loser like the farm and, well, next stop was the Hall. Or the foundation itself.

And Horace was sure Grundling's "other way to earn money" remark was aimed to cut him down to size: a big man, yes, but a poor man. Money, the great equalizer. Horace sat there, mouth dry, searching for something to say. Grundling's patient silence—knowing he had struck a nerve, a nerve Horace was working to suppress—irritated Horace even more. That, and the way Grundling knew, and knew Horace knew, Grundling had him by the balls.

"How can I explain this?" Horace was trying to temper his voice, but it rose and he inched forward in his chair as he spoke. "It's not about the money, John. It's never been about money. Jesus, John, does anybody do this for the money? If it was about money . . . I'm a historian. A living historian! It's about teaching. It's about teaching a boy about his heritage, about his culture. It's about grounding him in something, in something that is not somebody else's idea of culture, which, for kids these days, let's face it, is nothing but a bunch of shimmying exhibitionists and lunkheads scoring touchdowns or dunking basketballs or movies where aliens kill millions or girls get butchered. It's about teaching him the value of hard work. To let him see that land can be used for more than just throwing a ball around, or for building yet another consumer pig trough of condos and shopping centers. To let him build up some calluses on his hands—like these."

Horace thrust his hands palms-up toward Grundling and saw him flinch. And in that moment, just like that, Horace got some power back.

"Take it easy, Horace," Grundling said as he leaned farther back in his chair. "I'm not the enemy."

"I know, John, I'm just frustrated," Horace said as he withdrew his hands and lowered his voice. "Raising a boy these days, well, it's not easy."

"I'm sure it's not, Horace. And if he were sixteen, I'd love to have . . ."

"Michael. His name is Michael."

". . . Michael working here at the Farmers' Museum. But there are other concerns and issues. Liabilities. Insurance, for instance. Improprieties, or the appearance thereof. Other young people may want those jobs. Shouldn't we discourage nepotism to open ourselves up to the entire community? Maybe bring in a kid who really *needs* a job?"

So now, Horace thought, Grundling is using my "it's not about the money" argument against me.

"Bullshit, John," Horace said. "You know it and I know it. I've been here twenty years and every summer we carry at least one or two privileged offspring of *this* board member or *that* foundation trustee. And they have one thing in common with the underprivileged we bring in: they're equally lazy. These opposite sides of the economic spectrum share the common trait of entitlement. Difference is, *my* kid will *work*. And work hard. I promise you that."

Grundling said nothing, but his eyes moved around the office.

"Look, John," Horace finally said, not wanting to plead, but not able to tolerate the silence, "this is important to me. I feel my kid is drifting away. Sports. Rap music. The crap TV and Hollywood put out. It's not authentic *culture*. I want him to understand *his* culture.

His roots are here. Right here. His great-great-grandfathers planted hops. He should understand their lives."

Mid-spew, Horace realized how tinny and desperate he sounded with his Every Teen's Parent Lament. And, yes, even racist, which Grundling zeroed in on.

"Are you saying you don't want him exposed to 'urban' cultures?" Grundling asked. Horace thought he saw Grundling suppress a smile.

"I'm saying I want it balanced out," Horace said. "I can't change what comes at him through the TV or the Internet or the barrage of advertising my generation, by the way, never had to ingest. But I can make sure he sees the other side. I, we, have a culture, too. That fact gets lost these days in America."

Grundling leaned forward and put down the model.

"Well, then, Horace . . . since this seems to be such an important issue to you, I'll take it up with the board. I see the biggest stumbling block will be insurance, but I think I can make it work. We can work something out."

Grundling was going to ask for something in return, Horace knew. Everything with Grundling was like that. A negotiation.

But on his way back to the smithy, he noticed the season's first crocuses stretching to bloom along the farm's wide walkways and caught himself feeling surprisingly good.

In front of him, too far to call out, was Natalia in street clothes hurrying along with a patterned cloth satchel slung over her shoulder with her milkmaid dress spilling out. Horace picked up his pace to catch her but couldn't close the distance fast enough as she turned the corner into the dairy exhibit and cow barn. He went to follow her in, but she swung the door partway closed and he stopped, partially hidden behind a black-and-white Holstein, who looked at him with dumb ambivalence.

He could see only half of Natalia's body as she swooped her sweater over her head with her back to him. Next, down came the jeans, wriggling herself free. For an instant—no, an eternity—he took in the pink straps of her bra and one full naked globe of her butt, with a matching pink strip riding high on her hip. A milkmaid in a thong. He moved closer behind the cow, feeling more naked and exposed in the muddy yard than Natalia was in her underwear. And yet he watched. He watched as she bent down to retrieve the dress, revealing more of her ample, shapely ass. He watched as she fumbled with the dowdy material and raised it overhead, stretching out the body Horace wanted to embrace and, yes, mount, until the dress fell like a show-ending curtain from her head to below her knees. Horace turned and walked quickly to the smithy, hand concealing the beginning of a hard-on—like the schoolboy voyeur he was.

THAT NIGHT AS HE SETTLED INTO BED, Horace told Sally about his plan, expecting her approval.

Instead she let out one of her "that's the dumbest thing I've ever heard" sighs, like when he suggested they go off the grid.

"Did you ask Michael?"

Horace said nothing.

"Don't you think you should first ask Michael if he *wants* to work in the fields?"

"A little hard work will be good for him." Not to mention, a hundred years ago it was expected, Horace wanted to add, but didn't.

Sally fell back hard on the pillow, eyes on the ceiling, then popped back up.

Horace knew what was coming. Sally pulled the strands of hair back behind her ear, so that there was nothing between him and her stare.

"What happens if he doesn't *want* to work there? What happens if he thinks it will interfere with baseball? Did you think about that? This is his last summer of baseball before high school. Maybe he wants to work hard at that, to make a good impression on the varsity coaches next year. Did you think about that? What happens if he says, 'Dad, I absolutely *hate* the idea of working at the farm'?"

She fell back on the pillow.

"Michael doesn't use words like *absolutely*," Horace said, a little meek but with enough snide.

"Don't, Horace."

"Well, you're the one making it sound like I don't know my own son; like arranging for this job is some giant miscalculation, another episode of Horace-in-the-Dark. Michael has always loved it at the farm."

"When he was, what, seven? Eight? When was the last time he was there? Think about it, Horace."

"I don't know . . . his birthday, a couple of years ago?"

Horace knew he'd just stepped in shit, but it was too late. Sally was going to pile on.

"It was three years ago, when he turned eleven. Don't you remember? His birthday party? The little side-trip you arranged? It was miserable. *He* was miserable."

Horace remembered.

It was the year Horace began to see changes in Michael. The boy who once knew the night constellations, and the Greek gods they represented, switched his retentive skills to baseball statistics. He became bored with their sky watches and Sunday-evening hikes, where Horace taught him how to use a compass and coordinates to find his way. Michael wanted to stay home and watch sports.

Michael quit Boy Scouts, and his *Birds of North America* and *Mammals of North America* field guides and *Boys' Life* magazines were lost under piles of glossy sports magazines aimed at kids. The rock-collecting and fossil-dusting kits now collected dust. One night Horace went into Michael's room to try to convince him to stay in Scouts. He picked up one of the new magazines and flipped through ad after ad of outrageously expensive athletic shoes and other stuff. Nike. Under Armour. Adidas.

"Why is everybody a walking billboard these days?" Horace said as he flipped the pages, more to himself than to Michael.

But Michael answered.

"Because it's cool."

"Cool? Why? Because they say?" Horace said, pointing to a shoe ad with a player named Kamil Qawi shattering a backboard with a one-handed slam. The shoe was called the Kami-Qawzi. Was nothing sacred? Horace thought. All those World War II guys, spinning in their graves.

"Is that what makes it cool . . . that some big jock wears it? You know they pay these guys to wear these things, so they can sell them to you for more money. Don't you think that's a little dishonest?"

"I just think it's cool," Michael said, and Horace heard Sally's flatness in his voice.

"Maybe they should pay you for advertising for them. Like in the Depression. Eat at Joe's."

"Huh? Dad, that's stupid."

The words burned Horace. The death of respect. If he had talked to his father that way . . . but Horace let it go.

Michael wanted a baseball-themed birthday party for his entire Little League team. Sally put together a tour of the Hall, with cheeseburgers and ice cream to follow at the Shortstop, a '50s-style malt shop near Doubleday Field. After ice cream, the boys would go to Doubleday and watch a game between two out-of-town high school teams.

Horace did the math and figured it was a four-hundred-dollar day, even with his foundation discount. The money was one thing, the principle was another. Horace thought it was all overindulgent; video arcade parties, karate parties, sports parties, all in some strip mall or giant-sized aluminum shed, all contrived experiences done mostly for the financial benefit of the business owner, who did little more than put up a computer printout banner, serve some microwave pizza, powdered fruit juice, and a supermarket cake, and laugh all the way to the bank. Worse were the craft parties, where the kids were handed some cookie-cutter plaster sculpture or glued-together wood frame, splashed some paint on it, and were led to believe they had created something artistic, original, and worthwhile, as their parents gloated with their fixed phony smiles and glazed-over eyes, bloating the egos of their offspring with undeserved praise.

"Why don't we have something here at the house?" Horace said to Sally. "You know, an old-fashioned birthday party. We'll organize some games, have cake and ice cream . . . show his friends an *authentic* party for a change. Who knows, maybe we'll start a trend."

"He doesn't want that," Sally protested, "nobody does that anymore. He'd die of embarrassment."

"I don't understand this . . . what is so embarrassing about a game of horseshoes in the backyard instead of feeding quarters to some machines in an arcade parlor? What is so embarrassing about a homemade cake, instead of some cardboard-box thing?"

"You're right, Horace, you don't understand. It's his birthday. Why can't we just give him what he wants?"

"Because it goes against everything I want to teach him," Horace said, holding up his huge hands in Sally's face. "Look, I make things with these. Since when did *homemade* become a dirty word in this country?"

"Oh, Christ, Horace," Sally said, exhaling the burden of the conversation. "It's a birthday party, Horace! That's all it is! A birthday party!"

Horace let it go. But on the day of the party he announced he'd arranged for the boys to visit the farm museum before the Hall of Fame.

"For balance," he said. "We'll go through quick."

Sally was furious and objected, but Michael, sensing the tension between his parents, agreed with a shrug that a quick stop would be okay.

Horace took the boys through the machinery and tools exhibit, stunned by their ignorance of tools. He held up an antique claw hammer.

"Anybody know what this is called?"

"A hammer," they yelled in disunity.

"What kind of hammer?"

Only Michael knew.

Don't your fathers teach you anything? Horace wanted to ask, remembering his own father's organized tool bench with masking-tape labels so Horace knew what to get when sent.

Horace tried to make the boys visualize the hard manual labor their ancestors experienced but they quickly got bored, and the more rowdy among them began to fool around.

One grabbed a long-handled Amish scythe and did a Grim Reaper imitation. Another began pulling the levers on the 1923 Case Thresher, a rambling contraption of hundreds of irreplaceable moving parts. That same kid jumped, literally jumped, up on the running boards of a 1929 Model T milk truck.

"Boys, the signs say 'Do Not Touch' for a reason," Horace scolded. "These things are the last of their kind."

"These things are junk," came a reply from one of the boys, a wise-ass named Jacob something-or-other, followed by laughter from the whole group.

Horace looked hard at the kid.

"Hey, Jake, this is a museum where old-fashioned things are kept," Horace said, stepping up to him. "So, while we're in this museum, we do old-fashioned things like respect adults and listen to what they say. Got it?"

Horace glanced over at Michael, who looked away, red-faced and fighting back tears, either embarrassed or angry. He was in the awkward position of watching his friends irritate his father, then watching his father be harsh with his friends—and not being able to control either, or choose a side. Sally moved toward him, saying nothing, a silent witness to the chaotic unraveling of Horace's day.

Horace, though, soldiered on.

In the blacksmith shop he wanted to make a horseshoe right before their eyes, and let the boys take turns working the bellows, which they did with excited energy. Sally, from the back, pointed to her watch. Horace pulled a piece of grooved shoe iron from the stacks and held it over the glowing coals with a pair of long-handled tongs. When it was red hot, he moved it to the anvil with the tongs, and positioned it over the chipping block. He grabbed the hot set, a hatchet designed to cut the soft metal, and dug the sharp edge into the shoe-iron bar. Then he took a short-handled three-pound sledge, and with one heavy, measured shot, cut the shoe-iron bar in two. Some of the boys were impressed with the guillotine swiftness of the job and the video-game pyrotechnics of flying orange embers as they sailed like shooting stars against the darkness of the shop.

"Cool," he heard a couple mutter.

"That's how it's done," Horace said.

He took the shoe-length piece back to the hearth, where Michael, now on the bellows, had the coals spitting sparks and fire. With the tongs, Horace got the shoe iron glowing again, and quickly took it back to the anvil. Working with the cross peen hammer, he banged the metal into a curved shape around the anvil horn. It was shoe-shaped, and he should have quit there.

But instead he laid it down and flattened it out with a wide-base hammer called the flatter, blasted out six nail holes with the sharp drift and nail punches, made the blunt caulks at each end of the shoe and the cat's ear at the middle of the curve, oblivious to the boys' growing boredom. He explained that these last elements are what make the shoe fit, much like the shaped backs and toes of their own shoes. He thrust the shoe into a pail of water to cool it down, and handed the finished product to Michael.

"Here you go, birthday boy," he said, but saw tears of anger in Michael's eyes. The "quick visit" had dragged on and on. His dad's showing off by making the shoe took another painful half hour—adding to the time they wouldn't get to spend at the Hall of Fame.

"What's the matter?" Horace asked Michael.

"Nothing. I just got some smoke in my eyes," Michael said as he wiped his eyes, now further humiliated that Horace had brought his tears to the attention of his friends. In that moment, even Horace knew he'd lost his son.

That night after Michael was put to bed, Sally started with him.

"Really, how could you?"

"How could I what?"

"Oh, I don't know . . . ," she said facetiously. "Where should I start? How could you be so goddamned selfish? So goddamned insensitive? So thick-headed? How could you ruin your son's birthday?"

"He had a good time, I thought," Horace said.

"You think? You know what he told me at the Hall of Fame . . . in the half hour they had there? He said, 'Mom, I hate Dad. Dad's a jerk!' "

"And what did you say?"

"I decided it was best to not say anything. And I didn't say anything when he threw the horseshoe you made him in the kitchen trash."

Later that night, while Sally slept, Horace retrieved it and put it in a drawer beneath his blackened, coal-stained shirts, to give it to Michael at some far-off future point, when the boy grew to understand.

And now, as the summer before Michael started high school approached, there was desperation to Horace's plot. He wanted to make things right, the old-fashioned way, with Michael working by his side. For just a few hours a day, for just a few weeks, he wanted Michael to himself.

But here was Sally, already poisoning, already so sure Michael would hate the idea. Horace understood why a mother would cling to her only child, especially a son, as he rounded into his teenaged years. But preparing him for manhood, that was a father's job, and goddamnit, Horace was going to assert his right.

"Give it a chance, Sally," Horace said. "He's fourteen, old enough to have a summer job. You were working then, so was I. He's going to have to learn to work someday, might as well be now."

A FEW WEEKS LATER, Grundling stopped by the smithy. Horace was out back, sweeping up around the coal tunnel. Through a window he watched Grundling, who thought he was hidden in darkness, try to budge the 250-pound anvil. As Horace watched, he realized he had never seen Grundling in the shop before, nor had he seen him ever do anything physical. At least old Vanderoot would come down now and then and tinker with things, especially when he got close to retiring. Grundling gave up, then realized his hands were smudged, and he looked around for a place to wipe them. He began to move uneasily, as if he didn't want his clean, pressed khakis to brush up against the workbenches, grimy with coal soot and iron dust.

Horace came in and tossed him a rag, a silent admission he'd been watching, and Grundling's face got red.

"Horace! Good news!" he said, recovering. "The board said we could hire your son."

"That is good, John. Great, really. Thank you."

"You just have to sign a few insurance waivers, and we're all set."

"Waivers?" Horace asked.

"Yes . . . nothing too nefarious. If he gets hurt here, he will be covered by our insurance. The board just wants a waiver acknowledging your son is underage, and promising not to sue the museum or the foundation for negligence because we hired him knowing he was underage."

Horace took the papers.

"In my day," he said, gesturing around the shop, "my word would have been good enough."

"Yes, Horace, but when you walk out of this shop and into the twenty-first century, there's a million lawyers out there looking to sue a fat foundation like the Clark. You understand."

"Of course," said Horace. "Unfortunately, I do."

He signed the papers and said again, "Thanks, John, I appreciate you doing this."

"Don't mention it, Horace, it will be good to have your son . . ."

"Michael."

". . . Michael, right, aboard. There is, however, one little . . . stipulation."

"What's that?" Horace asked.

"Michael will be working as a general field hand and with you, in here, so in order to make room for him, I'm not going to hire the summer docent for the Cardiff Giant exhibit."

Back when Horace started, the Giant was in a circus tent off in a corner of the museum grounds, but had since been moved inside, near the main entrance and the hall of antique pickup trucks. Every few summers, the museum would repitch the tent near the Empire State Carousel, for a country-fair effect. This would be one of those years, Grundling said.

"We can't leave the tent unmanned all day," he said.

Horace knew what was coming.

"I saw a paper you wrote on the Giant almost twenty years ago in our archives," Grundling said. " 'American Rubism.' Very clever. With your knowledge of local history and legend, you would be perfect to give a few presentations a day."

"Jesus, John, I'm a craftsman," Horace said, not able to hide the irritation in his voice. "Can't you get some college girl to do that?"

"That's just it, Horace. I can't. I gave *that* position to your son. That leaves us short for the Giant."

"And what about my farm-and-baseball idea? I thought Michael and I could work on that. Remember, 'can of corn,' 'broad side of a barn,' and all that."

"Still in the works," Grundling said. "But, either way, I need you for the Giant."

Prick, Horace thought. Always a catch with this guy, he thought.

"All right. How many times a day?"

"Three, maybe four. Say, at ten, noon, two, and four."

"How long a presentation?"

"Fifteen minutes, tops, just enough to thoroughly tell the story with some good detail."

"Okay," Horace said, resigned.

"Good. It's settled, then."

"Yep. I'll tell Michael the good news," Horace said, embarrassed by a transparent, forced upswing in his own voice, a false note of cheeriness he used to convince Grundling—and himself—that it would all work out.

That night, he went home and told Sally.

She shook her head.

"Let's see what Michael says, Horace. I'm not sure he's going to want this."

"It will be fine."

"You win, Horace," Sally said, flat. "I don't want to talk about it anymore. But it might not be fine, Horace. It might not be fine."

Chapter Eleven

Sylvia Grudeck tried to put off the church board when they floated the idea of Meet Joe Grudeck Night to raise money for the new gym at St. Joe's. The plan was for a buffet and a silent auction of whatever memorabilia Grudeck would donate. And if he could stay for a couple of hours, well, that would be wonderful.

She objected by saying he was only there until sixth grade, "and he never really played much basketball," but some correctly recalled how he tore up the court in CYO before he discovered wrestling, and Sylvia knew. She was there.

So she reluctantly promised to ask.

"But don't feel you have to, if it's an imposition," she told her son over the phone.

"It's not, Ma," he said.

"I know you're busy, with the Hall of Fame and everything."

"I'm not, Ma. Not really. I go to spring training for two weeks, like every year, and I got a few other things after that. I'll check my calendar with Sal, but I think it's all right."

"If you can't, it's no big deal. You know I hate to ask . . . I told them the answer was probably no."

"Ma, it's no big deal. Tell them I'll do it."

The goal was to raise forty grand to make everything new, from floor to scoreboards. Two hundred tickets were sold, at fifty apiece; that was ten grand right there. Memorabilia sales would close the gap. A local Italian joint called Picatelli's would donate food in exchange for some photo ops with the star. It was a back-door endorsement, Grudeck knew; Picatelli's would plaster those pictures all over the restaurant, but what the hell.

Grudeck told his mother to tell the church board to contact Sal, who kept the stock; replica jerseys, signature bats, and boxes of photos: the McCombs knockout, the Series homer, and Grudeck, in a new uniform, waving good-bye to the crowd on his farewell night at Fenway, and others.

"I'll send good stuff for the silent auction," Sal told them. "But I'll also send cheap stuff, like balls and pictures, so everybody can go home with something."

Sal controlled most of Grudeck's memorabilia business and had rules. "We personalize everything. Makes it less valuable to anyone but the first owner. We don't want people trading on your good intentions." And when Sal said "we" he meant "we." Sal's *Joe Grudeck* signature was as good as Grudeck's himself, and Sal pre-signed everything for shows where he supplied the merchandise. They had a system. On each piece Sal wrote *To* . . . with a blank, then *Best of Luck!* . . . and signed Grudeck's name. At the event, Grudeck just filled in the buyer's name, to keep things moving. When Sal launched joegrudeck.com, everything sold on the Web was signed by Sal.

"It's only forgery without authorization," Sal once reasoned. "You're authorizing me to sign, so . . . okay, that's bullshit, I know . . . but I can't tell the difference, you can't tell the difference, so who is it hurting? Besides, it keeps your hand from getting worse. And half the stuff on the market is forged anyway. You know it as well as I do."

For the St. Joe's night, Grudeck told Sal to put up the uniform from his farewell night.

"That can be the big-ticket item," he said.

"You sure?" Sal said. "You could get a lot of money for that thing."

"I'm sure. Time to start—what do they call it?—downsizing," Grudeck said.

The uniform was mint; worn only for pregame festivities, the big standing O, then taken off before Grudeck fled the ballpark. The equipment manager had the uniform cleaned and packed in an airtight wedding-dress box, then shipped it to Sal, who put it in a temperature- and humidity-controlled storage unit with other stuff from Grudeck's playing days. The first mitt he wore in the bigs, the last one, too. Bats and balls from home runs 100, 200, and 300, all hit at Fenway. His 1,000th hit, an opposite-field single in Cleveland's old Municipal Stadium, his 2,500th, a two-out, nobody on, single in the eighth of a lost game in the Bronx. The Yankee fans booed. Sal sent that bat and ball, the Series uniform, and some other stuff to Cooperstown. Grudeck knew the rest would be auctioned off someday, not because he needed the money, but because there would be nobody to give it to.

The farewell night uniform would be the first, and easiest, to part with. It was like a marine's dress blues; never worn in battle, so it had little emotional value.

"You know what?" Grudeck added. "Send them the hundredth and two hundredth home run bats, too . . . and Sallie, one more thing: I don't want any surprises. Tell them if they're thinking of naming the gym after me, forget it. It's a deal breaker."

"Oh, you saw that one coming."

"Yeah. And I'm serious. Tell them I have a check for twenty grand to go toward the gym, but if they name it after me, I swear I'll tear the fucking thing up."

"So, you'll be the first guy in history to pay to *not* have a gym named after you," Sal said.

"Whatever," Grudeck said. "Make sure they know I'm serious. Gym namings are for dead or decrepit guys. I'm neither. Not yet."

Grudeck hated it all, especially when Sal talked about his stuff being a "good investment."

"Your price went up. The Hall of Fame does that, you know," he said. "We have to start charging more."

"I know, but I don't want to gouge people."

"There you go again, feeling guilty about it," Sal said. "Don't you understand? You're a good investment. Your stuff spiked after the Hall announcement. Just look at eBay. And when you die, God forbid, it'll go up again, like a maturing bond."

"Yeah, hot today, then would cool till I die, then get hot again," he said. "Then stone cold."

Time goes by, he thought, and pretty soon everybody who ever saw you play is dead, too. Then what? How valuable is all this crap then?

But for now, he was hot. A few weeks after the Hall news, Grudeck went to Boston for an already scheduled cash-and-carry autograph show. He never liked these things but agreed, thinking that if he didn't get in the Hall, it would make him feel less forgotten. Now that he was voted in, he regretted it; the trip up, the tacky hotel ballroom, the four hours of meeting sweaty-palmed, stuttering fans, all of it. There were five hundred already in line when he entered the room to big applause—"Please welcome Hall of Famer . . ."—surrounded by sports auction house organizers and six security guys playing hard-ass cops. He was cordoned off by Red Sox red and blue velvet ropes, and took a seat at a banquet table next to a pair of attractive young women, who handled merchandise and money.

It went the way it always went. "I'm your biggest fan . . ." "Hey, Joe, I was there when . . ." A signature. A handshake. A cell phone shot. Hand on shoulder, big smile, digital documentation that they met Joe Grudeck. Within minutes, on Facebook, Twitter, whatever. *Here's me and Joe Grudeck.* After twenty seconds, they were moved out by the security guys flexing minimum-wage muscle . . . *Let's go, people, thirty seconds, that's what you get. Keep moving.*

He was still uncomfortable—after all these years—with people sucking up to him like this, so willing to put themselves below him. Grown men, doing it right in front of their kids. Joe Grudeck idolized his dad above any athlete. Chuck Grudeck was Joey's hero. What kind of father so easily hands that over to some star jock, someone they don't even *know*? Not in Chuck Grudeck's day. The father came first, and the father was the role model. Not some ballplayer, even Grudeck. It depressed him.

The organizer, some Southie Irish guido named Lenny Something-or-other, bugged him all day, coming up several times an hour, talking low in Grudeck's ear simply to ask if he wanted water or something, acting as if they were co-conspirators. And at the end of the night, they were. There was a bag of cash from Guido Lenny.

"Here you go, Joey, five thousand, in fifties. That way the IRS doesn't know you got it or I gave it. Not bad for a half day's work, no?"

Grudeck excused himself to scrub his hands. Two of the rent-a-cops then escorted him to his car. He threw his brown bag of money on the passenger seat of his Cadillac, punched the gas, and got on the road. Nothing like a fast drive to blow back the conscience.

He was in a foul mood, pissed mostly that Guido Lenny had called him "Joey." Nobody called him Joey now except his mother and Sal, every once in a while, and some of the old folks in Union. "Joey" was off-limits to anyone who only knew Joe Grudeck, the ballplayer.

Three hours later, he was on Route 78 in Jersey, almost home, pushing the car at a buck-ten, then -fifteen, then -twenty, when he saw blue-and-red flashers pull out from behind an outcrop of Watchung Mountain traprock in the median. He thought for a second about outrunning the cop, but Grudeck pulled over.

It was a state trooper, not much older than twenty-five, lean and clear blue–eyed and crew-cut, a marine-like recruit. Typical Jersey trooper, all business, all thin blue line.

"License, registration, and insurance card, sir."

"Of course, trooper," Grudeck said. You never called a Jersey state trooper "officer." They saw it as a sign of disrespect to their paramilitary fitness, and if you were doing one-twenty, they'd write one-twenty—and reckless driving on top.

Grudeck handed over his papers and waited for his name to register, for the flashlight-in-the-face beam of recognition, for the "Okay, Mr. Grudeck, I'll let you slide this time, but you need to take it easy out here," and maybe even the "Can you do me a favor and sign this . . . ?"

But not on this night.

"Mr. Grud-eck, Groo-deck. Am I saying it right?" the trooper asked.

"Yes, Joe Groo-deck."

Still nothing.

Grudeck figured he'd give him a hint.

"I'll bet you were a pitcher in high school, huh, trooper?"

"Sir?"

"Did you play baseball . . . in high school?"

"No, sir, lacrosse . . . Mr. Groo-deck. This car is registered to, and insured by, MacIntosh Cadillac. Is that correct, sir?"

"Yes. I have an endorsement deal with them."

Still nothing.

The kid trooper flashed his light into the car and stopped at the paper bag on the passenger seat.

"Sir, do you mind telling me what's in the bag?"

He thinks I'm drunk, Joe Grudeck thought.

"Actually, it's money," Grudeck said, and held up the brown bag for inspection, ready to explain away the autograph show. "You see, I'm Joe . . ."

"Stay here," the trooper said, and walked back to his cruiser. Within minutes, another trooper arrived, same prototype as the first. They both approached, and the second stood in the shadows outside the passenger door, shining a flashlight on Grudeck, and around the cockpit.

"Step out of the car, please, sir," the first said. His hand was on his holstered service revolver.

"Whoa, sport," Grudeck said, putting up his hands and a weak smile on his face. "Take it easy."

His mind raced back to Syracuse, two girls, kneeling on the floor, bent over the bed, not fighting, just still.

Was this it? Did one come forward after the Hall vote?

"Keep your hands where I can see them and step out of the car, sir."

"Look, there's some . . . I'm Joe Grudeck . . . the ballpl—"

"Out of the car, sir. Right now, please. Hands where I can see them."

Grudeck wasn't halfway out when the kid spun him around, not rough, but with authority. The other trooper was there now, and grabbed Grudeck's right wrist.

Joe Grudeck flexed up, and protested over his shoulder.

"Hey, don't you recognize me . . . I'm Joe Grudeck, the ballplayer. I played for the Red Sox. The *Boston* Red Sox."

"No, sir, I do not. And if I did, it wouldn't matter . . . Sir, for my safety and yours, I'm going to ask you to put both your hands behind your back."

Grudeck yanked his hand free.

"Fuck this. I'm Joe fucking Grudeck. What is this?"

"Sir, for my safety and yours . . ." the first trooper yelled, and the second trooper came in with a nightstick under Grudeck's arm.

"Motherfucker, put your fucking hands behind your back, *now*," he growled. "Or I *will* spray you. I swear to *God*, I'll spray you."

"Hey! Hang on!" Grudeck said, still twisting away, but the nightstick was pinned hard against his back, pulling his arm up at an unnatural angle. "Okay, take it easy."

"Don't tell me take it easy," the second trooper said. "Put your fucking hands behind your back!"

Grudeck tried to pull free, but the old strength that let him do what he wanted, when he wanted, had diminished.

"You know, if this was twenty years ago . . ." Grudeck started.

"This ain't twenty years ago," the trooper said.

Grudeck relaxed, beaten, and they cuffed him and led him to sit on a guardrail.

"Sir, I'm going to ask your permission to search your car," the first one said. "If you refuse, and you have that right, I will have it towed and impounded, until a judge can execute a warrant for me to search it, do you understand?"

"Search warrant! For what? What is this?"

"Fuck him. Arrest him for resisting . . ." the second one said.

"For probable cause," the first one said.

"What the hell is going on?" Grudeck asked. He was embarrassed how afraid he sounded, but he was. Vulnerable. And overpowered. He thought of the two girls, his hands on their backs, the blonde's striped, little girl panties.

"Sir, we're going to only ask you this once," the second one said. "Are there any drugs or weapons in this car?"

Grudeck then got it.

"Drugs! Are you out of your fucking mind? I'm Joe Grudeck, for Christ sakes, the ballplayer. Joe Grudeck. Call your fathers and ask them who the hell I am if you don't know. Deal drugs? I made that money signing autographs . . ." God, he sounded hysterical.

"Calm down, sir," the first one said. "We're going to ask you one more time, in accordance with law. After that, I call a tow truck."

"Search the goddamn thing, I don't give a shit," he said, relieved it wasn't about Syracuse.

They popped the trunk lid and engine hood and bent deep into both with flashlights. Grudeck's golf clubs were taken out, the bag emptied and shaken. The first trooper got on his hands and knees, and shined the light up into the wheel wells and around the undercarriage. The other trooper then went through the cockpit, emptied the glove compartment and the console bins, and raked under the seats.

Another cruiser pulled up, and two sergeants emerged, older and thicker, but cut from the same cloth. The first trooper showed them the evidence—the bag of money—and Joe Grudeck's license, registration, and insurance card. He did most of the talking, often signaling back to the Cadillac with his flashlight.

After a few minutes, one of the sergeants came to the guardrail where Grudeck sat.

"Mr. Grudeck?"

"Yes."

"Joe Grudeck?"

"The same."

The light in his face turned out to be one of merciful recognition. "Okay, then, let's get you on up and outta here."

The cuffs came off and the apologies started.

"I'm sorry for my young colleagues', ummm, *exuberance*, but we get a lot of drug and weapons mules here on Route 78, going from Newark to Easton. You know, the luxury car, lotsa cash, the speed, you kinda fit some of the profiles."

"I'm a middle-aged white guy, for fuck's sake!" Grudeck said.

"You'd be surprised," the sergeant said. "The young man here was just doing his job."

"No apologies necessary," Grudeck said, cooler, but with an edge that suggested they damn sure were. "It was my fault . . . I was the one speeding, that's for sure."

"Okay, well, we'll let that one slide now, for your trouble. But try to keep it double digits . . . the trooper clocked you at one-twenty-two. No doubt you can handle that . . . it's the other idiots on the road we worry about."

The sergeant fished in his pocket for his own summons book and produced a pen. "Hey, while we're here, can you sign this for my son?"

Chapter Twelve

Meet Joe Grudeck Night was held on the last Saturday in April. Spring had arrived only on the calendar. Winter's damp hangover stuck in Grudeck's joints and knuckles, making them scrape like rust on rust. He wished the golf course were green and firm; instead, the trees were still barren against battleship-gray skies, and the fairways spongy enough to leave footprints. The only warmth Grudeck felt was from inflammation.

Grudeck parked in back, in the darkest part of the lot, and hoisted himself out. He was stiff and shook his legs out, not wanting anyone to see him limp.

The steps of the parish hall were lit, and Grudeck saw people hurrying in. He watched for a few minutes, hidden off. Each time the door would open, the noise from the party inside would drift out; laughter, loud voices, the sounds of a reunion. He had played before thousands in the stands and millions on TV without an ounce of self-consciousness, but now he was nervous. He was home. He began flexing his fingers and palms, a warm-up stretch for the handshake and signing that awaited him. It would be one of those four-Advil nights.

He started out across the blacktop, cracked and pocked in places, and felt the loose stones roll under his steps. He played basketball in this yard and kickball and four-square, and touch football and baseball, and it probably hadn't been repaved since. In the dark, he could barely see the faded white lines. He climbed the steps of the parish hall—a very plain stucco building where the children's Sunday Masses were held—and entered into the light.

Grudeck, through the ages, was everywhere. The walls were decorated with giant-sized pictures, Grudeck larger than life, playing in high school and the bigs. Grudeck and McCombs. The Series homer. Tipping his hat on Farewell Joe Grudeck Night. On either side of the crucifix over the stage/Sunday altar were Topps cards blown up as posters; Grudeck's rookie year, and one from down the line.

One wall was just from high school. Grudeck, returning state wrestling champ, arms raised over the whalelike mound of the black kid he pinned in the final. Grudeck slamming helmet-to-helmet with two linebackers at the goal line to win the state title game against Elizabeth. Grudeck trotting bases after one of two homers to beat Summit in the county final. Grudeck, always in the center, always the winner.

In all, there were a dozen such photos, hanging on every wall. Grudeck took it all in with his catcher's eyes before anybody noticed him. Good thing, because he couldn't have hidden his embarrassment at the excess.

For what it cost, they could have built the goddamn gym without his help, he thought. What a waste. They built a shrine. And for what? To create an atmosphere? They could have done with just one on each wall. Why go over the top? To impress him, their kid from Union? Did these people, his hometown people, forget who he really was? Them, too?

All that, and besides, it just illuminated the fact that he was no longer the kid or guy on the walls. He was older now. Creaky and gasping, feeling vulnerable, not immortal.

He stood at the door, unnoticed, for only a few heartbeats before . . .

"It's Joey!" came a shout from the crowd, the voice of an older woman.

"Joe's here!" came another, almost simultaneously, from a man. The gym lights were dimmed, and a brilliant white illuminated square from a computer projector went up on a wall.

The *SportsCenter* video from the day he got inducted began to play. Twenty years in the bigs, forty-six years on earth, his life, his *persona* edited down to a ninety-second segment of highlights and stats, narrated by one of the actor-anchors, dripping sentiment about how Joe Grew was one of the good guys, and one of the last of the lunch-bucket ballplayers, blah, blah, blah.

Joe Grew will be remembered not for his heroics or home runs but for how he played the game. With hard-knuckled heart. With body-racking passion. Joe Grew is a Hall of Famer now, a player for the ages, because, in baseball, love of the game never goes out of style.

The screen went dark, the lights came up, and the crowd broke out in applause. Showtime. All the years of meeting fans, all those interruptions in hotel lobbies and restaurants, in meet-and-greet memorabilia shows and charity dinners, Grudeck always put on a good face. Forced, but good. Maybe transparently phony, but the fans never seemed to notice, or maybe they just didn't want to believe it. That Joe Grrreww, what a good guy. But here, back in Union, he suddenly felt at home.

Crazy thing, though. No one approached him. Instead, they backed up slightly, as if to give him more room on center stage. All those years, all those strangers came right at him, but here at home . . .

Grudeck forced a smile, but his self-consciousness was expanding to fill the space. With his face getting hot, he made one big wave, and then walked into the crowd to stop the clapping. He felt moistness in his armpits and on his shirt collar, and hoped his palms weren't sweaty as he shook hands with old classmates and teachers and coaches and neighbors and his father's friends from Jenn-Air and mother's friends from St. Joe's.

There were smiles all around, but he saw something in their eyes . . . a nervous glance, a cloud of . . . what was it? Disappointment? Concern? He was forever young in the pictures and the video, but now, as they saw him with their own two eyes . . .

The crowd did not envelop him; he moved into them, and shook hand after hand, and offered his cheek to the women, some of whom grabbed his head with both hands to pull him down to their level. Some faces he knew. Others he recognized, but the attached names were long forgotten.

His mother came forward and grabbed his arm and led him to the Rosary Society ladies. He kissed their papery cheeks, which smelled of lavender powder.

He leaned down to say hello to shy children who were shoved toward him, finally brought to meet the man they'd heard about all their lives, Joe Grudeck, the living proof of all that was possible for someone from Union who worked hard and kept their nose clean. He moved forward, sweating his balls off in his charcoal cashmere pullover and black wool sports coat. These were his people. But still, he felt a distance. Something was not right. What was it? Him? Or them?

Were they puzzled by his open affection? Did they expect arrogance? As he opened himself up—no, threw himself into them—did they think his warmth was all show? Were they, too, blinded by his fame, even though they knew him before he attained it?

Or was it the opposite? Did they feel sorry for him, because, in truth, he was not who they remembered? He was middle-aged, losing breadth of shoulder and roll in his walk. He was no longer Chuck Grudeck's kid, the eternal boy of summer. He was now a sideline-sitter, just like them. In his smile and willingness to embrace, did they detect weakness, a need to be loved and not forgotten? Did they feel embarrassed for him?

Or was it simply that he had been gone so long, he was no longer theirs?

GRUDECK EXCUSED HIMSELF, chased by these swirling thoughts, and went to the men's room. It was unchanged since he was a boy. Old-fashioned Standard porcelain urinals that went right to the floor, gray-and-white-checked tile floor. Black tin partitions between the crappers, but no doors. Everything the same, just more dull and filmy.

He cupped his hands under the cold water and splashed some on his face, then downed the first two Advil of the night.

IN HIS FIRST FEW YEARS IN THE BIGS, when he returned to Union in the off-season, Grudeck walked among them and there was novelty in his new fame. He went to stores with his mother, to high school wrestling matches, and out to dinner and bars with his friends, on him. Everyone was always happy to see him . . . snapshots were taken, drinks were bought. But the routine soon got old—for him and the people of Union. The small talk that revolved around his career became stilted, he felt big and clumsy and conspicuous in the bleachers at the high school gym. He began to stay in more when he came home, spending his days eating his mother's cooking and resting his body.

Winter hung around like a feral cat, and as the gray, damp days dragged on, Grudeck couldn't wait to leave Jersey and drive south. Midway through the trip, somewhere in the Carolinas, he could turn off the car heat. Next he'd put the windows down, letting the lush, musky air of the Georgia countryside rush over him. By Florida, the air was sunshine-hot, and it blew through the car, blasting the chill of winter from Grudeck's bones.

He loved that drive: the twenty-four hours to Daytona. It was a test of his focus and endurance, and the durability of whatever machine he drove, from the Pontiac Grand Prix he bought after his second-year contract, to the high-end BMWs he owned when he was a star, to the final years in MacIntosh Cadillacs. And for those twenty-four hours, he never felt more free. Alone. Out of reach. Phone off. Best of all, anonymous.

All those bleary-eyed overnight gas station attendants on interstate access roads in Harleyville, Virginia, and Alcolu, South Carolina, and Intercession City, Florida, never recognized him. In all those years, only one guy, an old chaw-spitter in janitor green, said to him, "Ain't you a ballplaya?"

"No, a salesman," said Grudeck, out of the car only to piss, stretch his legs, and buy a Coke. "But some people tell me I look like one."

"Sho' do. Big dude like you. Like, wha-sizz-name? Dat big catcha boy. From Boston."

"Don't know," Grudeck said. "Don't follow sports much."

WHILE HE WENT ON WITH HIS CAREER, his friends went on with their lives. Those who went to college were around town less and less. Those who stayed in Union and worked locally started growing up. They got married (Grudeck would be invited, but could never make it). They had kids. They had budgets. More and more, the things in their lives were things Grudeck could not relate to. And Grudeck's life, to them, was pure fantasy—glory and money, women galore. Their friendships became good-old-days memories, and Grudeck became the guy on TV, or in the newspaper: someone everybody once knew, but nobody knew anymore. As Grudeck became more famous, winter in Union became his chance to hide. The constant assault of strangers during the season left him drained, so he withdrew from his friends just to recover.

So now, back in this crowd of familiar faces, Grudeck made the first moves. He stepped up to Eddie Spallone, a guy Grudeck had known since kindergarten, a childhood best friend. Grudeck grabbed him and pulled him in for a hug.

"Eddie, hey, Jesus Christ . . . how you been?" Grudeck asked, slapping his back.

"Not as good as you!" he said.

"Don't believe it!" Grudeck said. "You look great, better'n me."

That was the truth. Spallone still looked boyish, a young man in a mid-forties body. Quick smile, teeth white, wavy hair, black and intact. Why did Grudeck feel so old?

"How's . . . ahh . . . ?"

"Maureen."

"Right. Maureen."

"We got divorced five years ago."

"Sorry to hear that."

"Don't be. Best thing for everybody. Nothing was ever enough. Turned into a Class A, like her mother."

Grudeck wanted to hear more, especially about Maureen—what was her last name? Walsh?—and wondered if she ever told Spallone about those couple of times in the backseat of his father's Malibu. But he was grabbed by the elbow. It was Anthony Morello, the guard on Grudeck's football teams.

"I'm divorced, too," he said to Grudeck and Spallone. "I wanted to bring my boys tonight, but she wouldn't let me. Not my weekend. I said, 'There's fifty-two fuckin' weekends a year . . . how many times they get to meet Joe Grudeck?' You know what she says? 'You're always bragging what great friends you used to be . . . have them meet Joe Grudeck on a weekend that's not my weekend.' That's the shit I put up with."

The men began to swap divorce stories, and Grudeck turned to the growing line of people waiting to talk to him.

Mike Fitzgerald, another kid from grammar school; Jack Clancy, a wide receiver and a star pitcher; Stu Luby, the football center and a very good wrestler, who had to cut fifteen pounds to make 215 because he couldn't beat Grudeck at heavyweight; Jimmy Smithers, the tailback and center fielder, one of the few black kids from Vauxhaul who had white friends; Chris and Mike Damiano, the twin brother linebackers and mid-weight wrestlers. Grudeck caught up with them all.

Grudeck looked at each of his old friends, and tried to figure which one the years had beaten up the most. Was it him?

Each conversation ended the same way, "Let's get together sometime . . ." then just hung there.

After the boys came the girls, the girls, the girls. Some would never look better than they did at seventeen, all thin, tight, and firm, long hair shiny and soft, teeth white, lips flush pink. He remembered how they smelled. Like clean water. And he remembered their fake, blushing reluctance. Like Syracuse? No, not like Syracuse.

So now, almost thirty years later, the girls in the jock circle came out to see him. Grudeck remembered most of their names . . . Monica, Erin, Mary Anne, Patti . . . First names, anyway.

Some were with husbands and sons, who, depending on their ages, were either thrilled or oblivious.

The girls who married early had boys who grew up rooting for Grudeck. These kids, now young men, saw Grudeck at his long peak. Their mothers, looking small next to their mannish sons, introduced them by saying, "Oh, Ben [or Justin or Jake or Mike] here was such a big fan of yours. He had your baseball cards and your posters in his room. He thought *I* was cool because I knew you in high school."

The girls who married later had sons who were only ten, eleven, twelve years old now and a half generation behind Grudeck's best time; they said things like "Remember, honey, Mommy told you about the famous baseball player I grew up with. Well, this is him!"

The girls who came without husbands spent an extra minute on his arm, gave him a tighter hug and a hello kiss toward the lips. The girls with husbands turned it down a notch. Some of the husbands glanced around him nervously, knowing (or suspecting) this jock mountain of a man had once piped their wives in the back of a car or the dark bleachers or the basement rec room while her parents slept upstairs. High school stuff . . . except that Joe Grudeck didn't become some hazy memory. He was a star. Famous. Huge, in legend and body. Grudeck didn't let go. He was always there. In the newspapers, on TV; the talk and pride of the town. You didn't forget Joe Grudeck. You didn't forget his size. The weight of his body. The strength of his arms. Grudeck didn't let go.

On and on, it went like this, and after an hour or so, Grudeck's mood began to go south. After his circle of friends came guys whose names Grudeck couldn't remember. Bench warmers, losing wrestlers, kids Grudeck carried on his broad shoulders, kids who would have never played for a championship team, if Joey wasn't hitting home runs and scoring touchdowns. Kids who bragged about playing high school ball with Joe Grudeck to their co-workers, their new friends, their in-laws, their kids, and, someday, their grandkids. This is the gift Grudeck gave these guys. A hook into his legacy. He gave them moments, and then memories, and their own lasting athletic legacy, no matter how small. They played with Joe Grudeck, now a Hall of Famer. Otherwise, their careers were forgettable.

One after another, they came at him, remembering this game or that, verbal replays of highlights from Grudeck's high school days. Grudeck's face began to hurt from smiling. His right-hand ache was dulled by the Advil, but he could feel it just the same, and the oils from so many hands felt grimy on his own. He was hot, and the gym felt airless. Heavy beadlets of sweat amassed on his forehead and he felt rivulets trickling under his arms and down the middle of his chest. One after another, they came at him, an army of guys named Jack and Skip and Mike and Arnie, guys who made small talk and asked for a glimmer of recognition . . . "You remember me? I recovered the fumble in the Westfield game, senior year" . . . "Hi, Joe, you might not remember, but I wrestled one hundred six on jayvee the second year you won the states."

Now Grudeck's hip was full-blown killing him, a sciatic snake of pain radiating from his ass up his lower back and down his leg to the back of his knee. His feet hurt, too. Playing eighteen was easier than just standing there.

One after another, it was the same bullshit: a little small talk, Grudeck's feigning interest in their lives, them pretending they knew something about Grudeck's, a couple of smiles and back slaps, a pose for a picture, another flash exploding in Grudeck's face like a mortar blast from an old war movie. Flash after flash. Now came the eyeball ache, exacerbated by each new blast of strobe.

Grudeck moved through circles of people, groups clustered by old teammates, organizations, or age. He was embraced by his parents' friends who had patiently waited for him to arrive. He knew them all when they were his age; now the women had thinning hair swept up on their heads, their pear-shaped, overperfumed and powdered bodies stretching the fabric of their old-lady dresses. He felt lipstick residue on his face; medicinal Listerine breath was in his nostrils.

Mrs. Vezzosi . . . Gert Schumacher . . . Mrs. Przybylski . . .

The men, bent and bowlegged, had food stains on their sweaters or polyester sports coats and urine blotches on their pants. He shook their withered hands, sometimes calming their tremors with his grip.

Mr. Zabrinsky . . . Jack Ricciardi . . . Joe Mickles . . . Others, whose names he forgot.

They all came smiling, yellowed teeth or piano-key dentures wide open.

In him, they saw youth. In them, he saw death. It was coming.

I'm at my own wake, Grudeck suddenly thought. Except he was a walking, talking stiff—still alive to hear everyone's stories about him. He was enshrined, and entombed. A gloom began to coat him, like the sweat leaking from his pores, only black.

When the buffet line opened, Grudeck used the distraction to take another break. He went back to the men's room, where he exchanged pleasantries with an old guy he did not know who was just zipping up. Alone now, he looked hard into the kid-proof metal mirrors, now slightly warped and hazy, and searched for the boy in himself as he scrubbed his hands. It reminded him of Syracuse, when he looked into the steam-soaked mirror after he washed the girls off him, and saw someone different.

HE NEEDED AIR. Alone in the dark parking lot, Grudeck let the cool, misty April air chill the sweat on his body. He inhaled it deeply, then blew it out and watched the vapor dissipate like cigarette smoke.

He heard a car door shut, and the beep of automatic door locks. He'd started to move to an unlit corner, when he heard the sound of a woman's heels on the pavement. A slender, dark-haired woman in a mid-length black raincoat pulled tightly at her waist approached. Grudeck immediately recognized how she carried herself. After all these years. He moved out to meet her, deeper into the darkest part of the lot.

"Stacy," he said, surprised by the softness of his own voice.

He put his hands on both her shoulders and kissed her on the lips. It was quick and deliberate.

"I just promised myself I wouldn't do that, and then I did," he said. "I'm sorry."

"Same old Joe," she said.

"No! Well, yeah. But . . ."

"I know, I know . . . 'I'm different.' That's what you always said."

Stacy with the beautiful facey, that's what Grudeck used to call her.

Now he said it again. And she laughed.

"You're such a little boy. Still."

He wanted to kiss her again, but instead held her at arm's length to take her all in. She was better than ever, a more sophisticated version of her teenaged self. Her dark hair, always straight, was still long but shaped around her face. Those olive-green eyes, even in the dark, moved something inside him. A heart thump. A lung expansion. Something. Something not lust. Her face, always thin and petite, had filled out, taking away some of the prominence of her nose. She hated her nose in high school, Grudeck remembered, and Grudeck always pretended it got in the way when he kissed her.

"Stop. Be nice," she would say as Grudeck acted as if her nose had poked him in the eye.

Kissing was as far as it got. Grudeck never pushed, because he liked her too much, more than just another notch. More accurately, he didn't want to give up the other notches and didn't want to hurt Stacy Milo by cheating on her. Sometimes he thought it was the only admirable thing he'd done in his life. That was one part. The other part was that Stacy kept him at a distance because of his "groupies."

"Pathetic, vapid girls," she would say.

Grudeck knew what *pathetic* meant, but had to look up *vapid.* Still, he understood; the only way Grudeck would respect her was if she held him off.

Back in high school, she was an artsy but get-involved type. She wanted to be a photographer and was always lugging a camera. She was class treasurer, editor of the paper, and took pictures for the yearbook. That's how Grudeck first noticed her. On the sidelines, with a long lens on a monopod. At mat-side, she would get down on her elbows at action level. Always in jeans and a baggy workshirt or flannel over a tee. Her hair tied back, which showed off that Roman profile; the strong chin, the nose, and those serious olive eyes. Grudeck remembered.

Through freshman, sophomore, and junior years, the only time Grudeck spoke to her was when he threw a kid out of bounds during a wrestling match. The kid crashed into Stacy.

"You all right?" Grudeck said as he helped her up, touching her elbow with his sweaty hand.

"Yeah, sure," she said, eyes on her equipment.

That was it, until winter of senior year, when the school highlighted some of the artists in the class. Stacy had work hanging on three partitions outside the cafeteria. Stark images in lights and shadows, in black and white. Bare trees in winter. Lonely litter in an alley. Headstone obelisks against leaden skies. Dark clouds gathered around the City Hall Colonial clock tower. And two shots of Grudeck.

One was him standing alone under a gym light, up next to wrestle, his singlet pulled down off his shoulders, exposing the muscles in his back and arms. The shot was taken from the side, somewhat behind him, and the lighting gave his shoulders an enormous breadth while leaving his expressionless face in the shadows. Joey Grudeck, the sullen, teenaged Hercules.

The other was Grudeck the quarterback. He was standing upright in the pocket, his by-the-book throwing posture perfect, his clean white jersey and helmet gleaming against a gray sky, looking downfield, indifferent and high above the chaos of fallen linemen around him.

Grudeck, in his whiteness, glowed at the center of the photo, with the dark-shirted opponents and mud-stained teammates strewn at his feet. That photo, too, had a mythic tone, the high school football version of *Washington Crossing the Delaware*.

When Grudeck saw the photo exhibit, he didn't know what to make of it. Was she obsessed with him? She didn't act that way, saying all of two words to Grudeck through three years of high school. His buddies broke his balls. She was a stalker, they said. The paparazzi. But the photos were not intimate. Grudeck had no personality in the photos. He was an inanimate object. Trees, headstones, Grudeck.

The images grew on him. He found himself sneaking looks on his way in and out of the gym. If no one was around, he'd take a few seconds to study the magnificence of himself.

One night after wrestling practice, then weightlifting, Grudeck was alone in front of the two photos in the dark hallway. The school was quiet, except for the swish of the janitor's mop from a distant hall. Then there were light footsteps echoing, coming closer. Stacy Milo came around the corner, with a portfolio case in one hand, and tools to dismantle the exhibit in the other.

Grudeck was flustered at being caught, but at what? Being interested? Or self-indulgent? Either way, he feigned nonchalance. He flung his gym bag over his shoulder and headed in the opposite direction.

"Did I embarrass you?" Stacy said from behind him.

By what? Grudeck wanted to ask. The pictures? Or by catching him looking? But "Huh?" was all he said, as he turned to face her.

"The pictures. Do they embarrass you? If they do, I'm sorry."

"No. No. Actually, they're pretty cool," said Grudeck, now embarrassed by how Dumb Jock he sounded. "They're very . . . I don't know, intense," he said. Dumber still.

"Well, as long as they don't embarrass you," Stacy said. "That wasn't the intent."

"Don't worry. It's cool," Grudeck said, and turned again.

"Don't you want to know what the intent was?" Stacy asked. In her voice was a halftone of disappointment. Could Grudeck be that much of a lunkhead? Or did he really not care? Either way . . .

Grudeck stopped and turned toward her. Why didn't he think of asking? Dope.

"Yeah, I guess so," he said.

"There was no intent," Stacy said. "I just like the way they turned out."

"Well, they're nice," Grudeck said.

"You're easy to photograph. You'd make a good model," she said, and those words froze Grudeck. Models were girls. Or fems.

"What?" he said.

"Not like a clothes model, like a photography subject. The way you move. Your body mechanics, they make for good composition. The way you fill up a frame. You know, photography stuff."

But he didn't know. It was the first of many things he didn't know, but would learn, when he was with Stacy Milo.

"It just comes natural," he finally said, as if he had to explain.

Then, out of nowhere, he asked, "You wanna get some coffee, or something, with me?"

She said no, but he said "c'mon" twice, and she relented.

That's how it started. How it ended, Grudeck wasn't sure. But for a few months, he spent a lot of time with her. Like friends. Coffee and cheesecake at the Peterpank (for Panko) Diner. Nighttime walks around the running track, all bundled up in layers of sweat clothes and jackets. Sunday afternoons hanging around the downtown. He even went to a couple of plays with her at Kean College. Grudeck found her intriguing. She talked openly about things foreign to him: art, creativity, expression, self-awareness. Exceptionalism, which she said he had and she wanted. But she also thought sports were barbaric, and brought out the worst in boys ("being bullies and showoffs") and fans ("crowd behavior, like you see in those Hitler propaganda films") alike. The only reason she liked to photograph sports was because of the action ("it challenges my skills"). She called him Joseph, or Joe, never Joey. "Sounds like you're still in kindergarten," she would say.

He talked openly to her, too. He told her things he had never told anybody before, or since. Things that left him—what?—*vulnerable.*

When you're like me you're never sure if people really like you, or just because you're good at sports. I wonder if I'd have any friends if I sucked.

After games I hate when parents pay more attention to me than their own kids. I'm like, "Hey, your kid just played four quarters on the line. Go kiss his ass for a while."

One night after the diner, they were parked in front of Stacy's parents' house on Emerson Street, sitting in the Malibu. He was talking about the flip side of glory—the fear of letting everybody down—when she grabbed his arm tightly and said, "Poor baby!" and he felt the warm softness of her breast against his triceps. It was her first move, and Grudeck freed his arm and draped it around her neck in a gentle headlock, then flexed his arm.

"Feel that?" he asked.

"Yeah . . . ?"

"That's my second-biggest muscle."

"Don't be a pig," she said, pushing him away, but laughing.

Two nights later, after a walk—it was early May and the chilly air was heavy with spring dew and the musky smell of hyacinth—they ended up on the porch of the James Caldwell House, the town history museum. Grudeck told her the story of Reverend Angus, and she sided with the pastor.

"He was just trying to teach you something about the history of the town. You know, education?" she chided.

The porch had wicker furniture on it, and was shielded from the street by trellises and small hemlocks.

Stacy was shivering and Grudeck wrapped her up in his arms and kissed her. She kissed back.

"Joseph . . . I know what you do and I don't want it to be like that . . ."

"Like what?" Grudeck said, nuzzling her neck.

"Like that!" she said, squirming. "Like those other girls."

"C'mon, Stace, I really like you."

"And I like you, even though you're not my type."

"Type? I'm everybody's type."

"That's exactly the problem."

So there it was. Stacy wouldn't go easy, and in the end, not at all. Grudeck didn't force it; he wanted to prove he respected her. She was different. He wanted to protect her, even from himself.

A few nights later, they sat with their backs up against the concrete snack stand at the football field. Grudeck remembered how good it felt to be in the dark. Most times on that field, on so many brilliantly lit Jersey fall afternoons, he was the center of attention. This night, Stacy was the center of his.

With his maroon varsity jacket blending into the maroon-and-gold-trimmed snack-stand paint, and Stacy in a black turtleneck and open peacoat, they were invisible. And so small underneath the clear sky. Grudeck remembered the stars and the crescent moon, and himself not even a speck in that universe. He said this to her.

"It makes me feel, I don't know, kind of relieved. Like free. That's what I like best about you. You never talk about my games."

She looked at him and leaned her head against his shoulder.

"You know, I'm just as good an artist as you are an athlete," she said. "You should remember that while all these people are 'kissing your ass,' as you say. There's a million people out there just as good as you at what they do. It might give you some humility."

She paused and said, "You know . . . I really do like you."

And he knew she didn't mean like everyone else.

But he said it anyway.

"Right. Everybody likes me. Haven't you noticed?"

"I know, but I like *you*. You're interesting. More complicated than anyone thinks."

And at that moment, Grudeck liked her so much it might have been love. He liked her so much he didn't want to move. He just wanted to stay quiet, with her head against his shoulder, and figure out a way to feel like that forever.

That was thirty years ago. And he'd never felt anything like it since.

A few weeks later, the Red Sox called, and the day after graduation, Joey Grudeck was gone.

SO HERE WAS STACY NOW, trim in her black raincoat, looking less worn and more refined than their old classmates. He waited for her to ask why he never called when he was back in Union, or ever. He had an answer ready—"You were different"—but that answer would skirt the truth. The truth was harder, and Grudeck wasn't sure if he'd yet figured it out.

But she didn't ask.

"You look awesome," Grudeck said. "Better than the rest of us."

"Thanks," she said. "Yoga. Stretching—and stressing. It's the stress that keeps you thin."

She congratulated him on the Hall and asked, "So, what are you doing now?" He realized she was the first one to ask that night. Maybe the only one, besides his mother. God, how he hated that question.

Grudeck told her he lived at the country club, still "adjusting" to retirement.

"I'm not sure what I'm going to do," he said. "Seems I'm busy enough just being me. What about you?"

She still lived in town, in her old house. Her parents signed it over after she divorced, and they retired to Ocean County. She said nothing about her marriage, except she had a seventeen-year-old son, Wayne Jr., a senior at Union. She made "decent" money as the art director of a midsized marketing company in Springfield.

"So you're an executive?"

"Of sorts."

"You play golf?"

She laughed. "Lord, no."

"Maybe I should teach you, so you can schmooze with the boys."

"No, that's the sales director's job," she said.

"And I bet the boys schmooze you anyway."

"Some do . . . And I always have a conversation piece," she said.

"What's that?"

"That I went to high school with Joe Grudeck."

That was it? Went to high school? Not dated?

"I thought it was a little more than that," Grudeck said.

"Yeah, a little more," Stacy said, and let the words hang.

Grudeck shifted on his stiff hip.

"You still have those pictures?" he asked.

"Pictures? . . . Oh, the photographs of you. Yeah, somewhere . . . I used one of them in my portfolio for a while, back when I started," she said.

"Which one?"

"Oh, hmmm, I forget. No, it was the wrestling one."

The door of the hall opened, and people came out. Stacy looked over his shoulder toward them.

"How is it in there?" she asked.

"I don't know . . . kinda weird. In some ways, it's like I never left. In other ways, it's like I don't belong . . ."

"A familiar stranger?"

"Exactly," Grudeck said. "A stranger in my own town . . . *world.*"

"You've always been like that," she said. "Strangely lonely. Poor Joseph, nothing's changed in thirty years."

He couldn't tell if she was mocking him or not, and it left him stuck.

"The things I tell you," Grudeck finally said. "I don't know, they just come out."

Grudeck looked back toward the gym, then at her.

"Your public awaits. You'd better go back in," she said.

"Aren't you?" he said, gesturing her to walk ahead.

"No. I just came to say 'hi' and now I did," she said.

"Wanna make a run for it?" he asked. "With me?"

She took his jacket lapels and pulled them tight, like a mother bundling up a child.

"No," she said with a sweet laugh. "I should get going. And you should go back in. People are waiting."

"Can I see you later? Tonight?" he asked.

"No. You know that."

"Can I call you?"

"I'm still in the book. Same number after all these years."

He repeated it, to his surprise. After all these years.

Chapter Thirteen

Horace pulled "American Rubism" from an oak filing cabinet in the Farmers' Museum archive. It was his last research paper, finished the same month he picked up blacksmith tools. Now here he was again, fifteen-plus years later, brushing up on the Giant for his summer stint as circus-tent docent.

The paper—twenty-four pages, single-spaced—was an academic analysis of the Great American Hoax, a textbook case of what P. T. Barnum called "humbug."

In the post–Civil War days of seeing-is-believing, the Giant—a gypsum statue deliberately buried on a farm in Cardiff, New York, and unearthed a year later—was passed off as a fossilized biblical goliath to thousands of paying rubes, even after noted scholars in the fledgling sciences of geology and paleontology debunked it. Barnum tried to buy it, the owners refused, so Barnum simply made his own American Goliath. The parties ended up in court, countersuing each other as promulgators of a hoax. That put an end to it, and the authentic Cardiff Giant was sold a couple of times as a novelty, eventually ending up in his final resting place at the Farmers' Museum.

That was the ten-cent tour—a classic American parable of greed and arrogance with a litigious conclusion.

The ten-dollar tour—Horace's original academic treatise—wasn't so simple. Through his freshly master's-degreed lens of diminishing farm town culture, Horace played with the facts like a kid with a kaleidoscope, looking for patterns and symmetry, and made this case:

In 1869, the shift from agrarian America to industrial America was coming with the relentless march of an assembly line. Northern cities were growing full bore. Farmhands found better work in factories and offices, where big-city anonymity let them enjoy moral loosening they never knew back home. For veterans burdened with shrapnel or night terrors from Gettysburg or Bull Run or Antietam, the big-town vices of alcohol, opiates, and prostitutes lessened the pain.

As cities grew, America itself shrank. The golden spike was hammered at Promontory Summit, Utah, on May 10, 1869, marrying rail lines from east to west, a union from the Atlantic to the Pacific. The rail network webbed secondary cities through the east and brought more people to more places than ever before. As Americans became more mobile and exposed to cities, they aired a greater pretense of sophistication.

New transportation meant easier distribution of mass-produced consumer goods. The market explosion of these goods—and newspaper advertising to shill them—rendered handmade things old-fashioned and ordinary. Country folk—and the things they made—became backward in the national view. The roots of rural slurs—hayseed, hick, bumpkin, clodhopper, hillbilly, Okie, yokel, and rube—all trace back to these days.

The Giant, a crude sculpture not nearly as anatomically detailed as a human fossil would have been, gave America's new city folk reason to chide their unsophisticated country cousins. Decades after the Giant caper, it was still a popular trend, from Lewis's *Elmer Gantry* to TV's *Beverly Hillbillies*.

It was the dawn of America's ongoing thirst for new communication technology as Western Union wired the country coast-to-coast. Fast forward 130 years, Horace thought, and the dots and dashes of Morse code evolved into a new text-message language of abbreviations, and other bombardments of constant gadget-driven news, scores, games, social networks, and on and on. It was the continued exodus from the spiritual to the external. Contemplation, quiet time, and internal reflection were dead, dying in a white-noise wilderness of diversion. Where was the God within? As silenced as the mute stone Giant.

At the same time the first wires were being strung, America's fascination with natural sciences—including paleontology and anthropology—shook the long-held tenets of Bible-based religion in modern-thinking society. In God, America first trusted, but then science figured it all out. Creation was evolution. Religion was a lie, clung to by ignorant country folk. Horace's America was founded on the belief that its land and people were in God's favor. George Washington himself said the colonies were blessed by God's "Providence"; it was a land of abundant natural gifts, with infinite forests, rich soil, an endless wealth of iron ore and minerals deposited below.

But by 1869, the notion of a nation smiled upon by God had passed. The Civil War was hell on earth for the men who fought it; and the new generation of industrialists believed it was their own genius, not God's grace and loving hand, that made the nation prosperous.

One of these men was George Hull, a pronounced atheist and capitalist cynic, who hatched the Cardiff Giant plot as a way to embarrass the "biblically blind" of his day. In the Giant archive drawer, Horace found the cracked, leather-bound memoir of Hull's, which came to the Farmers' Museum through his great-grandnephew in Genesee, who found five copies of the self-published tale in an attic strongbox. Horace hadn't looked at it in twenty years, but when he started reading, he remembered how delightfully Hull told the story.

Hull was from Binghamton, New York, and inherited his father's cigar business; he found himself rich and bored. A family business will do that to a man, and Hull lived to escape by train on tobacco-buying trips to New York City, where he met Carolinians and Cubans who supplied him with leaf samples, dinner and drinks, and willing girls. But the trips to heartland cities such as Akron, Duluth, and Peoria where Hull's Grade B cigars were sold were not as vice-full, and Hull dreaded them.

On one such trip to Ackley, Iowa, where the cigar maker had set up a sales territory for his "half-wit" brother-in-law, Hull found himself at a formal dinner at his sister's house with a man he called "Reverend Turk" and several other prominent citizens.

Turk was a corn-belt Fundamentalist, a believer in the Bible as the Word of God. Old or New, it was to be read and consumed literally, as full Testament and Truth—not as a series of parables made up by hapless Jews who blamed an unpleasable God for their misery, and then later, followers of Jesus, who promised heaven to give solace to the earth's downtrodden.

Hull knew the type, because upstate New York was loaded with them.

Back home, there was a revival movement, started by Charles Grandison Finney, Hull wrote in his memoir. *He was tall and bearded in the Lincoln manner; dignified, until he started to preach. Then he transformed into a shaking, vibrating stem, like a tree hit by lightning, his arms whip-snapping like branches in a tornado, his voice a-thunder. He was a burning bush of hellfire and brimstone, a flaming beacon for lost souls! And he massed them together all spring, summer, and fall in any town that had five flat acres to pitch his giant tent. I went often when he came by Binghamton, not as a believer, but to be at once amused and repulsed by his believers. I do admit this perverse attraction; it is no more than the same curiosity that drew men to Barnum's New York museum or traveling sideshows.*

Reverend Turk, himself, had been influenced by Finney, and that night in Iowa, bored with the polite dinner chatter about corn prices and local charities, Hull asked Turk what he thought of T. H. Huxley's new theories on evolution, which claimed man and primates shared the same biological ancestors.

"I suppose this is all a contrived controversy to bring him scientific fame," Turk replied. "But it is heresy, and will earn him God's eternal shame!"

"But I think any book with such a weighty title—Man's Place in Nature—*must be plied to see if it contains any plausible truths," I countered, swirling my glass of port for emphasis.*

"The truth comes from a source far more knowledged than some English biologist, *which to me, is a fancy word for leaf-collector," Turk said, his impatience growing. "How can any man pretend to know more about the natural world than that very world's Creator?"*

"Yes . . . but doesn't that Creator hint to mysteries in the Bible?" I asked. "Three equal gods in one . . . a virgin conceiving a child . . . (at this, a few of the women coughed demurely) . . . Doesn't your Bible challenge intelligent men to unearth some of its mysteries?"

"My Bible has no mysteries," Turk said without pause. "It is the true Word of God, to be taken on faith," he said, his voice then rising up to preaching levels.

"I have always viewed the Good Book as a series of parables," I said. "But you're telling me you believe, for instance, that giants like Goliath actually roamed the earth?"

The Reverend closed his eyes and began to recite: "From Genesis 6:4: 'There were giants in the earth in those days.' Numbers 13:33: 'And there we saw the giants, the sons of Anak' . . . 'All the region of Argo was called the land of giants,' Deuteronomy 3:13. And, speaking of apes, sir, this biblical evidence of giants also refutes this fashionable 'survival of the strongest' theory, does it not?"

"You're speaking of Darwin," I said. "How so?"

"In this theory—I'm only told because I would not subject myself to such heresy—the biggest, strongest gorilla is king of the troop. In humankind, giants were invariably Philistines, and thus were overcome by smaller men who followed God's word. Hence, David slayed Goliath, as every child knows. And look no further than who rules our world! The Zulu warrior? The Tripoli pirate? Our own redskins? No, the civilized God-fearing man!"

The other guests gave him a polite smattering of applause, and I admit his mulishness left me speechless. All I could manage was, "Well, that's that," and he sat, smug and satisfied, having vanquished his own brute . . . me.

That night, as Hull lay restless in the quiet Iowa night, he recounted the episode, as people do after a conflict.

I thought of all the clever retorts I failed to come up with. I thought of ways to embarrass Turk and those like him, to expose their antiquated stupidity. I was fitful the night through. So desperate I was to rest I opened the Webster's Bible on the night table hoping its pedantic language would lull me to sleep. The book fell open to Deuteronomy, where my eyes fell on this passage.

"And the LORD shall scatter thee among all people from the one end of the earth even to the other; and there thou shalt serve other gods, which neither thou nor thy fathers have known, even wood and stone. And among these nations shalt thou find no ease, neither shall the sole of thy foot have rest: but the LORD shall give thee there a trembling heart, and failing of eyes, and sorrow of mind . . ."

I drifted off with thoughts of this vengeful God but awoke with a fresh idea! A god of stone! I would give the Turks and other sanctimonious preachers an Old Testament Philistine! I would take a gigantic statue and bury it, unearth him later, and pass him off as a fossilized human Goliath. His grotesque face would be contorted with the anguish of a death without Salvation, smitten by their angry Lord. Such a thing had never been discovered! I would do it near the roads the Holy Band traveled, and put up a revival tent over my Giant, then pass the hat among the Faithful. Oh, the Union-backs to be made! Here lies the Bible's Goliath! I would advertise him as such! An American Goliath! And I would take their fool money!

Hull spent weeks reading up on geology, archaeology, and alchemy, and studied sculpture from Mesopotamia to the Renaissance. He decided a soft, porous stone would best give his Giant an ancient look, but it could not reflect any definitive art period. The Giant was to be unique, like any human.

Ah, the study of rocks yields all the mysteries of the Earth. Once secure in my knowledge, I went back to Iowa to buy a block of gypsum, a hydrous calcium sulfate that contained vein-bluish strata, as if human blood once pumped through it. I told the quarry master the block was for a President Lincoln memorial I planned to donate for the county courthouse back home.

The quarry master told me he had been a corporal with Pennsylvania's 17th Cavalry and fought at Gettysburg. Michael Foley was his name, and he went west after the war, with his army severance and a half-pound of rebel shrapnel in his thigh. (I noticed the limp and made up the Lincoln story the moment I did.) He wanted to contribute to my cause and dropped the price from $75 to $50. This bit of serendipity got my scheme off to a rousing start.

Hull asked Foley if he could recommend a good sculptor who was looking for work, rather than one in demand. He offered up Edward Burghardt, who had a monument shop in Chicago but had higher artistic aspirations. Hull paid Foley, and arranged to have the block delivered by teamster and train to Burghardt's shop.

On the train from Iowa to Chicago, I had drawn rough sketches of the giant's face and his twisted body that came to me. Burghardt took these, and made some anatomical suggestions. I told him I did not want our petrified man confused with ancient art.

The next day I returned to examine his clay model, and it was exactly as I imagined. The body was strife-ridden, the face in muted torment; the silent scream of a man crushed in a catastrophic burial.

"This is art!" I told Burghardt, and gave him a modest down payment and a box of cigars.

When he returned to Chicago six weeks later, Hull saw a giant more convincing than he'd ever dreamed.

Burghardt proved himself a sculptor of artistic merit. My Giant was a masterpiece; a primordial man, like us, but greater in mass and bone. The thickness and breadth of his forehead and jawbone were not quite early man, but not yet modern. And Burghardt added a dimension of reality of which even I hadn't dreamed: It was the feet. The length and heaviness of those feet, the blunted thickness of the toes, were of a man who walked the earth. These were not the perfectly formed dainty feet of Michelangelo's David. These were the feet of an authentic Goliath, worn and tired and flattened out from years of supporting such enormous weight, ambling through life protected only by primitive sandals against earth's harsh elements.

Now it was time for the second stage—moving and burying the Giant—for which Hull had "lain the groundwork" with his second cousin, once removed, a vegetable farmer named Stubby Newell who owned fifty acres of dark-dirt land in the Onondaga Valley outside Cardiff, twelve miles south of Syracuse.

I asked Stubby to clear a plot behind his barn, hidden from the post road. Here, he could dig a shallow grave and leave the Giant to rest. A year, I thought, would be sufficient to age my Giant a few biblical eons; then we'd dig him up, and the sideshow would begin.

Now, I knew a crate that size, coming in by teamster, would draw local gossip, so I told Stubby to tell his neighbors, if they asked, that he got a new rotary cultivator from Deere & Company of Moline, Illinois.

"What do I say when I don't have a new cultivator, then?" Stubby asked.

"Tell them it was broke."

Stubby worked three days on the hole. When the Giant was delivered, Stub busted up the box and rented a team of oxen to drag it into the grave.

We harnessed and strapped them to the Giant, and the animals started to pull, Hull wrote. *I raised welts on their haunches with the whip as they snorted and strained. "Gidyap, goddamnit," I yelled, and I went harder with the whip to near exhaustion, tearing into the hides of those beasts until Stub grabbed me in a bear hug, and said, "Jeezum, George, them's borrowed animals!"*

The Giant would be "discovered" a year later, in mid-October, the most temperate time in the Onondaga Valley; clear skies, dry days, with the last warm breezes coming from the south before Arctic winds came down. It was after harvest season, when farmers had fresh money in their pockets and time for a little leisure. Those warm Indian summer days would entice the Syracuse crowds for one last country jaunt, before frost came.

I checked the Farmers' Almanac *and saw a glorious, dry two weeks predicted beyond October 16,* Hull wrote. *That was it then. Saturday, October 16, 1869, would be the resurrection of my Goliath. The Holy*

Rollers and Shakers and fanatics would trample the farm to see fossilized proof of their Good Book's veracity. Their unwavering faith in the Word would override the unblinking truth of the Eye, and convince them they were looking at something more miraculous than a plain rock, these worshippers of stonemen!

He planned to collect two bits from several hundred people, then bury the Giant for all time. But Hull underestimated the public gullibility. He underestimated the egos of preachers who rushed to Cardiff to rejoice and proclaim the proof of biblical accuracy, and the egos of the scientists who rushed to Cardiff to become the first to proclaim the Giant authentic or fake.

Most of all, Hull underestimated the power of the new wired world, which got news of the Giant to every Western Union depot in the nation, from major cities like New York and Chicago to outposts like Butte, Montana, and Yuma, Arizona. He underestimated the rolling momentum of such word, which once in this expansive public domain created something never before seen in America. A fad, a craze, a trend. Hype and hysteria. The Western Union wires did that, beckoning all who could to travel to Cardiff, and those who could not to follow the news. And they did.

WHEN STUB AND TWO FIELD HANDS unearthed the Giant on the prescribed day, Hull was on his way from Binghamton in a freight wagon, packed with a yellow-striped tent, a couple rolls of chicken-wire fencing, and printed flyers announcing the find, which he dropped off in every village along the way. He also had a portable strongbox for the proceeds, and a Colt six-gun to protect them.

In each village—places like Chenango Bridge, Marathon, Tully, Cortland, and Preble—he told them about the miracle up in Cardiff. The posters hit the porch of every general store, stage depot, and postal office. Before he ever got to Cardiff, hundreds of people in New York State's apple region heard the news or read the posters.

COME SEE!
THE CARDIFF GIANT!
Larger than Goliath whom David slew!
10 feet tall! 1,000 pounds!
An Amazing Discovery!
The American Goliath!
Ask for Newell's Farm on the Main Road in CARDIFF, N.Y.

As delivery wagons, mail coaches, and passenger buggies came and went that afternoon, word spread to Cazenovia and Pompey and Joshua and Lords Corner and all the other little villages on the east-west route.

When Hull got to the farm, Stub was sloshing the Giant with Borax and scrubbing him with a wire brush, just like Hull told him.

"Looks as good as the day he was born," Hull said. "Let's get to work."

They were still fiddling with the striped awning, driving in the final spikes, when the first out-of-towners arrived. The Cardiff folks all got there sooner, looking with *wide-mouth agapement*, Hull wrote.

We let the Cardiff folks view for free—they were neighbors, after all—but their astonishment and the high-volume speculation paid for itself in my joy. Children screamed in delight and pointed to the Giant's enormous genitals.

"Maybe we should cover that thing up," Stub suggested.

"No," I said, "such a detail exposes his authenticity."

All around Hull, he heard the arguments and theories begin.

"Everything . . . elephants, tigers, people . . . was bigger in them days."

"I seen a fella 'bout this size come up from Elmira back with the Twelfth Reg . . . think he got it at Chancellorsville, or maybe it was Antietam. Hit with Reb mortar, right in the chest, I heard. Didn't even knock him down. Was the bleeding that killed him."

"Lookit, there's the dent in his head where David hit him with the stone."

By night, the orange specks of a thousand lanterns swarmed like fireflies on an alfalfa field in July. The smell of kerosene polluted the crisp New York autumn air.

That night, John Clarke, a Shaker in the Temperance Movement, was on his way to Syracuse for a lecture when he heard about the commotion over in Cardiff. He ordered his driver to find the farm, where Clarke beheld the Giant in flickering lantern light and was convinced of his authenticity.

"His size is an allegory for the voracious and lurid human appetite of the vices," Clarke would tell an audience of teetotalers at the Wieting Opera House. "And his extinction makes a lucid case for moderation and temperance."

The moment was not lost on Hull.

A man of Clarke's stature gave the Giant credibility. Within a day reporters from the Daily Standard, Daily Journal, *and* Courier *came down from Syracuse. I herded the photographers in, and lightning went off all 'round the giant, and the smoke of burnt fireworks filled the tent. The next day he was laid out on the front pages of the three newspapers for all to see. The* Standard *called my Giant "the most wondrous scientific discovery of the century."*

In came the crowds, by foot, horseback, and wagon. The children of Cardiff sold them lemonade and cool water, their mothers rented rooms, and their fathers stabled tired horses. The crowds reminded people of Abe Lincoln's funeral train four years earlier.

By Tuesday afternoon, the *New York Herald*, *Tribune*, and *Times* sent reporters. "For believers, it is evidence of truth in the Book," Hull told them. "It's as if they have seen Jesus walk on water with their own eyes, or watched Him push aside the stone of His tomb."

A *Times* editorial reported, "Whatever it is, the discovery in Onondaga has begun yet another round of spirited discourse in the age-old debate between religion and science."

True enough, distinguished men from both sides rushed in with opinions.

A Presbyterian elder from Ithaca pronounced: "This is the proverbial biblical goliath, perhaps a descendant of the warrior Anak or the sheep shearer Nabal. Clearly these goliaths were not limited to Palestine, but walked all the continents of God's green earth."

An expert on Indians said he was proof of an ancient tribal legend of a giant warrior. A Yale biblical scholar said it was a Phoenician idol, proof America was discovered centuries before Columbus, or even Christ. The evidence was cloudy, yet clear: he was whatever the beholder wanted to believe he was.

Before the week was out, the Giant had a slew of newspaper nicknames—American Goliath, LaFayette Wonder, Onondaga Colossus—printed in rag sheets coast-to-coast.

Two thousand people a day were now coming to Cardiff. Hull was too greedy to shut down. Then Mr. David Hannum of Syracuse First National Bank arrived in a velvet-curtained carriage and Hull's scheme grew exponentially. The banker asked for an immediate viewing as people in line cursed about fairness. He had a proposition, he said. He walked around the Giant, even poked it in the ribs with his pearl-handled cane. He studied it, absently twirling his graying muttonchops, then scratched out some math in his ledger. He and four partners were willing to buy three-quarters of the Giant for $25,000, with Hull and Stubby keeping 25 percent. They would take the Giant on the road, to be exhibited in museums and convention halls. First stop would be Syracuse, then Albany, then New York City itself. Then west to Chicago, Kansas City, Denver, and all the way out to San Francisco.

I pretended to do some math scratching of my own, and asked for $50,000, with all due respect, Hull wrote. *Mr. Hannum thought $40,000 could be arranged and we hand-shook, sealing the deal between honorable men until the contracts could be drawn.*

Had I waited a couple of weeks, I could have sold the Giant outright to Mr. P. T. Barnum, who wired me a deal for $70,000 sight unseen.

THE GIANT WAS EXTRACTED from his grave by winches and pulleys and the muscle of four oxen—*He rose like a dandelion in the breeze, all feathery and air-light,* Hull wrote. *He ascended like magician's trickery, up he went like a cloud wisp instead of a ton and a half of carved gypsum*—and was brought by wagon to the Bestable Arcade in downtown Syracuse for two weeks in November. A cross-town trolley line was built from rail station to exhibit hall to accommodate the crowds.

Next stop was Geological Hall in Albany, where state legislators turned out en masse for the opening, with the Giant laid out on a sturdy wooden platform draped in deep purple velvet, worthy of a royal funeral. People came alone or in groups, from churches, ethical societies, and naturalist clubs. Artists came with sketch pads and notepads, leaving charcoal dust on the hall floor.

One constant visitor was Dr. James Hall, the state geologist. His first pronouncement that the Giant was "the most remarkable object brought to light in this country" had caused him woe in scientific circles, so he was determined to make a more clear-eyed, science-based finding on the Giant's origin.

He now scrutinized the Giant's every surface, noting the lack of nostrils, eardrums, and oral and anal cavities, and wondered how soft tissue of the penis, ears, fingers, and toes could have survived normal decomposition.

One morning he appeared with a loupe, and went over the Giant's surface like jewelers looking for flaws in a diamond, Hull wrote. *The next morning he came with rock chisels and chipping hammers and glass specimen containers.*

"You can't damage this!" I cried. "It is a natural wonder of the world!"

"Save it for your rubes!" Hall snapped at me. "I'm a man of science. I'll determine how wondrous this monster is."

But it didn't take long for Hall to identify the Giant's flesh as gypsum.

It was, without question, never human, he concluded. *Nor is it ancient. "Upon further study, I amend my earlier ascertainment of 'remarkable discovery.' I say now it is of very recent vintage, a sculpture, not a fossilized human. I now question if it was 'buried' with the sole purpose of hoodwinking the public."*

None of this mattered to Barnum, who made more overtures toward the Giant consortium. After his first offer of $70,000 was rebuffed, Barnum came back with $100,000.

Barnum was looking to the Giant to breathe new life into his burned-out American Museum, his "fairyland mixture of wonder," where the main attractions were the human freaks: Joice Heth, the 161-year-old nanny of George Washington; Constentenus, the tattooed man, a Greek prince imprisoned by the Khan of Kashagar and tortured by branding; Fedor Jeftichew, known as Jo-Jo, the Dog-faced Boy; Josephine Boisdechene, known as Madame Clofullia, the Bearded Lady; and Zip the Pinhead—whose skull was shaped like a football and who was billed as "A Missing Link and Wild Negro from the Darkest Jungles of Africa."

They were all there to astonish and entertain, and Barnum saw the Giant the same way. What was it? Barnum didn't care. Controversy equaled publicity and publicity brought customers. Even proof of fraud wouldn't kill the Giant. People would then line up to see the spectacle that had fooled so many. Yes, in time, Barnum knew, the public would become satiated, but not before he could turn a nice profit. And once the long lines diminished and the Giant fluttered down from sensation to curiosity to historical artifact, Barnum would retire him to a well-lit, cozy corner of the museum, and let him rest as testament to what once was.

Barnum met with investors in Albany, and Hannum began to proudly lay out the West Coast swing, after New York.

Barnum tapped his cane and interrupted, Hull wrote. *"Gentlemen, this is why you need me!" he cried. "You see the nation. P. T. Barnum sees the world! What about London, Paris, Rome, St. Petersburg, Istanbul, Persia, Bombay, Peking, Japan? The Holy Land itself. Are we not all humans? Wouldn't the world stand on line to look into the darkest abyss of history and find a true specimen of the Lost Race of Giants?"*

Barnum pulled a contract from his inside pocket.

"The figure below," Barnum said, "is not a misprint. It does indeed say two hundred thousand dollars for my majority ownership of the Giant . . .

more than I paid Joice Heth, General Thumb, and Zip the Pinhead put together! I'm confident he will bring more revenue than the tour I put together for Jenny Lind, without nearly as much overhead. The Giant, for one, does not require a different silk gown each night."

I implored my partners to take the money. Hannum was the first to object. "If P. T. Barnum is telling us it's worth that much, it must be worth double."

"The iron will never be hotter than it is now," I said. "And remember, we have men of science scouring our find. I say sell. I say let Barnum take the risk."

"The risk of what?" Hannum asked.

"The risk that our Goliath might be, in fact, an ancient manmade thing," I said, teetering on the edge of confession. "An archaeological artifact, nothing more."

"Let the debate continue!" Hannum said. "It only puts more asses in the seats!"

In the end, the partners outvoted Hull again. Barnum neatly refolded the contract and returned pen and paper to his breast pocket.

We told Barnum we rejected his final offer, Hull wrote, *and what came next, we should have seen coming.*

"Well then, gentlemen, you leave me no recourse but to find my own giant," Barnum told us.

"That's preposterous!" bellowed Hannum.

"Is it?" Barnum asked. "By whose standards? Not mine, sir. Surely you don't believe your Giant wandered this earth alone. There must have been a Mrs. Giant, and little Giants. And a grandpappy and grandma Giant. Somewhere out there is a colony of giants, all resting below the surface waiting to be discovered, studied, and scrutinized, waiting to help us peer down the dark, foreboding corridors of our ancestry, to shed light on our own beginnings."

The words had not escaped his mouth when I realized Mr. Barnum was way ahead of us. He had his own giant. He made a giant the way I made my Giant, and got one better. A Mr. and Mrs. Giant, a family of

Giants. A phony consortium of scientists to claim their veracity. My mind was reeling in this direction when Barnum announced:

"And I will guarantee I find my giant before you bring your Giant to New York next month. In fact, I guarantee my giant will outdraw your Giant when they go head-to-head in New York."

Hannum dismissed Barnum's braggadocio with a wave of his hand.

"The only reason, sir, your Giant will attract anyone," Hannum said, "is because there is a sucker born every minute."

"Hah!" Barnum erupted in laughter. "A sucker born every minute. Oh, I like that. I think I'll procure that, too!"

Barnum had already commissioned the famed New York sculptor Franz Otto to carve his giant out of black marble, a shiny, mineral-rich stone from New England far more exotic than the original's bland Iowa gypsum. Barnum wanted a giant with an aura of primitive culture: a petrified Zip the Pinhead, so to speak. The Cardiff Giant was scheduled to arrive in New York for the holidays at Apollo Hall, an ornate theater two blocks from Barnum's museum. Barnum, the thunder stealer, unveiled his giant to the hungry public and a well-fed press on December 6, 1869, one week before the Cardiff Giant arrived.

At the press luncheon for his specimen, he denounced the Cardiff Giant as "pure humbug! Look at the details of the man my scientists have unearthed. While men of science question the veracity of the Cardiff specimen, my team of scientists have authenticated the specimen you see before you."

It was Hannum's idea to sue P. T. Barnum for slander and fraud, Hull wrote. *I wanted nothing to do with it. True, his giant was a fake. But asking the court for a cease-and-desist order preventing Barnum from exhibiting his giant would bring more scrutiny to the origins of our Giant.*

I knew things would not go well for us, when the Honorable Elias Wilkerson opened the proceedings by saying, "Good to see you again, Mr. Barnum."

And here, Barnum turned the tables on the partners once again.

Barnum admitted his giant was "unearthed" in a quarry in Danby, Vermont, and said the "scientific light to be shed" was about the new science of geology.

Then his lawyers introduced evidence that the Cardiff Giant was a fraud. They produced the rock-solubility findings of Dr. Hall. They had investigated shipping records and traced the Cardiff Giant's beginnings from Fort Dodge to Stubby's backyard. They had an affidavit from the sculptor, Burghardt, saying it was his creation.

There comes a time to give up the ghost, Hull wrote. *And that was the time. I admitted to the whole plot, and explained my motive was to only debunk the Bible-thumpers, not hoodwink the public or exploit their gullibility for personal monetary gain, or get rich. That was just an unforeseen by-product, I told the judge as sincerely as possible, but my countenance was not helped by a stage snicker from Barnum. The judge was threatening to have me arrested for fraud, when Barnum intervened on my behalf.*

"Let's not be hasty here, Eli," Barnum said to the judge. "Mr. Hull here made no claims about the scientific veracity of his Giant. He left it open to interpretation by the men of science. As a man who has experiences in these endeavors, I see Mr. Hull's actions as simply furthering scientific debate. To charge him with fraud seems to punish his initiative to create such discourse. We now have two giants in our great city, and we are soon to be besieged by men of science and curiosity-seekers from all over the civilized world. Our good, mutual friend, Governor John T. Hoffman, approves of such spectacle for the economic health and robust tourism of the city. Great crowds will want to see the spectacle, and become part of the spectacle. We are about to stage an event that will draw people who simply want to say they were there. This isn't about truth, Eli, it is about entertainment, the expansion of commerce!"

The judge ruled Barnum could exhibit his giant as planned and was innocent of fraud, because, as a matter of law, no fraud was committed because there was no authentic Giant. In other words, there is no such thing as a fraud of a fraud. Life for both giants went on.

After the proceedings, I stood alone in the rotunda of the New York

City Superior Court, Hull wrote. *I had exonerated my partners during the proceedings to the judge's satisfaction, thereby making them immune to future charges. Nonetheless, they ditched me with nary a word, racing out to Centre Street and into a waiting hack without me. A few newspaper fellows crowded around Barnum, who told them all was well, and both exhibits would open as scheduled. He never mentioned my admission, although word did leak out over the next few days. But just as Barnum predicted, it did nothing to dampen the crowds. They came for weeks and stood in December's cold drizzle and wet snows, waiting in lines while Christmas bustle went on around them. They came and went between Barnum's giant and mine, comparing the two, often arguing over which looked more realistic, and which was more believable. Through the holidays, through January and beyond Washington's birthday, they came. Barnum was right; they came to see the spectacle and be part of the spectacle. That, in the end, was all that mattered.*

And in the end, it ended almost as quickly as it began, perhaps the first example of the abrupt flame-out of instant celebrity. Hull's Giant fell into obscurity within a year of Stubby's discovery. It never did make a national tour, let alone worldwide. It landed with such a thud, the partners sold it to the first taker, a Syracuse hotelier named C. O. Gott, who put the Giant in a corner of his eclectic lobby, nearby a suit of medieval armor and several examples of taxidermy, including a snarling black bear up on hind legs, an antlered mule-deer trophy, and a peacock in full blossom. The price? $5,000.

Hull's memoir ends there, as if he had no life worth living afterward. His final entry is boastful, but laden with regret.

But one thing I will never forget is my last conversation with Barnum as he left the courthouse flanked by his entourage of lawyers and associates.

"No hard feelings, I hope, Hull," he said as he shook my hand. "In fact, I admire you. We're kindred spirits, my friend, pioneers in a coming American industry. You may not see it now, but it is coming, my friend. The factory and farm machines and other inventions will give everyone from the field hand to the seamstress more leisure time. And how will they

fill that slack time? Piety? Searching their souls for God's mark? Doing good deeds? Contemplating the heavens? Philosophizing over the great mysteries of life? Mastering a musical instrument? Learning foreign tongues? No, sir, they'll fill their long evenings and days off with the humbug I bring them. They will look for lazy ways to be entertained and I will entertain them.

"I learned an important lesson from you, Hull. All this time, I put my entertainment in the big city, and expected the people to come to me. But you showed me this: I should take my show to every backwater hamlet and out-of-the-way village. You unveiled your Giant in a godforsaken place and still drew crowds worthy of Broadway and made headlines worldwide. It gave me an idea: I'm going to pack up my menagerie of exotic animals and human freaks, and travel the countryside, packing in all those people with time on their hands. It will be a Roman circus! A traveling Roman circus!

"Truth be told, you make a lousy cigar, Hull. Give it up and join me in the business of amusement and entertainment. Mark my words, it will one day be the trademark industry of this nation."

Hull declined.

Of the mistakes I've made in my life, the next was the biggest. Weary of the entire Giant affair, I wanted nothing more than to shrink from the public eye (and escape my partners' wrath), and return to Binghamton and the anonymity of my everyday business. I told Barnum so, and he stuffed his card into my breast pocket in case I ever changed my mind. And then, Poof!, he was gone.

WHEN HORACE WAS DONE READING, he dug through some of his old first-reference material and found this summary of the Giant affair by Andrew D. White, the president of Cornell at the time of the scam:

> *There was evidently a "joy in believing" in the marvel, and this was increased by the peculiarly American superstition that the correctness of a belief is decided by the number of people who can be induced to adopt it—that truth is a matter of majorities.*

Truth is a matter of majorities. Those words hit Horace in a way he hadn't seen earlier. The Cardiff Giant wasn't only about America letting go of its religious roots and rurality. It was about the birth of popular culture, with the mute Giant himself starring as one of the nation's first celebrities. A stone man, nothing at all like the public believed him to be.

Truth is a matter of majorities. Those words reverberated in Horace's head. He smiled, as if he'd just seen an old friend.

Truth, defined by majorities. Not God, not family, not some innate, internal sense of fairness or reason. Forget the lone voice of the individual soul, or the moral barometer of the God within; it is only an unheard whisper against the howl of noise around us. America, with no ancient, ingrained, or inherent culture, no Renaissance patricians to set high standards of value, no Michelangelos or Mozarts, was ruled by the tastes of the masses.

Horace took out a legal pad and began writing down all the modern measuring sticks. Nielsen ratings, box office numbers, Platinum records, sell-out crowds, Google searches, Twitter trends. All that truth in majorities, swamping all other art. Success deemed by numbers. The bottom line. Think of all that got lost in a world ruled by numbers. Artistic nuance and visions that did not appeal to the masses. Individualism. Esoteric expression. Niche products. Business became cutthroat; stock prices, not employees, not quality, mattered.

His presentation was forming and Horace wrote quickly: *A nation founded on the God-granted sanctity of the individual was now a nation of sameness, with a culture not decided by those with extraordinary talents but by the ordinary masses. The American standard for quality, for culture, is held in the numbers of acceptance . . .*

Ah, this is what's wrong with America! Those words, said often by Horace, never felt more *relevant* than right now, and he felt the joy of a choir singing the "Hallelujah" chorus bursting from his heart.

And at that moment, the door to the archive opened and in came Natalia, Natalia Piatrovich, the graduate student, not in a milkmaid's dress but in a pair of form-fitting jeans, and a tailored white blouse that muted the color of her pastel blue bra. Twenty-first-century lip gloss, eyeliner, jewelry, and heels. Heels, at the farm museum. Horace realized he'd maybe never seen that before.

"Beauty is hard work, Horace," Natalia said when a compliment got loose from his mouth before he could stop it. From there he recovered and stumbled through a sentence that ran the gamut of calling her "gorgeous" to expressing "admiration" for her work (which he knew nothing about) to an apology for saying something "inappropriate."

She laughed and waved off his political correctness.

"Women from Ukraine never go out looking like slob, Horace." She laughed again. "This how I dress, unless working in barn!"

The accent, the articleless broken English, and the way she said *Hooorace* quickened his heart and sent a pulse through his balls.

"So, Horace, do you mind if I work now, too? I'm researching thesis," she said.

"Please," Horace said.

Horace explained he had been the archivist before he became the blacksmith.

"So if I can do anything to help," he said, adding the Cornell degrees.

"Thank you. Very impressive, Mr. Ivy League," she said playfully, and went to one of the oak cabinets to retrieve several folders of her work. She dropped one and bent over to pick it up, and Horace got a chance to stare.

"So, Horace, what are you looking up?" she asked as she straightened.

Horace explained the situation, from asking Grundling to give Michael a job and being forced to give the Giant presentation, to his old research on the nation stepping away from God and country folks, to his gleeful discovery just moments before about "truth being a matter of majorities."

"Oh! Then I have something that might interest you!" she said with delight in her voice. "I have found similar things in my work!"

Now it was her exuberance for dead history that sent blood in both directions, and he felt himself becoming aroused. She sat next to him and pulled her hair behind the ear closest to him. He fixated on the perfection of that ear, the gold dangling earring, and the elegance of her neck. And the scent that rose from it. Cherry blossoms. No, something sweeter. She was that close.

"I, too, was interested in growth of proletariat taste during Industrial Revolution," she said. "So look at this."

Natalia opened a folder filled with copies of newspaper articles.

"Look. 1869. Year of your Giant, right?" she said. "Here. Broadway's first million-dollar show, *The Black Crook*, about black magic and the devil. See this? Religious groups protested, but show went on, even Sundays."

Exhibit A in the step away from God, Horace thought.

"Then I found this," Natalia continued, gently producing another clip. Horace stared at her fingers, long and a little thick but perfect, and the scarlet tips. "Look, Horace, here. Twenty-one theaters opened on Broadway. People started paying more attention to actors. Gossip columns started in papers. Like this."

She showed him an article about Lydia Thompson and her "British Blondes" burlesque troupe.

"There is some suggestion of backstage sex," she said. "Titillating? Right?"

Backstage sex . . . blacksmith shop sex . . . barn sex . . . archive sex. Was it a signal? Damn, he was rusty. He stayed put.

"In 1869," she said, shuffling more clips. "First boardwalk built in Atlantic City. First college football game, *Rootgers* against Princeton. First professional sports team, Cincinnati Red Stocks, *Stockings*, in baseball."

"The birth of popular culture," Horace said. "The birth of spectator sports."

"Yes!" she said, squeezing Horace's arm. "Birth of shopping as sport, too. Look what I discovered, just looking through old papers. Advertising. More and more. Then more and more newspapers. I did research. Seven hundred papers in country before Civil War. By 1869, five thousand! Magazines, too. In 1869, *Harper's Bazaar* and *Vanity Fair* started. First mail-order catalog, Montgomery Ward. Lord and Taylor opened, then Wanamaker's, all in 1869! Guess what was next? First advertising agency, Ayer & Son, in Philadelphia. All in 1869. Same year as your Giant!"

"The end of homemade goods," Horace said. "Shopping as a sport, as entertainment. I like that."

"You see! We're doing same thing. Industrial Revolution was also birth of pop culture! When I go back to Rochester in fall, I'm writing this as thesis," she said.

Horace again resisted the temptation to lean in and kiss her. Instead, he began to write with manic excitement . . . "the year was 1869, when America began the business of diversion." He crossed out "business" and substituted "industry," then settled on "economy." *An economy of diversion.* All of it, from smartphone games to movies to sports.

He thought of Michael's room, a pantheon to sports stars, and Hull's line about "worshippers of stone men." The modern pagan gods. He wondered if Michael could name an astronaut, or a Medal of Honor recipient from Iraq or Afghanistan, real heroes. Or if the frontier legends—Davy Crockett, Daniel Boone, Wyatt Earp, even Jesse James—spurred his imagination, as they did Horace's when he was a boy?

"We have raised a generation that believes athletes are heroes and sports results are history," Horace wrote.

He put down one of his favorite quotes. *In times of universal deceit, telling the truth is a revolutionary act*—George Orwell.

He would tell the truth, as he saw it.

He grabbed his head with both hands, trying to contain the bigness of his discovery. And Natalia's. And *Natalia.* The Cardiff Giant, an allegory for all Horace knew had gone wrong! Who knew? And how did he miss it the first time around? "You fucking idiot," he said out loud, laughing.

"And you," he said to her. "You fucking genius." Then he grabbed her head the same way.

His laughter was contagious to himself, and it became uncontrollable. Natalia looked puzzled at first, then began to laugh with him.

"Horace, the mad sociologist!" she said.

That thought made him laugh even harder. His head pulsated. His peripheral vision got fuzzy. He wanted to kiss her. In joy. In everything. When had he ever felt this happy?

Chapter Fourteen

Grudeck drove down Stacy's street, and braked for a group of brown kids kicking a soccer ball. Not a white one in the bunch. This part of Union—all of Union, really—had changed. This neighborhood was now mostly Indian and Hispanic, with a few Chinese. Grudeck saw it on the real estate signs. Donash Patel. Elmira Ramos. Li Xiang. Tells you who is selling, and who is buying. Back in the day, these blocks were filled with white immigrant factory workers or builders who came home to their 50-by-150 piece of the dream. The streets were rows of orderly, simple Capes, two bedrooms down and stairway up to a converted attic, like his parents' house. On other blocks were stunted versions of the storybook Tudor architecture so prevalent in the rich towns to the west, Maplewood, South Orange, Short Hills, and Summit. The Union versions were solid, with brick walks and chimneys, trowel-smoothed stucco sides, built by the same Italian masons and Portuguese handymen who lived in them. That was Grudeck's Union. Back in the day. When Joey and his friends played around here with a Wiffle bat and tennis ball, they used car bumpers and manhole covers for bases, and always tried to hit down the middle of the street so some guy in a guinea tee wouldn't come bounding off his porch with a can of Pabst in his hand yelling, "Watcha the goddamma car!"

The kids were in front of Stacy's house, so Grudeck drove about fifty yards down—not to protect the Caddy, but not to disturb their game.

As Grudeck pulled himself out, he saw the soccer ball flying toward him. He could have let it go, but what the hell. Holding a bouquet of flowers for Stacy in his left hand, he stretched for the ball with his right and stopped it dead, without so much as a noticeable bobble. Then, in one quick, graceful motion of perfected fluidity, he planted his left foot well out in front of his right and swung the full weight of his body forward. His arm came up, cocked over his shoulder, and then whipped down with the violence of a knock-out punch. He uncoiled his arm at the vortex of maximum thrust of his body, just as he climbed on the ball of his left foot and turned his hips and shoulders perpendicular to the target. The sportswriters called it machine-like, and it was. Grudeck made that throw thousands of times, in a hundred seasons, with a baseball or a football, and now this. The ball rocketed straight at the kids and only the oldest, a skinny Indian about sixteen, had the guts to stick out his hand to stop it. It smacked his palm and skittered off into the gutter.

"Whoa!" said one kid.

Grudeck, showoff that he was, walked toward them, arms out in apology.

"Sorry, old habit," he said.

"Dude, that was awesome!" said another.

"You okay?" Grudeck asked the Indian kid.

"Yeah," he said, rubbing his hand.

"Well, when you get home tonight, tell your parents you caught Joe Grudeck."

"Huh?"

Grudeck figured he didn't understand the baseball vernacular.

"Tell them you caught a ball thrown by Joe Grudeck."

"But I didn't catch it."

"Well, tell them you tried."

"By who?"

Now Grudeck understood the puzzlement.

"Yeah, mister, who?" asked another.

Then he saw a smattering of stifled laughing from the kids in the pack. One kid said something in Spanish and another busted out and a girl rolled her eyes. Two ran off to retrieve the ball, wanting nothing to do with the big guy coming at them, saying something they didn't understand, with a bouquet of flowers in his hand.

Grudeck felt a blink of embarrassment that escalated quickly to something akin to anger.

Yeah, mister, who? This was his fucking town, he wasn't going to explain himself. Fuck these kids.

"Forget it," Grudeck said as he turned up Stacy's walk. She was standing behind the glass-and-brushed-aluminum storm door, with decorative "M" across the center, smiling at the scene. She saw the throw and saw the kids laugh, but hadn't heard the exchange.

"Look at you . . . still the most popular kid on the block," she said.

"Uh, oh. Yeah," Grudeck said, handing her the flowers.

"You going to sign autographs?" she asked, then kissed him ever so briefly on the cheek. *A cousin kiss*, Grudeck thought.

Grudeck didn't answer and stepped inside.

He filled the frame of the foyer, ducking to avoid a lantern that hung from the stucco arch. He scanned the living room; paintings dominated the vibrant pastel walls. A home decorated to accentuate the art. On one sunny yellow wall was a giant lavender lily, painted on four canvases like pieces of a puzzle that hung a foot from one another.

The light green wall held a light brown bowl of orange fruit: tangerines, tangelos, clementines, navels, all detailed but cottony. The pink wall held a carnival scene, with the neon colors of the Ferris wheel and carousel softened and understated.

"Are these yours?" Grudeck asked.

"Oh . . . yeah, I still paint," she said.

Maybe I should paint, Grudeck thought. *Do something different.*

"They're beautiful. Really," Grudeck said. He searched for something else to say, but stood there, feeling stupid and unschooled, in art and everything else. For the second time in two minutes he felt clumsy and lost. *In my own fucking town.*

He moved into the room and saw the Mission-style console filled with photographs. Most were of the boy. *What was his name again?*

Some were school pictures, from cute in kindergarten to the awkward middle school years (mouth gripped to conceal braces) to the handsome young man sitting confidently for his high school portrait. There was a junior high graduation, where he was flanked by both parents. The estrangement was fresh and tension was apparent. Stacy's smile seemed forced. The ex didn't bother. Weak chin. Sandy hair. Wire-rimmed lawyer glasses. Grudeck tried not to look too long.

Others were clearly Stacy's work, with the boy shaded in the same contrasting light she cast Grudeck in some thirty years earlier. In one, her son was in a baseball uniform, kneeling on deck, bat slung over shoulder. Warrior waiting his turn.

"He plays baseball?" Grudeck said, picking up the frame.

"Wayne," Stacy said, knowing Grudeck had forgotten. "Yes, he does. Believe it or not, he's pretty good."

"Why wouldn't he be? We're a baseball town," Grudeck said. "We were, anyway."

"They do okay," she said. "It's not like the old days."

"What is?" Grudeck asked. "But, hey, if you want, I can give him some pointers."

Stacy let that one hang in the air, and Grudeck wanted to snatch it back. Too fast, too forward. Now, too late.

"Well, you know, if he was interested," Grudeck finally managed.

"We'll see," she said.

He put the picture down.

Interspersed with Wayne Jr. were pictures of Stacy's parents, from their Korean War–era wedding—him in dress Army greens, her in a white wedding dress—to very recent Thanksgivings and Christmases, and other Milo family celebrations, Stacy always at their shoulder. Grudeck suddenly thought of his own townhouse, neutral walls bare except for a few plaques and an ink illustration of the club's main mansion that came with the place. Not a nonsports picture of him. No pictures of his parents. All those years.

Toward the back of the console were a few photos of Stacy, through the years. Angelic in Holy Communion white. Sullen and dark-eyed in her Union High graduation portrait, maroon tassel hanging from ivory mortarboard. Smiling and beautiful, in the scarlet and black robe of Rutgers, standing between proud parents. Beaming but tired, holding her newborn in a blue blanket. In a black one-piece stretched out on the sand, sunglasses on, a Kodak moment from the Jersey Shore. One hand up, as if to block the shot, her mouth frozen in objection.

Grudeck picked it up.

"Stacy with the beautiful facey," he said.

"Stop. Wayne Junior took that one," Stacy said. "That's the only reason it's there."

"You were gorgeous. Really," Grudeck said, then caught himself. "*Are* gorgeous."

He looked at her face and, in that moment, saw all of her in it; the little girl, the high school sweetheart, the young mother, the woman she was now and would be. He wanted to hold her head in his hands, to pull her close and kiss her. A kiss not to make up for lost time, but to gently brush lips with all those faces of Stacy.

"Was. Maybe," she said.

"No. Was, and are, and will be," said Grudeck, in an unchecked romantic blurt.

It caught her by surprise. She reached and rubbed his triceps, the way friendly women do sometimes.

THEY WERE GOING TO DINNER AT THE CLUB, and he told her to bundle up.

"We'll open up the sun roof," he said. "You know, it'll be like all that Beach Boys stuff we never had in high school."

He turned out of Union, this way and that, and started the climb up Route 78 toward the Hobart Gap, which split the millionaire sections of Summit and Short Hills.

"I'm surprised you didn't move up here," she said as they drove through.

"Too close. I wanted to buy my folks a house up here, but they wouldn't leave Union."

"I know. I couldn't get my parents to move until Mom broke her hip. Then they *had* to have one floor," Stacy said. "They're down in Bricktown, in one of those Leisure Village places. They love it. My father said, 'I wish we did this ten years ago.' I was like, 'I wish you did, too.' "

She tightened her scarf as the car picked up speed.

"If you're cold . . . ," Grudeck started.

"No, it's fine. Fun. It's good to get out."

Grudeck reached over and squeezed her hand. She squeezed back and, like, thirty years just came off the clock. There was no pain in his hand, as he gunned it through both ridges of the Watchungs.

At the club, he guided Stacy through the dining room, nodding and shaking hands—"The mayor," she said out of the side of her mouth—but he got a corner table and put his back to everyone, to discourage them from interrupting. Mostly, he wanted to avoid the Joanie MacIntoshes of the club. Stacy would pick up on it, no matter how quick and superficial the pleasantries.

"So," Stacy asked, after the waiter opened a bottle of house Merlot. "Why am I here?"

"You asking me or yourself?" Grudeck asked.

She laughed, and it was so abrupt and genuine, Grudeck again wanted to just . . . just . . . *love* her.

"Both, I guess," she said. "But you go first."

"I don't know, Stacy," Grudeck began. "The life I've led . . . I've been away a long time. Sometimes I feel so . . . unattached, I guess. And you were always somebody I felt attached to."

"Me? Jesus, Joe, we haven't talked in almost thirty years," she said with a facetious wave. "And please don't tell me you dreamed about me all those long, lonely nights on the road. I think we both know better."

"No, I mean, back then . . . back then, I felt like you were somebody . . . I don't know how to explain it . . . somebody that really knew me. The real me."

Her eyes searched his face. He knew she was looking for sincerity.

"It's true," he added. "I felt closer to you than anybody back then. Maybe ever."

She shook her head in exaggerated disbelief, then laughed.

"Stop it, will you," she said. "Me, the closest? But when you left, that was that. Not a call, not a letter. Please."

She said this without anger or bitterness; it was more of a don't-bullshit-me statement of fact. Still, Grudeck felt compelled to say, "I'm sorry."

"Don't be. It's not like I was hurt or even disappointed. I didn't expect anything from you. You moved on, and the truth is I was right behind you. I never gave it that much thought. I liked you, yeah, but when you left, I knew you were gone. Even when I heard you were home in the winters, I knew you were gone."

"All those years . . ." Grudeck said absently.

"And in all those years and, I'm sure, all those girls, there was never anybody, anybody else you got close to?" Stacy asked.

"No, not really."

"Why?"

"I don't know. The years, they just went by, and I was always on the road. Like I said, I was kind of . . ."

"Detached? Alienated?"

"Yeah. Those are good words."

"By choice?"

"It's hard to explain. When you're famous . . . I guess I thought that's all anybody cared about." Grudeck fumbled with his dinner napkin, folding it in geometric patterns. "Yeah, so I guess I was, I don't know, *careful.*"

"Or closed off?"

"Maybe." He paused and gave this some thought. She was right, he was closed off. Yeah, he racked up numbers. But in the end, nothing amounted to nothing.

"All I know is you were different," he said. "When we used to have conversations like this, I felt I could tell you the truth about things."

But there was one thing he knew he'd never tell her. The night in Syracuse. He thought about it just as the word *truth* came out of his mouth.

Stacy searched his face, in that third-degree way, which made him feel strangely transparent and guilty, like she was certain he was lying. What do they call it? Women's intuition.

"I rarely use *men* and *truth* in the same sentence," she said. "Remember, I was married for twenty years."

"You can bullshit the fans, but you can't bullshit the players," Grudeck said with a small laugh. "But I'm being honest. You were always different to me. Special."

The skepticism showed on Stacy's face. Was this just another line? But then, why her, when he had a roomful of country club blondes? Maybe he was sincere. But so what? Thirty years, and his inability to directly articulate his feelings made her feel he hadn't changed much since high school. Worse—and she felt guilty about this—she was a little put off by him feeling sorry for himself. This was a guy who had every advantage in life. Who should have had *everything.* And now that he didn't, she thought, he's over there pouting, looking for something from *me.* Me, single mother, with a kid and aging parents, scraping by.

Want to know the feeling of being alone? she was tempted to say.

Instead, she said, "My God. You're lonely," and regretted the way it came out. Incredulous. Hard, with a touch of not-my-problem inflection, like she didn't need another boy in her life.

Grudeck tried to dismiss it.

"*Lonely* sounds . . . what? . . . so pathetic," he said. "Maybe I'm just tired of . . ."

"Being alone?"

"Being me."

"I guess I'm missing something," Stacy said. "It seems like you got exactly the life you wanted. And I'm having a hard time believing the one thing you didn't get was me, if that's where you're going with this."

"I'm not saying that, not exactly," he said, embarrassed now. "And I'm not complaining, it's just that something is missing and I'm not sure what."

He was quiet then. There was so much to say and he didn't know how to say any of it. Same thing with the goddamn speech. Everything was in his head, cloudy and unformed.

After a few moments, Stacy broke the silence.

"Joe," she said. "You never did ask me why I'm here."

STACY MILO KNEW THIS MUCH ABOUT HERSELF, as far back as high school: her own ego wouldn't allow her to stand in someone's shadow, and no one's shadow was larger than Joey Grudeck's. She liked him fine, when they were alone. He surprised her with his sensitivity, at times, and he could be very sweet. She always felt the kid just needed someone to talk to, just like now. In those times, when they were alone in his father's car, at the empty football field with the stars out overhead, the night he first kissed her on the Caldwell porch, and she thought, Maybe I should . . .

But in daylight, when the other boys and girls hung on him, he reverted to the big jock. And then she knew she couldn't, wouldn't, hang on.

She got a glimpse of the detachment he spoke about at dinner, thirty years earlier. When he was surrounded by other kids, a distance crept in. She knew if she joined that company, she would end up on that side of Joe's wall. She knew she was different. The question for her was always this: Could he pull himself away and be just him with just her? He answered it when he left. Now he was back, searching for something he'd lost along the way.

She didn't believe it was her. It was him. It was himself he'd lost.

"So, why are you here?" he asked.

"I guess I was curious about how you turned out," she said. "And I was curious about why you asked me. Now I know."

"That's it?"

"That's enough. What, you want more?"

"Yeah, a little. At least admit that you *like* me. A little."

Stacy laughed and reached out to pat his hand.

"My God, Joe, haven't you had your ego stroked enough in your life?"

"Yeah. Maybe just not by the right people," he said, and turned his hand over to squeeze hers again.

"Okay, I *like* you. There, I said it. You happy?"

"Happier," Grudeck said, and realized he was.

They were both quiet for a moment. Stacy broke the awkwardness.

"I guess there's one more thing," Stacy said. "The night at St. Joe's, I saw you before you saw me. You came out and snuck into that dark corner. You looked sad. More than that, you looked uncomfortable in your own skin. I could see it, even in the dark. I wondered how long that was going on. Then when you came up to me, and kissed me, I sensed you needed *something*. Maybe just a friend. Or like you said, someone who never cared that you were 'Joey Grudeck.' So . . . what is that thing?"

Grudeck fumbled more with the napkin.

"I'm not sure. But, see, I have to give this speech. For the Hall of Fame. And I can't stop thinking about it. It's really bugging me."

"Why?"

"Most are just bullshit. I want mine to be different. True."

"How?"

"It's hard to explain . . . but the guy from the Hall of Fame said their motto is 'Connecting Generations.' It got me thinking. Who do

I connect with? Who knows anything about me off the field? Truth is, the whole time I was playing—even now, too—there were always things that bugged me, but nobody ever talked about."

"Like what?"

"Like everything. The fans. Other players—the assholes, I mean. Autograph dealers. The reporters, hundreds of them, up your ass every minute. Steroids. I took stuff, too, just to compete, toward the end, when I started wearing down. But it wasn't banned then, so technically, I never cheated. I guess what I'm trying to say is the fun went out."

"So say that," she said. And made it sound so simple.

After dinner they walked out to the golf course, along cart roads to avoid sprinklers. The mist was illuminated under towers of halogen lights that lit the driving range and practice greens like day, and muted colors of the spectrum danced in the air. Grudeck looked up into the lights and closed his eyes, like a beachgoer facing the sun.

"I used to love stepping out onto the field at night," he said. "All that light. You could feel the warmth. And beyond, the sky was so dark. Pitch black. In springtime, and fall, those lights took the chill out of the night. In summer, they energized you, like they burned off all the humidity and made the night clear. All those years, I never had a bad night under those lights. It was when I walked away, out from underneath them . . . it was the stuff away from the lights that made me hate the game, sometimes made me hate myself."

The word *Syracuse* came to the top of his throat, but he swallowed it before it escaped.

Stacy thought of the irony: the man felt most comfortable and emotionally safest when glaringly exposed to the public.

She began to say that, when he abruptly turned to face her.

"Will you help me with my speech?"

She agreed. "Sure. I think your idea is great, Joe, to talk about things nobody sees."

She could work with him and see where it all went. Maybe they did have something, something that got lost way back when. Whatever he was looking for, maybe she could help ground him. And if they found a future in their past, well, whatever. Maybe she could do that, she thought, because his shadow was shrinking. He said so himself.

"How do you want to do it?" he asked.

"We'll sit down a couple of times, we'll just talk. You tell me things, tell me the stories. The more you talk, I've found, the clearer things get," she said. "Don't worry, Joe. We'll figure it out."

Chapter Fifteen

Horace knocked, waited a few seconds for Michael to answer. When he didn't, Horace opened the door enough to peek in.

Michael was stretched out, filling almost the length of the mattress. He was headed toward Horace's height, and seeing him suddenly dwarf his childhood bed made Horace think how fast it was coming. He held a gadget in his hands, his thumbs working as fast as a banjo player's. He was propped up on a few pillows, to see a game on his flat-screen TV. Horace saw players moving, and it took an instant for him to realize it wasn't a live game, but a digital version. On his chest was his cell phone, wired to his ears, and Horace could hear the tinny music coming from it, even as the animated sounds of crowd noise and players woofing one another blared from the TV.

"Michael . . . Michael," Horace said, loud enough the second time to get his attention.

"Dad! What up?" Michael said, not taking his eyes off the game.

"Nothing . . . I just wanted to talk."

Michael made a grunt, the sound affirmative, but Horace realized it was over something that had happened on the screen.

"Can we talk?" Horace asked again. *Why do I have to plead with this kid?* he thought. *I'm the father, goddamnit.*

"Sure. Let me finish this inning."

Horace took a look around while Michael played. Michael's desk was made of angular, heavy slabs of black laminate, a kit Sally bought at Ameri-Mart and Horace put together while Michael played baseball. (Horace wanted him to help as a lesson in tool-hood, but Sally wanted to surprise him.) His laptop computer was open, the screen waving fluorescent colors at him like a kaleidoscopic lava lamp from the old days. Yellow sliding into green, green to magenta, magenta to purple. Against the wall, perpendicular to the desk, was Michael's "entertainment center"—the new hearth, Horace thought. The old, mesmerizing dance of fire replaced by the mind-numbing flicker of television, the enjoyment of self-taught music on simple instruments as a diversion from a day of hard work replaced by a wall of sound and sight that could be ratcheted up to assault levels.

Michael's television was the crown jewel of the entertainment center; a flat-screen with a deep, radiant blue color, like a sapphire October evening over the western shore of Otsego Lake. The entertainment electronics made Horace think of a manned space fortress from a science fiction movie. And he was Rip Van Winkle, waking up in the Kaaterskill Clove of his own home, the black-and-white graybeard in a Technicolor world.

After a few minutes, Michael put the game down and pulled the plugs from his ears. "Thanks for turning it off," Horace said.

"I just paused it. I'm winning. Beating last year's All-Star team."

Horace broke a brief silence.

"You know, it's funny, but as I was watching you play, I realized that people, from the time we were cavemen, have always needed something to do with their hands and fingers. So we created primitive art, then invented tools, then musical instruments. Think of all the intricate artwork through history. Think of all the different crafts that evolved just to give people something to do with their hands. You know, kids in the nineteenth century played finger games with string, making elaborate designs. Interesting? Huh?"

"I guess."

Horace decided not to press the message: *If you spent as much time perfecting a craft or practicing a musical instrument as you did playing these fucking games . . .*

He wanted to tell Michael these things, but held back; Sally's critical chirping was always in his ear, whether she was there or not.

"So, Dad, what up?" Michael said, with a barely audible sigh of impatience, as he looked back at his paused game.

"I got you a job at the farm," Horace said.

"I know. Mom told me."

"She did? What else did she say?"

"She said I'd be working in the fields, and with the animals, in the blacksmith shop. She said it might tire me out for baseball, and I didn't have to do it if I didn't want."

"She did?"

"But I'll do it, if that's what you want. It's no big deal," Michael said, his eyes transfixed on the still screen.

The resignation in his voice was another Sally echo, a passive-aggressive tactic that always worked.

Horace, instead of saying "okay, well, good," and walking away with the win, elongated the conversation.

"Give it a chance. It'll be fun," Horace said.

"I'll give it a chance, Dad, but it won't be fun."

"I guess that's right. Hard work isn't fun, not in the video-game sense. . . . No, I take that back," Horace said, unconceding the point. "It is fun, to break a sweat, to build muscle. To feel tired satisfaction at the end of the day. It's work. It's life. It's more than life. When I look out in those fields, and into the eyes of those animals, I see God's work. It puts you in touch . . ."

"Dad. It's just a summer job," Michael said, again with Sally's exasperation in his tone.

"You can dismiss it as that, but you shouldn't," Horace said. "Tell you what . . . you think about it. A man should love his work. Work feeds your soul. Otherwise it's thankless labor."

A few weeks earlier, Horace had taken Michael to the town hall to get working papers "just in case."

"In case of what?" Michael asked.

"You're almost fifteen. In case you want a job," Horace said, holding back the museum part. "You know, make yourself a little spending money, so you don't have to listen to me say no all the time. A little work never killed anybody. . . ."

"I know, Dad. I'm not saying it did."

The idea of a job never occurred to Michael, but once he had the state-stamped certificate with his name and Social Security Number in hand, he thought it might not be a bad idea. His baseball practices and games were mostly at night, under the lights at Legion fields. He could work a little part-time job into his schedule and it would be cool to have his own money. No more asking his parents. No more lectures from his father about the apps, tunes, or games he wanted to buy.

"All this fingertip technology is making people's brains soft," Horace would say. "People don't know their own phone numbers . . . GPS is killing our sense of direction. We can't find our way without some gadget. That's a metaphor for the whole damn thing. . . ."

It seemed whatever Michael wanted—music, movies, sports, fast food, clothes, whatever—brought on one of Horace's "This is what's wrong with America" speeches. Michael and his mother even had a code joke about it.

It started one afternoon when Michael was about ten. He was out with Sally and wanted to stop at a McDonald's.

"Or is that WWWA?" he asked his mother.

"Excuse me?" said Sally.

"WWWA, you know, What's Wrong with America," Michael said.

Sally had to pull over, she was laughing so hard.

"Oh, that's beautiful, priceless," she said, wiping the tears from her eyes.

Michael loved that moment. He never saw his mother so happy. She hugged him and called him brilliant. So he used it again and again.

Now he could work and buy the stuff he wanted with his own money, and that's what's right with America, Michael thought.

THE DAY AFTER Horace took him to get working papers, Michael went into town to see if anybody was hiring, and hit the T-shirt shops and memorabilia stores.

Gone Batty was a narrow shop on Pioneer, with an inventory of replica bats of the most popular Hall of Famers, and a machine that could carve anybody's signature into a standard Louisville Slugger. Sally once gave one to Michael for his birthday.

Michael walked in and saw a pretty young woman, no more than twenty-five, hanging up baseball jerseys. He asked for the manager.

"Why?"

"I'm looking for a job."

"Well, if you want a job here, the first thing you have to do is be smart enough to think a girl might be your manager," she said.

"Sorry." Michael felt his face turn red, which made it turn redder, which made the girl laugh out loud.

"I'm just joshing you," she said, and patted his arm.

"*Joshing?*" Michael said, relieved. "That's a country word. My mother says that."

"Oh, look at you! So you give as good as you get. We like that here."

She smiled at him, and Michael felt his heart do something funny and the warmness spread from his face to his chest.

"I'm June," she said, and stuck out her hand, businesslike. Michael shook it, aware his hand had gotten clammy all of a sudden.

She said, "Follow me" and bounced off with a quick walk, lurching forward, which made the blond hair flutter around her neck and her butt stick out. Michael found his eyes drawn to it, in a way he couldn't help, like some animal instinct that made him ashamed. She gave him an application, and Michael struggled to make sure his handwriting was neat and not childlike.

She looked it over when he was done.

"Michael Mul-ler."

"Mule-er."

"You're a Cooperstown boy. Chicken Farm Hill Road? Really?"

"Yeah, it's on the edge of town. I can walk here," he said.

"Okay, hon. I think we can work something out during tourist season."

Something about the way she said "hon" deflated him. It made him feel like a little kid, like she was his babysitter or something.

She explained the job; stocking shelves and polishing bats. Keeping order in the shop.

"When would I start?"

"First week of June. That's when the tourists really start coming. We can use you right up till school starts. One thing, don't plan any vacation around Induction Day. We get busy as heck. And this year, we're getting Joe Grudeck in for a signing. You know who that is, right?"

Chapter Sixteen

Michael didn't tell Horace he'd applied at Gone Batty, because he didn't want to hear the WWWA lecture about the downtown stores.

"Tourist traps," Horace called them. "Fools and their money."

He told Sally, though, and that's when she told him about the farm job.

"What should I do, Mom?" he asked.

"You should do what you want."

Now, as Horace told Michael about the farm job, Michael had to tell him. He sat up on the edge of the bed.

"Dad, listen. I already got a job in town."

"Why'd you do that?"

"You said to get a job."

"I didn't say that. I said you should have your papers, in case. I got you a job."

"But I applied for this one first."

"Okay, so turn it down."

Michael was quiet, eyes back on the TV screen.

"Where's the job?" Horace asked.

"One of the souvenir stores. Gone Batty," he said, and knew what was coming.

"Gone Batty? I'll say. The whole goddamn town, the whole goddamn country's gone batty. Maybe I'm missing something, but I think the farm would be a better experience . . . I can teach you how to make things of iron with your own two hands, things that last a lifetime. Isn't that better than selling souvenirs made in China to tourists?"

"Most jobs these days are in stores," Michael countered.

"What? Is that your ambition? To work in Walmart? Or maybe Burger King? Is that it? To be in a polyester smock, poisoning people with crap food, or peddling shit products made in Asian sweatshops?!"

"Dad, it's no big deal," Michael said.

"That's where you're wrong, son. It is a big deal. It's bigger than big. Somebody has to make a stand before all the things we once valued are gone."

At that point, Sally, who had been eavesdropping, entered the room.

"My God, Horace, it's just a summer job!" Sally said. "Why do you make him feel like he's contributing to the downfall of the democracy?"

Michael tried to stifle a laugh.

"What? What the hell? What the hell's so funny?" Horace said, looking from son to wife.

Sally jumped in.

"Nothing, Horace. It's just that you're so predictable. We knew what you were going to say."

Horace felt rage. The way Sally said "we." Them. Them on one side, opposite him.

"Well, I'm glad I'm such a big joke to both of you . . . You know, Sally, goddamnit, all I want is to spend a little time, work time, with my son. *My* son. Show him something about the work his ancestors did. *My* grandfather. *His* grandfather. Show him where he came from, and goddamn you, you have to undermine the whole goddamn thing."

"Stop yelling!" Sally said. "It's his life, Horace, once and for all. It's not always about what you want!"

"Can you both stop fighting?" Michael said. "I'll work at the farm."

"No! No, you won't," Sally said. "We've been bullied enough around here . . ."

"Is that what we call a father, a man, asserting himself these days, Sally? Bullying? For *Chrissakes*."

"Dad, stop it. Stop yelling at her," Michael said. And Michael, asserting himself, even with the tears in eyes, left Horace no choice but either escalate the fight or retreat.

He went out the door, then onto the porch, where he grabbed his tools and headed to the woodpile.

Eight-pound maul, ten-pound sledge, three-pound wedge, and the double-bladed ax. All were sharp. Every two weeks, he brought them to the smithy and sat at the pedal grinder, pumping until the wheel spun so fast its coarse stone particles blended into one color. He laid the blades on the spinning wheel, and sparks of metal were spat out, stinging his hands and forearms.

Horace laid the tools down on the pile of tree-trunk pieces, cut by chain saw.

Damn Sally. She was probably in there right now, babying him. Telling him . . . whatever. What the fuck ever.

Horace took the wedge and tapped it down in the grain cracks near the center of the log with the sledge. He swung the hammer over his shoulder, arcing it around his head, with a torque twist of his body, then punched it down, arms straight, knees collapsing, with the force of all his practice and anger. With one shot, the log broke in half, except for a few thin bands of splinters, which Horace pulled apart with his hands.

He worked fast; whole logs became halves, halves became burnable quarters, some quarters were turned into kindling eighths. He didn't stack; he just threw them in a pile for now, near the rusted overturned wheelbarrow. Maybe Michael would come out and move them to the porch, as a way to make amends. Maybe, bullshit. As Horace broke log after log, he looked back at the porch door, waiting for it to open, knowing it would not.

The violence of the work usually calmed Horace; he took his anger out on the wood and soon found a calm rhythm, and saw the product of his labor in a growing cord. But on this day, every swing brought more frustration. Goddamn, Sally. Michael, too. Gone Batty. Sucking up to jock sniffers, every one of them. Something was broken. Now, in his own home.

He pulled a log he knew was too green and would kick back, either bounce the maul blade off its resilient surface or eat the blade and not let go. On his first shot, he buried the maul deep, but the wood did not give. He pushed and pulled on the handle, trying to twist it out. He felt a twinge in his back; the beginning of a muscle spasm. Getting old. His brute body, now, too, a traitor? The muscles between his shoulder blades burned, and there was a dull ache in his lower back and both hips. He couldn't free the maul, so he grabbed the sledge to drive it deeper and split the log. As he slammed down the hammer with all his force, he hit the maul at a bad angle, flat, without tension, and all that vibration zipped up the handle to his sinew and muscle, like an electrical current. The handle splintered and the pain radiated through his hands and wrists, up the flexors and extensors of both forearms. His elbows, God bless them, did their job as shock absorbers and stopped the pain's northward march, but the damage was done. He cursed himself for being distracted. He wheeled and threw the broken handle toward the house, hating everybody and everything.

He was out of breath, and his legs were shaky. Horace's throat was clogged with a clump of stubborn mucus. He tried to gob it up, but his throat was too dry.

He sat down on a log, and the chilly air caused vapor to rise off the sweat matting his hair.

Who the hell was she to judge him?

Horace hung his head and looked down at his stinging hands.

Hands that made things. That *made* things, goddamnit.

When did that become not enough?

All he wanted was to show his kid how.

And now everything was . . . lost. Fucking lost.

He practically had to beg Grundling to arrange the job and agree to do a college girl's docent work in the Giant tent. And now Michael wasn't coming to work. Horace knew that, for sure. He'd bet his life on it. He knew Sally was in there right now, coddling Michael, telling him he didn't have to do anything he didn't want to. He knew she was in there saying, "You do what you want, sweetheart . . . Don't worry about your father, I'll take care of him."

SALLY WATCHED FROM BEHIND THE THIN CURTAIN. Horace looked so defeated and alone, and though she tried to feel sympathy for him, she instead felt guiltily victorious. At least it wasn't Michael or her beaten down this time. Horace didn't break easily, and there he was, sitting on a log, head down, massaging his hands. He would come in soon enough, and go through his sullen act. He would move through the house, planks creaking underneath his weight, and stoke the fire in his beloved stove, pull up a chair and watch the flames through the grate. He would wait for her to break the silence, and she would. She always did.

But now, as Horace rose and headed toward the house, Sally saw something that frightened her. He had pulled himself up to his full height with his chest thrust out, and was walking fast. He picked up the shattered handle on the way, the splintered side sharp like the blade of a sword. Sally ran to the door. Lock it? Or go out and confront him, away from Michael? She went out.

"What, Horace? What are you going to do?"

Horace saw the fear on her face and it gave him some primordial satisfaction.

"I broke the sledge handle. I was going to throw it on the woodpile. Then I was going to talk to Michael."

"About what?"

"Since when do I need permission to talk to my son?"

Sally crossed her arms.

"You just don't see it, do you? You just don't see how you beat him down. How you beat us down . . ."

"I don't beat him down, Sally," Horace said, volume rising. "I just ask him to look at things a little differently. Why is that so bad?"

"Because you aren't helping him make choices! You're making him make choices. You're overbearing and relentless, you chide him until he comes around to your way of thinking. The almighty Horace way. Can't you see he doesn't want to work there? Didn't you see how proud he was to find his own little job? Can't you see that he doesn't want to disappoint you, but that every single little thing he does never meets your approval? You're driving him away, Horace. You're just too dense to see it."

"Enough!" Horace yelled. He slammed down the handle and gripped Sally by the shoulders. His hands surrounded them, and she felt his fingers digging into her shoulder blades.

"Let go of me! . . . What the hell are you doing?"

In all the disagreements and fights over the years, Horace had never manhandled her and she couldn't control the fear on her face. "Jesus, you're *hurting* me."

Horace didn't loosen his grip. He was looking at her with a concentrated anger, one that had been building for years, and now came exploding and spewing out.

"Now you listen to me, goddamnit," he said, shaking her to punctuate his sentences. "I'm sick of you making me out to be some kind of monster. I'm the man of this house, goddamnit. I'm going to say what I want, and voice my opinion on how my son should be raised and not be ridiculed or admonished for it. You think you have all the answers. What the hell do you know about raising a boy that I don't? When the hell were you a boy? What makes your way right and my way wrong?"

He let go of her abruptly, and only then did she begin to cry.

"I'm just afraid for him," she said.

"Of what? That he's going to get a blister on his hand? That he's going to learn something about his own ancestry besides all the crap they teach him in school? That he's going to learn to look at our garbage culture with a skeptical eye rather than become just another fat pig consumer? I want him to pull those *fucking* plugs out of his ears, to tear himself away from those *fucking* video games, to not kill whole weekends watching *fucking* sports on TV . . . to *think*, for fuck's sake! Tell me, once and for all, what the fucking *hell* is wrong with that? What in fuck's name, for fuck's sake, is *fucking* wrong with that!"

"It's the way you do it . . . just like you are right now. You're so harsh, you're so angry," she said, wiping the tears off her face.

"It's called courage," Horace yelled. "I'm facing this head-on, in my own house . . . I'd like to hear you say that you admire my courage, or you value my individuality. Just once! Just one *fucking* time!"

He picked up the handle, knowing it would menace her, then hurled it into the woodpile.

"You know something, Sally?" he said, now quietly. "I'm afraid for him, too. I'm afraid he'll grow up to be just another guy who thinks work means skimming as much money as they can, and then hides in all the idiotic diversions this once-great country now calls its culture."

"You're afraid of more than that, Horace," Sally said dryly. "You're afraid of a lot more than that. You're the one who is running away. You've buried yourself in this bizarre philosophy . . . this bizarre character . . . because you're afraid."

"What are you talking about?"

"You . . . you hide . . . you're in this safe place where you can snipe and criticize but not take the risks of trying to really make it in life. You have your little shop, and your little costume and your little salary, and you're nice and safe, tucked away to tell everybody else what's wrong with them. Well, I don't want to be like that and neither does Michael. I don't want to live like this and neither does Michael."

"Speak for yourself. Don't speak for him."

"He speaks for himself all the time . . . you just don't listen."

"Bullshit."

"It's true. You don't really know anything about him. You think you do, but you don't. Everything he says or does, you twist around—"

"That's not true. Don't tell me I don't know my own son."

"Okay. Who's his best friend? Who's his favorite teacher? What girl does he like? Who's his favorite band? His favorite ballplayer? Who's the coach of his baseball team?"

Horace stared at her for a beat or two.

"Look, just because I don't keep up with my son's social life doesn't mean I don't understand him—"

"Then what does it mean? What does it mean that you can't answer these questions?"

"This is the kind of shit I won't stand for," Horace said. "You say I'm scared? What about all the people out there—like you—who hide behind their kids? You gave up being yourself, being my wife, because it was easier to go around being Michael's baseball-bag carrier than to face your own grown-up life. So you dote on him, kill your weekends watching him play sports. All we talk about is him. Do you even know who I am?"

It was a question that, as soon as it came out of his mouth, he wished he hadn't asked. Sally turned her back on him.

"I thought I did. Now I'm not so sure." She waited for him to come to her, to put his arms around her. She wanted to sink into him, like she used to, and feel safe. She even let herself sway toward him, but Horace missed it. He stood his ground, and in that instant, Sally had a moment of clarity.

They were through.

"What is there to be unsure about? I constantly tell you who I am," Horace said. "It's all out there, in the great wide open."

"No, Horace, it's not. You, the real Horace Mueller, is in there hiding. You disappeared somewhere inside the blacksmith. You're right. I don't know who you are anymore, and I . . . I can't . . ."

She turned toward him and looked out at the sun going down over the ridge beyond Otsego Lake. It could be so beautiful up here, she thought.

"What are you saying, Sally?"

"I'm saying I've had enough. And I think you have, too. I'm saying I'm scared. I think you need help. I think you need to be alone for a while and figure out what is happening to you. I think you need to figure out what you're afraid of. I think you need to figure out who you want to be for the rest of your life. If you're going to be *this* man, this man so out of touch with me, Michael, and everything, I can't stay with you."

He walked past her without saying a word, and she looked straight ahead at the torch-lit western sky. She heard his heavy footsteps on the crying floorboards of the porch and waited for the violent slam of the door. Instead, Horace shut it quietly, and it closed with a gentle click.

Chapter Seventeen

Induction Day was eight weeks away, and Stacy agreed to meet Grudeck in his place or hers every week to hear his stories. Grudeck warned her he was lost—he didn't really know what he wanted to say—and was afraid it might be a waste of time.

"Don't try to figure it all out," she advised him. "Just talk. The more you talk, the more you'll figure it all out. That's why women have girlfriends."

"So you'll be my girlfriend?" Grudeck asked.

"More like . . . *we'll* be girlfriends." Stacy laughed.

God, she was still so cute, Grudeck thought.

On the first night, Stacy was struck by how antiseptic his place was. Spotless, without clutter, without anything.

She looked at the few plaques on the wall, a few pictures of him in action or posing in uniform.

"Where's all your stuff?" she asked.

"The rest is all in storage."

"You planning on moving?"

"No. Why?"

She started to say, but checked herself because she couldn't avoid using the word *empty*.

"No reason."

Grudeck gave her a quick tour. It was show-model stock: various shades of earth tones on the walls and floors and, since this was equestrian country, the hunter-green and foxhunt-red window treatments. His bedding matched, and once again Stacy got a glimpse of him as an unfinished man. A boy in a puffy-faced, middle-aged body.

"Okay . . . let's get started," she said.

They sat at the glass-top dining table and Stacy took out a folder and two legal pads. She pushed one toward him.

"I'll take notes, but if something else comes to your mind while we're talking, just write a word or two to remind yourself later," she said. "It will help unclutter your mind."

"Okay."

"So where do you want to begin?"

"It begins with you."

"With me?"

"Yes. You said something to me in high school that stuck with me. It was something like, 'I'm just as good an artist as you are an athlete.' Remember?"

"Yeah. I was trying to knock you off your high horse," Stacy said, but the fact that he remembered touched her like an unexpected gift of flowers. "I was saying athletes get so much attention, but there's millions of talented people who are just as good at their jobs."

"I got that," Grudeck said. "I'm not stupid. But here's my point. For years, I used that as a relaxation technique. Every time I would come to the plate, I would look up at all those faces in the crowd and think, 'Some of these people are real pros, too,' and for some reason it took the pressure off. It made me feel, like, regular. Does that sound crazy?"

"No," Stacy said. "Not at all."

"But then, that started to change. A few years in, when I scanned the crowd, I didn't see that in people anymore. I only saw the drunks and fools. Fat guys wearing my jersey really bothered me. Here I was busting my ass to stay in playing shape, working my whole life to earn it, and these slobs can buy the same shirt in Walmart."

Stacy first wanted to say he should have been honored but, the way he explained it, she got his point, and made her first note.

He told her a story about the first time he heard the chant "Grudeck sucks." It was in Yankee Stadium, so early in his career he was surprised that he inspired hatred from the enemy. But after a couple of clutch hits in a three-game series, there it was, loud and clear. "Grudeck sucks."

"My mother was at that game. And to her *suck* was a dirty word. I was embarrassed. I wanted to climb up in the stands and kick somebody's ass. It was like, to them, I wasn't a real person, like . . ."

". . . you were a man without a mother," Stacy said.

"*Exactly*. This is one of the things I want to get to. Athletes always lie and say the fans don't bother them, but when it gets personal . . . well, you want to kill somebody."

There was a particular night in Comiskey later that season, he told her, when he thought he figured out why crowds had changed.

"One thing I always loved about baseball when I started was this restless quiet that settled over a ballpark when nothing was happening," Grudeck said. "You could hear people moving around, vendors hawking, a conversation here, a lone clapper there, the voice of maybe one egomaniac yelling down. But mostly it was quiet. I'd look into the stands and see people checking their scorecards, talking baseball with the people around them."

It gave the game dignity, Grudeck always thought. Not like the forced hush of tennis or golf, because nothing rocked like a baseball stadium when there was something worth cheering about. But the sounds of 35,000, or 40,000, or 45,000 people waiting quietly for something to happen was always kind of . . . *civilized.*

"It wasn't like football. Nobody painted their faces or wore costumes to baseball," Grudeck said. "Baseball—and those old-fashioned organ riffs—had class."

But then it changed. It was as if the game itself wasn't good enough anymore. Fans had to be entertained constantly. Music raged between innings, now even between pitches. The electronic scoreboards exploded with graphics and horse-race games and Three Stooges bits. It told people when to clap. When to cheer. When to boo. In between innings there were fuzzy mascots running around or riding three-wheeled motorcycles, teasing the opposing players, busting the umpires' chops. Some of it was funny, Grudeck had to admit, but most of it was stupid. The towels, the thundersticks, all the gimmicks. It all felt cheap to him.

"Here's the point," he told Stacy. "All that noise let the assholes up there hide behind it and become more abusive. They could scream down at you and know you couldn't figure out who it was coming from. Unless they were drunk, then they'd stare and point at you, knowing damn well you couldn't climb over fifteen, twenty rows to pound the living shit out of them. Just once, I wanted to catch one in the parking lot or the hotel lobby."

"Then what?" Stacy asked.

"Then . . . I don't know. Maybe just . . . There was this time at Comiskey, when this pimply, stringy-haired skank started screaming at me after I hit a home run. *'You suck, Grudeck. You suck, you suck job. You fucking suck!'* On and on. The guys with her, these three college-aged mutts, were laughing along . . . *'You suck, you suck job'* . . . and high-fived her and each other. They were only ten rows in, and I really wanted to go over the wall and backhand her. Instead, I just put my head down and I felt the anger burn in my gut. She started again when I got up a couple of innings later, and when I struck out, she started, *'Siddown, Grudeck. You suck job. Siddown! Hey, Grudeck! Hey, up here. You suck, Grudeck, you hear me. You fuckin' suck!'*

"And I remember thinking that somehow, all these assholes, they won. And I lost."

"Joe, that's crazy . . ."

"But it gets worse. It was at that moment I saw I was just a ballplayer to millions of people. That's all. A ballplayer. Someone to be loved, or hated, depending only on what hat you wore. All these people, like this little foul-mouthed cunt . . . sorry . . ."

"It's okay," Stacy said, but winced inside.

"To them, I was either just . . ." Grudeck got stuck.

"An 'object of affection' or 'target of their ire'?" Stacy offered.

"Exactly. Even though they didn't really know the first fucking thing about me. That night, in the hotel, I couldn't get it out of my mind. I was lying there, in this air-conditioned room, but felt like I was smothering. I felt claustrophobic. It was one o'clock in the morning when I got up and started walking. I stopped at every bar in the Loop, looking for them. I played the scene out in my mind. If I found her, I swear to Christ I would have grabbed her by her skinny throat and shook her till she pissed herself. And if one of the boys wanted to play hero, well then . . . I could almost feel their noses crunching under my fist and see their blood splattering the bar."

Stacy squirmed a little in her seat, inside and out. She could see the anger roiling up in him, even now, and looked down to see both his fists clenched. She looked down at the notepad, and scribbled a few words.

"But here's the worst part. I knew that even if I found them I couldn't do anything. I'd get arrested. Then the headlines. Then the commissioner's office. Then the lawsuits. Here I was, six-three, two twenty-five, young and all muscle, and I knew I had to take whatever shit the fans threw at me. All of them. I was powerless and they knew it. They could boo you, throw beer on you—they used to throw batteries at Yankee Stadium; darts, seriously, *darts* in Chicago—curse you and your mother, treat you like you weren't even human, like you were made of stone or something, and there wasn't a fucking thing you could do about it because you were you and they were nobody. And then there was sports radio, and now they blog, tweet, whatever, and sports TV shows post them and they get attention for their outrageous, anonymous opinions. And we have to take it."

Grudeck got up and limped a few steps. "Got to move a little. Getting too creaky," he said wearily. "I'm really breaking down. If I was a horse, they'd shoot me."

Seeing his physical pain, her alarm over his anger dissipated immediately, replaced by some maternal instinct, or something close. His vulnerability, in bones and soul, made her a little sad for him. Big Joey Grudeck, hurt, because he wasn't liked by everyone.

"Is that what bothers you? That the fans are jerks?" she said, but it came out in a "poor baby" way, and, once again, she wished she could take it back.

The dismissive tone chafed Grudeck.

"I don't think you get it. How could you? You ever feel hatred from complete strangers? No. Nobody does."

"So is that what you want the speech to be about?" she asked, injecting a little more sincere empathy into her voice.

"That, and so much other stuff," Grudeck said. "Like the media. When I started, it wasn't so bad. There were the guys from the *Globe* and the *Herald*, a few from the suburban papers allowed in the locker room. The sportscasters from TV would come around once in a while. But then the media tripled, quadrupled—how do you say five, six, seven times? Soon there were more of them than us. Microphones and cameras, everywhere. I'd be sitting there, drying off my nuts, and suddenly there's five cameras on me. You have any idea what that's like?"

"No," Stacy said. "Especially the 'drying off my nuts' part."

Grudeck rolled through. "The TV guys always clipped what you said to fit their story and some of the stuff I supposedly said in the papers didn't sound like me at all. As if I were a fictional character. Sometimes, that's exactly what I felt like. All that coverage, nobody ever gets to what's wrong. Seriously, flip the channels someday. There's more talk about sports than war. And the way they whip up controversy, football players kneeling during the anthem . . . I mean, really, who cares? That much? Sports reporters are like those little tick-eating birds that ride on the back of the rhinoceros. They're parasites, living off the backs of stars. That's why, as much as I tried to get along and be accessible, I really couldn't stand them. Still don't."

He told her how the media “whipped up a controversy” over a kid named Dre Motley, who had a noisy holdout against the team several years back.

The kid had a big year and suddenly thought he was worth twice the many millions the team was paying him. No question, he was a good ballplayer, but he choked in the playoffs and the Red Sox were eliminated again. Most everybody was disgusted with themselves and couldn’t wait for the next season to start. Grudeck, then—what, thirty-five or thirty-six?—hit the gym harder than ever, and started taking andro to help his aging body repair between workouts.

“A few weeks before spring training, I’m flipping the channels, there’s Motley in front of his house up in Holmby Hills outside of L.A. It’s like Beverly Hills. Big money. Motley used to say, ‘We party so much up there in the off-season, the neighbors call it Homeboy Hills.’ ”

During the season, his friends from Compton had the run of the place. There was a drug arrest one night, and a small fire another. Once, Motley’s ex-girlfriend got punched in the mouth by one of his friends and lost three teeth. Each time, the sports TV, TMZ, and *ET* crews made it impossible to move in the locker room. Scumbag athletes were big news, and entertainment, and good for ratings. . . . That’s what scared him so much now about Syracuse.

When Grudeck first saw Motley on TV that off-season, the volume was muted, so he thought there was another crime. Motley was talking fast in gold-rimmed shades and giant chains, wearing a synthetic Nike jacket.

“The kid always bragged about the cash Nike gave him, but bitched because he always had to wear something with the logo on camera—headbands, crew neck undershirts, hats, wristbands,” Grudeck explained. “Said it cut into his style.”

Parked behind Motley was a glossy black Hummer Alpha and a fully chromed Porsche Carrera GT. Next to him was his agent, Marty Levinson, who had ten or fifteen top players. Levinson wore a black suit, and shirt with a tab collar fixed with a white pearl stud and no tie, what was left of his hair slicked to his head, racing shades plastered to his face, beads of sweat glistening on his forehead in the California sun.

"I turned up the volume and Levinson was doing an 'injured party' act. I remember him saying, 'My client is being exploited by a system that ignores fair market value' and 'The Red Sox should have the decency to pay the man what he's worth.' I wanted to puke. Except it got worse when Motley answered questions.

"He said something like, 'I thought slavery was dead, but I'm like a high-paid slave, see? I can't go work where I want. I can't go work for somebody who wants to pay me better. I got to stay on the plantation until my contract is up, see?'

"*Slavery?* What was the guy making? Eight or nine million a year to *play baseball*? I couldn't believe the press had nothing better to do than pay attention to this guy. Worse, no one in the media even challenged him. When the sports show cut back to their anchor desk, their 'baseball experts' started to argue the merits of his value, but none of them told the truth. None of them talked about honoring a contract, or putting that kind of money in perspective for regular people. If I was a regular working guy, like my father, I'd hate us, too."

This went on for weeks, Grudeck told Stacy, and during one press conference Motley said, "I know I'm worth mo' money. They know I'm worth mo' money. Just pay me the damn mo' money." The press ate it up. The clip ran all day, all channels. The *Herald* turned it into a back-page headline.

MOTLEY:
"JUST PAY ME
THE DAMN
MO' MONEY"

"So he finally shows up in Fort Myers, 'under protest.' The reporters circled him, like dogs sniffing each other's asses," Grudeck said. "I let it go, but it was starting to get on my nerves. It was *my* team, and he was a disruption. But you know the part that bothered me the most?"

"He was making more than you?" Stacy guessed.

"No. I didn't give a shit about that. Never did. No, what pissed me off most was watching all these reporters suck up to him. This bunch of little squirrelly white guys, nodding with these phony smiles plastered on their faces at all of Motley's jive bullshit."

"I don't think anybody says 'jive' anymore, Joe," Stacy said.

"You know what I mean . . . but one day he goes too far. He says the Red Sox want everybody to fit the same mold. He says, 'Boston ain't ready for a boy from Compton, see . . . they like the Joe Grudeck types, you know, that clean-cut, all-American, white-boy thing.'

"Now he'd brought me into it, the motherfucker, so when the sportswriters slunk over to my side of the locker room, I told them, 'Motley should shut up and play. That's what he gets paid for. Not to talk bullshit.' I was stupid. I took the bait."

The next day's *Herald* front page, not the sports page, but the *front*, read:

"SHUT UP
AND PLAY"
Grudeck lays down law to Motley

Grudeck leaned back in his chair, then leaned in, close to Stacy's face.

"Now this is where it gets stupider. The next day the reporters crowd Motley's locker and he gets in outrage overdrive. He says something like, 'If Joe Grudeck has somethin' to say to me, he should be a man and say it to my motherfuckin' face. I don't give a fuck how many motherfuckin' All-Star teams he made. He needs to show me some motherfuckin' respect."

"This is going to get ugly, isn't it?" Stacy said, cringing at Grudeck's attempt at black English like she did at the c-word.

"Oh, yeah," Grudeck said. "*Ugly* ain't the word. So he's over there telling the sportswriters . . . 'I'm no suburbs Little League champ, see. I'm from the fuckin' streets. Maybe that's how they do shit where Grudeck from, but where I'm from you stay out of a man's shit, *else he be in yours.*'

"When the sportswriters came back to me, I kept it simple. All I told them was 'I said what I had to say yesterday. He can talk all the shit he wants. I'm done.' "

He stopped there, and she was relieved. She didn't want to encourage him to tell more. His anger was off-putting, almost frightening. As for the unveiled racism . . . she was rolling that around in her head, remembering things he said back in high school. But she let it go.

Grudeck, too, held back. He wanted to go on and tell her about how sick he was of all the tattooed chest-thumpers in sports today, and their big fucking mouths. Especially in football and basketball. With their long hair coming out of football helmets like professional wrestlers, inked up like Hells Angels.

God, he wished he played back in the day . . .

But he left it unsaid. He didn't want to be judged by her. There's only so much truth a person can take. So he kept on with the story.

"I was done with the media, not with Motley. I was captain. It was my team. Nothing blows up a locker room faster than race stuff. When you're on a team, you should be team colors first, everything else second. I know that sounds like bullshit, but it's true. Now with all Motley's slavery talk, I could see a couple of black guys leaning his way, and now with his 'white boy' remark, he'd made it racial, in a big way. I had to put it down, right then. I had to clean it up, quick."

Grudeck's story was turning and, again, Stacy along with it. Asserting himself, his responsibility—his muscle, really—all that "my team" stuff stirred her in some innate way. Her expression must have changed, because Grudeck looked her in the eyes and threw her a wink. She blushed and quickly looked down at the notepad.

"I want to tell you something I've never told anybody before, not even my dad," Grudeck said. "I get this feeling . . . it comes when I know

I'm going to win. I don't know how to describe it. It's like adrenaline, but calm, and my hands feel light, and move like they have a mind of their own. I felt it with every touchdown pass in high school, every time I pinned a kid, every big hit in every big game I was ever in, from Little League to the Red Sox. That's how I felt that day with Motley."

Grudeck told her how he felt attuned to everything when he walked into the Florida sun that day. The bleached white City of Palms stadium shone brighter against the blue sky; the rustle of the outfield palm trees sounded crisper. He went through his morning stretches and warm-ups, making sure not to avoid Motley. He got next to him for calisthenics and when Motley went into the outfield to jog and sprint, Grudeck did, too. When Motley came in for batting practice, Grudeck joined him in the on-deck area. Motley said nothing and avoided eye contact. Grudeck made "goddamn sure" to not do the same. He looked straight at Motley a few times. This was Grudeck at his best. Being boss, and making fucking-A sure everybody knew it. At the end of the day, with the palms casting long shadows and the breeze turning a notch cooler, Grudeck called his team together.

"The coaches trotted off, and the equipment guys were clearing the field. I stood on the mound and looked around at my teammates. 'I only got one thing to say,' I told them. 'We're all in this together, right?' And I looked straight at Motley. 'Right?'

"Everybody started saying, 'Yeah, Joe,' 'Right, Joe,' and I said, 'Good. Now, if somebody's got something to say, get ready to say it now, 'cause I got something to say. And that's this: everybody here is paid to play, to be part of this team, not part of some asshole media circus. I'm talking to you, Dre, so if you got something to say, or any of you got something to say, say it now.' Nobody said anything, and I asked, 'One more time . . . if you got something to say, say it now. Say it fucking now, to the face of your teammates, not to a bunch of jerk-off reporters.' I was looking straight at Motley. He got the message: it was us against him. And that was that."

"That's it? That wasn't so ugly," Stacy said. "What happened next?"

"Nothing, really. It all kind of died down. He left camp, the team didn't budge and eventually traded him to Anaheim. And that was that."

Whatever it was Grudeck saw in Stacy's eyes moments earlier—admiration? love?—made him decide not to tell the rest of the story. He knew she wouldn't appreciate how he mopped up the unfinished business. Some things she just wouldn't understand. Like Syracuse. He could never explain that away, not even to himself.

She stopped writing and was studying his face, and a guilty look said he was holding back.

AFTER PRACTICE, Grudeck stayed in the shower, long after his teammates left, waiting for Motley, who he knew was dawdling to avoid him.

He waited, soaping and rinsing, for twenty minutes, letting the water splash off his massive shoulders and run down his body, pooling at his feet. The hot water turned his skin soft.

Motley finally came in, went to shower at the opposite end of the room, and turned his back on Grudeck.

After a minute, Grudeck broke the silence.

"So, now that it's just me and you, you got something to say?" Grudeck yelled over the clatter.

"Don't fuck with me, Grudeck."

"That's it? 'Don't fuck with me'? All the bullshit you gave the press about being from the streets . . . where was it? . . . South Central L.A.?"

"Compton, man."

"Whatever . . . So now, after all that ghetto bullshit, all you got to say is 'Don't fuck with me, Grudeck'? I was expecting a little more. A little more . . . I don't know what . . . *manhood.*"

"Look, Grudeck, I don't want no trouble with you, see," Motley said over his shoulder. "I don't give a fuck about you like you don't give a fuck about me. Let's leave it at that."

"That's where you're wrong, Motley. You may not give a fuck about me, but I have to give a fuck about you, because you're on *my* team. *See?*"

"Why you fuckin' with me, Grudeck?"

"Because you're fucking with my team. *My* team."

"Whatever, Grudeck . . . what-the-fuck-ever," Motley said.

Grudeck then started going around the room, turning every shower on full blast.

"Problem is, Motley, it's not that easy," Grudeck said, raising his voice over the steamy din. "You just can't say 'whatever' and be done with it, because it's not in your control anymore. You lost that when you called me out. What did you think? I was going to be intimidated? Shit, man, I've been beating black asses like yours since I was in seventh grade."

Motley ignored him, until he felt Grudeck's breath on his neck.

"It's in my control now," Grudeck said. "It's my team, and you called me out. So I got no choice."

Motley spun around with a wild hook, but Grudeck was already inside it, and his big right hand got Motley by the throat. His left forearm hit Motley across the chest and drove him hard against the tile wall, and, just as quick, Grudeck kicked out his legs from underneath him. Motley landed hard on the tile floor, back first, with nothing to break his fall. Grudeck heard a squeak from his chest, and slammed a knee into his solar plexus to hear it again. He buried that knee in Motley's gut, pinning him to the floor, and still had his throat. Motley frantically tried to pry Grudeck's hand off with both of his. This left Grudeck's other hand free, and he balled up his fist and cocked it right over Motley's face. Motley looked up at it, eyes bulging. At first, Grudeck wasn't going to hit him. But the terror in Motley's eyes was too good to pass up. Grudeck brought the fist straight down, alongside Motley's nose and under his eye. Bat-on-ball sound. So satisfying. Motley lurched and stopped struggling.

Grudeck let go of Motley's throat and got to his feet. Motley stayed down, coughing and rubbing his neck.

"Shut the water off when you leave," Grudeck said over his shoulder.

Motley bolted camp that night, and they never spoke again. He asked for a trade, and the Red Sox sent him home to play in California.

But soon after, Grudeck realized he'd been manipulated by the press and felt like fresh meat for the jackals that circled and yapped and whipped things into a frenzy. He felt like a kid in a schoolyard fight, egged on by cowards who only liked to watch fights, not be in them. He felt stupid. What if he'd hurt that kid? Or killed him, slamming him on a tile floor like that? Punching his head against it. People died from less. Or if Motley had come after him with a gun. They all carry guns, these sports thugs today. Then what? And for what? One night against the Angels, he thought of finding him after the game to apologize, then thought, Fuck Motley. Fucks like him ruined sports.

GRUDECK THREW HIS HEAD BACK and closed his eyes, blocking out the harsh glare of the kitchen track lights.

"What?" Stacy asked, putting down the pen.

"I'm just trying to think of the point . . . for the speech?" he said. "That's the problem. I want to talk about this whole thing with the media, but then again, it's the sportswriters who voted me in. Sal warned me, I could come across as an ingrate."

"Like a Motley," Stacy said.

"Exactly," Grudeck said, coming to.

"Maybe you can do it in a questioning way, not a harsh way. Something like, why, and how, did we become so obsessed with something just meant to be a diversion? Maybe, instead of sounding critical, you just pose innocent questions. Maybe you make yourself sound like a man looking for answers, rather than a man who has them."

That night, Grudeck stretched out on his bed, thinking how long it had been since he felt the lightness in his hands. When he walked Stacy to her car, he was hoping to get it, but his hands felt heavy and ached.

All this talk tonight, all the downsides of the game nobody saw, nobody but the people deep inside it. Amphetamines, steroids, and painkillers, the ballplayer's equivalent of pot, coke, and booze. Racial tension. Deep ethnic division. Hotel hookers and groupies, some who went willingly and some who got too drunk or high to resist. He learned in Syracuse how easy it was. He did it himself. But he was just a kid then. He looked at himself in the mirror that day and said, never again. Not like that. But it went on all around him. He heard the locker room stories. Girls pissed on and pissed in. Forced to take it in the ass. Gang bangs. The gold-chain guys loved that shit. Grudeck figured it was because half of them were closet fags, bisexuals, at least. No one wanted to believe it, but it was true. With all their macho bullshit. They'd stick it in anything that had a pulse. Look them in the eye hard enough and you could see it. Grudeck figured the guys who did gang bangs secretly got off on watching the other guy. That was the only explanation.

Plenty of times Grudeck saw girls staggering out of hotel rooms, disoriented and disheveled, mascara smeared, face blotched, eyes and lips blood-red.

And when one went to the cops, the world lined up against them. Grudeck saw how the public was so quick to give these scumbags the benefit of the doubt. Standing Os at games. And what did the guys in the media talk about? How it would impact the team. The girl? Nobody gave a fuck. That was sports today. A guy accused of rape gets cheered for hitting a home run. A guy not accused of rape gets booed for striking out. A guy accused of rape won the NBA MVP, another won the Heisman Trophy. What a world. What a fucked-up world.

How do you tell the world all this? How do you tell the dirtiest secrets, and not your own?

His brain flooded with disturbing images. The two girls in the door-light limping out of his room in Syracuse. What did Grudeck say? "Thanks for coming"? That was it. He was lying in bed, hands folded behind his head, sucked and fucked in his private porno, satisfied. "Thanks for coming."

Girls in the dark corners of clubs, in their tight black dresses, being spun around and groped by players. Party time. Their drunk laughter. A girl, Christ, she couldn't have been more than seventeen, on her knees in a private room, choking on someone's dick and then vomiting, while the players howled. Grudeck broke that one up, then went upstairs disgusted. He was old then, it was toward the end, and he knew if things were different he could have had a daughter that age. The locker room scenes, guys stretching and chubbing themselves before turning naked toward the pretty female sports reporters; on the street it was indecent exposure, in the locker room, it was tough shit. Should he tell Stacy all this? He was a pig, too, let's face it. Syracuse, and lots of girls, then paid-for "massages" when the groupies wore him out.

He lay in bed thinking about all the stuff that bothered him. The new spring training facilities looked like concentration camps, lined with fences to separate the fans from the players; he walked past thousands of people with their hands sticking through the chain link with balls and programs to sign, like Mexican street beggars, starved for a fleeting moment of attention while he ignored their calls, eyes straight to attention, acting indifferent and above them, but still wondering why they cared so much.

The night at Fenway where a man was beaten bloody by two Southie thugs, in front of his two little boys. Grudeck saw it so clearly. The Brewers were in town and the boys were wearing Milwaukee hats. A tourist family, a vacation nightmare.

The Sunday afternoon in New York where they passed an inflatable sex doll around Yankee Stadium like a beach ball, and the drunks who took turns abusing it, pretending to fuck it or have it blow them, or punched it repeatedly in the face. Grudeck remembered the look on one woman's face, a mother with two young teenaged girls and a prepubescent boy. It was a look of terror more than revulsion. At that moment, he remembered thinking, if she only knew the truth about her son's heroes in the dugout.

He was restless in bed, and in pain. Sweat pooled on his sternum. How do you tell the truth? He thought of the other induction speeches, and all the good-old-days stuff about the brotherhood of teammates. These days, teammates came and went. Mercenaries. Grudeck, the Last of the Mohicans, stayed. Grudeck, the last of the gold-watch men, twenty-some years in the same organization, the only organization. All those years, no best friend, no longtime teammate. No Billy and Mickey and Whitey. Just Grudeck. Joe Lonely, like Stacy said.

He flipped over and pounded his pillow, mad at the ingratitude even in his own mind. Somewhere along the line, he forgot how lucky he was. Lucky to be discovered, lucky to be brought up, luckiest to stick around as long as he had. A dream life. Without it, he'd probably be teaching phys ed and coaching at some high school somewhere, trying to mold spoiled kids and placate misguided parents.

But what was the cost? Seeing her, he wondered how "bad" a normal life would have been. To come home to the same place every night. Same woman, same four walls. Not whoever you picked up, not to whatever team hotel. How many women, how many nights? And now this golf course condo felt like an extension of that life. Rooms like those in an extended-stay suite hotel, maid service, meals out, Darlena for the in-home "massage." Grudeck being Grudeck, the ballplayer. Except now it was on a golf course, not the diamond. Was this it? If he wanted something different, time was running out. He decided their next session would be at Stacy's house. He concentrated on her face and tried to sleep.

Chapter Eighteen

"I changed over the years," Grudeck said at Stacy's kitchen table, watching her cut the stems of the spring flower bouquet he'd brought.

"So beautiful, Joe. Thank you," she said, then sat down with the same legal pad from the week before. "So where were we?"

"I was thinking about how they built fences at spring training to keep the fans off us," he said. "I keep coming back to it."

Grudeck told her about the All-Star game at Wrigley. It was his third; he was a recognizable, authentic star, no flameout.

There were chest-high, metal crowd-control fences at the hotel where the players stayed. Regular Chicago cops—the ones with the checkerboard caps—were stationed along the way. There were two guarding the players-only elevator, which was programmed to go to the players-only floor, and one at each stairwell door. For the two days, the fans lined these fences, reaching over with photos, balls, and bats to sign.

On the first day, Grudeck stopped to sign for a family with two boys, Cub Scout age.

"They had these little notepads, nothing fancy, and the pages were all blank," Grudeck told Stacy. "That's why I stopped. Those blank pages."

Grudeck shook fingers with the boys through the steel mesh and started to sign, then heard the father yelling, "Hey . . . hey . . . hey!" A crowd of grown men and older kids raced in, with bats, balls, and glossy shots they shoved at Grudeck. He knew what they were: memorabilia dealers looking to make a buck off his name. The family was being crushed, so Grudeck chicken-scratched their notepads and moved on, with calls of "Hey, Joe! No fair! . . . Joe, overhereoverhereoverhere . . . C'mon, Joe, don't be an asshole . . . You suck anyway, Grudeck, shoulda been Sanchez, not you . . ." at his back.

"Here's the point," Grudeck said. "It was the first time I felt caged. The bigger I got, the more . . ."

"You became a prisoner of your fame," Stacy said.

"Exactly. It was everywhere you went. People clawing at you, and if you gave yourself to them every time, there'd be nothing left. And when you refused them, they walked away thinking you were an asshole."

"Were you?" Stacy laughed.

"I tried not to be. But I changed. I became, what's the word . . ."

"Aloof. Distant."

"Yes. It was fun for a few a years, but after a while it seemed like my whole life revolved around keeping bloodsuckers off me."

Grudeck told her how he didn't do much in Boston but get to Fenway early, work out, then kill time before on-field batting and stretching. Once the game was over, he drove home past lines of autograph seekers, right into his building's garage. Going out to dinner, going for a walk, going for a run, going to a bar for a pop, all out of the question unless you wanted to be accosted. He ordered food in, using a phony name. He built a home weight room to avoid the health clubs, even though the camaraderie of the gym was something he enjoyed from the first time he stepped into the Union Y. Everything he did was geared to keeping his privacy. He did not tell her that's why he chose Asian massage parlors. The girls knew nothing about him except he was a very big man who said very little and tipped very well.

"At first, I thought, 'It's sick to live like this,' but the years went by and I got used to it," Grudeck said. "The years kept going by, and it just became who I was. Who I had to be, I guess."

"So, this price of fame, is it worth it?" Stacy asked, earnestly.

"This is part of what I want to say in my speech."

He paused, then said, "You want to hear something crazy? When I retired I did these 'Legends' autograph shows, and there would be players who had retired ten, fifteen years before me. And I would hear the fans say things like, 'Jesus, so-and-so got old.' As if he wasn't supposed to. I even had the same reaction when I saw guys like Willie Mays and Joe DiMaggio. Ted Williams. That's when it hit me."

"What?"

"We're not real to people. Not real humans. Just the images they see on TV, on baseball cards, at the ballpark. Sometimes I feel that way about myself."

He wanted to tell her about all the girls and the pressure and, now, the blue pills. He wanted to say how tired he got, 182 games a year at least, of controlling his face because he never knew if a camera was on him, and the snapshots and cell phone shots and video clips, and life being one long highlight reel from which he felt so strangely detached.

Instead, he just said, "I mean, look at my life."

Stacy absorbed that one for a good beat. His life. She wondered where it was going. He talked like it was over; that he wanted this speech to be like a eulogy for his career. But where to, after that? To her? She tried to envision it. He was, at heart, a good guy. And he cared about her. But something was missing. He talked about being one-dimensional in the eyes of the fans, but she wondered how much there really was to him. Sure, there were glimpses of sensitivity and thoughtfulness, but he was lost and was grasping for something. Stability? Love? A future different than his past. He'd said it once: "I'm tired of being Joe Grudeck." But who did he want to be? Mr. Stacy Milo? Suddenly, she felt a responsibility for him, and his feelings, that she did not want to take on. Joe and her; she did not see it. Not yet, anyway, because in his current state—in this suspension between being Joe Grudeck, ballplayer, and whoever it was he wanted to become—he was incomplete. He was falling for her, she knew, based on his romantic version of a casual, kissy-face, puppy-love thing from long ago. But she was done with her past; Grudeck, she knew, was trapped in his. Fame did that. It had stunted his emotional growth.

"Joe, what do you want? What do you really want?"

The suddenness of his answer surprised her.

"I want not to be forgotten."

"By who? Everyone?"

"No, by someone."

Stacy knew she was the one. She just didn't know what to do about it.

Chapter Nineteen

Now it was late spring, and Horace was alone. Sally said they both needed time to sort things out and Horace didn't disagree. She moved into a furnished condo in town with Michael, a sublet owned by a SUNY professor in Europe on sabbatical.

Horace knew Sally was going, but was still dismayed to come home from work one Saturday and find a note on the kitchen table with her new address. It was like the death of the terminally ill; expected, but sad just the same.

Horace walked through the house. He remembered the first time he saw it with a Realtor, how the creaks of planks reverberated through the empty halls and rooms. And now came those lonely cries again; echoes of a place unlived in.

He opened the door to Michael's room, and saw that all his electronics and entertainment boxes were gone. Left were remains of the boyhood Horace wanted for him: fossil-dusting and rock-collecting kits, a book on the Greek gods in astronomy, another on Otsego County geology, a pamphlet from the Fenimore Art Museum for an exhibition on the American flag used in Plains Indian art. In his bedroom, Sally's closet and chest were empty, her jewelry boxes gone.

Horace sat on the bed and looked around. She left. He knew that was the hardest part, the extrication, so he knew she was never coming back. That life was lost. This life, this house, was now his, alone.

For dinner, he boiled water and cooked a half box of Dutch noodles and smeared it with butter. Simple enough. As the sun set over the ridges beyond the lake, a chill settled into the house and Horace decided to fire up the woodstove.

He had used the last of the old newspapers to ball up under the kindling, so he searched the kitchen drawers for some paper. It was there he found Sally's folders, hidden under the woven placemats. He opened the envelopes, and the stern warnings bled before his eyes.

Legal action.
Foreclosure.
Tax lien.
Balance due.
Immediate attention required.
Attempts to collect.

"Jesus Christ, what has she done?" The numbers sank in. Credit-card debt alone equaled four or five months of his salary. She had taken out a second mortgage of $15,000 and maxed it out. All the years, all the work, and now this. The house would have to go, and there was no equity in it. Underwater, as they say. The mortgage-bundling recession saw to that.

Contact our loss-mitigation department, the letters said.

Loss mitigation. From here on, that's all that was left. Everything else was gone.

HE PULLED THE ESCORT up to the garden apartment and saw Michael peeking out of an upstairs window. Sally opened the door a crack before he knocked, and looked down to see the envelopes and papers in his hand.

"Let me in, Sally," Horace said. When inside, he waved the bills at her. "Is this why you left?"

"You know why I left," she said.

Horace shook his head.

"All this time, you've been working against me," he said. "Against us. You kept buying the things you knew I thought were worthless, knowing we were broke."

"We're not broke, just behind. And please lower you voice, we have neighbors now. And Michael."

"No, Sally, we're broke. Tapped out, flat fucking broke! They're coming for the house! And you didn't tell me?"

"Horace, please . . . Michael," she said.

"Michael should know, goddamnit. Life is a cautionary tale," Horace said. "He should understand how corrosive debt is. He should understand you just can't *have* everything."

He was seething and Sally moved away from him to the living room couch and sat down. Horace looked around the room. The couch was covered in a dark green plaid fabric, but still looked dirty. The recliner was beige velour. In the kitchen was a Formica-topped table and four wooden chairs.

"Is this what you want?" Horace said, his hands sweeping the room.

"I want a fresh start, Horace. This is just a first step."

"And what about the house? Our *home.*"

"It was never my home, Horace. It was what you wanted. Now it's yours. Do what you want. The bank will work with you. They certainly don't want it."

Horace moved toward the door; he felt the fuzzy weightlessness of anger in his head and hands. He gripped the knob to tether himself, to keep away from her. He wanted to break something. He wanted to punch himself in the face, to grab her by the throat. All was lost. Why not more? He closed his eyes and leaned his head against the door and took two deep breaths. Sally said nothing, and everything was still except the buzz of the fluorescent kitchen light.

"So, that's it?" Horace finally said, and Sally was relieved by the calm tone.

"I'm sorry, Horace."

"And Michael?"

"He's old enough to decide what he wants. You can see him anytime you want. I'll never stop you from being his father."

Two thoughts came to Horace: *You already did* and *You never will.* But he said neither and left.

Back at the house, Horace took all the bills, late notices, and foreclosure warnings, and stacked them in the stove. He took two handfuls of dried oak splinters, hatcheted down from quarter logs for kindling, and laid them across the crumpled papers in an X pattern. Dusk was settling in, leaving the room, furniture, stove, and Horace, too, in various tones of gray. He took the box of kitchen matches he kept on the mantel, lit one, and an orange glow flared through the room. He put the match to the paper in three places, each end and the middle. What was it she said? A fresh start. Here it was. All those bills, all that debt, turned to ashes. Up in smoke. Dissipating, disappearing, bellowing up the smokestack. Horace put on a few logs, sat in a chair, and watched the fire through the bars of the metal grate, as it roiled and spat hot embers, like an angry prisoner. Within minutes, the room was warm. He went to bed, but the stillness and silence of his house was almost unbearable. He couldn't wait for summer, to hear the throaty conversations of the cicadas. He lay there, as the night closed in, and found himself short of breath. His heart was banging hard, too. He checked his pulse and it was strong, but too fast. Scary fast. He felt like he was being smothered and sat up, then stood. He took deep breaths and felt around his chest, as if searching for the absent pain. His hands hurt, as always, but they weren't numb. Anxiety attack, he thought. Of all the fucking things. He lay back down and began to calm himself with his morning prayer: "God, help me continue my meaning." He repeated it, over and over, if nothing but to regulate his breathing and try to drift off into an unconsciousness that would decelerate his head and heart. Finally, he relaxed and his mind moved to the quiet, early dream state of sleep. It was then that he heard a bare whisper in his ear.

"Dad."

It was the higher, softer voice of a child.

"Dad" was all it said.

Chapter Twenty

Monday was a dead day at the museum and Horace was always off. He would spend a few hours in the woodpile, replenishing the cords for winter. It was never too early to start, and now, in the late spring as the musky smell of wild hyacinths filled the air, Horace felt restless and unsettled. He took his log-splitting tools out to the pile and began to work. In a short time his hair was matted with sweat and weighed like a damp towel around his face and neck. He chopped and hammered for hours, and the skin on his hands, scarred and toughened as it was, turned red and tender, and the yellowed, hardened calluses began to crack.

He worked, thinking of how much he wanted Michael with him, outdoors like this. Working, and traipsing into the woods behind their house, for sticks and logs, taking what the winter had timbered.

Horace thought back to the times when Michael was little, before sports, when they hiked the trails of Glimmerglass State Park at the north end of Otsego Lake. Along the Beaver Pond Trail, in spring and summer, on days just like this, Horace would point out to him the plant species with whimsical names that sounded like they came out of a Beatrix Potter book: devil's beggartick and Parlin's pussytoes, bearded sprangletop and Kinnikinnick dewberry. Michael's face lit up at the funny names and he squeezed Horace's hand as they walked, quick-stepping to keep up through the forest.

"Trees are just like people. A lot of different kinds live together in the same place. If one falls, it can hurt the others," Horace said as he showed him the leaves and needles of different maples and pines.

In the fall, when the autumn leaves blazed in contrast against the soft, refracted evening light, Horace made Michael giggle as he pretended to be confused over the colors.

"Now let me get this straight," Horace would say. "There's yellow leaves on the black oak and white ash, and red leaves on the silver maple and black gum, and brown leaves on the red and white oak . . ."

They searched the soft forest floor for deer and bear tracks, scanned the skies for dive-bombing hawks and circling turkey vultures. Michael especially loved spotting the skittish woodland critters: gray squirrels, striped chipmunks, and, at dusk, the first nocturnal showings of the possum and skunk. They found mammal and bird skeletons, but it was the carcasses, animals deflated to skin over bone by maggots, that at once most fascinated and horrified Michael, who would poke them with a stick. Horace explained the food chain. The decay of the dead creature creates bacteria that feed plants that feed animals that die in the woods and continue the cycle again and again.

"Now, this is real," Horace would say. "Real life. Real death. Real colors, real sounds. Not the made-up stuff you see on TV."

Horace guided Michael to see the natural world's yield of forest colors and sunset shades: a painter's palette array of autumnal leaves. Hues of reds and yellows unnamed by man, the torch-fire glow of the western skies at dusk, where orange and pink faded seamlessly into sky blue and light purple, and clouds burned or cooled with such colors, depending on their distance from the horizon.

Horace would pick up a dry leaf.

"What color is this?"

"Brown," Michael answered.

Then he'd grab a pinecone or acorn.

"And what color is this?"

"Brown."

Then a handful of path dirt.

"Brown."

"All brown, but all different," Horace said. "Even drab, lowly brown comes in more shades than we can describe with words. That's what I want you to understand. The world around you is full of things to discover."

Horace did similar experiments with sounds: bird calls, the different tinkles of water in feeder streams to Otsego Lake, the crunching of their feet on the forest floor of pine needles and decomposing mulch.

"Close your eyes and stay quiet . . . ," Horace would say. Then ten seconds later, "Now, tell me all the things you hear . . ."

"Birds. Some other kind of chirping, maybe squirrels. Wind. I can hear wind. I hear a stream."

"Now, if you listen long enough it kind of makes a song, doesn't it? The stream is the background. The wind is, too, but not as constant. Then in come the birds, and they go back and forth. The sounds are layered over each other. It's how you make music."

That was fatherhood, Horace thought, as he slammed a sledgehammer into a wedge with a clean hit, watched the log split evenly in two, from top to bottom. He picked up a half, and divided it again with the same swift skill. He worked through the afternoon, turning thick, round hunks of timber into four or eight burnable pieces. He stacked them, alternating two down, two across, building stacks of square towers with good airflow so the splintered logs would be seasoned by winter. He tried to think of the last time Michael worked with him on the woodpile. He was ten, maybe eleven, and Horace told him it would improve his baseball swing.

"Whip an ax or a maul for a few hours and you'll be hitting 'em out of the park," Horace said.

Michael gave it a few hours, then struck out every time the next day. Horace said it was just a coincidence, but Michael's coach told him the motions were different; that the vertical swing of the ax was nothing like the horizontal swing of the bat. Horace argued that it would at least make him stronger, and he could swing the ax into an upright tree as much as he wanted when the work was done, but Sally said he should listen to his coach.

Now spring was here, another baseball season and another few months of Horace working by himself. This time, though, he was so alone. The sound of the ax seemed to echo more, and there was no movement in the dark, dead windows of the house. Everything was changed. His son was gone. At the end of the day, Horace suddenly felt tired and beaten, without enough energy to move or even stoke his anger. He sat down on a pile of uncut wood. The Pugilist at Rest. Samson, blind and enslaved at the grindstone. He was breathing too hard and his loneliness terrified him. He felt weary, and his weariness weakened him, from his soul out. He snorted back the gob of snot that was choking him and swallowed it. He closed his eyes and asked God to help calm him. He let the evening air cool his sweat, and thought of a happier time.

He saw Michael with him at the farm, when he was little. Horace let him duck under exhibit ropes to climb on the horse-drawn buggies and sleds, antique tractors, and Model T trucks. Michael knew he was breaking the rules, and delighted in it. Horace took him into the smithy, let him shovel coal into the hearth, then helped him muscle the bellows. He liked it best when Horace gave him the tongs. Horace covered Michael's hands with his own, and together they would dip a piece of red-hot pig iron into the cooling vat. The hiss and explosion of steam made the boy think he'd done something magical. Horace remembered the day they looked across the farm museum valley, past the lake to the mountain above it.

"We live up there," Horace told him, pointing to the hill. "And every day when I'm at work, I look over at the mountain and know you're there at home."

Horace saw him on his toes in the apothecary, looking at the jars of licorice and peppermints, the choice all his. He remembered how he mastered the ball-and-cup toy from the general store, maybe the first sign of his gifted hand-eye coordination. He was allowed to hand-feed the goats and horses, collect eggs from the chickens, and watch the cow milkings. A little man about the village, polite and inquisitive, well liked by the rest of the staff.

"He's one of us," Jim Tremont, the cattle master, said to Horace. "Not like those spoiled little pain-in-the-ass kids who come in from out of town."

Nancy Schneerer, the small-animal and poultry caretaker, who also played the minister's wife in holiday celebrations at the church, was especially nice to Michael. She let him bottle-feed the goats and sheep and baby calves. At shearing time, Michael was allowed to gather the wool in baskets to take to the spinning shed.

Even old Jacque Angstrom, the German keeper of the draft horses, let Michael get pretty close to the big boys under his supervision.

"Hees a goot boy, dat Mikey. He haf reschpect for da beast."

One year—was he six or seven?—he played an eighteenth-century farm boy during "family life" days. He wore an authentic straw hat, high-waist woolen one-button pants with suspenders, and a plain cotton shirt, like he came out of *Tom Sawyer*. Michael showed visitors how to pet lambs and billy kids without spooking them, gaining trust with a cooing voice and a palmful of grain. He demonstrated chicken feeding, sowing the ground with shelled corn, roasted soybeans, and nutrient pellets from a tin bucket, as hens and roosters flapped and squawked around him. Michael did this unafraid, even as birds crowded him and pecked at his feet. He stood tall, showering them with feed, a little lord of the fowl. The other kids and parents marveled at Michael's command of the animals, and Horace watched, proud, like the father of the star player.

And that's what Michael was now. Maybe Sally was right. Not *right*, exactly, but maybe she had a point. Horace's distaste for the things Michael later enjoyed forced him to withdraw from the kid's life. Horace thought of his own father, now old, but always a little stoic, distant, and authoritarian. Early on, when he talked, Horace listened.

Later, the more he talked, the less Horace felt understood. His father was outside his life, a judgmental and irrelevant voice. Horace drifted away. Like fathers, like sons. And yet Horace came back in his own way. He was the keeper of the family culture, dead as it was.

What he gave to Michael in those early days was still in there, somewhere. But what Horace was taking from Michael now—a father's attention and approval—could never be replaced. He saw this only now that Michael was gone, and he was ashamed of himself for drifting away from his son. Maybe Michael didn't yet feel the hole, that recessed blackness in the soul that came with the absence of love, but Horace knew it well. All those years with Sally. Lonely in his own bed. Empty arms, emptying heart. Horace ached for his boy, and knew the pain that would one day come to both of them if Horace didn't fix this. The tears that came to his eyes brought more, and more, until they ran down his face, and deep sobs shook his massive back. He cursed himself for his strength and weakness; his strident conviction of a man making his stand in the world was all fine, until it brought this sadness and isolation, and reduced him to this.

"You big, fat fucking baby," he said out loud, wiping his eyes and nose with his dirty long johns sleeve.

He prayed again, asking God to rescue him, to quell the whimpering mess his insides had become.

"Fix this," his own voice said. "Get off your ass and fix this."

He stood up, walked over to the leafless silver maple with the ax, and took a mighty baseball swing, burying the blade into the bark.

Chapter Twenty-One

The next day after work, Horace walked into the Verizon store in a local strip mall, in full blacksmith garb, hands and face blackened from the coal soot.

"I need a cell phone, the cheapest thing you got," he said to the first red-vested clerk he saw.

"You have to check in at the help desk."

"I don't need help. I need a phone."

"They'll help you. They'll check your account and the status of your upgrades."

"I don't have an account and I'm not upgrading, goddamnit. I just need a phone."

The clerk seemed confused, and maybe a little scared. "Still, you have to go over there."

When his number was called, he was put in the hands of another clerk. The kid began to spew words Horace barely knew: apps, Google, Instagram, Twitter, Siri, Snapchat, Wi-Fi. All these silly names, Horace thought.

"All I want is to make calls."

"No texting? Nobody really talks anymore," the kid said.

"Okay, then. Texting."

"Let's see, I think we got a few flip phones left . . ."

This was the first step into Michael's world. Or a try, at least.

In the weeks since Sally and Michael left, the only calls on the answering machine she once insisted they needed were from collection agents. Horace wanted to tear it out of the wall now, but he didn't want to miss a call from Michael. He played it every night in the empty kitchen and hoped to hear Michael's voice, returning Horace's messages. When the clerk said "nobody talks anymore," Horace thought maybe it wasn't so much rejection, but Michael being afraid of how the conversations would go. Texting would be stilted, but efficient.

Can I see you? Horace clumsily thumbed out on his new phone.

K.

When?

Game, t'nite. Legion Fld. @ 7

See you then.

K, c u.

Later he got a text from Sally.

change first please.

This was an old wound. Horace knew his work clothes embarrassed Michael. Sally's terse words made him remember the first time he saw that shame in Michael's eyes. He was in fourth grade, excited for the school's Halloween parade and party. Horace argued with Sally over his costume. He wanted to help Michael make something with his own hands out of the rag bag. A pirate. A cowboy. A farmer. Michael wanted a store-bought cartoon-character costume, Ninja Duck, or some bullshit like that. Sally backed him, and Horace was irritated even more when Michael was one of five Ninja Ducks in a class of eleven boys. So much for individuality, he said to Sally, who ignored him.

Horace left work for the noon parade, and watched in his blacksmith garb. In the classroom later, parents served jack-o'-lantern cupcakes and store-bought cider—even though there were at least a half dozen cider mills operating around Cooperstown in those days. Horace stood, towering over the miniature desks, muzzling his thoughts. The teacher, a pretty young woman with earnest intentions, clapped her hands to get the children's attention and thanked the parents for their efforts.

". . . and I see Mr. Mueller even came in costume!" she said, cheerily, pointing to Horace as some of the kids giggled.

Horace didn't let it pass.

"It's not a costume. These are my work clothes," he said, his voice with more edge than he intended.

He looked at Michael, whose eyes reddened and tears gathered. Then he looked at Sally . . .

Before this moment, Sally always handled comments about Horace's appearance and work with humor, in mild defense of him.

"Horace works as a blacksmith, the Pony Express wasn't hiring," she'd say. Or "Horace works at the farm museum, but his hobby is time travel." These little comebacks left room for a "how interesting" remark and Horace would explain his work.

But on this day, Sally turned away, toward Michael, and Horace saw she not only shared Michael's humiliation but was angry her boy was hurt. It was a moment of clarity for Horace. She was pulling her support, joining forces with the "them" he railed against.

THINKING OF MICHAEL'S GAME, Horace walked into a strip-mall hair-cutting place after work, ignored the stares, and settled in on a vinyl couch. Soon a Dominican girl with purple nails summoned him and led him to a washbasin.

"No, it's okay," Horace said.

"It's the rules, Papi," she said.

Horace sat as she hosed hot water over his head and lathered up his scalp. He felt her nails through the long mat of hair and the latex gloves as she dug in. It felt good and he closed his eyes. He heard the jingle of her gold bracelets next to his ear, and felt the brush of her black nylon smock against him.

"It's been a long time, hmm, Papi," she said, in a low murmur.

"Yes, it has."

She took a warm towel and dried his hair with the same vigor, then sprayed it with a detangler. She led him to her chair and covered him with a black cape. She buttoned it on the back, then moved to his front, and pulled and straightened the hem out over his lap. She moved behind him, gathered his damp hair in both hands, and pulled the residual strands out from underneath the cape. She took her hands and moved them from his neck out across his shoulders, ironing down the cape fabric.

"Strong," she said. "A very big man."

She gave an approving nod, then moved to her workstation in front of him, and bent slightly to pick up shears and a thick comb. Her eyes met Horace's in the mirror, after she caught him dropping his glance to her butt.

"So what are we going to do?" she said, moving behind him again to stroke his hair with the comb. He told her he wanted to keep it long to the shoulders, but not this excessive. Beard, too. Trim 'em up.

She went to work, and clumps of strands fell to the floor, or into his lap. He closed his eyes again and said, "Samson and Delilah."

The girl laughed, surprising Horace that she understood the reference, and said, "Isn't that always the way?"

AT HOME, HORACE CLEANED UP. He threw his half-used bar of Octagon in the trash, and unwrapped a bar of deodorant soap. He got in the shower, washed his hair and body with a shampoo Sally had left behind. He scrubbed under his arms, smelling them every few seconds until he was satisfied the stench was gone. He dug out blue jeans and a light flannel shirt from his drawer and looked at himself in the mirror. He saw, underneath the added muscle and few strands of gray, pretty much the Cornell student he once was. That was not the intent, and for a second, he worried that Sally might see it that way: an attempt to get her back. It might move her to consider reconciliation, and the idea threw a chill in Horace. He thought of changing back into his blacksmith garb, to protect himself. The truth was he didn't want her back. All he wanted was his son, for a few hours a week, if that's all he could get, free of Sally's interference.

And then there was Natalia. Smart, like-minded Natalia, who seemed to respect what he stood for. Now he was free; a man abandoned. Separated. A sympathetic character. She was winding down at the farm, heading back to Rochester for the fall semester. Still, there was time. He'd been watching her from the iron storage room at the back of the smithy; he could see across the muddy goat pen into the cow barn.

A few days earlier, he walked over while she was giving a milking demonstration to a group of Girl Scouts. Horace stood at the back of the group and watched with carnal fascination as her hands delicately but firmly pulled and stretched the long, supple teats of an oblivious Holstein. Was it his imagination, or when she saw him, did she yank it to a greater length, and playfully manipulate the tip? He felt himself getting hard. She smiled at him with a warmth long missing from his life, then raised her eyebrows, then bit her lower lip, as if she knew the effect she was having on him. What the hell? Even one of the Girl Scout leaders picked up the vibe, and her eyes inadvertently went from Natalia's hands to Horace's face. He got out of there. Back in the smithy, he watched from the privacy of the dark storage room through a sooted window, got a clean rag and took himself out of his breeches, and thought about those hands working on him. Jesus, how long had it been.

HORACE DROVE TO LEGION FIELD, tucking the Escort behind a monstrous new Chevy Suburban with its tail end plastered with magnetic stickers for Cooperstown kids' sports and cheer teams. Michael was in the outfield with his teammates, tossing the ball. He was the tallest boy and Horace saw how they congregated around him. But there was no laughter; Horace was surprised about how serious they all looked. Michael more so, and every few throws, his face would harden and he would unleash the ball with ferocity into the glove of an equally intense teammate. It was after one of those throws he saw Horace and waved his glove; a friendly, if slight, gesture of acknowledgment. Horace returned an equally understated wave, and felt, at that moment, he and his son shared the language of men.

It had been a while since Horace saw one of Michael's games, but Sally more than made up for it. During the first few years of Little League, she was the Team Mom. She brought snacks and drinks, huddled the boys for pictures. She wore their colors to games.

No such things happened in Horace's baseball days; he would walk or ride his bike down Route 20 over to the lumpy LaFayette High School fields near his house to play on Saturday mornings. Most kids came alone. No mothers toting coolers of Gatorade, no fathers handling baggage. No matching uniforms with embroidered names and numbers. Horace remembered his "uniform": cheap T-shirts usually donated by a local business, canvas sneakers, and whatever pants his mother scratched off the good clothes list. Horace's mother never came to a game, dedicating Saturday mornings to cleaning the house, and his father was busy with yard work or some other home-improvement project. Once in a while, he would show up in the late innings and maybe treat his hot, dusty boy to a vending machine soda from a nearby Esso station. They never talked about the game; instead, they talked about the home project his father was doing, and how Horace could help.

His father never complained about Horace's playing time to coaches, or bitched about a bad call. It just wasn't that important to him. And Horace liked it that way. Men in his generation said more with silence.

Truth was, he hated the inanity of the parents around him at Michael's games. All the talk, on and on and on, centered around their kids; the world beyond didn't matter.

And the overindulgence! Concrete dugouts. Manicured fields, some with grass infields, all with freshly limed batter's boxes and foul lines.

Electronic scoreboards and lights for night games. Fences with advertising banners. A snack stand that sold adult-sized Cooperstown LL hats, T-shirts, and replica jerseys. A loudspeaker system that announced each batter and blasted rap between innings, which Horace viewed as assaultive.

"Do they have to do this?" Horace asked a beefy guy stuffed into a league golf shirt, whom Horace knew to be one of the league officials.

"The kids like it."

"What about the parents? Do we count?"

"Afraid not," the beefy guy said, curt enough to make Horace want to square up.

Worst of all was the schedule; three, sometimes four games a week. It dominated family life. School, church, dinnertime, working around the house, it all came in second to sports.

"You know how many nights I've eaten alone while you're off watching Michael play until dark?" Horace complained to Sally.

"You could come, too."

"That's not fair, Sally. I just don't believe I have to be there every inning of every game. God forbid a parent misses a game nowadays. I look at all those people sitting there hour after hour. Do you know what forty grown-ups could collectively accomplish in all those hours?"

Sally threw up her hands.

"I can't believe how you twist things around. There's a social aspect, Horace," Sally said. "It's being part of the community."

"What are you saying, Sally?" Horace asked, but he knew. He was an outsider.

So now Horace was back. The kids were older, and grown out of their childhood looks. Horace didn't recognize a single one.

He walked to the nearest bleacher and sat. There was Sally, across the diamond, chatting with a few other mothers. Horace was on the wrong side, and began the long, self-conscious trek to the other. As he approached Sally, she turned to him and made a face of pleasant surprise.

"Well," she said, with an uptick in her voice.

"I took your advice."

"Good, Horace . . ."

She didn't finish the sentence, but Horace knew the end. Because now Horace didn't stand out. He almost blended in, almost like a regular dad. Anger flamed up in him, and he tamped it down by clenching his jaw and saying nothing. Sally saw it, too, and let it go. Horace moved down the row and they both turned and looked toward the outfield, where Michael was warming up.

The other men were grouped along the fence, away from their wives. A couple of them had their hats on backwards, like the kids. You could see separation among them; almost like high school. The men whose boys were stars, the taller, more confident-looking men, were clustered together at the fence. The others stood in pairs, constantly checking their cell phones. Horace nodded to a few he recognized from seasons past.

My generation of men, Horace thought, scorned for sins of generations past, unable to shape generations of the future. In the end, we're either too strong or too weak, and reduced to spectators in our children's lives. He wondered how many of these fathers ever made their son miss a game for the opening of trout season, or to go camping, or to visit a historic site or museum. He knew the answer. None.

There was a sucker's game going on around all these sports: the chase for college scholarships. Horace heard it from Sally, the minute Michael showed promise. If they paid for *this* pitching coach, or put him in *that* conditioning program, or let him join *these* travel teams, it would help him get a scholarship. But Horace knew a scam when he saw one. An industry sprang up around these dreams. Camps, training centers, club teams, private lessons.

"Tell him to put all that time into studying," Horace would tell Sally, "and he'll get plenty of scholarships. Like you."

He was thinking all this when Michael, batting fourth, got up in the first inning with boys on first and third, and hit a ball that went to the fence in a straight line. It died with a rattle against the chain link. By the time the ball was thrown back to the infield, Michael was slowing up, cruising into third. The group of jock fathers at the fence erupted when the ball was hit. Horace heard his son being called "Mike-O," and one dude dad cupped his hands over his mouth and shouted, "Beeassst."

"That's what they call him, *Beast*," Sally said as she turned to Horace, expecting a derisive potshot.

But Horace said nothing and didn't look in her direction. Instead his eyes were back at the plate, trying to savor the mental picture of his boy, back foot dug in, hips and shoulders rotating as one, chin tucked, arms extended in a compact but horizontal swing of brute force. It was a thing of beauty; it was Horace in the woodpile. A perfectly controlled violent stroke. Michael was his boy. His boy after all.

AFTER THE GAME, Horace stood aside as other parents congratulated the boys on their win. Horace noticed how some of the jock dads congregated around Michael, slapping him on the back. "Beeasst," a few more said, and fist-bumped him. When the small crowd dissipated, Horace approached his son, and Sally, mercifully, said, "I'll meet you in the car," over her shoulder and left them alone.

"Good game, Mike," Horace said. "What did you have? Three hits."

"Two. One was a fielder's choice."

"Still, a pretty good day."

"Thanks, Dad."

Michael slung his bat bag over his shoulder and they started walking toward the parking lot, his cleats scraping the pavement.

"Want to get a burger with me?" Horace asked, hoping there was no desperation in his voice.

"Dad. You? A burger?"

"Sure, why not?" Horace said. "No lectures. Just a burger."

Michael looked toward his mother's car.

"I should ask Mom."

Horace swallowed the words—*you don't need her permission to see your father*—and instead said, "Yeah, that's probably a good idea."

In town, they walked down Main Street. Horace stopped at a baseball-themed bar and grill, but Michael led him away.

"You'd hate it there, Dad. It's okay."

Instead they went to the Cooperstown Diner, brick-faced, railroad car–style, with a counter and a small TV usually tuned to the weather. Horace's speed.

They ordered—two cheeseburgers, fries—from a matronly waitress in plain black pants and vest with a name tag that said "Sunny."

"Dad, I'm sorry about the farm job," Michael said.

"Don't be. You have to find your own experiences and define their value. Work at the bat shop, and see how you like it. Me, I wouldn't. Cooped up in a store all day, placating tourists. But you're not me, then, are you? That's the thing I have to start to learn."

"Dad, don't you *placate* tourists at the museum?"

Horace bristled, then forced a phony laugh. "I'd like to think I educate them, too, but you're probably right."

Michael's eyes flashed over Horace's face, a quick evaluation of his father's sincerity. Horace had recovered quickly, genuinely happy they were actually conversing.

"But that's a brilliant observation, Mikey," he said, meaning it.

"Thanks, Dad."

"So when do you start?" Horace asked.

"I started already, just learning everything. But in a couple of weeks, when the tourists start coming, I'll work weekends when I don't have a game, then more in summer."

"What's the job, exactly?"

"Stock, mostly. She told me I could learn to work the register for when we get busy in the summer."

"She?"

"The manager. June."

Horace saw the look in his eye, and the blush. A girl. That was it. It wasn't him, it wasn't the farm. It was the girl.

"So, how old is this *manager*?"

"I don't know . . . twenty-five. Around that."

"Pretty?"

"Yeah, I guess."

"You guess? That look on your face says you know."

Michael's blush deepened.

Horace looked at his son and wished he was back there, too, just starting out in a world filled with girls you wanted to get near, to inhale the clean scent of their flesh, pure as fresh water. Girls you wanted to touch so badly, you dug yourself into the mattress at night imagining the firm softness of their skin. Girls who made your mouth go dry. Girls who made you think if you were older, better-looking, more athletic, or had a cool car, they might pay attention to you. Girls you *wanted.* How could Horace tell his son that men were condemned to that want, a pervasive longing for love to fill the emptiness inside? And it never went away. Now he was getting it for Natalia, as someone to reach for and cling to. Horace wanted to tell him there is a hidden, dark place in every man's soul that, if he's lucky, a woman will reach once, maybe twice in his life. But she would never stay. He wanted to tell him that women, ultimately, sooner or later, break your heart. Even after you've married and lived together and built a life, they withdraw in the natural, conspiratorial bond between mother and children. Men are left on the outside, with a hollow gut of alienation, looking in. You love your wife and children, but they love each other more. Horace now understood why generations of fathers before him were sullen; and his own generation humiliated themselves by being buddies, not fathers.

He wanted to tell his son that all those adolescent emotions, that optimistic, romantic tachycardia Michael was now experiencing, were something to cherish and enjoy, but to never, ever hold on to as real expectations. Even strong men, like Horace, were weakened by these fantasies. He wanted to warn Michael that June, the Gone Batty girl, like life itself, would show him unintended but nonetheless painful cruelty. Because June, Sally, Natalia, no woman, from Ann to Zoe, ever cured the inherent ache of a man's loneliness. They soothed it for a while, but in the end made you realize you were never too far from being alone.

These were things left unsaid, from father to son. Societal order demanded it; if these things were said, the frail pretense of domesticity would degenerate into chaos, Horace knew. If young men were told enduring love didn't exist for them, they would move from woman to woman, abandoning the children left behind. No, it was the civilized man's job to prop it all up, and keep his mouth shut.

"Well, just be careful," Horace simply said.

Chapter Twenty-Two

In the next weeks, the postgame burger would become a ritual. Mostly it was small talk, about the game, about school. On weekend mornings, Horace would pick him up and drive him to work.

They were an odd pair. Horace in his circa 1860s woolen pants and high boots and loose, soot-stained cotton shirt; Michael in a cranberry golf shirt with the Gone Batty logo over the left breast, a pair of Walmart khakis, taupe or light brown. The new American uniform, Horace thought. What'd they call it? Business casual?

The first time Horace drove him, Michael asked to be dropped at the corner.

"I can walk from here."

"It's okay, I'll take you."

"No, Dad, you have all those one-ways. Just go straight. I'm good. It's no big deal. I have to pick up coffee at the Bean Ball anyway. Part of my job."

Before Horace objected again, he got it. He looked at his son, hair trimmed neatly around his ears, bangs brushed neatly to the side, blemishes scrubbed into oblivion. *June.*

Michael didn't want to be seen getting out of the smoky Escort, driven by a man whose beard, hair, and clothes would take some explaining, explaining Michael would rather not do, especially to June.

A FEW DAYS LATER, while Michael sat in front of a half-eaten cheeseburger, Horace said he wanted to drop in to his job—not in blacksmith's clothes.

"Why, Dad?"

"They should know you have a father. Someone who's looking out for you, making sure they're not skimming your paycheck."

"Why do you do that, Dad?"

"What?"

"Make everything so negative. Mom says you're cynical."

"Put Mom aside for a second. *You* should give me a little more credit for understanding the world. I've been in it a lot longer than you. And maybe Mom should . . ."

"Why do you always make her out to be so bad?" Michael's face hardened, and in it, Horace saw Sally's fed-up expression.

"I don't," Horace said. "It's complicated, Michael. But somewhere along the line, I feel your mother stopped respecting who I am."

"What? A blacksmith!?"

Horace took a breath, to let the conversation cool.

"What's the matter?" he said, pointing to the plate of cold meat and fries. "You usually want another."

Michael picked up one fry with his fingers and put it in his mouth, staring down at the table.

"Mikey. What's wrong?" Horace asked.

"I don't know, Dad . . . you and Mom are getting divorced, right? She says you'll never change," Michael said.

"Maybe she's right. But I'm trying. You see that, don't you? Like, I just asked you if I could stop in to your job. The old me would have just shown up," Horace said.

Michael continued to stare down, and made a move toward another lone fry. Here it was, the Sally silent treatment, and Horace, as always, broke the silence.

"You know, Mike, maybe she's the one who changed. I feel I'm still the same guy who married her. Same values, same beliefs. Maybe I dug in a little too much. Maybe I didn't explain myself well. But your mother has been unhappy with me for a long time, and that's not an accusation, just an observation. Do you understand that?"

Michael said nothing.

"I know it's tough for you. It must seem weird living in that apartment."

"Not really, Dad. It's kinda cool. At least the whole place doesn't smell like smoke."

Horace let that one go, too.

"Well, the old house is your house, you can stay anytime you want," Horace said, knowing it wouldn't be long before the house was lost. "You can come back to live. Or just weekends. Or never. Whatever you want. You're my son and I love you; I'm not going to let some divorce lawyer treat you like a piece of chattel."

"You mean cattle?"

"No, chattel. Like a piece of furniture, or something like that, that your mother and I might fight over."

SALLY WAS TRUE TO HER WORD, reasonable in this regard. Horace, too. He took a change of clothes to work every day Michael had a game, showed up, and took him out after most times to the little diner. The few times Michael opted to go with friends, Horace was careful not to pout. He knew he had to relax his hold on the kid, and it ate away at him. He was no longer the man, the father he wanted to be. He was at the end of his son's string. He felt unassertive, even passive, beaten into plow-horse obedience. But he had no choice. He was getting Michael back, and this was the only way. Still, he couldn't accept it as redemption or compromise; to him, it was defeat. And he had to swallow it. And swallow it again. Maybe he'd write a paper, "American Manhood in the Twenty-first Century," as a secret diatribe, an outlet for the disgust he felt for giving in, and as a way, at least on paper, to not give up.

On the woodpile, Horace found redemption for his masculinity. He split and stacked three cords in the weeks after Sally left, working into the warming, lengthening nights. It was invigorating, and like a fighter in training, he felt strong, fit, and ready for the coming tourism season. He was the blacksmith, damn it, he thought as he admired himself shirtless in the mirror each night and when he massaged his hands back to life each morning. He was going to make a move on the milkmaid, pretty Natalia, before she left for Rochester.

It was in this state of burgeoning renewal that Grundling called him to the office one day. Horace sat and picked up the miniature Conestoga wagon to fiddle with.

"Now, remember, Horace, we had a deal. I cleared a billet for Michael, so now I don't have the summer docent for the Cardiff Giant presentation. Has he changed his mind?"

"No, John, he was lured into one of the tourist traps downtown."

"Too bad."

"Do I really have to do this? I'm the blacksmith, goddamnit."

"I know. But I'm actually happy it worked out this way. I think we need an expert, not a college girl. Didn't you write a paper once?"

"Yes. 'American Rubism.' "

"Well, why don't we republish it and put it in the tent as a handout? And you can give a talk, say, four times a day."

Horace wanted to crush the Conestoga model into splinters and tell Grundling, *These are not the hands of a docent.* But he thought of all Natalia had told him, and all he wanted to say. Grundling was giving him a platform.

"Okay. I want to alter it somewhat, though, make it more relative to modern popular culture," Horace said. "You know, 1869 was an interesting year."

Grundling gave a nod Horace saw as dismissive approval, his way of saying, "Whatever."

ON THE LAST SATURDAY OF SPRING, Horace picked up Michael to take him to Gone Batty. He was wearing a new logo shirt, this one freezer-pop blue.

"Summer uniform?" Horace asked.

"Oh, yeah," Michael said, looking down at the shirt. "Hey, Dad, June asked me to pick up some posters at the print shop on the way to work today. Is that okay?"

Dad as errand boy, Horace thought, but instead gave a cheery "Sure. Why not?"

He drove to the outskirts of town on Route 20, to a print shop in a strip mall. Horace was a little ticked—he was going to be a few minutes late for work now, and wished Michael had let him know earlier—but he didn't want to start the day with a reprimand.

He waited in the car and saw Michael through the window, looking at a small stack. He picked one up, eyeing it carefully, then nodded to the man behind the counter. He slid that poster into a bag with the rest, then bounced to the car, and propped them up against the backseat, with only the tops peeking out.

In the rearview mirror, Horace saw the words *Exclusive Appearance*.

"What's that?" he asked.

"Oh, this is pretty cool," Michael said. "You know that guy Joe Grudeck? The guy going into the Hall of Fame? He's going to do a signing in our store during Induction Week, and I'll get to meet him."

Summer

Chapter Twenty-Three

Grudeck sat at the club bar, a matted pile of fifties in front of him.

"Good day out there, Mr. Grudeck?" asked Pete the Greek, one of the regular bartenders.

"Yes, Pete, it was. Raked in a few Grants."

Pete leaned in and said in a low side grumble, "Between you and me, Mr. Grudeck, I love it when you take some of these fucks."

It was late and the place was emptying out. The three executives he played with were long gone, heads heavy by Dewar's, wallets lighter by Grudeck. Now Grudeck sat and vigorously stirred his club soda with crushed lime to flatten it. He took three of the fifties and pushed them toward Pete, as if it were his cut of the hustle.

"There you go, my friend," Grudeck said. "Ulysses . . . S . . . and Grant."

Pete, now straightened up and toweling off a glass, put up no resistance.

"Better than Jesus, Mary, and Joseph. Thank you, Mr. Grudeck," he said.

"My pleasure, Pete. After all, we're both workingmen," Grudeck said, and gave him a wink.

Grudeck was a scratch golfer. Every time he played in a pro-am benefit, the pros would tell him he was good enough to get a PGA card when he retired. At one event, he was paired with Dom Iosso, a tall, silver-haired, self-made New York apartment-house developer who branched out into resorts and first-class country clubs. He took distressed properties like old estates, even Victorian-era mental hospitals, and turned them into clubs with top-ranked golf courses.

During their round, Iosso told Grudeck about the club he was building in "New Jersey equestrian country."

"I did my homework: You're a Jersey boy, am I right, Joe?" he asked. "So while some people might laugh at the idea, you know the appeal. Wealthy area. The foxhunt and steeplechase crowd. Amazingly beautiful countryside, especially autumn."

"That's not the Jersey I'm from," said Grudeck. "But I've heard."

And so that day's hustle was on.

Iosso said he'd sunk ten million into restoring the mansion alone, converting it to a clubhouse with a legitimate four-star restaurant. Off the mansion were two wings of twenty-five luxury townhouses. One of the townhouses would be divided into separate living quarters for the club pro and a celebrity-athlete to play with members and draw new ones.

"And that is where you come in," Iosso said. "To raise the profile, give the place a little athletic panache."

Iosso finished his pitch: free condo, unlimited expense account at club restaurant and bar, annual salary of $75,000—all for playing about fifty, sixty times a year to fill out foursomes of members and prospective members. Grudeck didn't have to live there; "consider the condo," Iosso said, "your own luxurious private locker room."

"I know seventy-five grand is chump change for you," Iosso said. "But we're both workingmen, so you get this. I'm paying to put your name on the list of charter members, and I'm paying you a little extra to do what you would normally do: live, eat, play golf. Just do it at my place."

It was the "workingmen" line that sold Grudeck. Like him, Iosso was a pretender in a rich-guy world. Underneath his dress and manners and curse-free, deliberate enunciation was a subversive streak. He beat the privileged at their own insider games, and now they kissed his ass to play at his clubs.

"And there's one other thing," Iosso said. "While we officially frown on gambling at the club, every now and then the subject of Grants or Franklins, even Clevelands, comes up during a round. These are grown men. Do what you will."

The deal was signed, Grudeck's name went out on all sales brochures as "Charter Member," and he moved into the completely furnished and decorated townhouse. All he had to do was unpack his clothes and his most valued trophies, and nail his plaques to the walls—actually, a club handyman did that. Grudeck signed a few autographs for him and tipped him a grand. That was the beginning of the country club life, and he never bothered to find another place to call home.

HE WRAPPED HIS HANDS AROUND the glass and the cold sweat cooled his palms, swollen and red from the two rounds of eighteen he played. The first was with the top pyramid from Johnson & Johnson, the second was with two hedge-fund guys and a whale they were trying to impress: a trim, compact guy named Stein-something, a New York acquisitions-and-mergers lawyer, who wore a navy-blue Y cap and hinted about his national championship squash days at Yale and the New York Athletic Club.

"Seems we're both hall of famers, Joe," he said, amiably. "But I had to give up my game to make money. If only I'd picked a revenue sport."

Every time, with these fucking guys, Grudeck thought. Every time, there was a left-handed comment like that. As if Grudeck had won the lottery and didn't bust his ass in the weight room, run bleachers in the off-season, spend a million hours in the batting cages, and fight to keep his weight down since he was a sophomore in high school. Like his strength and athleticism—and therefore fame and money—were some God-given gifts that didn't require work. Just show up, and make the

Hall of fucking Fame. Like he was the guy with the unfair advantage in life. Not them, the Ivy finance types. The entitled. Generation after generation of expensive prep schools and passes into Princeton, Harvard, or Yale. The "best and the brightest," they called themselves, as if that legacy wasn't bought and paid for by their fathers and grandfathers, as if they worked as hard for their connections as Grudeck did to be a top athlete. Best and brightest. That's how they justified their salaries, even when their companies tanked. Grudeck wanted to come right out and say: "If I had a couple of seasons in the shitter, I'd be coaching high school baseball, not negotiating a multimillion-dollar golden parachute. Best and brightest? Fuck you guys." Or when they talked about how "fierce" corporate competition was. "Take a fastball in the kidney, piss blood for a week, and tell me about me your dog-eat-dog world," Grudeck wanted to say.

So when the Yale squash man offered to "make it interesting," Grudeck shot back, "How interesting?"

"It's your course," said one of the hedge-fund guys, afraid of the answer. They'd played with Grudeck before.

"Five hundred a hole; carries until there's a low score," Grudeck said. Prick.

"Not that interesting," said the other. "How about a hundred?"

The Stein guy played it cool, making sure he didn't blink as Grudeck looked at him.

"Whatever you guys want," Grudeck said. "I'm just a hired hand."

"Hand or gun?" the Stein guy said.

"I guess we'll find out," Grudeck said, knowing he sounded like an arrogant asshole. Fuck 'em.

They settled on the hundred, and Grudeck offered to hit first. He teed up, and whipped the club with that big arcing swing of his, with a violence he knew made them wince, and posed for just a second to watch the ball disappear like a round rocket into the sky, knowing they were either watching the ball or the expanse of his huge, muscular back straining the fabric of his golf shirt. And by the time the ball touched down some 300 yards down the fairway, on a straight line between tee and flag, Grudeck was walking nonchalantly to his bag (no cart, no caddy for Grudeck), never watching the shot or turning around to see the look on their faces. Like, business as usual. Like, shove *that* up your ass.

And that's how Grudeck always played it. To win. Big. No bullshit. No tanking, no stroking egos. No handicaps, no playing just to play, or to get loaded or to talk business or stock prices or mergers or about Grudeck back in the day. This wasn't lunch. This was a collision at the plate.

Grudeck shot six over, won every hole, and beat the execs by double digits. After sinking a ten-foot putt to win the eighteenth, he shoved six more fifties in his pocket, invited the group for a couple of drinks, saw them off in their cart, and began a slow, almost mournful walk back to the clubhouse. The thrill of winning, that boost of adrenaline or shot of testosterone and whatever primal urge it satisfied, was wearing off faster these days, and the Advil pops were more frequent. As he limped along, he wondered, how many more times? How much longer, before time and age and his fading place in people's memories reduced him to an old-timer, a mere glad-hander, rather than the force of nature some people still called Joe Grrreww.

GRUDECK KEPT PLAYING WITH THE BUBBLES. Stirring, watching zippers form and float to the top and die in a fizzy explosion. He stared into his drink, wondering how many millions of guys in the world right now were doing the same thing. Sitting alone at a bar, staring into a drink, thinking about a woman. Stacy. Stacy with the beautiful facey. What to do about Stacy? For Grudeck, this was new territory. *Forlorn.* That was the word, wasn't it? Jesus, what was happening to him? He knew. He was going stale; same shit, different day. Breakfast at the club. Golf. Lunch at the club. Golf. Dinner at the club. Drinks at the club. Get laid. Sleep. One man's dream becomes another's drudgery.

Since seeing Stacy again, he thought about those two words he never once before considered. *Settling down.* If you loved somebody, shouldn't they call it settling up? With Stacy, it was definitely up. She had lived somewhere in his consciousness for three decades, and now had come forward. And now the truth presented itself, right in front of him, unavoidable and pressing and confusing. She was the nearest thing to love—whatever it was—that he'd ever known; as close to filling that gray vacancy in his soul as anyone. And he wanted her to love him back. But he sensed a distance; worse, a distrust. He deserved it. He left, and never looked back. And if she ever found out about Syracuse . . . he knew she couldn't live with that, and there was no way he could explain it. Not to her.

What to do about Stacy . . . *she* came to St. Joe's that night. Why, if she didn't have feelings for him? And she was helping him figure out the damn speech, putting in time, listening to his stories, over dinners, during walks around the course. He held her hand; they kissed, a little. She told him he was sweet. He wanted to take her home and engulf her with his size and strength, but resisted, sensing her hesitation.

Grudeck smashed a few more bubbles with the straw. How could he get her to trust him? An absolution of modern sins? Maybe she would eventually detect that. Maybe she would see the change. Maybe then, she'd give him a chance.

Since he started seeing Stacy, he'd eliminated the "get laid" part of his routine, which wore on him as much as performing for the execs on the golf course. No more catering-company waitresses, or members' wives, ex or current. And no more Darlena; Grudeck was feeling dirty about the whole thing now, like he was cheating on Stacy.

He decided to end it one night, just like that. She came through the kitchen door, putting large hoop earrings back in her ears now that she was off. She glanced at him and gave him a smile no more than polite, professional recognition that only they knew said, "See you later." She cashed out with Pete, changing the cumbersome singles and fives into bigger, more manageable bills. Grudeck caught up with her in the parking lot.

"No more for now, okay?" he said. "But let me know if you need anything."

He handed her all the money in his wallet, at least one thousand dollars in hundreds and fifties.

"Okay, Mr. Grudeck," she said. "Thank you."

And she pocketed the money without another word.

A FEW DAYS LATER, Grudeck had a date with Stacy to work on the speech, but when Grudeck picked her up, he said he was tired of it.

"Let's go for a ride. You pick the place. Take me somewhere I haven't been."

Stacy sat in the passenger seat of the Caddy and tied back her hair. It was a warm June day and the roof was open. She thought for a moment.

"There's a place I used to paint. Down the shore. You want to go that far?"

"Baby, I've crisscrossed this country a thousand times," Grudeck said, knowing it was irrelevant as soon as it came out of his mouth.

They headed down the Parkway, over the bridge that spanned Raritan Bay.

"I haven't been down this way since high school . . . my summer job always got in the way," Grudeck said as he looked at the expanse of central Jersey from the bridge peak. Below them, an oil refinery, a power plant, and a railway bridge, but off in the distance were the white sails of dozens of boats skimming the green, open waters. He pointed them out to Stacy.

"Yacht season," she said.

He looked at her, strands of loose hair flying around her face, sunglasses pushed up tight against her eyes, bathed in the light from the roof. She felt his gaze, looked over, and smiled. He had never seen her look so beautiful.

"What?" she said.

He wanted to blurt out, "I love you," but instead said, "Nothing. You're just so beautiful."

They got off the Parkway onto Route 36, a state two-lane highway that ran though the bootheel towns of the Jersey bayshore. At the west end, there were weathered trailer parks, roadside bungalows, and a couple of go-go bars. The town names seemed familiar to him, Sayreville, Keyport, Hazlet, Keansburg, but he had never been to any. No, Sayreville. Played them in a state game. But that was it. It struck him suddenly, how little exploring he had done in his life. There was never time in high school, and in all those minor league and big league towns, all he knew was the hotel-to-ballpark route. And here, less than thirty miles from where he grew up, it was all foreign to him.

"It gets prettier down the road," Stacy said.

They detoured off the highway and drove along the bluff overlooking the bay and the marinas. The sailboats and catamarans populated the briny water, and sliced silently through green-gray whitecapped swells whipped up by the bayshore breeze.

"You ever think of getting a boat?" she asked, and hoped it didn't sound like a monetary probe. She knew Grudeck was a millionaire, and millionaires bought boats, but she was only trying to gauge his interests beyond baseball and golf.

"No," he said. "No reason. Just never thought of it."

Stacy talked about a tucked-away fishing village called Belford, and a seafood restaurant only locals knew about. From the road, she pointed out the six-mile-long barrier island called Sandy Hook that she said was a miniature version of Cape Cod.

"In the geologic sense," she said.

Grudeck sat dumbly, wondering about the world he never saw.

In the far distance was the Oz-like New York City skyline, the neighboring squat profile of Brooklyn, and the Verrazano Bridge. It was late afternoon, and the setting sun glistened off the glass-and-steel and sandstone towers of Lower Manhattan, giving them a pink glow.

They came to the crest of the hill and the great blue expanse of the Atlantic presented itself.

"Whoa," Grudeck said.

"Just wait," Stacy said.

She pointed to a brown sign up the road that said, "Twin Lights Historic Site."

"Turn there, and go up the hill."

The road up was steep, pitted, and narrow, and overhung with trees. It curved up the hill; along the way were a few houses, with glass walls and decks facing the view. Toward the summit, the heights of the lighthouse towers could be seen over the trees. The two square monolithic castle turrets of dark brownstone were capped by the ornate glass enclosures that protected the Fresnel lens, and crowned with decorative metalwork.

As they got closer, the whole structure appeared. It looked like a fortress or prison from Civil War days, dark, looming, and isolated, on the windswept hill.

"Whoa," Grudeck said again.

"Isn't it amazing?" Stacy said.

They parked and followed the path up to the building, where Grudeck noticed the cornerstone: 1870. The walkway took them to the front, where the bay and sea were laid out before them. Out on the horizon, tankers and cargo ships seemed still as they dotted the shipping lanes into New York Harbor. To the left was the full, long arm of Sandy Hook, with beaches exposed to both ocean and bay sides, thick with scrub vegetation in the middle. Straight ahead was big blue; the never-ending Atlantic. Below, to the north, was Highlands, once a fishing village, now compact with bungalows and marinas. South was Sea Bright, which had a seawall on its doorstep and the Navesink River as its backyard, sandwiching a stretch of oceanfront beach clubs and mansions.

"Jesus, you can see forever," Grudeck said happily.

The upbeat tone took Stacy by surprise, and she wondered why.

Then she realized it was the first time she'd ever heard joy in his voice. She took his arm and guided him toward a bench. After they sat, Stacy gathered her light jacket tight, up at the neck, crossed her arms, and gave a forced shiver.

"Are you cold?" Grudeck asked, and moved close and put his arm around her.

"It's windier up here than it was in the car," she said.

"Here, I'll warm you up."

They sat, quiet, for a few moments, listening to the muted crash of waves a few hundred yards below, and the wind in the trees on the slope.

"Joe, can I ask you something?" Stacy finally said.

"Sounds serious."

"It has to do with your speech."

"Sure."

"Did you enjoy playing?"

"What?"

"Did you love it? I mean, any of it. Or did you just do it because you were good?"

"I loved it. Of course I loved it."

"No, just think about it for a second," she said, patting his leg for emphasis. "Because I remember, even back in high school, it all just seemed like work to you. Serious work. Those pictures I took of you, you were never smiling, or even seemed happy. You were always so . . . *grim.*"

"That's a crazy question," Grudeck said, turning to face her. "Of course I loved it. I wasn't grim. I was intense."

"Don't dismiss it so easily," she said, pulling back against his arm. "Did you really love it, or were you just so damn good at it, you had no choice? Because now that I think about it, it wasn't only high school, it was all the times I saw you on TV, too."

"I took it seriously, if that's what you're asking."

"No. It's beyond serious. You always looked . . . like I said . . . *grim.*"

"Stop saying it like that . . ." Grudeck said. He turned back toward the ocean, and now the wind seemed cold to him, too. "Like I was in prison."

"Were you?" she said.

Grudeck was quiet.

"Or golf? Do you *enjoy* playing golf?" Stacy asked. "It is fun for you, or more work?"

"Where are you going with this?" Grudeck asked.

"The whole speech, all the stories, they all point to the same thing. It seems you didn't enjoy any of it."

"You're not going to give me a bunch of psychological bullshit about my father, now, are you?" Grudeck said, making sure he added a laugh to not offend her. "'Cause I don't want to hear it."

"No way I'm going there . . . that's between you and up there," she said, tapping her index finger against his temple. "But since you brought it up, did you ever get a chance to be good at anything else? Or learn that you might have other passions? Look, I'm not saying it's anybody's fault. It's just what happened, and all with good intent, I'm sure."

"If you're asking me if I ever wanted to quit, the answer is no," Grudeck said. "If you're asking me if my dad forced me to play, the answer is no."

Stacy saw she was headed up a dark alley, one Grudeck might not follow her through. She wasn't confident he would accept the concept of childhood self-worth being so tied to parental approval, especially mother-to-daughter and father-to-son. It was unspoken coercion.

She stayed quiet, except to say, "Well, just think about it."

Grudeck looked at the horizon, now diminished in the fading light. She could see him thinking, those wheels spinning in there. His look reminded her of her son a decade earlier, head bent over the kitchen table, struggling with grammar school math. Joe Grudeck, big, strong, famous, Hall of Fame Joe Grudeck, still had enough confused little boy in him to bring out something maternal in her, something like protective love, and she wasn't sure that was good.

"I see what you mean, though," Grudeck said. "The first few years after I retired, I helped an old coach with a baseball camp for kids, like twelve and up. They were like robots, programmed to get scholarships, or at least try. Their parents would line the fences, living and dying with every strike, every error. I stopped because it was depressing. Like you said, all the fun was sucked out of it. My dad wasn't like that. At least I didn't notice. But I can't sit here and pretend I didn't know it was important to him. So maybe I got stuck in it, a little. But I was one of the lucky ones, 'cause it paid off. Sometimes I wonder what would have happened if it didn't. How my dad would have felt. How I would have felt about letting him down. When I would go to those camps, I would see all these parents with unrealistic hopes. Not just unrealistic. Insane. And the money they spent? Craziness. The fathers would pull me aside . . . 'Joe, you think so-and-so has what it takes?' And you know what I wanted to say? 'Takes for what? Takes to be happy? Takes to become a doctor or a teacher or whatever? Takes to be a pretty good high school ballplayer?' Because that's what almost all of them were ever gonna be. And there is nothing wrong with that.

"But that's sports today. My dad told me being strong and good at sports was part of the measuring stick of a man. Now it seems to be the only measuring stick. The fans today, they cheer guys accused of doping, of sex assault, beating their wives, beating their kids, drunk driving. Then you see people, with kids, asking these guys for autographs. It's sick, when you think about it. So I guess you're right. Maybe all the joy went out of it. I don't know . . ."

She let him reflect on his own resignation for a moment, especially after he turned away to look up the coast.

"Well, on the bright side," Stacy said, "maybe that's the speech. Maybe that's what the speech should be about."

STACY GOT IT. GOT HIM. That night at Twin Lights, she figured it out. The next night, he was back at the club bar—same s., different d.—

stirring another club soda, after another thirty-six holes with two sets of execs. Another stack of their money; these guys Grudeck took for two Gs. He was tired of this world. Tired of being Joe Grudeck. He couldn't get that view from the shore hill out of his mind. This big world out there. His was reduced to foul lines, and now fairways. He wanted to move around in the big world, anonymous. He wanted to do it with Stacy. He'd call Dom Iosso, and tell him he'd rather be a regular, paid member than a glad-hander, and get free of this. After the Hall induction, he would opt out of all those "Meet Joe Grudeck" obligations. No more autograph sessions, no more spring training visits. Old-timers' day? Fuck that. Okay, maybe. He didn't want to become completely forgotten. But here was his chance to change his future, to answer questions he'd spent his life trying to avoid. He'd figure it out.

Behind him, the laughter from a table of women, three martinis in, was getting very unclublike.

"Maybe I should calm them down," Pete the Greek said. "Or maybe I should just let them embarrass themselves. Life's little dilemmas."

"Life's little dilemmas," Grudeck repeated.

Just then, he heard heels approaching on the hardwood bar floor, then fingertips playing piano on his back, then the mild scent of perfume, mixed with gin and vermouth breath, in his ear.

Joanie MacIntosh.

"Hey, stranger," she said.

"Stranger? I'm here every night."

"Buy me a drink."

"I don't think you need another drink, Joanie."

She moved her lips closer to his ear.

"Is it that obvious?" she said, low, from her throat.

That small moan, the exhalation of breath, went right to where he didn't want it. His scrotum.

He turned toward her, but she pivoted to keep close to his ear. Still, he could see the black sleeveless dress tailored and tight where it counted; her hair seemed lighter, or maybe it was the salon tan.

"Why don't you come over and meet some of the girls. The not-so-young and restless. With gin and Xanax, you never know what can happen. You might hit a double."

"No, Joanie, I'm okay here. Me and members' wives, it's a violation of my contract."

"Oh, stop!" she said, and playfully slapped his arm. "When did you become such a choirboy?"

"Truth is, I'm seeing someone. I'm trying to be good."

"Oh, okay . . . so it's discretion you want. Well, just leave your door unlocked."

"No, seriously. Joanie. You're a lot of fun, but I can't."

"Oh, you can, baby," she said. "You can."

She turned and walked back toward her friends, tossing her hair back in his direction.

Chapter Twenty-Four

Sally hoped Horace wouldn't notice the two scouts from Archbishop Moeller, but they couldn't have been less discreet in their silky navy-blue jackets with MOELLER BASEBALL embossed in gold letters, with *Cincinnati, Ohio*, embroidered in script.

It all came together so quickly. Michael's Legion coach knew a coach who knew a coach who knew *the* coach at Moeller. Sally was called a few days before, and they all agreed to keep it secret. Sally didn't want him to tell Horace. The Legion coach didn't want Michael to feel pressure. The Moeller coach didn't want him to get his hopes up. Moeller was regarded as the country's best high school team in the north, the coach told her. "Barry Larkin and Ken Griffey Junior played here. One is in the Hall of Fame, and the other should be. Certainly, if we like your son, our school is a pathway to bigger things."

The names meant nothing to Sally, but she saw opportunity for herself, too. New city. Fresh start. Horace-free. And Sally had already plotted concessions to make it easier for Horace to let go; Sally would ask for no child support or alimony, and she would send Michael back for a couple of weeks a year. Horace was welcome to come to Ohio for the same.

She had hoped the scouts would blend in, but instead they came in those screaming jackets. During warm-ups, all the boys eyed them, and when Michael jogged in, he caught Sally's eye, tapped his index finger against his chest, and mouthed, "Me?"

Sally shrugged, but she knew her huge smile gave it away.

Horace arrived for the game, and began the long walk from the parking lot down the right-field line. When he stood along the visitors' side fence, Sally couldn't help but notice how his shadow, in the late afternoon, seemed to reach the foul line.

Michael delivered. Line drive up the middle in the first, then again in the third. It was 5–0 by then and he'd driven in three runs. In the sixth, as the ballpark's overhead lights glowed down on the field, he showed he could go to the opposite field, and the ball reached the right-field fence on two bounces for a stand-up triple. In the ninth, he put one over the left-field fence into the now-dark evening. Four for four, six RBIs. Quite a day.

Sally's enjoyment only lasted beyond the third hit. By then Horace saw the scouts making notes on Michael's every move and he came to the seat next to her, taking the bleacher steps two at a time.

"So, who are those guys?" he asked, purposely unaggressive.

"I guess they're here to see Michael."

"You guess? Or you know?" he said, still even.

"His coach invited them. That's all I know. They say they're the best high school baseball team in the country. In the North, anyway."

"Jesus, Sally, from where?"

"Ohio. Cincinnati."

Horace stared down at them.

"Cincinnati? What are we talking about here, Sally?"

"It's a long shot," Sally said.

"What if they want him? Then what, Sally?"

"We'll cross that bridge . . . But if they want him, it would be a great opportunity. He'd get a scholarship and they play all over the country. They make one trip to Texas, Arizona, and California, and another down South and Florida. The coach said most of their starters play Division One somewhere, and get full rides."

"For someone who doesn't know a lot, you know an awful lot," Horace said, the bile rising. "When were you going to tell me?"

"I didn't want to upset you unnecessarily . . ."

"Or was it that you just didn't want to deal with me. I mean, don't I have a say in this? I'm his father, for Christ's sake."

Here we go again, Sally thought. She wanted to launch yet another "it's Michael's life" speech, but didn't want the thing to escalate. Not here, not in the bleachers, not surrounded by other parents.

"Horace, please . . ." she said, lowering her voice as if to plead *not now*. "Let's just see what happens."

"Let's see what happens?" Horace said, his voice lowered, too, but with edge. "Here's what's happening. We've got a mountain of *your* debt, a house going into foreclosure, and you're going to run off to Cincinnati and I'm going to be left here to clean up *your* fucking mess. *Your* fucking mess."

"No one said anything about me running off, Horace. This is about Michael," she said.

Sally stared straight ahead, into some unknown but hopefully better future, knowing Horace was more than a little right.

When the game ended, Michael was waved over by the scouts. They talked briefly, shook hands, and one of them clapped a hand down on his shoulder while the other reached down into a navy-and-gold *Crusader Baseball* equipment bag and pulled out a T-shirt and sweatshirt for Michael.

Michael pointed up to his parents, still in the bleachers, the men gave a quick wave, and that was that. Michael then climbed the bleachers two steps at a time like his dad.

"They said they'll be in touch," Michael said.

Over that night's burger, Michael told Horace he knew nothing about the scout visit, and Horace believed him. Sally, so fucking duplicitous.

"So what's next?" Horace asked.

"They said they had to talk to the head coach, and they might bring me to Cincinnati to meet everybody."

"When will that be?"

"I don't know, Dad."

"Do you want to go?"

"I don't know, Dad. I have my friends all here, and I'm looking forward to high school. I'm just getting used to the way things are with Mom and you."

"What do you mean?"

"I mean this is okay. The way things are."

Horace felt elation in his chest. The way "things are" was better than the they way were; Michael being haggled over by his parents. Now both had their own time with him, and Horace felt Michael drawing closer to him without Sally's interference.

"So, if you went, what would it be? Like college? Would you live in a dorm?" Horace asked.

Michael had a mouthful of burger and stopped chewing.

"Didn't Mom tell you? She would move to Ohio."

For fuck's sake. The words almost escaped, but Horace just leaned back against the booth and said, "No, in fact . . . forget it."

"That's what she said."

"So you and your mom would move to Cincinnati, and what? I stay here? Or am I supposed to go, too? How do you see it, Michael?" Horace said this in the most measured way possible, without sarcasm or anger.

Still, Michael asked, "Dad, are you mad?"

"No, Mike. I just want to understand what everybody's thinking."

"I don't know, Dad. I guess everybody just does what they want."

That night, Horace told Michael he wanted to swing by the house before he drove him to Sally's.

"There's a few things I'd like you to have," he said, not adding that those things would end up in a Dumpster when the bank reclaimed the house.

They came up the long dirt driveway, the Escort's headlights bouncing, illuminating the woods in bursts of yellowed light. A whitetail deer with a fawn stood motionless in one frame, like a still-life painting.

The house was dark, a black box against the midnight-blue Otsego Lake sky.

"A great night for stars," Horace said, as they got out of the car.

He put one arm heavily around his son's shoulders and pointed north to the darkest part of the sky over the lake, then traced an outline, a million miles away, with his finger.

"See. Perseus. Remember?"

"A little."

"He was the Greek hero who killed Medusa, and used her head to turn his enemies to stone. You have a book inside. It was one of the things I wanted to give you."

They sat at the kitchen table, with the buzz and flickers of the old fluorescent lights overhead. Horace went into his room and came out with the Greek mythology constellation book, the local geology book, and the pamphlet from an old exhibit at the art museum on the American flag in Indian art.

"I remember this," Michael said. "This was pretty cool."

It was eight or nine years ago—a childhood—already. Michael was a little boy, soft and impressionable, with a spongy brain willing to absorb the world around him. Horace tried to fill that head with his view of the world, like any father. Now Michael was lean, and long-muscled like his father, with the same head of wild, dark hair.

As he looked through the pamphlet, the old wonderment returned to his eyes. There were pictures of a horse blanket with beads of the Stars and Stripes sown in, a teepee with the flag painted on it, a large weave where Old Glory was the centerpiece, contrasting the turquoise, red, and brown patterns that zigged and zagged around it.

"I remember you told me the Indians thought the design was cool."

"At first," Horace said. "Then came the killing, and the resettlements. But things like this, about their early curiosity, are the little things that make history so fascinating, aren't they?"

The center of the book was a two-page print of Thomas Cole's *The Last of the Mohicans*.

"I remember the time you asked me what 'Mohicans' meant," Horace said. "I told you, and you said, 'Oh, I thought it meant 'pests.' There was some brilliance to that."

Michael laughed. "I was a goofball."

"No, you weren't. You were smart . . . you are smart. You were interested in all these things," Horace said, with a wave of his hand across the tabletop.

He pointed to the Cole picture again.

"This is what the land looked like before the big towns, highways, and strip malls," Horace said. "Remember when we used to hike in the woods? These were the same woods James Fenimore Cooper used to hike in as boy, after his father came up from Jersey and built Cooperstown out of the wilderness. Back in those days, this was the frontier, home of the Iroquois. That's why he wrote the Leatherstocking books. His imagination, as a boy, took hold as a man."

"We had to read some of them in school," Michael said. "I thought they sucked."

"Maybe, but you should know local history," Horace said, "and how local history sometimes influences bigger things. Like in this case, Natty Bumppo was the first American fiction hero. A loner who got the job done. It's been that way ever since, from Wyatt Earp to Batman. Of course, it's kind of been that way forever. Cooper stole it from the Greeks."

Horace picked up the mythology book.

"When you were little, you used to love these stories," Horace said. "Remember this stuff? Orion, who killed all the wild beasts on his island. Perseus, who freed the flying horse by beheading the lady with the snake head. Hercules and the twelve impossible labors.

"Of course, when you were little, I didn't tell you the rest of the stories. The bad stuff. Orion got blinded for loving the wrong girl. Perseus killed his father-in-law. Hercules murdered his own wife and children. The Greeks didn't believe in happy endings; they believed in cautionary tales. They knew that the same things that made somebody great could also lead to their downfall. They knew misery was right around the corner for everyone. That's a fact of life."

"That's kind of messed up," Michael said.

"The other thing was this. Orion, Perseus, Hercules, they all did all those heroic things alone, and after they were cheered and worshipped, still ended up alone. The Greeks knew, in life, you mostly go at it alone. You're not always surrounded by friends or teammates, not forever, anyway. They believed loneliness built character, it was not something to be afraid of. You find your own path, lonesome as it might be, and you don't take it because someone wants you to, or because there's a reward in it. You take it because it's yours. Do you understand what I'm trying to tell you?"

"Are you telling me I shouldn't go to Moeller? Or I should?"

"I'm saying you should decide for yourself. I'm saying if the things you love are here—your friends, our community, its history, the landscape, even—stay here. That's what I did. I chose this life, crazy as it might seem to people, because this is not only what I love, but who I am. I'm saying there's more to life than sports, believe it or not. All these things you learned when you were little, the stars and the woods and the art, they give . . . *texture* . . . and context to your life here, in Cooperstown, where you grew up. Sports teach lessons, too, but I want you to think about your world being bigger than a baseball diamond. I want you to seriously consider that before you make a decision."

Michael decided to spend the night at the house. He called his mother to tell her, and Horace could hear her voice through the cell phone speaker.

"Is your dad brainwashing you?"

Michael smiled up at Horace.

"No, Mom, he said I should do what I want."

That night, Michael quickly fell asleep in his own bed, in his quiet room expunged of electronics. Horace looked in on him, how he filled the twin-sized bed, even curled up. Horace wanted to lie next to him, and pull him close, to hold him like a small child one last time. One last time, before he left. One last time, before he became a young man. His boy. *My son.* The words came to his lips, and he said them silently. The love he felt—and the fear of losing him—collided at that moment and overwhelmed him. Tears came to his eyes, and he stood there, half in, half out of the doorway, and cried. Only when he could no longer completely muffle his sobs, and the hollowness in his gut drained the warmth from his soul, did he turn away.

In his own bed, he listened to the June cicadas as they surrounded the house. It was hot and humid, and he lay awake. The air was thick and smothering, and he could feel the plaster walls sweat, like he could feel the poison of despair running through his veins. He repeated his prayer for purpose, his morning mantra now offered in the black night to find some anesthesia in sleep. And again, just as he finally drifted off, he heard the ghostly child whisper—*"Dad"*—just as he had every night since it first happened.

Chapter Twenty-Five

"So, you want my opinion?" Sal said.

"Always," Grudeck replied, truthfully.

"Okay, let me take a look."

Grudeck took the 8 ½-by-11 yellow envelope and flipped it onto Sal's desk. It slid across the glass top and stopped when it hit Sal in the gut.

"So, the bucks stop here," Sal said, and took three typewritten pages, double-spaced, out of the sheath.

"Stacy helped me write it," Grudeck said.

"How's that going?"

"Good," Grudeck said. "I'm working on her."

Sal raised his eyes at him.

"To what end?"

"I don't know, Sallie. Maybe some kind of future."

"Want my honest opinion?" Sal asked, without waiting for an answer. "Be careful. You're a rich man, Joe. She may have the best intentions. You, too. But if the time comes—and I'm not saying it should or shouldn't—I won't let you get married without a prenup. This is Jersey, she'll get half of everything, right down to one of your nuts. Think I'm kidding? I'm not. Worse, you'll pay her lifetime alimony out of your half. Lifetime. That means forever. Guys like you go broke because of shit like this . . . and you know my old joke about my office."

Grudeck had heard it a million times. Sal shared a plain-brick-and-glass-block professional building with a urologist, a marriage counseling group, and a matrimonial law practice.

“One-stop shopping,” Sal said. “First, the wife breaks a guy’s balls, then gets him to change through counseling, then decides he’s not the man she married so she wants a divorce.”

“All right, all right, we’re a long way from there,” Grudeck said with a laugh, holding up his hands in mock surrender. “First things first. Just read the speech, please.”

As Sal read, Grudeck picked up the glass-encased World Series ball he’d signed for him two decades before. “To Sal, with love, Joe Grudeck,” it said. Grudeck remembered the incongruity of signing his last name underneath “with love.” On the one hand, it sounded stupid. On the other, he wanted people to know it was authentic, which was dumb in itself because only a blind man could enter Sal’s office and not see he represented Joe Grudeck.

SAL HAD BEEN HIS FATHER’S LAWYER; the usual stuff. The mortgage on the Stuyvesant house, his will. Taking care of this and that. They were men of the same generation, Sal a few years older, from Newark’s North Ward, the section of hardheaded Southern Italians who stayed long after the riots. Chuck Grudeck was from the Polish section of Elizabeth, an enclave next to Peterstown, the goomba section where Sylvia D’Angelo grew up.

When the colleges came after Joey, Chuck Grudeck knew he was in over his head. The NCAA had rules upon rules, and Chuck Grudeck couldn’t figure them out. He was afraid he would screw up and hurt Joey’s chances, so he went to Sal, who figured it all out for him. Grudeck remembered how he folded his hands on his desk and began to rapid-fire the facts, looking alternately at Joey and his father, and calling them “you” as if they were one person.

“Here’s the deal . . . right now you’re getting letters from all over. Penn State and Boston College want to turn you into a linebacker.

Iowa State and Minnesota want you for wrestling. Rutgers will take you for anything. Seton Hall and South Carolina want you for baseball. You have to decide what you want to play. My advice would be baseball, somewhere it's warm. Wrestling ain't taking you anywhere, financially, that is. Football can leave you crippled. You get hurt, bye-bye scholarship, and you're back home, taking night courses at Union County College. Baseball's easier on the body. You play, you get your education, and in the end, maybe, just maybe, you get drafted."

But then came the pro scouts and the Red Sox were first with an offer; a $100,000 signing bonus on top of the minor-league median salary, rather than the minimum.

Chuck brought it to Sal.

"I don't know this stuff," Sal said, pointing to his Seton Hall law degree on the wall. "I'm a simple town lawyer. Go find him a trustworthy sports agent."

"That's the problem," Chuck Grudeck said. "Trustworthy."

"Okay, let's think this through. A hundred grand. It's a lot of money," Sal said. "So if you want to play baseball, take it. If you don't, don't. It's that simple."

"What about his education?" Chuck Grudeck said.

"Colleges aren't going anywhere. If things don't work out in baseball, you can take English 101 in a couple of years. No big deal. Best part is this: You can still wrestle or play football in college even though you've been a pro in a different sport. The NCAA allows that."

"What about waiting to see what else comes in from baseball?" Joey asked. The Red Sox wanted him to catch; he wanted to pitch.

"You can do that, but if nothing else does, the Red Sox may rethink your value," Sal said. "Here's how I look at it: right now, they've shown good faith, so show good faith back. Makes for a better long-term relationship. But then again, I don't know nothing about sports.

"But here's what I do know. First, it's a big step but not irretraceable. Nothing is. Second, one hundred grand is a lot of money. It's twice what your dad makes in a year, right, Chuck? You can invest it and begin to set yourself up for life. Third, if you don't take this chance, you might regret it forever."

Sal's clear-eyed view helped Joey figure it out. He was ready. He thought about it overnight, then put himself through a little batting cage test just to make sure, then asked Sal to be his agent.

So Sal went to work, charging only billable hours rather than percentage. The NBA and NFL put caps on agent takes, about 4 percent. But baseball didn't regulate it, so who knew? And they all took about 15 percent of endorsements. Right up front, Sal said he wouldn't slice up Grudeck like that, not that Grudeck would have minded. Sal did right by him. When millions started getting made, in salary and endorsements, Sal tried to keep his billable hourly rate, but Grudeck doubled it, then doubled it again. Sal objected.

"Joey, first off, you already made me rich. Second, it's your talent. I'm just the guy who walks in the door first, makes the deal, then makes sure the taxes are paid on the way out."

"I'm not just paying you for the deals," Grudeck would say. "I'm paying you for the trust. And the advice."

Even before Chuck Grudeck died, Sal had become the common-sense, no-bullshit voice of moderation and maturity in Grudeck's life; he made no decisions without him. Even while his father was still alive, there was no one else Grudeck could count on for the truth.

Sal promised him that, day one.

"The one thing I won't be is a sycophant," Sal said, and then explained what *sycophant* meant.

Above the cherry leather couch in Sal's office were three pictures: the famous one of Grudeck over the prone McCombs; Grudeck and Sal on the field at Fenway sometime in the late '90s; and Grudeck and Sal at Winter Haven, third year in, after he signed his first contract with the big club.

NOW, AS SAL RAN HIS INDEX FINGER over the lines of Grudeck's speech, Grudeck studied the pictures. There was Sal, mid-forties, in the Winter

Haven picture, with a comb-over of still-black hair, wearing a white cabana-boy shirt, open wide at the neck, over a pair of Bermuda shorts. There was Grudeck, lean, barely out of his teens, in practice pants and navy-blue RED SOX T-shirt, hair a little long, brushed across his forehead. Sal was smiling. Grudeck was squinting in the sun. Both were somewhere they'd never dreamed of. Sal, the local lawyer, had just made a deal with the owner of a storied major league team. Grudeck was penciled in as starting catcher on the same spring training field where Ted Williams and Carl Yastrzemski played.

But there he was, face contorted almost into a grimace. He thought about what Stacy said about no joy. Maybe she was right. He tried to remember how he felt at that moment. He wasn't thrilled, that he knew. He wasn't nervous, either. He felt . . . competitive. Like he had something to prove, and there was no doubt he would prove it. Confidently competitive. That was it. Different than arrogance. Arrogance was feeling you were entitled to succeed. For Grudeck, there was always this chip on his shoulder, an innate fire to prove himself.

No joy?

She was probably right.

Who had time for joy?

Grudeck shifted in his chair, which matched the couch. The decorative brass upholstery nails created mounds of cushion and pockets of none, and Grudeck's hips began to seize. He stood to stop the spasms, and Sal looked up from the speech.

"What? You in a hurry? Because we got a lot to talk about," Sal said, waving the papers at him.

"No, just stretching. You ought to buy more comfortable chairs," he said.

"Nah, that way I keep my billable hours to resemble real hours. Otherwise, people come in and bullshit all day. Speaking of . . . let me finish reading."

Grudeck watched Sal go through the speech and thought how little he changed. Yes, Sal's hair was grayer and thinner, the comb-over more obvious, the face a little doughier, and the bargain-store sport coats, usually mauve or some kind of brown plaid, were replaced by charcoal-gray or navy tailored suits. Grudeck's "billable hours" did that. But no matter how you dressed him, he was pretty much the same old Sal. Trim. Clear eyes. Quick hands, always gesturing, and a quick mouth, to the point. No bullshit. Speaking of . . . Sal was frowning. He shook his head, not demonstratively but like an internal reflex.

"What?" Grudeck said.

"I'm still reading."

Next he made a few clicking sounds with his mouth. Clear disapproval.

"All right, what??" Grudeck said.

"You want my honest opinion?"

"Yes."

"Honest opinion?"

"C'mon, Sallie."

"Okay. Sit down."

Grudeck obeyed.

"It doesn't feel right, Joe," Sal said. "Scratch that. It feels bad. I mean, really, Joe, what the fuck is this: No joy in Mudville?"

"I want to tell the truth."

"Jesus Christ, Joe. Haven't you learned this by now: Nobody wants to hear the truth. About anything. They want to be entertained. They want to get away from the shit that scares them: cancer in the food, economy in the shitter, the fucking ice caps melting. And not just that, they want to be part of something. Rotary. Knights of Columbus. Hells Angels. They need a team. So they buy a Yankee hat, or the Cowboys, or the fucking Vancouver Canucks.

"I've been telling you this for years. Merchandise has gone through the *roof* since you've been playing. You know why? People want to *belong*. Jews wear yarmulkes, Muslims wear skullcaps, and Americans wear baseball hats with somebody's logo on it. Arabs wear dishdashas, Indians wear dhotis, and Americans wear T-shirts with somebody's logo on it. Yankees, Notre Dame, Abercrombie, Harley.

"Sports is the second-safest universal topic of conversation after the weather, so everybody buys in. Everybody wants to sit at the jock table. Same with the sponsors. You're a millionaire today because Budweiser charges the regular Joe an extra quarter a six-pack to be the official beer of baseball and buys TV time . . . and then here *you* come, Mr. Not Regular Joe, Mr. Hall of Fame, Mr. Made Twenty-five Million, to *piss* on all that?"

"Not piss on it . . . just . . . I don't know, I'm tired of it all," Grudeck said. "It's like a farewell."

"You mean a parting shot." Sal looked back at the speech. "Like this . . . 'We've taken all the joy out of sports.' Says who? You know what the average fan is gonna say to that? They'll say, nobody put a gun to your head and said, 'Play.' Nobody forced you to sign those big contracts. They'll say if you hated it—and *us*—so much, why didn't you just *quit*. And you know what? They'll be right . . .

"No offense, kid, but you've taken all that's come your way. The money, the girls, the fan worship. You took it all. Now you're out, and you want to say, 'This was all wrong.' It will sound hypocritical. That's how people will see it: Joe Grudeck got his, now he's telling us it's out of control. It's like these old rock stars who find Jesus: 'I got stoned all the time, I screwed a million girls, I bought exotic cars and mansions in Hawaii, and now that I'm broke I realize how empty my life was.' "

"Are you done?" Grudeck asked. An uncontrollable, deflated expression of disappointment came across his face. He'd hoped for approval, but instead got this. Sal saw it and softened a little.

"Look, kid, I know things are screwed up. But is it up to you to fix it?"

"I don't know . . . Somebody's got to tell the truth," Grudeck said.

"And that has to be you?"

"Why not?"

"Why is the real question," Sal said. "What does it get you?"

Sal's hands were out in front of him and he flicked out a finger with each point he made.

"Respect? You already got that. From players, from fans, even the media. A clear conscience? That's between you and God. All these things you say, you think people don't know?"

"Maybe they don't," Grudeck said.

"Like what?" Sal said, starting a new finger count. "That Bonds took steroids? That Tyson raped a girl then fought for the title? That the kid from Florida State might have raped a girl and still won the Heisman? Want me to keep going? Nobody cares. Why do you think they call it hero *worship*?"

The word *rape* made Grudeck go cold. The two girls in Syracuse, they got drunk with him, didn't they? What did they expect?

Grudeck gathered himself and said, "That's my point, Sal. Things are broken. Out of control."

"Of course they are!" Sal said, keeping his voice patient. "Some of the things in the speech are right."

He shuffled the papers looking for certain points.

"No one can argue about greed. Or bad fan behavior. I even like that line, *the beauty of the game has been ruined by loud music and cheap scoreboard entertainment in our stadiums*, although I would change 'beauty' to a word like *serenity*. But some of this other stuff—like memorabilia. Jeez, Joe, you're still doing cash-and-carry autograph shows! You're booked into a mess of signings around Induction Week alone. All those little stores up in Cooperstown are stocking up on your stuff. Hillerich and Bradsby is making five thousand—five thousand!—'authentic' Joe Grudeck souvenir bats to sell online and in Boston and Cooperstown. You get a three-buck slice of every one. This place in Cooperstown ordered five hundred and they're paying you a grand to sit there and sign the damn things for a couple of hours. You see where I'm going with this? You'll come across as a hypocrite."

The word scared Grudeck. What if the Syracuse girls came forward *because* of the speech? Hypocrite.

"What if I canceled everything?" he asked.

"To prove what? That you're a reformed star? That you're swearing off your celebrity? Then what? You going to return the millions you made playing ball?"

Grudeck was quiet, and Sal softened his approach even further.

"And so here's the next big question. Say you get up there and you say all this. Then what? What will it change?"

Grudeck again shifted in his chair, thinking what to say.

"Let me answer for you, then," Sal said after a few beats. "Nothing. Nothing at all. Let me tell you what will happen. *SportsCenter* will clip your speech and show excerpts and God knows what it will end up sounding like. Sincere. Flip. Stupid. Whatever *they* decide. A couple of sports columnists and TV guys will say Joe Grudeck is absolutely right, and a couple will say you're completely full of shit. In the end, nothing changes. Nothing good comes of it. The truth is, it's too far gone, Joe. The good old days ain't coming back."

Grudeck shook his head.

"It's not that simple, Sal, it's—"

"It is that simple, Joe," Sal said. "Don't complicate it. You're a ballplayer, not a sociologist. That's what people love you for. Baseball, not social commentary."

Grudeck felt dismissed, and it fired his temper. He wanted to point to the pictures on the wall, the mahogany desk and the cherry leather furniture, and remind Sal who made it all happen. Sal was studying him, and knew that Grudeck was struggling to keep himself in check.

"Go ahead, say it," Sal said.

Grudeck leaned up in his chair.

"You know, I'm just trying to do something good, goddamnit, and you make me feel like an idiot," Grudeck said. "Like it's the stupidest idea ever."

"Lookit, Joe. I'm just afraid you'll come across as self-righteous. You want out? Fine. But you don't want to go out like this. Americans hate hypocrites as much as they love athletes. And trust me, once one of the media jackals rips into you, the pack will follow and tear you apart."

Grudeck shifted in his chair, trying to think of the right words, but was distracted by pain in his hips and thoughts of Syracuse becoming public. In his gut, he knew Sal was right. No good could come of it. But Stacy admired him for wanting to do it. Could he punk out now? Things needed to be said. Maybe there was a better way to say it.

Sal must have read his mind.

"Talk to your girlfriend. Try to lighten it up a little. Less pontification. Speak from your heart, not the pulpit," Sal said, then paused. "But Joe, kid, promise me something."

"What, Sal?"

"Think about your reputation. If you want to run off and be a hermit, fine. Just don't tear down the guy you built up on the way out. People love Joe Grudeck. You don't want to kill that guy."

"What if I'm not that guy?" Grudeck asked.

"It doesn't matter. Not to your fans. Not to the rest of the world. To them, you're the guy they think you are. Let 'em think it."

GRUDECK WAS SLOUCHED in a corner of Stacy's sofa, with her in his arms. She was curled up facing away, so her breasts rested near his hand. He opened it up wide, spanning both, nonchalantly, and she relaxed against him. In his pocket were two pills, just in case, wrapped in a piece of toilet paper. But with the warmth of Stacy's body, and the way her breathing resonated in his lap, he didn't think he would need them. Not to get started, anyway.

Wayne Jr. was at his father's for the night, and Stacy had made a simple dinner of kraut and kielbasa.

"*That's* what you want?!" Stacy said.

"Yeah. Like my mother used to make. You don't get that at the club."

Now it was evening, and the light in the room had turned gray, muting the pastel walls and Stacy's paintings. Only the neon of the carnival scene held its color in the diminishing light.

Stacy offered to turn on a lamp.

"No, this is nice," Grudeck said, then bent his head to kiss her hair, then moved to nuzzle her ear. He stroked her neck with his other hand.

She made a soft sound, one that went right to Grudeck's soul.

"Come with me to Cooperstown," he said.

The suddenness surprised her, and she reacted with another involuntary murmur.

She turned in his lap and looked up at him, unsure what it all meant.

"Come with me to Cooperstown," he said. "I want you there. It's the biggest day of my life, and I want you there."

Stacy reached up and touched his cheek.

"That's very sweet, Joe. Very sweet."

"But . . . ?"

"But I'm not sure I belong there."

"Why not? You'll be my guest. We can bring Wayne Jr. Front-row seats."

"I'm not sure," she said, imagining photographers taking pictures of the three of them together, Joe Grudeck's insta-family.

"Why? What?" Grudeck hadn't been prepared for this. "It'll be fun."

"It's your day, Joe. It's your thing," she said, now sitting up.

"But I want you there."

"And I'd want to be there if . . ."

"If what, Stace?"

"I don't know . . . if we were further along. If we *get* further along. You know what I mean."

"C'mon. It'll be *fun.* And you'll probably get on TV. They always show the guy's family when he speaks," Grudeck said.

"That's exactly the point," Stacy said.

She sat up and tried to face him, but Grudeck pulled her in close and guided her head to his shoulder. He didn't want to see the look on her face when she started to explain herself.

"It just seems like the place for a family, a *wife*," she said.

"Or girlfriend," Grudeck offered.

"No, not a 'girlfriend,'" she said. "Girlfriends come and go. The person with you should be someone who was by your side all along, who supported you, who held things together when you were on the road half the year. That wasn't me."

"But you helped with the speech."

"But it's your speech, Joe. It was your life, Joe. Not mine. I wasn't part of your baseball life; neither of us wanted that. If we did, it would have happened. But it didn't. You went off, and I didn't chase you. There was a reason for that. Do you know what that reason was?"

"No."

"Think about it, Joe," Stacy said, now moving away to look at him. "What did I always tell you back in high school?"

"That you didn't want to be just another girl to me?" Grudeck said.

"That was only part of it. The other part was that I didn't want to be swallowed up . . . by your hugeness," she said, and playfully slapped her hands against his chest, trying to lessen what she feared was an emotional blow. "That wasn't your problem. It was mine. I knew you were going to be big. Bigger than any of us. But I had my own dreams, and maybe I was too afraid that if I became Joe Grudeck's girl, that was all I would ever be."

Grudeck thought this over, thankful the faded light masked what he felt was a stupid look on this face.

"So instead you became Mrs. Wayne . . . ," he said, and the "I'm sorry" came even before he got the last name out. "That was a shitty thing to say."

"Yes, I married another man, and had a child, and tried to be a family," Stacy said flatly. "And maybe it wasn't the smartest thing, or the best thing, but it was the thing I did. But along the way . . . oh, never mind."

"What?" Grudeck said. "Don't do that, Stace. What?"

Stacy shook her head. What could he possibly understand about her life, and all it had entailed since high school? She felt herself getting irritated. He went off to play baseball, and detached himself from all else. He had no wife, no child. He never held a little, helpless life in his hands and felt the unrelenting burden of its survival. He never had to please a woman beyond their chemical-attraction expiration date, or partner with her for the long haul. He never made himself vulnerable; he never stuck around long enough to get dumped, or cheated on, or to feel the relentless, obsessive emotional pain of a broken heart. There was no "she" in his history, no relationship regrets, no "one that got away." Stacy wanted to ask him: Did he ever *long* for anybody? Did he ever lie there at night, feeling the distance, arms empty, with that feverlike sensation of abject loneliness in the chest? Did he ever cry over a woman?

And then there was the day-to-day drudgery. Did he ever struggle to pay bills? Make a doctor's appointment? Grocery shop? Keep a junker running? Did he lie awake some nights, worrying about how he would pay for his kid's college or his parents' nursing home?

No, he played baseball. Sal took care of his taxes and expenses. The team carried his bags. He ate in hotels or in the clubhouse. His mother cooked for him in the off-season. Retirement didn't change much; the clubhouse was now the country club.

But now something was changing and she understood. His induction, his so-called sports immortality, was really the first step to obscurity. He knew it, and he was scared, and he wanted to be grounded. With her. A mirage from the past. The first thing that came along. Just like that. Easy, like everything else that came his way.

"What, Stace? What?" he asked again.

"Joe, sweetie, this is your thing. Not mine. You go. You give your speech. And when you come back, and you have some time to absorb it all—where you are in your life and where you think you want to be—I'll be here, and we'll see what's what."

Grudeck fell asleep holding her, but woke when she, also sleeping, nestled down in his lap. Her head rested in his crotch, and he came up, throbbing. He stroked her hair, softly enough to not wake her but enough to put gentle pressure on his erection. He didn't want to leave her, and go home alone. Since they started up, he felt lonelier than ever when he was by himself. He was afraid of the nights, when he returned to his empty condo, determined to keep faithful to her but with no warm body to cling to. All those women, even when he paid. They all staved off the isolation he'd always felt. But now his fear of being alone was becoming oppressive and left him short of breath at times. And now this moment, peaceful as it was, brought him closer to that fear. He would have to leave her house soon, and return home. Alone.

He had decisions to make. About himself. About her. About the speech. But he didn't know how. All his life, he went where his talent took him. He didn't make decisions; he just followed along. When he decided to sign with the Red Sox, he never gave her a second thought. He wanted to wake her now and apologize, and confess that he was the one who created the distance, staying just out of reach. Not just from her, from everybody. From his high school friends to all the women to all the fans. He mastered being there, but not being there. He did it so long he wasn't sure if there was a "there." Stacy wanted more; he knew that. And now in the dark, with her head resting on him, he didn't know if he had it. He felt empty inside and was clinging to the hope he could fill the hole with Stacy. But she had turned down Cooperstown. It was his moment, like she said, but she didn't want to share it with him. Maybe it was her first step away. How did she say it? "We'll see what's what." And who he was, or wasn't. He was paralyzed by fear and life suddenly felt harder than ever. After a few minutes, the weight of Stacy's head made his hips hurt and he squirmed to find a place of less pain.

Soon, he would go home alone.

He would go to Cooperstown alone.

What did Sal say? The whole party, just for him.

Chapter Twenty-Six

When schools let out, the summer season at the farm museum officially began, and Horace was duty-bound to trudge up the grounds from the blacksmith shop several times a day to give the Cardiff Giant presentation. As much as he first dreaded it, it soon became his favorite part.

It got him out of the smithy, a slab stone building where the masonry walls sweated in the summer humidity. Their natural coolness was overcome by the hearth fire when the bellows pushed the coals to metal-melting temperatures and transformed the shop into a smokehouse sauna.

The walk to the Giant's circus tent near the carousel gave Horace a chance to breathe deeply some fresh air, and let the valley breezes evaporate the perspiration from his shirt and cool his skin. The tent itself was bright and airy; the yellow and white stripes cast a light, ambient glow and the large doorway flaps at either end, when pulled back, let the Otsego Lake breezes flow.

On a table near the entrance was a stack of Horace's revised archival treatise, reworked with sharper teeth. He'd renamed it: "American Rubism: The Cardiff Giant and the Birth of Pop Culture." Some visitors picked it up, scanned it, and put it back down. But more kept it, folding it into a back pocket or purse.

Then there was the stone man himself, the historic relic, mute and unaware of all the fuss he had once caused. Horace developed a protective affinity for him, like a treasured possession. Sometimes he got to the tent early or stayed late, just to study him. He saw what Hull meant about the feet; large and heavily flat, as if they had walked thousands of miles on the earth's unforgiving terrain, bearing the burden of the Giant's great weight. He stared hard into the Giant's face, and understood how the post–Civil War rubes might have wondered if there was once a man under that contoured-rock coat of armor. The Giant's bed was a wooden platform, surrounded by a white picket fence, and his posture looked as uncomfortable as the oak planks that served as his mattress. His left arm was pinned to his side, his right crossed over his body, almost touching the opposite hip, which jutted in the air, making his left leg rest on top of his right. This was not a relaxed pose. It was twisted, like a soldier who had fallen where shot. At times Horace wanted to reach over and wrestle free the limbs of the Giant's wrenched and contorted body, like some nursing home orderly trying to bring comfort to a geriatric patient in the final, fetal stages of Alzheimer's. The anguished face, the "silent scream" George Hull described, added to that image.

And yet, even as Horace told the story of fraud and deceit, visitors looked at the Giant as if he were once alive and they were laying eyes on a mummified human, like something out of the ancient Egyptian tombs. All these years later, Horace thought, the Giant still delivered George Hull's original intent.

"Step right up and see what was once the most famous man in America," Horace told them. "A national sensation. Featured on page one of every major newspaper. People traveled miles—by foot, by horse-drawn carriage, by steam-powered train—just to see him. They lined up for country miles and city blocks and paid their hard-earned money to watch him . . . do absolutely nothing. In this respect, he was America's first 'reality' star. Not only was he a celebrity with no talent, he wasn't even alive!"

This always got a few laughs from the crowd, especially the middle-aged.

"Yes, folks, you are looking at the Cardiff Giant! The American Goliath! The Onondaga Colossus! And, yes, the Great American Hoax! The Leviathan of Flim-Flam! The Behemoth of Humbug! The year was 1869 . . . Does anyone know what happened in 1869?"

And this being sports-driven Cooperstown, someone might raise their hand and mention the Cincinnati Red Stockings, or the first college football game.

And Horace, being Horace, grabbed the moment to say, "Yes, 1869 was the birth of diversion, the American economy of entertainment as we know it today."

He checked off his evidence, supplied by the lovely Natalia, like a lawyer's opening statement: baseball, football, Broadway theaters, the explosion of newspapers and magazines, tawdry gossip. A record year, fourfold, for patents of consumer products and gadgets; Edison's cylinder phonograph and the creation of recorded music was coming, as was his kinetoscope to show moving pictures.

"Our modern American entertainment industry was being hatched, like some medieval dragon that would parch the countryside," Horace concluded.

"The year was 1869, and the nation began its march away from the simplicity of 'God and country' to the so-called sophistication of consumerism and city life. The figure that lies before you, the Cardiff Giant, the LaFayette Wonder, epitomizes all that. He is a small parable of a larger story.

"The year was 1869 and a New York State cigar maker named George Hull wanted to make fools of the God-fearing, religious fundamentalists of the rural heartlands, so he tricked them into thinking this sculpture was a fossilized man from the biblical race of Goliath."

At this point, Horace studied the faces in the crowd; some would nod in approval, others would be impassively disguising their discomfort, as he delivered the punch line of "a first example of the nation shucking its Christian roots, a process that continues today."

Horace knew these were dangerous times to talk about religion publicly, so he was not surprised when he was called to Grundling's office a week or so into his presentations.

"Horace, I've gotten a few complaints," Grundling said, while turning the Conestoga wagon over in his hands. "I'm sure you can guess why."

"Yep. I stepped on one of the third rails," Horace said. "Religion. Race. Homosexuality. And to think, we were once a free-speech nation."

"This is a public venue," Grundling said. "Well, not exactly, but we take public grants, so we have to be a little more . . . benign."

"And what about historical accuracy, John," Horace said. "Doesn't that count in the world of being . . . benign?"

"Is it accuracy? Or are you getting into the gray area of interpretation?" Grundling said.

Horace wasn't in the mood.

"You asked me to rewrite the paper. I did, and you approved it. The talk is based on the paper," he said.

"I'm not challenging your interpretation, Horace. I respect your research and intellect. I'm just asking you to tone it down. A little. We're in the history business, but we're also in the entertainment business. Don't you agree?"

"I'd call it the education business, but you're the boss, John. I'll tone it down."

Still, Horace told the story, rich in detail; the secret deals Hull made with the Iowa quarry master and the Chicago sculptor; the comic burial and unearthing at Stubby Newell's farm in the Onondaga Valley breadbasket. He told of the stage lines that traversed the valleys of New York State and brought the first few thousand gawkers. And how the rage of it all brought out the consortium of bankers who bought into Hull's scam. Finally, he talked about P. T. Barnum's imitation giant—and Horace correctly gave credit to Mr. David Hannum for the "sucker born every minute" line—and the absurdity of lawsuits and countersuits that brought the whole thing crashing down.

Horace concluded each presentation by reading the quote from

Andrew D. White's piece about the Giant's meaning in American society, hitting hard on the words *joy in believing* and *truth is a matter of majorities*.

"In that way, the story about the Cardiff Giant isn't so much about one man's folly or the gullible rural public or the assault on religion or the emergence of natural sciences," Horace said. "It's about how we measure our culture. The commercial, pop culture forces count the number of people who watch a game or show on TV, go to a movie, download music, all to say, 'This is what the public wants. This is who Americans are.' But . . . who is counting you today? Who is counting all the people at museums or library talks or pursuing interests outside the realm of popular culture? Think about that, and how our identity as a people is manipulated and shaped by the 'truth of majorities' rather than the individualism that guided our earlier years."

Natalia came to one of the early presentations in her milkmaid dress, and as Horace delivered this last line, she began to clap with joy and the other visitors timidly followed.

She lingered as the tent cleared.

"That was wonderful, Horace. Very powerful," she said. "Very convincing."

He moved toward her, fighting every urge to wrap one arm around her waist and pull her to him.

Instead he offered to walk her back to the cow barn. As they emerged from the tent, Horace looked out over the farm museum and the valley. From that vantage point, there was nothing he could see that didn't date back to 1869, except for a few tourists in their twenty-first-century clothes. And here he was, the village blacksmith, courting the milkmaid next door. He purposely brushed her hand several times as they walked, and wished he could return to the days, and age, of innocence.

Chapter Twenty-Seven

Grundling appeared in the Giant tent the next morning as Horace was winding down his first presentation.

"Quite a specimen," he said as he admired the Giant, after the half dozen people filed out.

"Yes, he's the man," Horace said. "Visitors seem to like him."

"Ah, visitors. That's why I'm here."

Horace braced himself for another "tone it down" speech, but instead Grundling asked, "Do you know how many people visit the Hall of Fame every summer?"

"I don't know . . . a quarter million?"

"Precisely," Grundling said. "Now guess how many visit us. I'll tell you; less than a tenth of that, including school trips."

"What is this, John, another round of budget cuts?" Horace asked.

"No, not at all. This is something good. The board met last night and decided to do some cross-promotion, museums helping museums."

"They took my 'rural roots of baseball' idea?" Horace asked.

Grundling looked puzzled.

"Remember. Flat fields? Can of corn? Broad side of a barn?"

"Oh, right. Well, not exactly."

Horace braced himself. Whatever was coming, he knew would be hokey.

"You've seen those 'Cool, Cool Cooperstown' billboards, no doubt,"

Grundling said. "Well, the board wants to include us, and Folk Art, in the campaign. We decided to play with the theme a little. They're going to make some farm animal cartoons like the baseball one—and the Giant, too—all on the same billboard. They're going to dress up the Last of the Mohicans the same way."

"Wait a minute . . . ," Horace said, his voice rising more than he wanted. "They're going to put cartoon sunglasses and that stupid logo over a classic piece of American art? Are they crazy? Cooper and Cole will be spinning in their graves. And the Giant, too? That's the most inane thing I've ever heard."

"Actually, the Giant was my idea," Grundling said. "And before you accuse me of sacrilege, let me tell you we *must* bring up our numbers. Not *try. Must.* These are tough times, Horace. The stock market put a big dent in the endowment, and we're scrambling. The battle for entertainment dollars has never been more fierce."

Entertainment. There's that word again, thought Horace.

"Even the Hall's attendance is down," Grundling said. "Ours is worse. If we don't come up with solutions, we're going to find ourselves in part-time jobs."

You mean me, not you, Horace thought, but said nothing.

Grundling filled the void of silence.

"Okay, well, there's more to this. We're going to do some cross-promotion during Induction Week."

Horace waited to hear it.

"You know who Joe Grudeck is, right?" Grundling asked.

"Yeah, I saw his name on the sign," Horace said. "He's doing something at Michael's job, too."

"Well, during Induction Week, the Hall is giving their customers a coupon for an official Joe Grudeck miniature bat, free . . ."

"What makes it official?" Horace deadpanned.

"That's not the point," Grundling said. "Point is, *we* are going to give them away. The people have to come *here* to get it. And I decided it was best not to give them away at the door, because the people could just turn around and leave. I figured we'd put them out here with the Giant. That way they'd have to see at least part of the farm collection and the carousel. Might get them to walk around a little. We'll have a sign at the Hall, 'Come See *Our* Giants.' "

"I don't get it," Horace said. "What does this have to do with us, with our mission?"

"Nothing, it's a play on words. You know, Giants. San Francisco. Baseball's Giants, our Giants." Grundling was smiling, looking for approval, but Horace wasn't giving.

"I get that . . . but the whole thing seems like a stretch," he said.

"Now you got the idea . . . seventh-inning stretch," Grundling said, and clumsily slapped Horace's back and forced a smile.

Horace shook his head, grim.

"You don't have to do anything," Grundling said. "We'll put a box by the entrance, and the fans can grab one as they come in. Simple, right?"

"In every sense of the word," Horace muttered.

"Try to have a good attitude about this. It will be cool," Grundling said.

"Cool? I've always prided myself on being the Anticool," Horace said.

"Look, Horace, the museum consortium is trying to be aggressive about this. We even bought ad space in the 'Dreams Park' guide. They get ten thousand kids a summer. Maybe we'll get some residual traffic.

"Pray for rain, Horace," he said as he left.

Horace thought of all those SUVs and minivans he saw clogging Route 28, license plates from all over the lower forty-eight, windshields scribbled with "Cooperstown Bound!" as if they'd done something more than write a check to earn the trip. "Cool, Cool Cooperstown" was coming to his dignified museum, to be overrun by hyper kids, disinterested in anything but getting one more useless souvenir, a miniature version of a bat used by a washed-up player. Worse, his dignified museum was kissing their asses to come.

THAT AFTERNOON, MICHAEL SURPRISED HORACE in the smithy as he stacked pig iron rods. Horace was drenched in sweat, and his hair was matted against his face. His linen shirt was stained coal gray, and his leather apron and breeches were smudged the same. Michael stood in his bright white Legion uniform, looking almost fluorescent in the dim blacksmith shop.

"Mikey! I'm just about to knock off and get ready for your game. You're in Hartwick tonight, right? I'll drive you over."

"That's okay, Dad. Mom's waiting in the parking lot."

"Oh, okay . . ."

"Dad, I got something to tell you. Moeller offered me the scholarship."

"And . . ."

"It's cool, Dad. They travel to the South to play during winter breaks, and all summer there's a travel team most of the kids play on. They want me to go out in a few weeks to join that team. The coach said Legion ball wasn't doing me any good."

"And . . ."

Michael averted his eyes, making Horace realize the kid had already made up his mind. Horace decided to make it easy on him.

"When do you leave?"

"The end of July."

"Your mother, too?"

"I think. She has to find a job."

Horace tried to fight off the lonesome pit that was spreading through his insides, that sick feeling of abandonment he got when Sally took Michael the first time. He didn't want to put guilt on the boy, but he also didn't want to appear nonchalant or resigned, in case Michael was even slightly conflicted. In case all was not lost.

"Are you sure that's what you want? To leave home?"

"I think it is."

"What did your mother say?"

"She said I should follow my dreams."

"I agree. My question is 'Do you have to leave home to do that?' Now, at fourteen?"

"Mom and the coach say it's the best chance to get a college scholarship. But they want me on this travel team now. They even found a sponsor to pay for me."

"To pay for you? How much?"

"Mom said it was two thousand dollars, but when she told the coach we couldn't afford it, he said not to worry."

Horace was now at another fork: Should he caution the kid about false hope and look like he was squashing Michael's dreams, or stay quiet and pretend he was oblivious to the realities and corruption of the long-shot youth-sports world?

He was stuck there, and suddenly angry that Sally had sent Michael in alone to do the dirty work, with no advance discussion. He knew what she was doing: daring him to say no to the kid, to once again be the guy who denied everything to everyone. Horace the heavy. The bad guy. He was trapped and his mind was scurrying, a rat in a corner.

Horace slammed an iron rod down on the stack harder than necessary and it snapped.

"Dad, are you mad?" Michael asked with a timidity in his voice that shamed Horace. Here he was, the bully Sally always made him out to be. And before he could check it, Michael added, "Mom said you would be."

Horace took a deep breath, not realizing it puffed him up to his full imposing height, chest out, shoulders expanding. Michael shrank back.

"Mikey," Horace said, trying to calm his voice. "I'm not mad. I'm irritated at your mom. She should have told me."

"She wanted to, but I thought I should," Michael said. "It was my decision."

And now the circular conspiracy of mother-and-son fit Horace like a crown of thorns. Sally tried to run interference for Michael, who was now defending his mother. And they were right. Michael did the right thing by not hiding behind his mother and coming to his father man-to-man. And yet Horace still bled, cut by their intertwined alliance, with Horace as odd man out. Suddenly that expression made sense to Horace in ways it never had. Here he was, in a costume from Civil War days stained with bituminous coal, railing against . . . *everything* . . . fighting to remain relevant. And employed.

An odd man.

And there was his son, in spanking white, now the beneficiary of his mother's successful grand scheme and coup. She was *right*! Baseball, not real work, had paid off. He had a sponsor, and a scholarship. At fourteen. Horace's work was not only obsolete but a dead end. *See?* All these years, she was right to let him play and not help his dad. She was right to not make him work at the farm. Michael was getting opportunities Horace's grunt work would have never provided; Horace was proven wrong. *She* showed *him*.

Odd man out.

"Ah, goddamnit," Horace said, unconsciously.

"What's wrong, Dad? I was hoping you'd be happy. I mean, for me, at least."

Horace moved from the stack to the back tunnel, where the coal was kept. It was the darkest place in the shop, the best place to hide his face. He grabbed a shovel and began to push some coal around, and the scraping of blade against brick was the sound of his blackening mood: a harsh, irritating scream in his head he couldn't make stop.

He was the father, goddamnit.

Why didn't he act like it?

Just tell the kid, "No."

Michael was too young to carry the weight of such a decision. A good father—the father Horace wanted to be—would have stepped in. But Sally had so long denigrated Horace's role with all her "it's Michael's life, not yours" bullshit that he backed off. In his last conversation with Michael about going away, Horace told the boy he should decide for himself. Now that he had, Horace was angry with his choice, but more furious that he, Horace, had abdicated his responsibility. He was the father, but he punked out. He shied away from the very essence of his character: the blacksmith, the strongman, the man out of time forging ahead with his own values and identity.

He made a mockery of his own morning prayer—"God, help me continue to find my meaning"—by abandoning it himself. He thought it would win Michael back, but now he'd lost Michael—and himself. All these ideas bounced and slammed in his head, and he suddenly understood the lure of blowing your brains out. Or somebody else's.

A man filled with the lethal combination of uselessness, rage, and despair.

He took the shovel and speared it into the coal, and moved back into the shop near Michael.

"I am happy for you, Mikey . . . if this is what you really want," Horace said, trying to keep his voice even. "But I have to tell you I'm a little concerned. You're only fourteen, and maybe you're not ready for such a big decision. To leave your home, your friends, like this. And if your mother goes, too, then, let's face it. That's your new home. Cincinnati."

"I can come home, Dad, on vacations."

"Vacations? You just said you play down South in winter and on a travel team all summer."

Horace thought of all those out-of-state license plates on the road to Dreams Park, and saw himself in the junky old Escort, spending hours on I-81 to get to some citrus town or heading west on I-80 into the flatlands to see Michael play. No, not to see Michael play. To see Michael, over lousy meals in state highway fast-food restaurants. Travel team, travel dad. This was not the fatherhood he wanted, being a spectator in his son's sports life. The very idea disgusted him, and now he was disgusted with himself.

"You're fourteen, and you're joining the vagabond circus of travel teams," Horace said.

Michael knew where this was going, another WWWA speech.

"Dad, you're forgetting Moeller is a good school, too. I'll get a good education. It will help me get into a good college."

"Your mom and I both went to Cornell without running away to some out-of-state private school," Horace said. "We both got there on our brains. We built a life here, near our homes. Maybe things didn't work out the way we expected, but this town is our home, your home. Cooperstown. For better or worse. When you leave—and take your mom with you—that all changes. I'm not saying you should stay forever, or not eventually find your own way, but I'm not sure it's a smart thing to do at fourteen, to pull up your own roots."

Michael was quiet.

"Sorry, Dad. I thought you'd be excited."

And now the shame of ruining the moment attacked Horace and he again saw how he lost to Sally. No doubt she was ecstatic, hugged her boy and congratulated him, told him how proud she was and voiced not a scintilla of caution. One hundred percent supportive. Horace, on the other hand, was Mr. Bubble-Burster.

Now his soaring anger crashed just as quickly, into a twisted wreckage of regret.

"No, no, Mike, I am," Horace said, as he moved to hug his son. "It's just my job to give you all sides. And to worry about what's right. For everybody."

He held Michael tight, and felt the boy sob against him.

"C'mon, Mikey. Don't. It's good news. It just caught me off balance," Horace said. "It will all be okay."

He squeezed the boy hard, his strong arms trying to tamp down Michael's heaving chest and soothe him.

"It will all be okay," Horace said again, in almost a whisper into Michael's ear.

He held him that way for several seconds, until Michael relaxed and gently pushed away as Horace simultaneously let go. And even in the dim smithy light, Horace could see he'd left coal smudges on Michael's clean uniform.

Induction Week

Chapter Twenty-Eight

Grudeck forgot to close the room-darkening curtains, so the brilliant morning sun over Otsego Lake illuminated his suite at the Otesaga Hotel. He was alone in the largest room in the hotel, with a king bed, a pullout couch, four upholstered chairs, a desk, an entertainment center, a dry bar, and three basins in the oversized bathroom. The room was floral in décor, with pink flowers—they might have been orchids. Stacy would know. But she wasn't there.

On the antique nightstand was a booklet of Grudeck's itinerary for the week. It was waiting for him when he checked in the night before, swarmed by valets and deskmen and managers despite arriving well after midnight. He was supposed to be there much earlier but couldn't bring himself to leave New Jersey, hoping Stacy would change her mind.

In the weeks since she declined his invitation, Grudeck woke every morning with more than the usual pains. There was a feverish, weak sensation in his arms and chest, the physical manifestation of loneliness. It was a deeper ache, one without acute parameters or cure. He felt adrift, desperate to pull her into him to make it go away. Alone in his condo, he could sleep it away until it was time for golf and a date of some type with Stacy. But he dreaded the week in Cooperstown and being away from her. She said it would be good for both of them, "to give us some clarity," and those words made Grudeck think that once the speech was done, and she got a little distance, well, she would break free and keep going.

He had Sal call the Otesaga to let them know he was running late, and would not check in until way after a scheduled dinner with league brass. He had Sal relay apologies to the commissioner and the rest. It was late afternoon when he asked the golf club manager to send up two banquet waitresses to help him pack. He opened up the first suitcase himself and put the manila folder that contained his speech in a sleeve compartment. Stacy helped him buy a new black suit, one that required less tapering in the gut, and Grudeck was thankful he didn't have to wear those puke-yellow blazers the NFL guys had to wear. The girls helped him select other clothes and organized everything neatly, except for his underwear, which Grudeck thought prudent to handle himself. He had one go to a chain drugstore to buy him fresh travel toiletries, because he didn't want them rummaging through his bathroom, where they might discover his blue pills. He was leaving them home anyway. *Joe Grrreww*, on the straight and narrow. When the girls were done, he tipped them each three hundred.

He made a last call to Stacy around dinnertime.

"Are you sure? It's not too late," he asked, then cursed himself for sounding desperate. "You still have time to pack."

GRUDECK HEADED WEST INSTEAD OF EAST on Route 78, and took the long way up to Cooperstown: heading out Route 80 into the West Jersey sunset, up I-81 through the moon-silhouetted Endless Mountains of northeastern PA, and then back east across I-88 to Cooperstown. The drive reminded him of his trips from Union to Fort Myers for spring training. He shut off the interior lights and killed the music to immerse himself in the black and quiet cockpit, with only the droning, muted road noise as a bass line for his thoughts. It was a smaller space, a moving capsule, in which to feel less lonely, and less anxious about the speech. Unlike those trips, he stayed in the right lane, keeping within the speed limit, not blasting through the night at triple digits. He was in no hurry to get there. The opposite, in fact.

Somewhere near Clarks Summit, Pennsylvania, this thought occurred to him: all those twenty-four-hour races down south were part of his long journey to Cooperstown. And now here he was, making the final leg to baseball immortality. Whatever that meant. He suddenly grew afraid of the return trip home; still alone, beginning the second half of his life, on the road to irrelevance. An old-timer, getting older, year after year. And maybe not such a popular one, if he delivered his speech.

He pulled off for gas, and the access-road convenience-store parking lot was busy with teenagers, boys and girls together, sitting in and on cars, with naked arms all over each other on this warm July night. He moved through them to get a Coke, unrecognized, just another solo stranger on the road through their town, soon to disappear in the dark.

At the junction of I-81 and I-88, the overhead signs told of the coming split; Syracuse to the left, Cooperstown to the right. He thought of the girls back at the highway stop, just kids; small-town girls bored with their high school boys and their big talk of dreams they all knew would never come true, girls who might want to have some fun with a guy they thought had even a little chance to be famous, like a minor league ballplayer. Grudeck looked at himself in the rearview mirror, oncoming headlights illuminating only his tired eyes, equally scared of a past he could not change and a future he could not grasp. Joe Asshole. You deserved what you got.

NOW IN THE VILLAGE SUITE OF THE LUXURY HOTEL, the light flooded in and brought new thoughts of Stacy. What to do about Stacy? He was afraid she was relieved he was gone. He was afraid she would be gone. He was in a room big enough for a family, but he had none. Only his mother and Sal. Two old people. Everyone else seemed to have their hand out for something, just to touch him, to claim a piece of him, from cell phone shots to endorsement deals. All those hands.

Those sweaty, sticky hands, reaching for him. He felt the residue just thinking about it.

He picked up his itinerary, two pages of commitments.

During Induction Week, all 133 rooms at the Otesaga were booked by the commissioner's office and filled with league brass, TV network execs, and corporate sponsors—all those official *whatevers* of Major League Baseball. Everyone in the hotel was connected. Golf outings, lunches and dinners, autograph signings. Meet Joe Grudeck here, meet Joe Grudeck there. The Budweiser brunch, the Frito-Lay lunch, the Bank of America dinner. Eighteen holes on Leatherstocking with Chevrolet today, with Under Armour tomorrow, a round each with Coke and Pepsi. Joe Grudeck, the official glad-hander of Induction Week, meeting all the high-bidders, all the deal-cutters, all the winners of the sponsorship sweepstakes who passed their cost of being "official" on to consumers, like Sal said.

Then into town for memorabilia signings, the stores all stocked with Joe Grudeck this or that, lines of everyone unconnected out the door and down the street. His hands cramped from signing balls, photos, cap brims; handshakes and smiles. Grudeck's frozen smile forever on thousands of cell phones, masking the squirmy desire to wash his hands.

Then over to Doubleday Stadium to throw out the first pitch for this or that league championship. Senior Little League. Babe Ruth. American Legion. Signing cap brims and balls, sweaty, grubby hands reaching for him, touching him. *Mr. Grudeck, Mr. Grudeck, Mr. Grudeck, over here, over here.*

He remembered what Sal said when the announcement came back in the winter. "The whole party's gonna be for you." Now his hands hurt, just thinking about it. Yes, he could feel the grime on them, those oily moving germs. From the silver-haired, manicured corporation CEO to the dirtiest Little Leaguer, Grudeck hated their hands equally.

If only he could give his speech first, and tell them all the truth. If only he could do that, then leave town with their stunned silence at his back.

He lay in the bright room, paralyzed by thoughts of the coming days—the crowds, the speech—finding comfort only in imagining Stacy stretched out beside him, until there was a quiet tapping at his door.

"Mr. Grudeck," came the voice from the other side. "It's John Smythe from the commissioner's office. We have an eight o'clock breakfast scheduled with the commissioner and the people from Rawlings . . ."

He didn't want the distractions. He just wanted to think of her. He wanted to imagine her face in front of him. He wanted to see her dark hair spread out on the floral bedspread, in this room clearly appointed for a woman.

"Mr. Grudeck . . . are you there?"

Chapter Twenty-Nine

Grudeck stood at the podium in the main dining room, sweating in his blue suit, even though the air-conditioning was humming and the doors to the expansive porch were thrown open to let the evening Otsego Lake breezes in. Some of the women were chilly and wrapped shawls, sweaters, or their husbands' jackets around their shoulders, but Grudeck stood under a ceiling-mounted studio light, sweating his balls off. He could feel the sugary perspiration from a day's worth of Cokes leaking from his pores. One at breakfast, three on the golf course, another two in the bar after, and two more at dinner. Sugar-sober. Clear-eyed for all introductions to important people, and all those cell phone shots. The blue suit was only a couple of years old, but he should have had it let out. He felt packed into it. Claustrophobic was more like it. It felt straitjacket tight across his back and gut, and the pants crept up on him, the crotch seam uncomfortably splitting his testicles.

He whispered this to Sal—"my nuts are killing me"—just before he got up to speak, before he walked through the standing ovation of three hundred people there for the United Way. It was their show—they were announcing a new partnership with Major League Baseball, like the one they had with the NFL—but Grudeck was the star, the honoree, the keynote speaker. The board chairman introduced him "as more than a great player, but a role model for our youth, which we need so badly today." Grudeck made his way through the crowd with a big smile on his face not for the compliment but for leaving Sal cracking up at the table.

At the podium he shook hands with the United Way guy, reached into his inside jacket pocket, and pulled out the three index cards Sal had slipped him before dinner.

"It's the usual bullshit," Sal said when he handed him the cards. "Make them feel good about what they give, then guilt them into giving more. Make them feel they can do more than those football assholes.

"And don't forget this," Sal said, and handed Grudeck a bank check made out to United Way. "A hundred grand from you, like we said."

The applause continued as Grudeck adjusted the mic, and someone yelled *"Joe Grrreww!"* from the back of the room, which drew some laughs. Grudeck looked toward the yeller and saw Jimmy MacIntosh giving him a big thumbs-up. Next to him was Joanie, her hair freshly lightened and illuminated by the overhead lights. She waved, and Grudeck reflexively held up both hands, to at once acknowledge and quiet the crowd, like some late-night TV host.

Grudeck took the moments while they sat and settled to look over Sal's notes. *Start 'em off with the Yankee joke . . . then tell stories about stuff like visits to Boston Children's Hospital and the Big Brothers/Sisters days at Fenway, about the looks on kids' faces. You know the drill. Swing into how their generosity makes it all possible . . . then zing them about how they are the most fortunate and with all that good fortune comes responsibility. Tell 'em more is needed. Tell 'em to step up to the plate. Say "Join me and step up to the plate." Then announce you're dropping a check for 100G on U. Way right now to get the partnership campaign started.*

Grudeck looked into the crowd, and all those faces trained on him, the baseball execs and owners and sponsors, the people who made the game go, the same crowd that would be there on Induction Day when he dropped his bomb, or maybe someone dropped the Syracuse bomb on him. The thought of both made his mouth go dry, and he reached for the bottle of water that had been left for him. He looked at the crowd, unable to speak. All those millionaire, billionaire owners getting their ballparks built off the backs of taxpayers, then bilking those same suckers—their fans—for everything from parking to beer to seats. And, what, a few thousand bucks to the United Way would clear their consciences? What consciences? Cocksuckers. And he was part of their racket. Making millions, signing autographs for cash. He looked at the check in his hands. What? Penance? Was it enough? For his life? For what he did to those girls? Could it ever be enough? Joe Lucky Fuck? What was the price? He was alone up there among strangers except for Sal. Not another friend, not even a teammate, for fuck's sake. No Stacy. Just Joanie and Jimmy Mac.

These bad thoughts cascaded down him like the sweat trickling under his arms and inner thighs. He looked at the crowd and realized the moments had turned awkwardly long. Looks of admiration turned inquisitive. A woman muffled a laugh off to his right; the clinking of silverware sounded like crickets on a dead-air summer night.

He cleared his throat, and weakly mumbled, "Excuse me." In the back Sal was leaning forward in his chair, nodding his head and rolling his hand in a "Let's go!" sign, like a father whose kid forgot his lines in the grammar school play.

Grudeck smiled at Sal's worried urgency and spoke into the microphone.

"Well, um, thank you. Thank you, very much. I guess there aren't many Yankee fans here tonight . . ."

The crowd laughed, and Grudeck was on, reading from his innocuous script.

THEY FOUND A DARK CORNER in the hotel's Hawkeye Bar after the dinner. Grudeck faced the wall, putting his big back to the rest of the room. Sal ordered a gin and tonic, Grudeck ordered another Coke with extra lime.

"I need my vitamin C," he said to the pretty waitress, who didn't crack a smile but instead said "Yessir" in a passive, subservient way.

"What's bothering you, kid?" Sal said. "Have a drink, for Chrissakes. All this soda is making you jumpy."

Grudeck shook his head.

"Got to be on my best behavior. Remember, I'm a role model for the youth."

"If they only knew," Sal said.

If you only knew, thought Grudeck.

The drinks came and Grudeck stared into his glass, playing with his stirrer, bursting bubbles.

"Jesus, Joe, this is your party. You act like it's your funeral."

Grudeck didn't look up. Maybe it is, he wanted to say. Passing from one life, but hitting a wall to the next. His own Purgatory. What was it they called it back at St. Joe's? Limbo.

"Not now," Sal said to a couple of guys in golf shirts who approached the table.

"We just wanted to tell Joe how much we loved watching him play," one said.

Grudeck turned to them in his chair.

"Thanks, guys," he said. "'Preciate it. But we're doing a little business here. Catch me later."

"Can we buy you a drink at least?" another said.

"Taken care of," Grudeck said, holding up his soda. "Thanks anyway."

The men left, looking hurt.

Grudeck turned back to Sal.

"I can't wait to get the fuck out of here. I feel smothered."

"Smothered? Jesus, Joe, all these people want is what you just gave them. A little acknowledgment. What's the big deal? I'm starting to believe you're a misanthrope."

"A what?"

"A misanthrope. Someone who hates people, maybe even themselves."

Grudeck laughed.

"After all these years, you finally got me pegged," Grudeck said.

"Salut!" Sal said, tipping his glass toward Grudeck's.

They were quiet for a few seconds before Sal said, "I hate to bring up a touchy subject, but what about your speech? The commissioner's press guy was asking."

"It'll be okay."

"Want me to take a look again?"

"No, Sallie, I got it."

"Joe, I gotta ask you. You doing it for yourself, or for her?"

"What?"

"Burning the bridges. Are you pissing on your past life—the life that made you rich, famous, and respected—to prove something to her?"

"Like what?"

"Like you're done with it. Like you're going to give up your celebrity, and all that comes with it. Like all the broads. Like all the attention. Maybe she can't handle you being famous, you ever think of that?"

"She's not behind it, Sal. It's me. And I'm not even sure what I'm going to say yet."

"Be smart is all I'm saying," Sal said. "That thing between your legs ain't a leash."

When Grudeck got to his room, there was a big security guy from the commissioner's office in a black suit sitting on a dainty antique hotel chair.

"Secret Service?" Grudeck cracked.

"They just want to make sure you're left alone."

"You here all night?"

"No, sir, just till one. They figure everybody's asleep then."

"I'm good," Grudeck said. "You don't have to hang around."

"Those are the orders, sir."

"Okay. Well, good night."

"Good night, Mr. Grudeck. Let me know if you need anything."

Grudeck shut the wooden door behind him, hearing its lone echo in the hall.

He called Stacy, but it was after midnight and her cell phone went right to voice mail.

THERE WAS A SOFT KNOCK ON THE DOOR. Grudeck looked at the digital clock, glowing 1:38 in green. Stacy?

He got out of bed and found his underwear, but not before the knock came again, this time slightly louder, more urgent. At the door, there was a flesh-colored blur covering the peephole.

"Guess who . . ." said the voice from the other side in little more than a whisper. It was Joanie MacIntosh. "C'mon, Joe, let me in. We don't want to wake the neighbors."

"Joanie, no, I . . ."

She knocked again, just as soft as the first time.

"C'mon, Joe. Don't make me throw a tantrum."

He opened the door halfway and she did not push in, but stood there, heels in one hand and an unopened bottle of wine in the other. "Don't make me drink alone."

"Joanie, this is a bad idea," Grudeck said, hiding himself behind the door.

"Aren't you the shy one?" she laughed, and came through. Grudeck didn't stop her. She threw her arms around his waist and let her shoes and the bottle fall to the carpet as she pushed down his underwear and went to her knees.

"You seemed so . . . tense . . . tonight," she said before her hand and mouth went to work on him in a practiced rhythm.

He didn't stop her; Stacy should've come.

Joanie stopped, stood, and turned so he could unzip her dress, wanting him to be complicit in the act. He did and she wiggled out of it until it was a puddle at her feet.

Chapter Thirty

Horace played with the words while he sat in traffic on Lake Street. Induction Week. Dysfunction Week.

Now it was Wednesday, and the simple routine of getting to work was already a pain in the ass. Lake Street was always jammed because the Otesaga was baseball headquarters and the hotel hired police to make sure everyone trying to pull in was a registered guest, not just regular fans who wanted to chase ex-players for autographs or watch them play golf.

To mitigate this unfriendly act, the cops told the rejected drivers to park up the street, in the Farmers' Museum lot. From there, they could see the greens of the eleventh and twelfth holes at Leatherstocking, the hotel course, and the tees on nine and ten. Across Lake Street, on the hotel side, were the third green and the fourth tee and fairway. So not only was the street a mess, the parking lot was overrun by crowds hurrying to the best vantage points and standing on the museum's rock walls to get a better view.

Horace sat in traffic, and the Escort engine heated up and started to smoke oil. He lost patience at one point and swung around a line of cars into the empty oncoming traffic lane. Luckily, it was an old Cooperstown cop, not a New York trooper, that halted his progress.

"Whoa! Horace. You're going against the grain here," he said.

"Just trying to get to work, Billy."

"I know, but we got rules . . . Here, let me wave you up."

Billy motioned to the trooper up the street, who waved Horace forward.

Another simple, successful act of defiance, Horace thought. He drove past the line of stopped cars on one side, and fans lining the walls on the other. But just as he got to the entrance, the crowd jumped down and ran in front of him.

The trooper yelled, "Wait!" to both, then let the crowd cross, as Horace fumed. So many sheep, thought Horace, surrounded by the flock. When the trooper finally motioned Horace into the lot, the Escort backfired and left a noxious fart of blue exhaust in the faces of those still at curbside, which made Horace smile. At least something went right today, he thought.

When he got out of his car, a few fans brushed past him.

"Why all the bedlam?" Horace said.

"Joe Grudeck! Joe Grudeck's on the green!" said a middle-aged, red-faced guy.

From the crowd, Horace heard calls of "Joe!" "Hey, Joe, over here!" People had their cell phones out, extended over their heads, to capture the moment. Some had binoculars. Horace thought the whole scene was silly, but it was the calls and chants of *"Grrrewww"*—which reminded Horace of how the dude-dads called Michael *"Beasssst!"*—that, for some reason, made him want to get closer.

He strode, giantlike, across the parking lot, towering above the Red Sox T-shirt crowd in his leather breeches and coal-stained linen shirt; a stone-faced, shaggy giant of a man, a glowering curiosity of a man, slinging a long-handled splitting maul over his shoulder, just for effect.

He thrust himself up on the wall, among the shorter, paunchy fans just in time to see their hero miss a long putt. The ballplayer, this Joe Grudeck, raised his face to the sky and shook his head, mocking himself, to the groan of the crowd. One of the other players stepped forward and slapped him on the back, which put Grudeck's size in perspective. The other guy had to reach up, and Horace realized Grudeck was tall and broad, but he moved stiffly and without the athletic grace Horace expected. His body resembled the man Horace saw in the posters downtown, but with a few layers of thickness added, made more obvious by the strain of fabric in his synthetic golf wear.

Grudeck sank the gimme putt and the crowd cheered. He labored to bend over and retrieve his ball, and stumbled a bit as he straightened up, and Horace detected a slight limp as he waved to his adoring fans. But it was a short acknowledgment; one quick hand raised and minimum eye contact with the hundreds staring at him. The men in his foursome clucked around him, feeling superior to those being held at a distance. But Grudeck put his head down and walked ahead, alone, a silent figure as indifferent to the people around him as Horace's own stone Giant. Horace suddenly felt demeaned by watching, and had no idea why.

DRAPED ACROSS THE CLASSIC FIELDSTONE edifice of the museum was a banner that read "Come See *Our* Giants" and, just like Grundling said, there was a ridiculous cartoon sign of a shades-wearing draft horse and bull in the "Cool, Cool Cooperstown" motif. Both were wearing Red Sox hats. A separate sign posted on the ground said, "Come See a Real Giant," and the farm's own stone man was pictured, lying in his box with a superimposed Red Sox pennant coming out of his hand. The messages were tortuous on so many levels, Horace thought. Giants and Red Sox. Animal and human. Stone and real. It was flat-out stupid, and Horace felt embarrassed for his museum's pathetic attempt at "coolness." And yet, at the same time, it gave him a chance to revel in his anticoolness, as he told Grundling. He was the blacksmith. Recalcitrant and unapologetic.

Grundling was out front, watching the crowd overrun the parking lot and run to the best vantage points to follow Joe Grudeck. Several of his co-workers, in nineteenth-century costume, were circulating through the lot, handing out flyers with discount coupons. Natalia was not among them, which made Horace happy.

"We're seizing this moment!" Grundling said.

Horace almost didn't say it, but the whole damn scenario was so . . . *humiliating.* He leaned in toward Grundling, close, talking directly into his ear.

"Why are we groveling, John?" he said, sweeping his hand out over the fans. "For *them*? We're begging *them*? Look at them, John! They think history is a home run, for fuck's sake!"

Grundling's eyes darted from Horace's face to the maul on his shoulder, and he took a step back.

"I wish you'd play ball here," Grundling said. "Now's not the time to stand on principle. We need bodies through the turnstile."

"Goddamnit, John! There is *never* a time to not stand on principle," Horace said, almost shouting.

"We need the bodies! *Any* bodies. What don't you understand about this?" Grundling said, hands up, exasperated.

"Ah, so there it is! 'Truth as a matter of majorities,' the American way," Horace spat. "We're only as valuable as *they* say we are. America, the *Mediocre.*"

"What? What are you talking about?" Grundling said, eyes back on the maul.

"We're whoring ourselves out, John, and I'm not sure I want to be part of it."

"That's your choice," Grundling said, taking another step back. "Nobody's forcing you to work here. If you find what I'm trying to do so offensive, then by all means . . . go be a blacksmith somewhere else."

Horace could barely contain his rage.

"That's your answer? 'If I don't like it, leave'?" but he sputtered because Grundling had raised the stakes, then called his bluff. There was no "somewhere else" to be the blacksmith. Not full-time, with benefits, anyway. And they both knew it.

Grundling didn't push the point. Instead he softened, to placate Horace.

"Look, Horace. I admire your passion, and you're the most authentic reenactor we have . . ."

"And a craftsman," Horace said, slighted.

". . . and a craftsman," Grundling echoed. "And a historian. Let's try to get through this. Work the Giant tent for the next few days, give away the Joe Grudeck bats, and let's try to teach some history and win some fans."

THE MINI SOUVENIR BATS were stacked at the entrance of the Giant tent, "Made in China" stamped not-so-discreetly on each box. Horace ripped open the cardboard and marveled at the cheapness of the bats. The wood was flimsy pine, dentable with a fingernail, and the red stain uneven and blotchy. The *Joe Grudeck* signature was not engraved, but stamped in white paint that could have been smudged with a thumb.

"Crap," Horace said out loud. Crap that was an insult to all the durable artifacts in the museum, from centuries-old primitive iron tools to the American-made nineteenth-century contraptions like balers and threshers that still worked when prodded.

Horace gave the presentation to the first group of these new fans without enthusiasm, and lost the small gathering of people almost immediately. They took their souvenirs and ran. Alone in the tent, he took one of the toy bats and snapped it in half, then shoved the pieces back into the box to cover up the crime.

A second group and third group came and went, and shared with Horace their mutual disinterest; they in the subject and he in them.

He was alone with the Giant, like the sole mourner at a wake, when Grundling appeared.

"I just learned there's another round of golf later this afternoon," he told Horace. "So the fans will be back. Hopefully traffic will pick up."

Grundling left, and Horace looked deep into the Giant's face, into his open mouth, as if the gypsum throat held some rock-bound secret, some buried, ancient wisdom that evaded Horace. Somewhere, deep in that stone, was the sliver of an imprisoned soul.

"Speak to me, goddamn you," Horace said. "Go on, tell me."

And the Giant did.

Chapter Thirty-One

"Behold the stone man!" Horace told the Thursday crowd, back in carnival barker mode. "Behold this mute sensation, as famous in his day as the men in the baseball shrine you've come to see. Like many of them, he is a dead relic; a museum curiosity. But the stone man tells a story that peers into America's soul, certainly more so than any washed-up ballplayer. The stone man warns of false idolatry, of heathen gods, of the foolishness of the masses. He is a fallen celebrity—yes, perhaps America's first—exposed as all hype, a fraud. But, in this, he serves as a cautionary tale."

He was reenergized. His mind revved and spun like a grinder's wheel. It spat out stinging sparks of ideas to put a sharp, bloodletting edge on his delivery. Ah, bitterness, thought Horace, an unappreciated quality. One worth exploiting.

Staring into the Giant's stoic face helped him make sense of the Wednesday sighting of Silent Joe Grudeck. Grudeck's deaf ear to the crowd, his detachment, reminded Horace of his own stone man—dead, still, and oblivious to those who flocked to him.

But this Grudeck, he was alive, and his arrogance seemed purposeful, as if he held himself out as some kind of pagan god. His fans were blind to this; they worshipped his mute presence, despite being shit on.

As the ideas sparked and caught fire in Horace's brain, he took a walk through the Grudeck crowd, yes, for inspiration, and yes, to see what he had missed. A historian, like a detective, must uncover fresh evidence, and Horace saw it during his lunchtime venture. The parking lot had turned into a tailgate party of sandwiches and soda, people dipping into coolers outside their cars with license plates from Massachusetts, New Hampshire, Vermont, and Connecticut. Men, women, and children in silly Red Sox shirts and hats. Like Barnum said, to be part of the spectacle. Just like 1869, outside the village of Cardiff.

A new narrative screamed in Horace's head; later he would speak of the parallels between the "awestruck nineteenth-century rubes who rode stages and lined the dirt roads of Stubby Newell's farm" and "modern-day dupes in minivans who traveled great distances to stare wide-eyed at the bronze men at our own Hall of Fame."

"Long before your own 'Joe Grrreww,' or whatever you call him, there was the Cardiff Giant! The American Goliath!" Horace told them.

He ignored—perhaps didn't even notice—the headshaking and muttering in the crowd.

"This guy's crazy," one Little League dad whispered to another. Horace heard that one, but plowed ahead.

"Crazy? Maybe. But someone has to tell the truth."

"Let's get out of here," another dad said, and half the audience, wearing orange Nashua Indians shirts, left.

"Choose ignorance!" Horace called after them. "Take another bat! Help yourselves . . ."

But as Horace forged ahead about the abandonment of "God and country" in favor of "consumerism and city life," one of the Nashua Indians returned to announce Joe Grudeck was now visible on the back nine, and the rest of the crowd ran out.

HORACE WAS HOME THAT NIGHT, alone, exhausted, and naked, stretched out on his bed. The summer humidity pressed in on him, a head-throbbing, smothering force that just exacerbated how trapped he felt. The house would be taken, because the debt at his salary was insurmountable. His conversation with Grundling—"go be a blacksmith somewhere else"—unnerved him. A precursor to another salary cut? Or downgraded to part-time, no benefits? Or fired altogether? Insecurity, the capitalist's tool. Fuck Grundling. Maybe it was time to go. Start over. See what was in Ohio. Go west, just like in his day. Or maybe out to Rochester. Natalia was going back to teach in just a few days. Maybe he'd follow, see what happened.

He'd find something. He said so, every day, in his own smithy presentation: *The blacksmith is ancient, but he endured, because he is the epitome of self-reliance . . .*

He sat up and looked out the window at thousands of fireflies alighting on the long grass, flickering in the black night, and the beauty of the scene erased some of the darkness in his soul. He picked up his new phone and called Michael.

Michael was supposed to leave on Saturday, but Grudeck's autograph signing at Gone Batty was that afternoon and Michael wanted to meet him.

"I thought we could spend Saturday night together, after I get out of work," Horace said.

"Okay, Dad, I'll walk up after the store closes," he said.

"Come to the farm," Horace said. "I'll wait for you in the shop."

"Okay, but I can't hang out long, Dad. Mom is packing up the car and we're leaving at four in the morning, so I can make the team practice in the afternoon."

Horace, last in line. Behind Sally, behind his new team, even behind this fucking ballplayer, this Joe Grudeck.

He lay back down in the dark, perspiring. He stayed that way for hours; still, on his back, his hair matted, sweat pooled on his sternum. Somewhere in the middle of the night, he again sat up and looked again out the window, but the lightning bugs were gone. He fell back again, trying to calm himself with his prayer of purpose. He drifted off to images of Michael and again heard the whisper of a child. *"Dad."*

THERE WAS MORE GOLF, and more fans, on Friday. Horace stayed on the attack, in the name of "educating" and "challenging" them, as he told Grundling, who came to him with complaints.

"Some of the people say it's insulting. Dial it back, Horace. We're not here to make enemies. And, really, I'm not going to tell you again."

"You won't have to, John," Horace said.

But Horace continued, undeterred. Fuck Grundling. Fuck the fans.

"Baseball wasn't born here, my friends," Horace told them. "What was born here was the cozy business relationship between beer and baseball that continues to this day. The Busch family, yep, the Budweiser people, owned thousands of acres of hops farms right here, and their summer estate was right up the street. So you can thank them for all the drunk idiots you see at games . . . this Bud's for them. . . ."

"Now let me ask you boys a question. What makes a hero?" Horace would say. "A ballplayer? Do they really do anything heroic? Do they rush into a burning building to save someone, like a fireman? Do they stop crime, like a cop?"

Then to the fathers, "So you raised boys who think athletes are gods, and you come to our Pantheon to baseball, and buy souvenir junk like the suckers that paid two bits to see the stone man one hundred fifty years ago."

Grundling was back at closing time.

"Suckers, Horace? Really?" he said.

"It was said in the context of the Barnum quote," Horace said.

Grundling shook his head.

"Okay. Whatever. But tomorrow's the last day before the induction ceremony. There's more golf, and we're expecting a lot of fans."

Grundling looked long at him.

"Are you up to this, Horace?"

"Never better, John. Why?"

"You seem . . . out of sorts," Grundling said. "Everything all right?"

Horace rejected his phony concern, and quoted Orwell.

"*In times of universal deceit, telling the truth is a revolutionary act.* I'm just giving the other side to the story."

"What?"

"*I am the voice of one crying in the wilderness*—John the Baptist, John 1:23," Horace continued.

"Horace, I have serious concerns here," Grundling said. "Just keep things cool."

"Ah, *cool.* There's that word again," Horace said. "I keep telling you, John, I'm the Anticool."

"You know what I mean," Grundling said.

"I do. I know exactly what you mean."

HORACE HOPED SATURDAY would fuel his indignant energy, and it delivered. Traffic was miserable, the parking lot crowd was unruly, and, in the tent, his aggressive presentation was met with more derision. He saw several people shake their heads and throw side glances to each other. Perfect. He was doing his job, the way he wanted.

"What a bunch of b.s.," he heard one guy say as he left midway through.

"Choose ignorance!" Horace said after him, happily.

When he concluded the talk and asked if there were any questions, one father leaned down and whispered something in his son's ear. A mischievous smile came across the boy's face as he punched his hand in the air.

"Yes?" Horace said.

"Are you a homeless man?" the boy asked, and whole group laughed.

Horace, so steady, said, "That's a very, very good question, and I'm going to answer it," in a tone that took the smile off the kid's face and made the room go quiet. The father put his hands on the boy's shoulders and started to turn him toward the exit.

"Whoa! Where are you going?" Horace said. "Your boy asked a question. Now let me answer it. Let me *educate* him."

With all eyes on the man, he stayed put.

"No, son, I'm not a homeless man. I'm a blacksmith. I dress like this because it's hard, dirty work, and rural men in the nineteenth century usually had long hair and beards. Since this is a historic farm, we try to give our visitors an accurate picture of how people lived. Now, here's another example of how people lived back then. Know what it is?"

The boy shook his head no, frozen in fear.

"It was this: kids didn't ask rude questions. They weren't encouraged by their fathers to be smart-asses. They were taught to be respectful and polite, and if they weren't, they'd get a smack on their wise ass. Now, does that answer your question?"

The boy, near tears, nodded his head yes. His father stared at Horace and shook his head in disgust, but silently guided him out.

HORACE COULD SMELL BEER on several of the men during the last afternoon session on Saturday, and their preteen boys greedily attacked the box of bats, elbowing and shoving for position. Joe Grudeck was done for the day, so the tent was now full, with several teams of boys and their fathers, and other guests. The group wearing powder-blue uniforms stampeded toward the bats, overrunning smaller kids and the handful of senior citizens. Two uniformed boys elbowed past a stooped old-timer in khakis and white diabetic shoes. The fathers, dude-dads all, did nothing to stop it, but instead recounted among themselves a shot Grudeck made for birdie on the twelfth.

"Let's control your kids, folks," he said. When he was ignored, he shouted, "Hey! Settle those kids down, goddamnit!"

That got their attention, all right, but Horace wasn't done. He moved quickly to the bat display, and got between the kids and souvenirs. The boys shrank back, menaced by his size, appearance, and intent.

"Get in line! I'll hand 'em out," Horace ordered, grabbing a big fistful of bats, "instead of you acting like a bunch of animals."

One of the fathers began to object, but Horace took a step toward him and cut him off.

"This is an old-fashioned museum, and we do old-fashioned things here, like watch our kids and make them behave. Fair enough?"

"There's no reason to call them animals," the man said.

"There isn't now," Horace shot back, as the boys grew quiet, unnerved by the confrontation between the big angry man and the dad. Horace, a head taller, stared hard at the man, who averted his eyes and said, "Okay, boys, line up," as if it were his idea.

When the bats had been given out, Horace went back to the front and began his presentation, but was interrupted when one boy tapped the Giant's penis with his bat.

"Don't do that!" Horace said. "This is a historic artifact. Have a little respect."

Horace continued, but a minute later the same boy took his bat and stood it up on the Giant's penis, like a long, skinny red erection. The other boys, and some of the dads, all laughed.

Without saying a word, Horace pounced toward the boy, grabbed the bat out of his hand, and snapped it in two. Just like that. The tent grew stone silent and Horace thrust it toward the boy's father, jagged edges first. The man leaned back, hands up.

"Here! Take it! Here's his souvenir."

The boy began to cry and Horace wheeled on him.

"What's wrong, funny boy?"

One of the other fathers in the group came forward. Horace sized him up as the alpha dad, the chief meathead.

"You're out of control," he said, arms folded across his puffed-out chest over his gut.

"Control? Control your goddamn kids. Got it, coach?"

"Where's your boss? I'm going to your boss."

"What? You're going to *tell* on me?" Horace said. "You step up like some tough guy, and that's the best you got? To *tell* on me?"

Horace took a step toward the guy. With a hard stare, he held his blacksmith's hands up to the guy's face, knuckles out. Horace felt the rage rush to his head and the rush of blood in his ears made everything buzzy and muffled, bass drum thunder. The man held his ground, but his eyes darted back and forth to Horace's hands.

"You want to try me?" Horace said, close now and quiet, like he was telling a secret. "I've been working hard with these for twenty years, not sitting behind some fat-ass desk."

The guy started ushering his group out, and said over his shoulder, "This isn't the time or place, pal."

"Then you name it, Chunky," Horace said. "I'm not hard to find."

HORACE DIDN'T WAIT FOR GRUNDLING. He went to get his car and noticed Grundling's was already gone. Management, Horace thought. But this was good. It would give Horace access to his shop and maintenance barn after the museum closed. He walked to the cow barn, where Natalia was closing up.

"I might be leaving here, too," he said.

"Why, Horace? Are you all right?"

"Never mind all that now. I might be going to Ohio. Or Rochester. Can I look you up in Rochester?"

"In Rochester, sure," she said. "Horace, what is wrong? You seem . . ."

"Out of sorts? That's what Grundling just said."

"Yes. Out of sorts. Angry. Very angry."

"No, I'm fine. I just have some things to do, then I have to leave. If I come to Rochester, can I see you? Can I call you in a few days?"

She said yes, but even Horace knew, at that moment, she wouldn't have dared to say no.

HORACE WAITED AS THE EVENING shadows arrived and the lightning bugs started to blink on the fields. He then drove to the barn on the tire-track path at the ass-end of the farm. The Escort bucked and kicked up dirt, but he was alone on the grounds. He drove into an open bay, hidden behind draft horse stables, where the museum's Econoline vans were parked. He grabbed a heavy-duty chain saw, topped it off with the oil-and-gas mixture, and pulled it to life. The 60cc engine fired right up, and spat out its two-stroke whine. Horace shut it right down, and hustled it into the back of the Escort. He found a fresh can of lamp kerosene and put that in the car, too.

Are you a homeless man?

"Not yet, you little fuckhead," he said to himself.

At the shop, he loaded his personal tools into the car. A second maul, a two-headed ax, a long-handled sledge, several sizes of ball peens and mallets and tongs. The things he made that decorated the shop, everything from breadbaskets to candlesticks to ox yokes and hoist chains, he left. Time to travel light. He got a coal fire going in the hearth, stoked it with the bellows until the sweat poured out of his body, then sat and watched it, feet up on a second chair, relaxed like a man content, and waited for Michael.

Chapter Thirty-Two

Grudeck decided to drive himself to the bat store. The league had a limo waiting, and Sal offered to go, but Grudeck just wanted some time alone. Sort things out.

He called Stacy from his room and left a message, and wondered where she was. Maybe she was on her way up to surprise him, he thought. But he'd thought that all week, and still no Stacy. They last spoke on his second day in Cooperstown and she told him, "Just enjoy yourself. Don't worry about me," as they said good-bye. He'd rolled that sentence around in his head ever since, and felt pushed away. Hurt. And felt stupid for feeling hurt.

Then in comes Joanie MacIntosh and Grudeck takes what comes his way. Same old Joe. He felt most guilty about not feeling guilty. Stacy, back home, trusting him. But did she even care?

All this thinking put Grudeck in a shit mood. All of it, on his nerves: the rounds of golf with the jock-sniffing "corporate partners" of the league, and the obnoxious fans yelling out his name. Both embarrassed him. He couldn't move around the hotel without someone up his ass, and he couldn't hide in his room because of his "itinerary." And people from the league always at his elbow. Both elbows. Sponsor dinners. Meet-and-greets. Drinks. More drinks. Joanie MacIntosh at the door, on her knees, then on top. Always on. The price of celebrity. No one understood the exhaustion. If Stacy had come, he'd have a place to rest.

After he limped off the golf course on Saturday, he skipped a VIP cocktail hour and instead ordered room service, ate, took four Advil, and stretched out. He dozed off to Stacy's face as the inflammation in his hips and hands subsided. But in that brief dream state, the girls from Syracuse, black silhouettes in a doorway filled with light, visited him, and he snapped to, unnerved. The phone rang. "Yes, Commissioner, I'm feeling okay. Yes, I knew there was a cocktail hour."

Sal called. "Yes, I know I have a signing downtown. Yes. I'm getting ready."

"You sound like you're lying down," Sal said. "You sure you don't want me to go?"

"I'm okay. Take care of my mom. She's coming in tonight."

Grudeck languished in the shower, blasting hot water that turned his skin meaty and red, and dressed in casual black. He took the fire exit stairs to the parking lot, sunglasses already on, found his car without a valet, and took off.

The signing was from 6:00 to 7:30, so he had a half hour to kill, by design. He drove north on Lake Street, away from the downtown, and made a left on Glimmerglen Road, into the wooded hilly countryside. He wanted to get lost, to just follow the twisting pavement, mesmerized by the yellow lines, to wherever it took him, however long it took to get there.

MICHAEL HELD THE TWELVE-FOOT stepladder while June climbed. When her behind, snug in cuffed khaki shorts, was at his face level, she turned around and said, "Don't be fresh, now." Michael got red, and she leaned down and gave him a little tap on the shoulder.

"I'm just bustin' ya," she said.

She handed down boxes of Joe Grudeck stuff she'd ordered specially for the day, and the times their fingers would touch, he would feel the same thrill he felt when she reached up and the raspberry-blue Gone Batty shirt would stretch to outline her breasts. Maybe someday, he thought, when I'm a baseball star. When she climbed down, he held out his hand for her as she neared the last step.

"Thank you, kind sir," she said, and smiled. She took his hand and bounced down, almost into his arms, so close, and she looked like one of those Alabama or USC cheerleaders he saw on TV, all blond and smiley and so beautiful, but somewhere else, far away. Still, at that moment Michael thought he could never love a girl more. He wanted to tell her, so badly. Or just go ahead and kiss her. But he knew what would happen; she would say he was sweet, and tell him she was flattered, and that if he was older . . .

But he wasn't. He was just a kid, and there was nothing he could do but wish otherwise, and think that maybe, someday . . . when he was a baseball star . . .

That's why he told her about the scholarship first, even before his dad, to prove he was more than just a kid with a summer job. He had potential. She was happy for him, and when she said, "Well, we're going to miss you," Michael heard, *I'm going to miss you*, but instead of a kiss or a hug, he got the firm handshake of a store manager.

Now here it was, his last day before he would leave for Ohio. He had volunteered to work until the signing was over, because he wanted to stay until everyone left, and linger with her as long as he could, and trade cell numbers and become Facebook and Snapchat friends, and promise to stay in touch. He knew he was supposed to meet Horace, but he texted to say he would be late. Horace replied *okay*, and Michael shut his phone off so he wouldn't be bothered.

The store was closed while they arranged tables of Joe Grudeck memorabilia: reprinted baseball cards and frame-ready photos. June put authentic Grudeck jerseys on hangers, and made a display of Red Sox hats. Michael was glad to be alone with her, to help and just watch her be so happy, especially when the line began to form outside as early as noon, six hours before the signing.

But when she said, "I am so excited for this; I just *love* Joe Grudeck," Michael suddenly felt small and envious. And when she went out the back door of the store and returned with a six-pack of Samuel Adams Boston Lager to put in the fridge, he felt tiny and excluded. A few minutes later she opened the store, and the Red Sox fans crashed in. Some shopped, ransacking the clothes June had just folded, and some just stood in line, sweaty and breathing all over one another. Michael resented them for killing his alone time with her. He thought of his dad always complaining about "fat, T-shirt-wearing tourists," and it made him smile.

GRUDECK TRIED TO TURN ONTO PIONEER STREET, but was impeded by people with "B" hats and Red Sox shirts. Only then did it register; they were there for him. The line stretched a full block from the bat store and spilled into the street. It was still fifteen minutes till showtime and he wondered how long they'd been waiting. If he tried to walk past them, he'd be swarmed, so he found the side alley that led to the back door and parked there.

The back room of the store was shabby. An old table, a washtub sink and bathroom no bigger than a closet. Boxes of T-shirts stacked crooked like building blocks, and crates of unfinished wood bats. Through the opening to the main store he saw a cute blond girl in tight tan shorts with her back to him, bent slightly over a banquet table, laying out Sharpies and straightening piles of photos. A tall dark-haired kid stocked a row of bat racks along the main aisle with Grudeck's replica stick; the thick-barreled Louisville Slugger, the thirty-five-inch, thirty-four-ounce, red-stained white ash. Grudeck stood watching for a while outside the back door, watching her move around the table, setting up two chairs, putting out the cash box, smoothing the Red Sox–blue tablecloth. Sweet thing, Grudeck thought, then tapped on the window. The girl turned, pretty face, orthodontic smile, and bounded back to let him in. But she first shut the door between the store and back room.

Grudeck was surprised when she held out both hands for his, but obliged. She took his hand not at all firmly, and let it linger, and introduced herself as the manager.

"It is such a pleasure to meet you," she said.

She explained the layout and offered him a quick beer. He declined.

"Well, maybe after," she said.

"Maybe after," he replied.

She led him out front and introduced him to the tall kid, who was almost Grudeck's height. Grudeck figured right away the kid was a good athlete, because he had a self-confidence about him. He didn't hem and haw or smile nervously or flinch in any way, but just looked Grudeck in the eye and said, "Great to meet you, sir."

"Mike is quite the baseball player, too," June said. "He just got a scholarship to Saint—"

"Archbishop Moeller. In Cincinnati," Michael said. "Ken Griffey Junior and Barry Larkin went there."

"Ah, good," Grudeck said. The kid was all of what? Fifteen, sixteen?

"A little young to be leaving home, aren't you?" Grudeck asked.

"I'm fourteen," Michael said.

"Fourteen! Wow! You grow 'em big out here," Grudeck said to June as he clapped a hand on Michael's shoulder.

"Still," he said, looking back at Michael, "that's a big move, when you're young. I was eighteen . . . ," he began, and then trailed off, his mind distracted by cinematic snippets of "what ifs." He saw Stacy's face in high school, just a girl. What if he'd stayed? What if he'd matured a little before he was let loose on the world as a ballplayer? He thought of the Syracuse girls. He saw his father dying in the hospital, their relationship never reaching the depth of man-to-man, but remaining stuck on the surface of proud-dad-to-star-son. Even Ma. Jesus, did he even know her? What if he'd stayed? Would he have had a family? Joey, Stacy, and the kids at Ma's kitchen table? A life beyond this, greeting five hundred strangers who want to be your friends, friendless yourself? Here in Cooperstown, where—after Ma was gone—his only permanent home would be a fucking museum.

The kid was looking at him, wondering where he'd gone. Grudeck tightened his grip on his shoulder.

"I left early," he said. "And things worked out. But I missed a lot, too."

The kid was quiet for a few moments, as if he understood, then said, "My dad says the same thing."

"Then your dad's a smart man," Grudeck said.

THE GIRL SAT NEXT TO HIM, so close he could inhale her clean-air scent, so fresh it was overwhelming. She would take the fan's money, ask their name and spelling, then repeat it in Grudeck's ear for him to sign. "Larry." "Billy, Jr." "Sherri . . . S-H-E-R-R-I . . . I not Y." Each time she did it, in a low, heavy voice just above a whisper, it sent a tingle down Grudeck's leg. They touched legs at first, and he reflexively jerked away, but eventually came to rest his on the bare flesh of her thigh. *How old is she? Half my age, at most. Stacy at home. She should've come.*

The girl was pleasant to all the customers . . . "Of course he'll take a picture, that's why we're here." . . . "Yes, he can sign it to the McElroy family, how do you spell it?" . . . "No, sir, I'm sorry, the bat is fifty-nine ninety-five unsigned, autographed is eighty-nine ninety-five."

And attentive to Grudeck. Water? Coffee? She laid her hand on his bare forearm at one point and asked, "Do you need a break?" with such intimate concern he felt himself get slightly aroused. The second time she asked, he agreed. The girl summoned Michael to the front and announced, "Mr. Grudeck will be right back," to the fans. She followed him into the back room, offered him a beer.

"Better not," he said, and excused himself to use the bathroom to scrub his hands. The fullness he felt when she touched him was gone, and Grudeck spent a moment trying to revive it after he pissed, but gave up. When he came out, she was holding one of his bats, not in her fists, but with her fingers spread longways up the barrel. Was it his imagination, or was she actually caressing it? He thought of Stacy. Goddamn, she should have come.

"Can you sign this for Mike?" she asked. "He's leaving tomorrow. I want to give him a little present."

Grudeck's mind raced. Watching her fingers. She was just a kid. No, she was a grown woman, this . . . what was her name again? He took the bat and signed it.

IT WAS AFTER 7:30 and the line was still out the door. June told Michael to tell the people outside they weren't going to get in.

"Be nice, but if they give you any trouble, come get me," she told him, and Michael felt embarrassed. It was said in front of Mr. Grudeck, who might think Michael wasn't man enough. Not for the job, not for June.

Michael saw the way she fawned over Grudeck and patted his arm, like they were a couple. At first Michael thought she was just being nice, but then he saw it was more. His ears got hot. He was too young, sure, but Mr. Grudeck was *old.* How could she like him like that?

She told Michael to lock the door, then stand by it, to let the customers out and no one in.

"It's kinda early," Michael said. "We're open till nine."

"It's been a long day," she said. "And a good one."

WHEN THE LAST FAN LEFT, June and Grudeck went into the back while Michael folded up the banquet tables and straightened up the store.

He heard Grudeck say, "I should get going," but they each popped open a beer. He could hear June giggling from time to time, punctuating something Grudeck said in a husky voice.

When Michael was done, he went into the back, hoping Grudeck was on his way out. But they were both sitting there with a fresh beer and Michael felt a thing in his stomach he'd never felt before. Like weak. And sad. And kind of lonely.

"Are you all done, hon?" June asked.

"Yep," Michael said, and stood there, awkwardly.

Grudeck reached into his pocket, pulled out two tickets to the induction ceremony, and handed one each to Michael and June.

"They're not in the VIP section, but they'll get you in," he said. "Come by if you can."

"I will!" chirped June.

"Thanks anyway, Mr. Grudeck, but I'm leaving in the morning," Michael said, and tried to hand it back.

"Keep it. As a souvenir. Or give it to one of your friends. I got a bunch."

June then looked at Michael and said, "Okay, well, I have a little something for you, too," and handed him the bat that was leaning against the table. "Mr. Grudeck signed it for you."

"Thank you," Michael said to both, then, "Thank you, June."

June . . . that's right, Grudeck thought, thank you, kid.

Michael just stood there, feeling uncomfortable, unwanted, uneverything. Frozen.

"Well, okay, Mike," June said. "It's been great having you here, and you come back and visit, okay?"

She got up to give him a good-bye hug, and Michael barely touched her with his arms because he was afraid if he squeezed her, he would never let go.

"You did a good job here, hon, and good luck to you out there," she said, letting go quickly.

Grudeck rose and shook the kid's hand.

"Thanks for the bat, Mr. Grudeck."

"Sure thing, kid. And when you get bigger and stronger, maybe you can try it in a game," Grudeck said.

The words stung Michael, but Grudeck didn't notice the burst of anger in his eyes.

Michael went out the door. He was supposed to meet Horace, but figured he would circle the block a few times, and come back after Grudeck finally left. He would get June alone, and tell her all the things he rehearsed but was always afraid to say.

The streets of Cooperstown were happy. It was the night before Induction Day, and people milled around, families with children gathered outside the baseball-themed ice cream parlors and the other souvenir shops, all still open. Some had lines for other signing events, with old Hall of Famers sitting at tables autographing merchandise like Grudeck. Everyone had full shopping bags and the stores were all lit up in the diminishing evening light, and for some crazy reason, it made Michael think of Christmas, Cooperstown's other big holiday.

Michael slung his Joe Grudeck bat over his shoulder and walked. He was going to miss this place. Maybe his dad was right. Even Joe Grudeck said he was a smart man.

THE CAPS CAME OFF the third beer and the girl said, "I really shouldn't, I'm already a little woozy."

Grudeck didn't have time to encourage or discourage her before she brought the bottle up so fast, the foam spilled out of her mouth. She laughed and wiped it away with her hand, her eyes following Grudeck's to her lips, and then to her fingers as she squeegeed the neck of the bottle.

"I should shut out the front lights," she said. "So people know we're closed."

Grudeck watched her walk away, noticing the little athletic swivel from being up on the balls of her feet. Within seconds the whole place was dark, except for the glow coming out of the bathroom. She appeared in the doorway, backlit only by the light from the streets of Cooperstown, and the image drew Grudeck back to the Syracuse girls in his motel doorway.

"Oh, I didn't mean to do that," the girl said, and fumbled for a switch.

"Don't," Grudeck said, and he was on her. He scooped her up in his arms and kissed her hard, openmouthed. She was aggressive with her tongue and grabbed his head with both hands to lift herself to him.

He grabbed that gorgeous little ass of hers with both hands, roughly, and pulled her in, and she ground against him.

"Is there a place we can go?" he said.

"I have roommates," she said.

"Shit," he said. The hotel was out, obviously.

He spun her around, thrust his hand down her shorts, and found the right place with his finger. He held her tight around her belly with his other arm, exposing that sweet spot, and she felt his strength and it made her feel weightless and powerless and it didn't take long. She tried to spin back toward him, but he carried her over to the table like that and bent her over it. He undid her shorts and yanked them down, revealing a red thong, and he took each side of her ass in each hand and squeezed as hard as he could.

And still nothing. Rubbery-numb down there. She pushed into him, rotating her hips in a clumsy circle, to make something happen.

And this is what Michael saw.

The girl he loved, barely visible in the bathroom light, facedown on the table with Grudeck behind her, grinding themselves into each other. At first he thought Grudeck was hurting her, and he was about to take the bat and smash in the window, but then June got up and turned around. She undid his belt and pants and crouched down in front of him. Michael couldn't see everything, it was too dark, but in a sliver of the bathroom light he saw her blond hair bobbing and he knew what she was doing and couldn't watch anymore. He took off for the farm museum, running to see his dad.

Chapter Thirty-Three

Nothing was working. The girl was all mouth; she didn't know the hand rhythm like Joanie MacIntosh, and Grudeck wasn't responding. This beautiful girl, sucking away, and still nothing. Dead. He reached down and pulled up her shirt, to expose her naked back and her hip line, and the image of her blond hair and all that skin and the red thong over her naked ass exploded hot in his head. He'd never wanted anyone more. And still nothing. He felt for her breasts, encased in a flimsy bra. They were girl-firm and the nipples hardened and jumped in his hand. And still nothing. Fucking *nothing.* He didn't bring his pills; yeah, the straight and narrow. He closed his eyes. Concentrate. But his mind tumbled, all bad thoughts. Cheating on Stacy. The speech. The goddamn speech. The Syracuse girls, teary, telling their story. This girl, now, had a story, too. *"Oh, and by the way, big Joe Grudeck couldn't get it up."* No pills. No lead in the pencil. No pressure in the fire hose.

He pulled her to her feet and smoothed her shirt back down.

"I'm sorry," he said. "But this isn't right . . ."

"Am I doing something wrong?" she asked, now tugging him with her hand.

"No, no," he said, extricating himself from her grip and zipping up. "It's just that . . . you're so young. Really young. Like, young enough to be my daughter. I feel like a creep."

"What do you think? I'm a virgin?" she asked.

"No, I don't think that," he said.

"Then what?"

"Look, sweetheart, you're a beautiful young girl, but I'm a middle-aged, broken-down guy," Grudeck said, searching for the right words. "You had a few beers, maybe got some stars in your eyes, and I'd bet you'd regret this in the morning, and I would, too, like I took advantage of you."

"I know what I'm doing . . . ," she protested, but Grudeck stopped her, putting a finger to her lips.

"Tell ya what. On Monday before I leave, I'll stop by and take you out to lunch, and we'll see where it goes from there. Okay?"

"Sure, I guess," she said, embarrassed and hurt, as she pulled her shorts up, shaking her head. "I guess."

He kissed her on the cheek and quickly left, forgetting his money.

Chapter Thirty-Four

Joe Grudeck fucked June.

Michael muttered it to himself, over and over, feeding the rage and betrayal in his head.

Joe Grudeck fucked June.

He walked, then ran, then walked again, then sprinted, face red with anger and sweat, with tears mixed in. But no matter how fast he went, he couldn't escape the sentence pounding in his head.

Joe Grudeck fucked June.

How could she? He was gross. Old fat bastard. He wanted to break the bat in a million pieces. Smash fenders, shatter car windows, just whack it against all those tourists' cars parked along Pioneer and Chestnut. All those Boston fans here to see that asshole, Joe Grudeck.

Michael was crying, bent with that hollow weakness in his gut, trying to straighten up when people approached. Families with children, headed to the souvenir shops and to get ice cream. Little kids, boys and girls his age. Girls his age. They looked at him with concern. He didn't care. Let them see him cry. How could they be happy?

Joe Grudeck fucked June.

He started to run up Lake Street, where the road wound out of the business district and past the last few in-town Victorians, but lost his breath on the hill between the Otesaga Hotel and the farm museum property. Now, with no one around, he swung Grudeck's bat into the jagged edges of the rock wall every few steps.

Joe Grudeck fucked June. Whack. *Joe Grudeck fucked June.* Whack. *Fucked June. My June.* Whack. The vibration stung his hands, making him even angrier. He climbed the wall and ran hard across the fields up to the Cardiff Giant circus tent to find his dad.

Michael rushed breathless into the tent, but Horace was gone. He saw the box of red, cheap souvenir Grudeck bats, and flipped it off the stool, letting them spill all over the grassy floor. He ground them into moist earth, some snapping under his foot. Pieces of shit. Just like Joe Grudeck. With big bat still in his hand, he chopped down on the rest, breaking as many as he could. Now it was time to finally crack and splinter his "gift." He held it high over his head and brought it down in the pile of little bats, but it only mushed them into the ground. He did it again, and this time a broken piece of the souvenir bat kicked up into his face, and it stung like a slap. *Joe Grudeck fucked June.*

The Giant was the only rock around, the only thing hard enough to bust the big Grudeck bat. Michael swung it over his head the way he saw his father swing an ax a million times, and brought it down with all his might. A stone divot flew off the Giant. He did it again, and again, and the crimson wood stain of the bat left blood-colored smudges on the Giant. Finally Michael heard a satisfying crack and saw it run through the wood, but it wasn't broken. His hands were raw, but he did it again. *Joe Grudeck fucked June.* And again. *Joe Grudeck fucked June.* And again. *Joe Grudeck fucked June.* And again, until the barrel was a mash of dents and the handle splintered enough so he could twist it apart and rip it in two. He threw the pieces into the pile of broken little bats, then went down to the blacksmith shop hoping to find his father, leaving the Giant desecrated by a dozen pockmarks the color of an open wound.

HORACE WAITED FOR MICHAEL. When the hearth fire died down, he stoked it, and as time passed, he distracted himself by melting some of the candlesticks, plates, and other household items he'd made. He gloved up and held the pieces over the fire with tongs until they glowed red, then hammered them into dense lumps of iron. Destroying evidence. Burning bridges. One day he was there, the blacksmith, the next, gone; all traces of his craft reduced to first-year-metal-shop paperweights. *There comes a time in every man's life* . . . , he thought, but couldn't finish it.

When it was apparent Michael wasn't coming, Horace packed the hearth with coal and, in his last planned act of defiance, bellowed it to an inferno. He shut the exhaust vents to let the dense, particulate-filled smoke quickly engulf the shop, leaving its chalky gray stain and stench on everything. Horace emerged from the blackness, ready to start his new life. He shut and locked the door, then took in a deep breath of fresh, heavy dusk air, made moist by evening dew, and looked down at Otsego Lake, dark green now, long past its last blue shimmer of daylight.

He felt peaceful, not even too disturbed that Michael didn't show.

He'd see him soon enough in Ohio.

He'd surprise him, stay for a few days, catch up with Natalia in Rochester for a while, then head back to Ohio. A new life.

Horace drove off, lamp kerosene cans, chain saw, and tools rattling in the back. Through the open car window, he heard several cracks echoing through the farm museum valley and figured someone was in the hillside forest, chopping wood. He steered the Escort, struts groaning under the trunk weight, through the downtown, slowing for the crowds of tourists. He went past Gone Batty to see if Michael was still working, but the store was dark.

MICHAEL FOUND THE SMITHY DOOR locked and the inside dark, so he pulled out his phone to call Horace. He forgot it was off, and when it powered up, he saw all the missed text messages and calls from Horace, and figured his father was too angry to deal with now. He decided to call his dad in the morning, after he and his mom were on the road to Ohio.

Ohio. Suddenly, the thought of leaving scared him. He thought of all his dad had said about home, this place, his friends. What did he say? Something about the context of your life. Michael looked down at the lake and the green mountain behind it. It was a beautiful place; his dad taught him that. Maybe he shouldn't go.

Even dumb-ass Joe Grudeck seemed to have regrets; Michael saw it in his face when he said, "I missed a lot, too."

Michael walked to the bench, the one in front of the plain white church, and sat and gripped his head with his hands. So many thoughts. So much ache.

His mom wanted to go, but why? Was it just for him? Was he being selfish? Or maybe she was trying to get him away from his dad? Was that it? The thought of Horace left back, alone in the old house, made Michael sad, and it washed out some of the anger and betrayal he felt in his gut. But there was a new quiver. He wanted to see June again. He wanted to be near her, even just at work. Ohio would be so far away. He would miss Cooperstown. People came from all over to be here, and he was moving away. Something about that didn't make sense. He thought of what his dad said. *You can get where you want from right here.*

"Dad." He said the word out loud, surprised by the childlike sound of his own voice.

AS HORACE TURNED UP HIS DIRT DRIVEWAY off Chicken Farm Hill Road, he remembered he'd forgotten to take the last copies of "American Rubism" from the Giant's tent. He'd planned on using them to start the fire, *destroying evidence, burning bridges.* Better to keep them anyway. He wanted to give extra copies to Natalia, because she was credited in the footnotes, so he'd just go back in the morning and get them on his way out of town. Besides, it would be fitting to take a last look across the valley and lake to the mountain, and see the smoke rising over the trees as his house burned down.

In the house, he went to work. He packed his few clothes in plastic garbage bags, and collected Michael's mythology and nature books. He got the fireproof box with birth certificates, Social Security cards, and other important papers, and packed it all in the car. All except his marriage license. He put that on top of the wood-burning stove with more foreclosure notices and collection agency threats.

He crammed the woodstove with those papers, and then some live pine kindling, which would spit embers like gobs from the mouth of Satan. He neatly arranged eight dry quarter logs on top, leaving enough air between them for good ventilation. It would be a hot fire, a hellfire. If the embers failed, the heat alone would ignite the kerosene fumes. But for tonight he threw open every window in the house, then got a mop and spread the lamp kerosene evenly on the hardwood floors like polish. It would soak in overnight, and the airflow would not let the fumes accumulate. But in the morning, he would lay down a fresh coat, close the windows tight, put a match to the stove, and get the fuck out of there. Kerosene had a low flashpoint.

There comes a time in every man's life when . . .

Horace drove downhill to the end of the long driveway, parked, and slept restlessly in the car.

Chapter Thirty-Five

Grudeck got back from the bat shop and called Sal, and they met in the same dark corner of the Hawkeye.

"I'm in a Jack Daniel's kind of mood," Grudeck said, hoping to burn out the snot-lump of frustration and shame in his throat. Frustrated because he wanted it badly, and couldn't do it. Shamed because she was just a girl, and Stacy was home, and he couldn't do it. Joanie MacIntosh. Now this. All the guilt. He fell off the straight and narrow, crashed with a thud. No, a dud.

Three drinks in, Sal said, "Take it easy, Tiger. Big day tomorrow."

"Like I haven't had big days before, huh, Sal?" Grudeck snapped.

"Whoa. Whatever bug is up your ass, I didn't it put it there."

Grudeck didn't apologize, but when he said, "Don't worry, I can handle it," it had a conciliatory tone.

They were quiet for a few moments and Grudeck's mind drifted to Stacy. What to do about Stacy. He wished she'd come. All this, the speech, the girl, all the bullshit up here . . . if only she were here.

"Joe."

"Yeah, Sal."

"What are you going to do tomorrow?"

"What?"

"The speech, that's what. I'm worried you're going to commit hara-kiri up there."

Grudeck shook his head, drained the Jack, and summoned the waitress for another, pointing to his glass.

"Joe. What's going through that thick head of yours?"

Grudeck leaned back in his chair and put both hands on the table, as if he were laying out cards.

"Truthfully, Sal, I have no fucking idea. When I get up there, I'll see how it feels."

"Joe, listen to me, damn it. This isn't getting to the plate, looking for a fastball, and hitting a curve. This is serious. This is your reputation, your image."

"My *image* . . . ," Grudeck said, down-turning the words, and his mind went to the Syracuse girls in the doorway, and the bat-store girl tonight. "My image . . . my image, Sal, can come crashing down any minute. Any fucking minute. Everybody has a past. Anybody can come forward with—what's the word?—allegations. Alleg-fucking-gations. You know that, that's the way of the world today. The media up somebody's ass every second. Better I do it myself."

"What the hell are you talking about . . . unless there's something I don't know . . . Is there something I don't know?"

Grudeck chucked the last of the Jack down his throat, winced, and said, "No."

"You sure? A few years ago your mother came to me worried you were a fag. 'Why doesn't he have a girlfriend?' she said. I almost said, 'Sylvia, if you only knew.' It's nothing like that, is it, kid? I mean, if it is, well, the world's different today."

"Jesus, Sal. For Christ sakes. No."

"Then your image is golden, kid. It's money in the bank. And you earned it. You're one of the good guys. Don't you see that?"

Three Jacks later, Grudeck teetered to his suite; the baseball security guy was still there.

"All quiet?" Grudeck said.

"All quiet, Mr. Grudeck," he said.

Grudeck pulled out his wallet and took out a couple of hundreds.

"Here you go. Thank you for your service. Your secret service."

The guy took the cash as easily as Darlena the waitress had.

"Are you all right, sir?"

"Fuck! I'm fine! I'm a baseball immortal!" Grudeck said with transparently phony glee.

GRUDECK SLEPT FOR SHIT. The booze didn't take the edge off, and all the golf had his joints screaming. He got up to piss three times, finishing each trip with another two Advil. In the dark, ghosts and regrets, old and new, came to him. Hazy teenaged girls with smeared makeup, helping each other into the bleached white of a Syracuse summer morning. Stacy's face on the porch at the history house, young and bright and beautiful, and now with looser skin on her neck and sadder eyes, but beautiful just the same. Still putting him off, pushing him away. The night he asked her to come to Cooperstown, to see him through this. *It was your life, Joe. Not mine.* That's what she said. The bat-shop girl, so, so young, red thong and blond head in rhythm, still calling him Mr. Grudeck.

He listened to his heart pound; it shook his entire chest cavity. He had to get back in shape. But all the pain. He drifted off, half awake, half dreaming about the end.

GRUDECK CALLED A FASTBALL, low and away, but the rookie threw it high. And hard. Ninety-four, maybe ninety-five. Wild pitch. Grudeck popped up to pull it down. He should have let it go. Nobody on, late-August game, pennant out of reach. But it was reflex. Of all those Joe Grrreww moments, that's the one he wished he could take back. The pitch hit all wrong, square in the palm, not in the glove web. The impact quaked through the sponge; the smack of hard ball on pliant mitt was followed by a dull shock that radiated up his hand to his elbow through the fault lines of his bones. The aftershock was a sharp pain right above his wrist. He threw the glove off, the only time Grudeck ever showed pain, in all those years.

The trainer came out and took him out, but not until Joe Grudeck made a scene of wanting to stay in. He jammed the glove back on this throbbing hand and started to pull on his helmet and mask. The trainer tugged at his arm but Grudeck pulled it away. He put up enough of a phony fight to get the crowd rocking, then went off as they chanted, "Grrrr-ewww . . . Grrrr-ewww . . . Grrrr-ewww."

That was six years ago. He knew he was done. He was breaking down. There was a surgery and rehab, and a lazy off-season. He couldn't catch again; the hand wouldn't stand any more pounding. In spring training, they tried him at first base, then as DH. He could still hit pretty good, but felt lost not running the defense. He was out of the game, even when he was in it. Then people around him got quiet, and he knew a shot in the head was coming for the old horse. He talked it over with Sal.

"Don't hang on. Don't humiliate yourself, or let them humiliate you. Go out on top. Protect your reputation." Same old advice. Grudeck took it, and retired.

Opening Day was also Farewell Joe Grudeck Night. He came out in the new white uniform, as thirty-five thousand people stood and cheered. He did his Lou Gehrig thing, sans tears, tipped his cap, and disappeared into the dugout. He changed and drove out of the players' lot before the first inning was over. That was it. And just like that, one day you *are* Joe Grudeck, the next day you *were* Joe Grudeck.

THE HAND WAS KILLING HIM. It was under the full weight of his sweaty head, crushed into the pillow, and the pain woke him. It was four o'clock, and there, in the darkest part of the Otsego Lake night, Grudeck was suddenly filled with a sense of dread. Lonely dread. Today was the last day of his old life. In a few hours, he would be inducted as a baseball immortal, and then, just like that, he would be a ghost of baseball past. It was coming. The relentless march toward irrelevance. Lonely irrelevance. Grudeck lay there, listening to his heart pound, taking inventory of his pains and aches, not being able to envision a future beyond this day, Induction Day.

Induction Day

Chapter Thirty-Six

At dawn, as the caw of crows rang out through the trees like cries of some tortured, woods-lore ethereal ghost, Horace got up and pissed out in the open. He checked his phone for messages from Michael, but his battery went dead during the night. He got his tools together and went to work. He moved the car almost to the street, a good two hundred yards from the house, farther than any pumper truck hose could reach. He fired up the chain saw, and began to drop small trees over the driveway. His expert angled cuts insured they fell where he wanted, creating a timber blockade to keep the town's fire trucks away. The last thing he needed was some dumb volunteer fireman walking into the inferno. An arson warrant was one thing; manslaughter was another. They might not chase him for burning down a worthless house. Hell, it would save the bank some demolition costs. But for a dead fireman, they'd find him.

After a few small trees, Horace was still worried the trucks might flatten them to get to the fire. He chose a fifty-foot pine a few feet into the woods, and he timbered it with ease, as the jagged metal saw chain tore through the soft wood like shark teeth on flesh. It fell across the driveway in a crash of snapping branches, dust, and flying needles. Horace noticed a few old bird nests, now dry and empty, spill out and break apart on impact. He dropped two more trees like it, and a third he sawed into thick logs. He rolled one out, split it in eighths with ax and maul, stacked it, then did another. He left the tools there, to give the impression he'd taken down the trees for firewood—not to stop fire trucks—and it was work in progress.

He walked up to the house—no way those fat town volunteers were going to drag hoses up this fucking hill—and sat on the porch to catch his breath. It was just after noon, and the late-July sun beat down on the house. He was perspiring and his hands were sticky with pine sap, and raw from the ax and maul handles. He massaged his aching joints, and thought about the last night there with Michael, looking at the stars, and Horace's lesson of going your own way. It wasn't all bullshit. Horace believed in it.

This was his journey. It cost him his wife, his home, his job, but it wouldn't cost him his son. Quite the opposite. His journey—his choice, his way—would take him to Ohio, to follow Michael, yes, and fight to be his father. This would be the greatest gift he could give his son; a definition of fatherhood Michael could use to anchor his own adult life. Wives, homes, jobs may come and go, but being a father is permanent. It is the *relevance* Horace fruitlessly sought in other places; in Sally's arms, in the smithy, in his character. All the time it was right in front of him. He knew it, damn it, and should have been less forceful and more forgiving. He would have won, the way he was winning now. Because two days ago, he felt beaten. Now he did not. He was no longer afraid. Everything was lost, but he was free. With great loss comes great liberation. That's the only way to look at life. Without Sally, a house, a job, he was free to be the father, the man, he wanted to be. If it had to be in Ohio, well, so what?

There comes a time in every man's life when he . . .

It was time. Horace went to the kitchen sink and washed the sawdust off his face, neck, and arms. He walked through every room, empty of everything of value, except the stove itself. This was not the time for sentiment. A new life, new memories awaited him; this place was as cold and barren as Sally became to him.

It was time to let it go. Horace opened the second can of lamp kerosene and spread it sloppily this time, leaving pools in the room near the stove. He put the empty cans—Exhibit A—on the porch; they would have to be ditched far away. He went back into the house and slammed shut all the windows. He knew the first blast would blow the thin panes out, and the flames would inhale and gulp air, and exhale it in fiery colors of cobalt blue, red, and orange, and leave nothing but black, black, black.

At the stove, he took a wooden match from the box and struck it on the worn strip of flint. It sparked to life; this spontaneous combustion of red phosphorus, sulfur, and potassium chlorate. He lit their marriage certificate first and a foreclosure notice second, and only stayed long enough to see the flames move up to the kindling. He left the grate open and ran to the door. It wouldn't take long for the fire to spit an ember, or for the stove temperature to reach one hundred degrees, the flashpoint of kerosene fumes. Christ, it was already ninety, so Horace had to be way clear, quick.

He was halfway down the driveway when he heard the deep, guttural howl of a gale-force wind and the shatter of glass. He turned to see the flames erupt from the windows and felt a wave of heat on his face. After that, he never looked back.

SALLY WENT TO SHAKE MICHAEL AWAKE AT 5:00 A.M. She'd been up since 3:00, packing the car. Life came down to this. One carload. This was not what she'd dreamed of but nonetheless it was liberating. She felt unencumbered, about to make her escape from Horace and the house and all that went wrong in Cooperstown. In a few minutes she would put her sleepy son in the car and drive away. All that open road, all that expanse of highway, of opportunity, of adventure. She had already lined up three job interviews in Cincinnati and booked herself into one those extended-stay hotels near the school. In ten hours, she would be in her new city, Michael would be with his new team, and who knew what the future would bring.

"Mikey. Baby. Time to get up," she said close to his ear.

But he was awake, troubled all night by the thing he had seen, and that he didn't get a chance to see Horace.

"Let's go later, Mom," he said.

"No, no, no, sweetheart, we have a plan."

Michel had a plan, too. He wanted to see June, one more time, at the shop or the induction ceremony. Maybe those tickets Grudeck gave them were next to each other. Then he would go to the museum and say good-bye to his dad. And somewhere deep inside him, he was hoping his dad would talk him out of going. He didn't tell Sally about June, or that maybe he didn't want to leave after all, just about seeing Horace.

"You were supposed to do that last night."

"I missed him. My phone was off, and then he didn't answer his. Maybe he was asleep."

Sally didn't like the sound of this. Something was changing, and she could feel Michael's trepidation.

"We should go, Michael. You have practice. We'll call your dad from the road."

"No, Mom, it's no big deal if I miss one practice."

"Mikey, please."

Michael heard the slight desperation in her voice, and it confirmed his suspicion: leaving Cooperstown wasn't for him, it was for her. He thought of his father's words again, *This town is our home, your home. Cooperstown. For better or worse.*

"What's one more day, Mom? I just want to say good-bye to my dad."

Chapter Thirty-Seven

Grudeck slept in again, till late morning, lulled by the overworked hum of the air conditioner. He woke choked by thick mucus that clogged the back of his throat. In the bathroom, he hacked it up, gobbed it out, then pissed again. Two more Advil. Fuck it, three. He looked at his face in the mirror, framed by the bright floral wallpaper that conflicted with the darkness of his mood. He looked gray. Puffy. Tired. "Kid, it ain't your day."

His phone vibrated on the nightstand. Stacy.

"Joe. Hi. Did I wake you?"

"No, I'm up. Just groggy. I'm moving. Got to get there pretty soon."

"Well, I just wanted to tell you good luck today," she said.

They were both quiet, and Grudeck tumbled back onto the bed, head fuzzy, exhausted.

"You okay?" she asked.

What do you care? The words of self-pity formed in his head, but he stopped himself.

"Yes. Fine. Just about to go over the speech."

"You're going to do it?"

"Sal keeps telling me not to burn bridges . . . ," Grudeck said, not adding he was in a bridge-burning kind of mood.

More quiet, then Stacy tried again.

"Well, how's it been? Are you having fun?"

"Fun?" Grudeck said flatly, hoping to mask the resentment in his voice. "Not exactly. Playing golf with sponsors. Too much. Shaking a lot of hands. Too much of that, too. Dinners. Drinks. Like Sal said, the whole party's just for me."

"You sound down," she said.

"Down and out," Grudeck said.

"My God, Joe, this should be the happiest day of your life! This is everything you worked for."

"I worked to play. Not to be a bronze plaque," Grudeck said. He stopped. She couldn't possibly understand.

"Joe, please, just try to enjoy it."

"I am . . . but something doesn't feel right," he said.

"What?"

"I don't know. I can't put my finger on it," Grudeck said. And that was true. It wasn't just her, or all the handshakes, or all the smothering attention, or his limp member, or feeling old on the cusp of being forgotten. There was something else. Some sense of doom.

Even when Stacy said, "Well, maybe the day will bring a pleasant surprise. You never know, right? Anyway, I miss you," it didn't soothe Grudeck's unease.

Stacy was the surprise. She was on her way, calling from the road about two hours south of Cooperstown. She hadn't planned it but when she woke on the morning of Induction Day, the first thought that popped into her mind was *Cardinal Sin*. Joe wanted her there. It was a big moment—maybe the defining moment—of his life. She should have been there. Maybe not front and center, but at least to witness it and show herself later. In a restless night, she thought that her refusal to go might alter a future she was still trying to figure out. It would give Joe a reason to run again, armed with the excuse that she just didn't care. But she did. Was it love? Or comfort? Or just a deep friendship forged in the hazy adolescence of coming dreams? Joe lived his. She shouldn't hold that against him any longer. She was going to be there. Somewhere in the night, she felt that if she wasn't, he might slip away.

GRUDECK WENT TO THE CLOSET and pulled out the black Cerruti suit she'd helped him pick out and laid it on the bed. He showered and dressed. It was time to go, to meet Sal and his mother in the lobby and board a stretch limo to the ceremony. The air conditioner clicked up; the straining motor was the only sound in the room, and it reminded Grudeck he had not yet opened the room-darkening curtains to see what kind of day it was.

He went to the large window that faced the lake and pulled open the drapes. Otsego Lake was deep blue, the golf course lush green. Carts moved along the fairways and a tour boat was docking. Life, going on. Below him, on the extensive restaurant patio, the guests of baseball were finishing brunch, wearing blue blazers and summer dresses, attired for Grudeck's big day. To his right was the expanse of lake, tailing off to some unseen corner, shadowed by a long mountain. To his left was a lakeside motel, with children splashing in a small pool while their watchful parents lounged on the deck. It was peaceful, and quiet, with all the noise drowned out by the air conditioner buzz. It all seemed so picturesque, so perfect—marred only by a long column of black, roiling smoke rising above the treeline midway up the mountain.

Chapter Thirty-Eight

Stigmata. *Stigmata.* That was the word. Horace's fingers probed the Giant's bloody divots, the red smears on his gypsum skin. The anguish on the Giant's face, that twisted, silent scream, now cried pain. Ribs and arms broken by a baseball bat; nose chipped and smudged scarlet like that of a battered heavyweight.

The old guy didn't deserve this, Horace mourned. Requiem for a . . . Whoever took the bat to him . . . those cowardly bastards . . . whoever did this to a defenseless . . . Horace knew, and his grief rocketed to rage.

Boston fans. Cowards. Bastards. Motherfuckers. There wasn't a word to pen Horace's anger.

There was only this: *What goes around comes around.*

They'd vandalized his stone man. He'd vandalize theirs. Grudeck's bronze plaque.

What goes around . . . The idea came as quick to him as his mood change.

But for Horace, the blacksmith—*the muscles of his brawny arms are strong as iron bands*—there would be no skulking around under the cover of darkness. The blacksmith—*a mighty man is he*—would do it in the open—*and looks the whole world in the face, for he owes not any man.*

His rage flipped to glee and he felt a rush of joyousness, bathed by golden purpose. Ah, this was sent by God. This is what his whole life, his *whole world* came to; this, this, this defining moment. This moment of *clarity.*

He would deliver a message, one strike from Thor, good old *Donnerstag*, the god of the hammer, of strength, of courage.

One strike, like the *voice of one crying in the wilderness.*

One strike, his *revolutionary act of truth* against the false *truth of majorities.*

One strike, against all he despised, against the things that stole his son, against the culture of cheapness and idiocy that decayed this great country, *his* great country, against all those who mocked him. One strike against all those under the anesthesia of the diversion-makers, those too numb or dumb to tune out the siren song from its whores in the media.

The blacksmith, *a mighty man is he*, would stand. He would stand, and be seen, in all his physical and mental muscularity, and be counted. One truth. The truth, not of a majority, but of the lone man. The outcast. The blacksmith.

He took the remaining copies of "American Rubism" from the stand, and shoved one in his back pocket to leave at the scene of his farewell act, his calling card, his written speech, his *fuck you*, if anybody cared to understand.

He stepped across the broken bats on his way out, feeling the cheap wood snap under his feet. He did not bother to inspect the shards of the big bat, on the barrel of which was scrawled this message: *To Michael—See you in the big leagues—your pal, Joe Grudeck.*

Horace raced into town and could hear the fire truck horns bouncing across the lake, their circular echoes crying that they were lost, trying to find the fire on the mountain no one bothered to report.

On Susquehanna Avenue, not far from where the induction ceremony was being held, Horace could smell the smoke. It was stale and old already. As he looked north, he saw a wispy gray haze enveloping the hillside where he lived. Used to live. The stratus cloud now formed by his grand bonfire had a fog-blanket effect, far from the smokestack billows of black he saw from the farm museum valley. The old clapboard house, pretreated for arson, had burned quickly and efficiently. By the time the volunteers found it, it would be charcoaled timber, gutted, and in a red-hot smolder. No reason to fight it, just let it burn out.

Toward the Clark Sports Center, traffic stalled as police slowly waved latecomers into the jammed parking lot. Horace jumped the curb on the opposite side of the street, turned the car behind a rock wall, and drove two hundred yards undetected through a hay field leading to the old stables. He pulled into the circular driveway, tracking mud from the pasture. Old Hank was there, sitting in a lawn chair behind orange cones that kept fans from parking on stable property.

"Horace, what brings you here?"

"I got a job to do," he said, and popped the trunk hatch of the Escort. He reached for the long-handled hammer with a five-pound sledge. That ought to do it. And because his hands were raw from the earlier work, he pulled on a pair of leather mitts he had used to go elbow deep into the fire at the smithy.

"Something for the museum?" Hank asked.

"You could say that," Horace said, thinking *respect*. Or *revenge*. A nose for a nose. What goes around comes around.

The induction tent across the street was half the size of the soccer field it was pitched on, and loudspeakers carried the ceremony to the overflow crowd.

While Hall of Fame execs droned on and some awards were given out, Horace grew impatient. Enough with all this self-congratulatory bullshit. Time was being wasted. He wanted to strike, escape, and head to Ohio. He leaned on the sledge, his battle cudgel.

Hank gave him the skunk eye. "So, what's that for?"

"The job," Horace said.

Before Hank could ask another question, "Please give a Cooperstown welcome to our newest inductee . . . ," and the frantic applause and cupped-hand yells of "Grrrewww!" and cowboy whoops drowned out his name. Horace got in the Escort, started it back up, got out again, and told Old Hank to "leave it running."

At that moment a car drove up. An attractive dark-haired woman rolled down the window and asked Old Hank, "Can I please park here? Please? I'm so late . . ."

"Well . . . you ain't supposed to but I'm a sucker for a pretty face."

He waved her in next to Horace's wagon, looked down at the plates, and said to Horace, "Wouldn't you know it . . . Jersey driver."

But Horace was already moving quickly, long gone before the woman told Hank, in a way of explaining herself, "I'm a friend of Joe Grudeck's," and pressed a twenty-dollar bill in his hand.

Horace jogged across the street, calm, the sledge bootlegged, to a side entrance. A female ticket-taker tried to stop him, but Horace squared his shoulders and just kept going. Poor girl. She didn't want to make a commotion, Horace knew, because Almighty Grudeck was already at the podium, thanking the fucking world. Horace felt no eyes on him. He only saw his target; the bronze tablet with Grudeck's expressionless face in perpetuity. No smile, no silent scream. Stone man, stoic mug. Horace brought the hammer up, horizontal at his waist, rifle-style, and double-timed up the side aisle. He was locked in on the plaque, and soon the stage was in front of him, a last hurdle to be cleared, and Horace did it with an ease and grace that surprised him. He scrambled up, then quickly got to his feet, and then there was nothing between him and his revenge. The plaque was secured on a sturdy platform and Horace was on top of it in two strides. He launched the hammerhead while still moving, and the strike was solid. The sound was a satisfying, rich clang, a lone funereal reverberation. *Requiem for the Giant.*

The sound was so, so luscious, Horace wanted to hear it again. He twisted himself back as far as his spine would allow, then uncoiled with every ounce of torque he could ever coax out of his body. *A mighty man is he.* He swung with unleashed rage and frustration, but with a perfected pivot and arc, and with all that power, the centrifugal force of the hammerhead pulled him off balance. And when it hit, there was no musical tone. This was a deadening *splat!* Ax on wood, meat clever on bone, fist on nose, guillotine on neck. There were metal-on-metal sparks, where the hard steel sledge head hit the soft bronze throat of Joe Grudeck, and a lightning-bolt slash ripped through the plaque. It broke in two, and fell, not with the sound of a crashing cymbal, but of a dropped bowling ball. Horace's work here was done.

He tossed the hammer, shook off the gloves, and gave Grudeck a go-fuck-yourself look. Grudeck. Dumb ass. Standing there with his mouth agape. Ape. The dumb-ass ape then tossed the podium in some theatric display of jock macho and Horace dug in. *A mighty man is he.* A mighty man does not run. He stands, oaklike. Horace braced for Grudeck, stuffed in his suit like a sausage in membrane casing, and his aggressive pounce wasn't catlike, it was cattlelike. Horace easily straight-armed him, but Grudeck dove for his legs and Horace simply stiffened and collapsed on him, and heard him panting like a tired dog. In this first moment of stillness, Horace saw cops coming from all sides. Time to go. He hammer-fisted Grudeck one, two, three times, maybe more, to free himself but by then someone had him in a headlock and there were hands all over him. He toppled backward, pulled by the cops, and Grudeck landed on top of him. Horace was done, but Grudeck went for his throat, and when Horace saw the crazy rage in his eyes, he got Grudeck's neck and held tight, *with large and sinewy hands, and the muscles of his brawny arms are strong as iron bands.*

The power Horace felt at that moment was redemption for all that ate at him. He squeezed against the false hero worship of the Joe Grudecks of the world and the blind idiocy of their fans; he squeezed to defend his authentic, historic culture against the shallow, mind-numbing diversions of the modern world; he squeezed hardest to get his son back and to assert his own fatherhood—his own manhood—in these times when the whole fucking world seemed stacked against it. With this power, this Samson strength, he lifted this famous lug of a jock almost effortlessly and shook him to punctuate his physical superiority. *A mighty man—he is!*

But then there was a nightstick across Horace's chest, and too many arms at him. Horace yielded again. *Easy, now, easy.* When they said, "Turn over and put your hands behind your head," he did. *Easy. Take it easy.* Then he felt knees crash down on him driven by the full weight of men, while others twisted his arms and cuffed him too tight. He was yanked roughly to his feet. Tough guys, these cops who always had you outnumbered, with their billy clubs and stun guns and automatic weapons. Horace thought all that, and went quietly, but not meekly, into the crowd of cowards now rushing toward him. *I do not fear*, he thought. Instead, he relished the moment as cups and programs flew, and they mocked him, this king of chaos, loathed by pagan worshippers. He stood tall above them, proud, upright, and unbeaten—the lone voice, the blacksmith, *a mighty man is he*—even when the bat smashed down mightily on his head.

Horace fought off the black flash of unconsciousness.

I, too, am a stone man.

The blood of their sins trickled into his eyes, but through it he saw new light, the sunlight from outside the tent that illuminated the crush of faces, red, meaty, twisted, angry faces, cursing, slobbering, bellowing like wounded animals of a human subspecies.

And from that light and crush of hating faces came an urgent sound he'd heard many times as he contemplated his purpose and sought peace in the bleak of night.

"Dad! Dad!"

It was Michael, who had come to rescue him.

Fall

Chapter Thirty-Nine

There was deep sleep, dark and infinite, something close to death. He was still and naked, stripped of uniform and fame, at the mercy of hired hands, some tender, some not so. They washed him and adjusted his tubes. He felt hands work on him, not pulling at him, not asking anything from him. When the hands were gone and there was silence in the room except for the constant blips and hums of medical machines, he went deeper into the hole of himself. Some cavern of brain and soul. There he found himself through the ages. The him in his first conscious moments, taking in the world with wonder. The him on colt legs and with fledgling balance stumbling from chest-high coffee table to couch cushion. Joining the world of other children, oblivious yet nervous, discovering there were many others like him in that world. The him that was just another Joey, before he became Joe Grudeck.

There were moments, too brief for memory, when he did not sleep. It was then that he heard the murmurs of voices, or the rhythm of a machine, wheezing in and out, and the pedestrian beep-beep-beep of another. In these first hazy moments of consciousness, he fought to move or call out. But he could not, and fell back into the black hole of coma. There, in a jumble of memories and images, he found an essence, a baseline of himself, lonely and adrift. He was separate from a crowd, people he knew, his parents, Stacy, Sal, old coaches and teammates, through the ages. He wanted to join them. He held out his arms and waded in and they embraced him.

He slept. He heard his mother's voice. She was telling stories about him he'd never heard or barely remembered. Always first to shovel snow for old Mrs. Ippolito, a neighbor, or help carry her groceries, always first to volunteer for the nuns. Made his mother proud.

There were other stories, these from Stacy. Yes, she was here! He heard adjectives like *gentle* and *kind*. He picked up fragments—"I knew he was different"—and his mother agreeing and affirming.

"Joey, I'm here." It was his mother.

"Joe, I'm here." It was Stacy.

He wanted to cry out, "I'm here, too." But he could not.

He felt more hands on him. Tape being pulled off skin. A warm rag washing his nuts. Something hard down his throat. Wake up, he told himself. But he slept. Through the ages. He heard his own voice, mocking and self-loathing. "You got what you deserved, prick. Fuck you." But it was shrill and weak. A stronger voice came. One of peace and serenity. Guilty, but forgiven. Wasn't that the way? Wasn't that what Jesus promised? It came to him in those coma dreams.

He saw the surrender in the big guy's eyes as the cops took him away and the crowd pelted him. Did the big guy see the surrender in his? Was he the Messenger of Humility, sent by the Holy Ghost? Grudeck heard the voice of God. "Yes, asshole."

His hand hurt. It was being squeezed. He was alive. Pain meant that. It was the hand McNulty broke.

"Joe, I'm here, baby." *Stacy. She called me baby.*

He slept more. His head hurt. Then he slept again, numb to all the pain.

The skin on his back felt raw, then many hands pulled him up, while other hands rubbed cream on his back. "God, this guy is heavy," a woman said, but Grudeck felt weightless, drifting in space. He slept again. Then, some unformed time later, Stacy again.

Check Out Receipt

Bernards Township Library
908-204-3031
www.bernardslibrary.org

Monday, February 11, 2019
4:23:24 PM

Item: 0100403386079
Title: Gods of wood and stone : a novel
Material: Book
Due: 02/25/2019

Total items: 1

You just saved $26.00 by using your library!

"I'm here, baby." She was close, there to take care of him. Even in this muted stupor, he slept, satisfied.

"I'm here, baby." But then he wanted to see her and he forced his eyes to flutter, and then he slept again, and then he got his eyes to open and everyone was there. Stacy, Ma, Sal. People in green scrubs. All to take care of him.

"Welcome back, Mr. Grudeck," one of the green people said.

Medically induced coma to reduce brain swelling is how it started.

"But you must have liked it there, so you stayed longer than we anticipated," the doctor said. "This concussion on top of the old ones made your brain vulnerable."

There were things he had to know. The surgery scar. The stiffness. Some numbness in the face, left side. The slight loss of "motor skills" and weakness, also on the left.

"The average person might not notice, but you will. It will bring your coordination level down to, say, mine," the doctor joked. "Eighteen holes of golf might be tough, and your scores might climb. But seriously, you're a lucky man."

Grudeck looked in the mirror. He saw the slight droop in his face. He thought of the girls in Syracuse. It was the face he deserved. A public penance for his private sin. Or was it still secret?

He asked, "Who was that guy?"

"The police said he was some local eccentric nut," Stacy told him as she held his hand at his bedside. "His wife left him and they were having money problems."

"Tha's it?" Grudeck slurred. "Tha's all?"

He was safe. His reputation intact. Ancient history.

Sal was right. The speech was a bad idea. No one would have understood. The big guy saved him from himself. And for that, the big guy was forgiven.

He got his legs back under him in physical therapy, his limp now a slight drag, and learned how to dab at the drool on the side of his mouth before it got noticeable. They packed him up and sent him back to Union, to stay with his mother for a while until he figured out the rest. Before he left the hospital, he signed autographs all around, leaving a signature that looked shaky and craggy, like from an old, feeble hand. They wheeled him out a side door, dodging the cameras, into a waiting limo. He struggled to lift himself from the chair, with his mother on one side and Stacy on the other.

One day you were Joe Grudeck, the next day you were not.

Chapter Forty

The judge said the system had a special place for a man with Horace's unique skills. Downstate in Wallkill, a minimum-security prison housed a program where inmates cared for retired thoroughbreds, to teach the gang members and thugs about responsibility and care. Horace thought it was a joke at first, but sure enough, they needed a blacksmith.

Horace would do his time there after pleading out; five years for arson, and five years for simple assault, reduced from aggravated. The tapes supported his claim that he had no intention of attacking Joe Grudeck himself, and only acted in self-defense. His public defender said it was good deal; Horace didn't disagree. The sentences would run concurrently, since Horace had no priors and always held a job. In three years, he'd be eligible for parole. His prison salary would go for restitution of the destroyed Grudeck plaque and the cleanup of the blackened rubble that had been his house, now on bank property.

The horse farm was two hours south of Cooperstown, and Sally promised she would bring Michael down every few weeks or so, from home. That's what Michael wanted, to stay home, near his dad. Horace felt vindicated in that alone. Michael visited three times while he was being held in the county jail awaiting sentencing. He never asked Horace why he did it, and Horace never explained. It was just something that happened. Michael didn't seem bothered by it, so they left it at that. Someday Horace would tell him the truth: I did it for you.

Natalia came once and held his hand through the bars. He kissed that hand, like a nineteenth-century gentleman, before she left for Rochester, promising to write. Whether she did or not didn't matter much to Horace. He had his son. He'd won back his son.

On the kind of autumn day that brings tourists into apple and wine country, Horace was transported to Wallkill. The long white Dutch barn that sheltered the horses was illuminated by a brilliant, cloudless sky and almost shimmered in the light. Horace had never seen a sky so blue, or a barn so white. He looked over the rolling pastures and the dirt exercise tracks and decided he would like it here.

Dressed in an orange prison jumpsuit, he went to his old work.

His co-workers were men in similar costume. Their faces mapped the journey of their hard lives. Broken and bent noses, scars from knives or knuckles. The drug addicts all had bad teeth. The dealers had gold caps. Teardrop tattoos on the faces of the Bloods, swastikas on the necks of the Aryans, MS13 on the forearms of the Spanish.

Among them, he felt unease at first, but never fear. His size, and access to the tools, made him safe. Then he heard the whispers, "That's the dude who fucked up that ballplayer." He had made the news. He was one of them.

Because of his tools, he was caged off from the others behind a locked gate when he worked. The fire of the smithy, too, had to be kept far from the hay of the stables.

The horses were all thoroughbreds, retired racehorses whose chests once heaved on spindly legs down dirt or muddy tracks, carrying a man and the wagering hopes of many. But they aged out, or were losers, and were destined to some shit-heap farm or slaughter. The jail rescued them, as it did their caregivers. The men renamed them, with their own pet choices, forgoing the race program names christened by wealthy sportsmen. Now they had names like Street, 12 Step, Muchacho, Boss Man. They renamed Horace, too. They called him Blackie. Not imaginative, but simple. And somewhat dangerous. Horace liked that.

Horace watched the convicts through the wire mesh as they groomed the horses with care. These animals, once worth thousands, still had the glossy coats of privilege and once-regal stature of their breeding. But their muscles were softer now and less defined, and there was an arthritic gimp in some of their halting gaits. Their heads, once held high, bobbed lower as they walked, a sign of age and weariness. Horace understood.

And the men with hands that once punched or choked or stabbed or pulled triggers or raped or stole now caressed and brushed animals as used up and broken down by life as they were. The men brought the horses to him, blacksmith and farrier, and held their legs still as he fitted and nailed in metal shoes.

The barn was a quiet place. Sometimes the only noise was the snorting of the horse and the echo of Horace's hammer. The men rarely yelled or cursed or even laughed. All was calm. They took their cues from the muted dignity of the animals. The men had peace—or was it surrender?—in their hardened criminal faces—*God grant me the serenity*—and the barn was their place of solace, far from the chaos of the streets where they grew up and the other prisons where they served time.

That peace settled on Horace, too. His anger dissipated, turning to silent purpose. It was the work. Always the work.

He was the blacksmith, always the blacksmith, now behind different walls. No tourists, no talk, just work. Each day, he pulled on old long-sleeved leather gloves and shoveled coal in the hearth. He started the fire, got the bellows blowing, and let the ring of his hammer echo over the countryside.

Acknowledgments

Many authors write, "this book wouldn't be possible without . . . ," but in the case of my editor, David Falk at Touchstone, there are no truer words. David believed in the book from our first discussion and inspired me to finally complete this fourteen-year stretch of hard labor. His deft touch on the work can only be described like this: every single suggestion he made responded to an unspoken, nagging thought in my head that those areas needed help. We have an uncanny writer-editor relationship that I have only experienced once in my forty-year journalism career. To that point, the book's title, *Gods of Wood and Stone*, was David's suggestion after I wrote two versions under different names. The current title did not come easy. David and I kicked several around until this one stuck. And it is perfect.

I would also like to thank his wife, Sara, for the lost family hours David put into the book. It's a good thing she likes me—I think.

Thanks to the many good people at Touchstone/Simon & Schuster who've helped polish, design, and shepherd this book you hold in your hands, including Brian Belfiglio, Jessica Roth, Susan Moldow, Tara Parsons, Meredith Vilarello, Isabel DaSilva, Kelsey Manning, Cherlynne Li, Kyle Kabel, Sarah Wright, Amanda Mulholland, and Mike Kwan—passionate readers and champions of the unknown writer.

Likewise, my agent, Peter McGuigan of Foundry Literary + Media, was steadfast in his belief in this book. He read the first sixty pages as soon as he received the manuscript via email and called right away to sign me up. For an unknown novelist that kind of response puts a gust in your sails.

My children, Anthony, Michelle, Stephanie, Matthew, Mark, and Laura, have endured my journalistic writing their whole lives. There were times it simply had to come first. It's called deadline. Rather than feeling neglected, they instead learned something about work ethic and dedication to craft.

Several of my former *Star-Ledger* colleagues must be thanked: David Tucker, an award-winning poet who was my longtime editor and the catcher in our writer-editor acrobatic team; Rosemary Parrillo, my current editor, an award-winning playwright who, like Tucker, was always encouraging and never reluctant to show pride in my work; Robin Gaby Fisher, a *New York Times* bestselling author and two-time Pulitzer finalist in feature writing, whose complimentary encouragement broke all bounds of generosity; Amy Ellis Nutt, a Pulitzer Prize winner in feature writing, who also worked hard to convince me I had a gift.

My friend, author Wendy Wyatt, has guided me through dark periods in my life. She is always there, as is my lifetime best friend, psychologist Ted Batlas. His degree has come in handy over five decades of friendship with me. And finally, my sister-in-law Annette Kaiser, who evolved into a best friend and helped me reach a place of faith and humility that added great humanity to the finished version.

All of these people have love and hope for writing. And I thank them for that.

About the Author

Mark Di Ionno is a lifelong journalist and a Pulitzer Prize finalist in news commentary for his work on the aftermath of Hurricane Sandy. He is also a four-time winner of the New Jersey Press Association's first-place award for column writing. His columns appear regularly in *The Star-Ledger* and in its online partner, nj.com/starledger, with an estimated daily readership of over 1 million. Prior to becoming a front-page columnist at *The Star-Ledger* he was an editor of the paper's Pulitzer Prize–winning coverage of Governor Jim McGreevey's abrupt resignation.

Di Ionno began his career covering sports for *The New York Post*, where he broke many significant sports stories, including parts of baseball's case against Pete Rose and the undoing of Mike Tyson. His first novel, *The Last Newspaperman*, was published by Plexus Publishing. He is an adjunct professor of journalism at Rutgers University and a single father of six children.